MW00940634

THE FARMER'S
Daughter

THE FARMER'S
Daughter

JERI LE

XULON PRESS

Xulon Press
2301 Lucien Way #415
Maitland, FL 32751
407.339.4217
www.xulonpress.com

© 2021 by Jeri Le

All rights reserved solely by the author. The author guarantees all
contents are original and do not infringe upon the legal rights of
any other person or work. No part of this book may be reproduced
in any form without the permission of the author.

Due to the changing nature of the Internet, if there are any web
addresses, links, or URLs included in this manuscript, these may
have been altered and may no longer be accessible. The views
and opinions shared in this book belong solely to the author and
do not necessarily reflect those of the publisher. The publisher
therefore disclaims responsibility for the views or opinions
expressed within the work.

Unless otherwise indicated, Scripture quotations taken from the
King James Version (KJV) – *public domain.*

Paperback ISBN-13: 978-1-6628-2084-7
Hardcover ISBN-13: 978-1-6628-2085-4
Ebook ISBN-13: 978-1-6628-2086-1

Acknowledgements

*T*o my Heavenly Father that poured this story into me allowing me to use my life experiences as a farmer's daughter to share His unconditional love with all who read this novel.

To my parents that were hard working farmers and faithful Christians teaching me the importance of faith, family and love.

To Cindy who began this journey sitting next to me in journalism classes during college. She developed editing skills as I created stories. Thank you, Cindy, for your patience, attention to detail and editing expertise that turned this manuscript into a story I can be proud of.

To the Xulon publishing team that started with inspiration and encouragement from one of their authors, to walking alongside of me step by step to fulfill this dream. God brought each new person to the team at just the exact moment that was needed to complete this project. Thank you to each and every member of the Xulon Press team.

To Steve, Tallis, Tyler, Ty, Shaeffer and Walter who love me unconditionally and encouraged me to step out in faith to complete this dream. Thank you for believing I could do this.

Prologue

"We are all created for a special purpose. Accepting and fulfilling that purpose brings real joy and contentment." The Teacher's final words were strong and powerful. As the hillside class ended Teacher invited Evelyn to stay behind. Evelyn was excited to hear her name called. Receiving this invitation was an honor that all students worked towards. She gathered her things and approached the podium.

"Evelyn, I think you are ready to fulfill your purpose," He said calmly.

"Teacher, what is it?" she asked.

"I need someone to teach unconditional love," He stated. "We have studied this topic extensively. I observed you in the community with others and I think you are best suited for this assignment."

"How will I go?" Evelyn inquired.

"Just as I did, swaddled as a baby," was His response.

"Will You be with me?" she asked.

"Not like here, but yes I will be with you always. Where I am sending you, we will communicate through your heart." He spoke quietly and touched His chest.

"Through my heart, Teacher?" Evelyn was confused.

"Yes, there they call it prayer. When your heart speaks to Me from within, I will hear you, comfort you and guide you with the wisdom needed to complete your tasks." He spoke reverently. "They also have a guidebook. You will not have trouble finding one; it is called the Bible."

"When?" Evelyn asked.

"Soon, but first you must meet with my mother. She is best suited to teach your final lesson, enduring the pain of unconditional love." Teacher turned and walked away.

Chapter 1

J. C. turned left off the county pavement and brought her car to a stop under the big walnut tree on the gravel driveway at her parents' farm. The front lawn still had six inches of snow from the February 6th snowstorm. A few rabbit tracks created a design in the perfect white blanket over the rolling lawn.

The quiet hum of her Lexus LS engine mixed with the jazz music from Sirius Radio soothed the tension in her chest and stomach. J.C. knew this was more than a visit. She had been coming to the farm one weekend each month since her mother died eleven months ago. This time she was here to stay... her mind stopped. How long would she be here?

The past four weeks seemed like years as she had made life-changing decisions. At the age of fifty she took early retirement from IBM in Des Moines, Iowa. The one and only company Jacquelyn Caine Mason (J.C.) had ever worked for. She had started working for them straight out of Iowa State University and spent twenty-eight years with the organization. The past year had been hard on the IT Industry and as the Midwest Regional Sales Manager, some difficult financial decisions needed to be made.

J.C. could have moved again and taken a promotion with a larger territory. But doing that would have prohibited her from keeping a promise she had made to her mother, in those final weeks of her mother's battle with breast cancer. Instead, she looked at the sales projections for her team, completed evaluations on which of her team members could be successful without her and which ones needed to move on to other opportunities. With that knowledge and the need to fulfill her promise, J.C. traveled to the corporate headquarters in New York and presented IBM management with a proposal that allowed her to take early retirement.

She requested a twenty-four-month severance package worth eighty percent of her current compensation package and full benefits. The plan included a restructure of her Midwest regional teams into the surrounding territories. It eliminated six sales positions, two that were currently open and four of her lowest performers; all of which would receive six months' salary and full benefits severance packages. She would close the Des Moines, Kansas City, Minneapolis, and Chicago offices allowing all sales staff to work from home, eliminating the overhead cost of brick and mortar. Corporate accepted her offer with the contingency that when she was ready to re-enter the work force; IBM would be her first call and if they needed a similar evaluation of other territories then they could call on her to complete an analysis of those areas.

J.C. returned to each of her Midwest offices and communicated the upcoming changes which included her departure and worked through the paperwork for transfer and closure of the four offices. Now with that behind her, here she sat in the front seat of her car at her father's farm knowing that the job ahead of her was more difficult than any business deal she had ever closed in her twenty-eight years at IBM. J.C. turned off the engine, released the trunk lid and opened the door of her Lexus.

CHAPTER 1

J.C. placed her computer bag over her head and right shoulder, pulled two large suitcases out and balanced her weight between them. She looked down at the smaller bag and boots in the trunk and decided this was a two-trip job. She did not want to drag her bags through the snow and mud to the house.

J.C. walked slowly toward the old grey two-story stone farmhouse. It had a long porch across the front with four square wood pillars that held up the sloped roof over the porch swing and two rocking chairs. When she got to the porch she stopped and let both suitcases drop. She returned to her car and grabbed the smaller overnight bag and her boots, closed the trunk, and returned to the porch. J.C. took a big breath before turning the knob of the front door that opened into the dining room of the square two-story style farmhouse.

It originally had four rooms on the first and second floors. Inside the front door was the shoe mat; her mother had insisted that all shoes be taken off and left before entering the house. J.C. dropped her boots there and set the small bag on the wood floor in front of the mat. She turned and pulled the two large suitcases into the dining room. Slowly closing the door behind her she bent down, untied her shoes, and left them on the mat. With each breath, she took in the smells of the old farmhouse. Her dad must have had bacon for breakfast, she thought, smelling the lingering grease in the air. The 'old' smell hung heavy in the air along with that of the oil furnace that pumped heat throughout the house from the basement.

J.C. picked up the small bag and one of the large suitcases and moved through the dining room towards the living room. The house was perfectly square. All four rooms on the main floor were 16 ft. x 16 ft. originally. The kitchen which was directly behind the dining room had been remodeled by her grandparents in the 1950s. They had put in running water, kitchen cabinets on the north wall and sectioned off a small

3

bathroom on the south wall that included a stool, sink and bathtub. When J.C. was in high school her parents updated the bathroom with a shower/tub combo, new stool, and sink. It was the ONLY bathroom in this old house.

Her mother had also made other updates to the kitchen during her lifetime. One of the last changes made was the conversion of a lean-to porch on the southeast corner that was made into a mudroom/laundry room. This was the entrance that her father used to come and go to the barnyard. The living room was parallel to the dining room that laid behind the long porch. It too, was a square room. It had her father's recliner, the couch and her mother's chair. An antique secretary desk along with a television that was never watched, completed the furnishings. Her parents' bedroom was directly behind the living room.

J.C. opened the door leading to the upstairs. The cold air hit her in the face. She was not surprised that her father had not opened the floor registers to allow the heat to rise upstairs. She pulled the large suitcase behind her as she maneuvered up the narrow stairs. The first ten stairs laid against the north wall. She reached a small landing that turned right to climb another four stairs to the second floor.

At the top of the staircase was a small room that her mother had converted into a walk-in closet/dressing room for J.C.'s sixteenth birthday. It was nicer than the master walk-in closet at her condo in downtown Des Moines. She set her small overnight bag on the counter inside the doorway in front of the full mirrored wall. She pushed the larger suitcase into the center of the room before going back downstairs for the second one. As soon as J.C. had all her bags upstairs, she moved into the front room of the second floor.

The north room on the second floor looked like a study with a desk, small couch, and television. She laid her computer bag on the desk. This room had also been a surprise that her mother created during her senior year in high school to provide a place for her girlfriends to hang out with her when they came over. She walked over to the center of the room, reached down, and opened the register to allow heat to rise from the first floor. She walked through the doorway into her bedroom. Her queen-sized bed was a welcome sight tempting her to flop on it and stay for a week or two. Instead, she opened the register in that room as well to make sure the frosty temps would decrease in the next couple of hours.

She then walked to the south windows of her bedroom and pulled the curtains back. Her windows overlooked the farm from the driveway, across the barnyard and to the grain fields. Her father had grown up on these one-hundred acres that his great-grandfather had purchased from the government when he arrived from Ireland. Her grandmother was an only child and inherited the farm when her parents passed away. That pattern followed to her father when his mother passed away. Now J.C. was here to begin the preparation of documents and the next transfer of ownership from her seventy-five-year-old father to ...? Her mind went blank. J.C. did not want the farm but knew some legal paperwork needed to be completed.

Her eyes focused on her father's back that leaned on the fence, separating him from a cow that was held in the cattle shoot of the corral. A tall dark-haired, broad-shouldered man was obviously tending to the leg of this animal and then she noticed a pickup parked next to the corral confirming that the veterinarian was there. Her mind stopped to catch up with information that she had learned over her last eleven months during visits to her hometown.

This must be Vince Martin who had grown up six miles north. Vince was three years older than J.C. and the star of the local high school. He was smart, handsome, athletic, and nice beyond words. He too had gone to Iowa State University and graduated from the School of Veterinary Medicine. He married a sorority girl, moved back to his parents' farm, started his practice, and started a family. Unfortunately, he was widowed when his wife was killed in a car accident.

According to her high school girlfriends that remained there, "he was the most eligible bachelor of all times!" To hear some of them talk they would gladly give up their current spouse if Vince would give any of them a second look. Oh, yea, she thought, he was too NICE to break up anyone else's life just because his had abruptly changed. She shook her head to stop the mental tangent and decided it was time to begin the immersion into the plan she came to complete.

She returned to the dressing room, opened her suitcase, pulled out a pair of jeans and some boot socks. After changing out of her workout clothes and slipping into her jeans she headed downstairs, sat down on a dining room chair, and put on her boots. Standing up, she headed through the kitchen into the mudroom. Her farm jacket was hanging on the hook where she had left it. Swinging it around her shoulders she pushed her arms into the tan Carhartt, opened the door and walked confidently to the corral. Vince saw her coming and greeted her with a big smile, "Hi, Jacquelyn!" he said with all the niceness she remembered from those years of bus rides and passing in the hallways at high school.

She said, "hello," and asked what they were up to?

"Well, this one has some inflammation in its leg, and we are just giving her a shot to hopefully reduce the swelling." Another big smile from Vince. Will (William John Mason) did not move, speak or acknowledge J.C.'s presence in any way. J.C. did not expect him to. She was conditioned to her father's lack of communication which had been a part of her life since she was 10 years old. The tall, broad shouldered rugged man was focused on his animal and not distracted at all by the conversation that was beginning to take place around him.

"So, what brings you out to the farm in the middle of your work week?" Vince asked.

"No more work weeks for me; I took early retirement," J.C. responded.

CHAPTER 1

Vince pulled his head up and raised his eyebrows, "Really?" you could hear the question in his voice. "You really left big blue?" Iowa State alum had always referred to IBM as 'Big Blue'.

"Yes," J.C. said with a smile and stared into Vince's big brown eyes – not certain why. She really did not want this line of questioning to continue. They both stared for another moment and then, J.C. asked, "Is this the only cow that is having problems?"

"Yes, I think she might have twisted it sometime this fall and the tendons got inflamed," Vince responded. "We have been keeping an eye on it for a couple of weeks now and I think it is improving. Don't you agree Will?" Again, trying to pull Will into the conversation.

"Sure," Will mumbled under his breath.

Vince began putting his instruments back into the case, took off his sterile gloves and hit the release bar to allow the cow to return to the lot with the other animals. As he walked through the gate and towards his pickup, he asked over his shoulder, "How long will you be around Jacquelyn?"

"It's J.C.; no one has called me Jacquelyn since grade school," she replied.

"OK, J.C. but how long?" Vince responded with another smile.

"Not sure," J.C. replied with complete honesty. She really had no idea how long she would be at the farm. She owned a condo in a downtown high rise building in Des Moines that overlooked the river on one side and the Civic Center on the other. Her building was connected to the skywalk system that created miles of tunnels that linked businesses, retail, and housing for most of downtown Des Moines. Now, she was here. Forty-five miles west of Des Moines off Interstate 80 on a farm that needed her attention. She was no farmer and had no intention of becoming one, but her father was seventy-five years old. He had experienced a couple of health issues before her mother passed away, so something had to be done. Her business background was filled with experiences of disgruntled clients, acquisitions, financial and legal matters so J.C. was confident that she could assess this situation, put a plan together, and have things wrapped up in a couple of months. Yet, there was an uneasiness deep inside that she could not let go of.

Vince was locking down the side case on his pickup when J.C. realized her mind was lost in another tangent. "Will, 1 will stop back in three days. She should be fine by then. If you notice more limping or other issues, you can call the office and they will send me out sooner. J.C., hope you enjoy your retirement." Vince stepped up into his pickup, backed away from the corral and was gone.

Chapter 2

"*D*ad, I am going to make myself a sandwich for lunch. Can I make you one too?" This was J.C.'s attempt to say hello to her father.

"No, I still have some work to get done," Will said softly.

J.C. turned and walked back to the house. She left her jacket on the hook in the mudroom and her boots on the boot rack. She surveyed the kitchen and started preparing a grocery list. At least there was some sliced ham in the meat drawer. She grabbed the loaf of bread out of the cupboard. Really! Cheap white bread she thought. I am sure that is not the best diet for him with diabetes and heart issues. Whole grain bread went on the list. With a glass of milk and a sandwich, J.C. sat down at the dining room table to eat. She kept the grocery list next to her in case other items came to mind that she would need when she headed into town later to pick up a few things. Her mind began to wander again.

J.C.'s mother, Evelyn Caine Mason, could light up a room with conversation about nothing. How in the world did she ever end up with William John Mason?

J.C. wrote Nadine Crawford at the bottom of the grocery list. Nadine was her mother's closest friend. They had been girlfriends prior to getting married. Nadine was widowed at a young age when her husband was killed on a worksite accident. He was in construction work, but J.C. did not know the details behind his death. All she knew was no matter what went on in either one of their lives–Evelyn's or Nadine's–they both knew about it and shared everything.

Nadine had never had children, and not sure why; but J.C. was like an adopted daughter to her. Whenever she had practice after school and missed the bus home, J.C. walked to Nadine's and stayed until her mother could come pick her up in town. Sometimes if Nadine knew it would be an hour or so they would walk up to Main Street and get a treat at the drugstore. As a young girl, J.C. hoped every time when she got to Nadine's, that would be the case. When J.C. was in high school, occasionally Nadine would let her go on her own to meet up with some girlfriends. Each time when Evelyn got to Nadine's, they had a cup of coffee and talked non-stop about everything. J.C. wondered what it would be like to have that kind of friend. She had a few girlfriends in high school and others in college but no one person that she could just talk to endlessly.

Some days Nadine would come to the farm, and she and Evelyn would pick beans, peas, strawberries or whatever was in season and then spend hours on the front porch tending to them. Again, what a strange phenomenon J.C. thought. She had lived her entire adult life in the business world and could not think of one person she would call or spend time with like her mother and Nadine did.

J.C. finished her milk and sandwich and put her glass in the sink. She knew as soon as she left for town her father would come in and make himself a sandwich; so, she decided to head out. After grabbing her coat from upstairs, she put her shoes back on and walked out onto the porch. She quickly surveyed the barnyard but did not see her father anywhere. Back in her car with the smooth sound of jazz playing, J.C. backed out of the driveway and headed north into Stuart,

CHAPTER 2

Iowa. 'Home of 1,500 Good Eggs and a Few Stinkers' was on the sign at the edge of town. J.C. stopped at Al's grocery store and filled her cart with the items on her list. She carried out two full bags and set them down on the floor behind the driver's seat. She looked around for a minute or two before backing out and heading down Linn Street where Nadine lived.

Nadine was delighted when she answered her door to find J.C. there. "Honey, it is not the weekend, I am surprised you are here. Is everything all right? Did something happen to Will?" J.C. held up her hand to stop the questions and showed Nadine a tray of cookies she had picked up at the grocery store. "Come in, come in!" Nadine said with a big smile.

"I took early retirement from IBM," J.C. told Nadine after they poured some coffee, opened the tray of cookies and both sat down at Nadine's kitchen table. Nadine looked a little confused. She was extremely sharp for seventy-seven and following Evelyn's death called J.C. weekly to check on her. "I know I could have told you what was going on these past two months, but I just needed to work through all of that before coming home." J.C. paused, and Nadine narrowed her eyes.

"Home? Are you moving back to the farm?" Nadine asked.

"Oh, no, no!" J.C. said quickly. "You remember that Mom wanted to make sure that I took care of the legal and financial paperwork for dad. He was never very good with that stuff, she would say. So, before tax season is over, I thought we should get the process started. I got a great retirement package from IBM, so I can stay here for a few months to really get a sense of how much longer he should remain on the farm, get the papers drawn up, and make arrangements with the nursing home for when it is time for him to go."

Nadine pulled her shoulders back and widened her eyes. "I see," she said with some hesitation in her voice. "Have you told Will this plan?"

"Yes, three weeks ago when I was here for the weekend," J.C. responded.

"And what did Will say?" Nadine asked, still sitting straight up in her chair with her chest out and eyes widened.

"Nothing!" J.C. replied. "Exactly what I expected him to say."

"Well, it is not going to be easy to convince that man he needs to stop farming, leave the only place he has ever lived, and to do what? He doesn't play cards, he doesn't talk to people, he doesn't listen to music, he doesn't watch TV or participate in any social activities; so, I am certain the nursing home is not a place he plans on going anytime soon," Nadine said with a slight chuckle.

"No, he does not do any of those things. He just reads his Bible, and he can do that there where they can keep an eye on him, watch his diet, and make sure he takes his medicine." J.C. could tell the pitch of her voice was elevated. "I just need to get his affairs in order before I start looking for a new job. The likelihood of me finding another job in Des Moines is not very promising. I wasn't going to just move off and leave him out there to be trampled by his livestock when he has a heart attack." J.C. sighed hoping she had made her point.

"Well, honey take a little time to get to know his situation before making any drastic changes right away," Nadine advised sternly.

J.C. took a big drink of coffee and a bite out of her cookie. Get to know his situation! How do you get to know someone who has not spoken more than a dozen sentences to you in the past forty years? The situation is clear. He is old, and getting older, he will not be able to take care of himself forever. He does not want her around and she does not want to be here any longer than she needs to be. If he was not her father and she had not promised her mother to do this, she would have taken a transfer back in September and be living in New York City by now with a portfolio of high-profile clients. This was not something she wanted to do. It was something she had to do; just like all those business decisions that were hard to make. She reviewed the numbers, the facts and made the best decision possible for the organization. Her plan was to apply those same skills to her father's situation.

Nadine interrupted her mental tangent with a new question. "Have you started going through your mother's things yet?"

"No," J.C.'s breath caught in her chest. She looked at Nadine and then down at the floor. "Why?" J.C. said meekly still looking down.

"Well, there are a few things I might want if you are just planning on taking her clothes to Goodwill. A couple of jewelry pieces would be nice to have. And, her garden basket, unless you plan to keep it." Nadine talked about these items very casually J.C. thought.

Interestingly, J.C. had not given any thought at all to her mother's things that were still in the house. She really had not thought through the final process of what would happen to the personal effects of her parents' things if her father ever agreed to this plan of sending him off to the nursing home. Her face flushed as Nadine filled her coffee cup.

"Nadine, I might need your help with that," J.C. said cautiously.

"Sure, honey, your mother and I talked about some of the items and where she wanted them to go. I would be more than happy to come out and help you go through them. One stipulation! You must tell Will before we start. I do not want to go into his room and remove any of her things until he is aware we are going to start that process," Nadine spoke sternly, with those instructions.

J.C. finished her coffee and set the cup down. "OK," she said weakly. She gave Nadine a hug and left the remainder of the cookies for Nadine to enjoy. "Hey, is there a workout place in Stuart yet?" J.C. asked.

"No, but the middle school is open weekday mornings from 5:30 a.m. to 7:00 a.m. for anyone who wants to walk or workout in the gym there," Nadine answered.

"OK, I just realized today that I brought a lot of workout clothes and will probably not need all of them." J.C. was mentally admitting to herself that her plan already had a few flaws in it.

Chapter 3

J.C. pulled out the roast beef and potatoes around 6:30 p.m. and began setting the dining room table for dinner. Will came out of the bathroom in his robe after showering and headed to his bedroom to change. When he returned to the dining room he sat at the head of the table, bowed his head, and quietly prayed. For the first fifteen minutes, they were completely silent. J.C. remembered that her mother spent every evening meal updating Will on the details of what was going on in the world, neighborhood, church, town, school, or lives of people they knew. J.C. tried to recall if his expressions ever changed. Did he want to know the information Evelyn shared each night? Sometimes Evelyn would pull J.C. into the nightly updates to talk about her school day.

It was not until J.C.'s final years of high school that she recalled dinners had not always been silent. Will, Evelyn, Jacquelyn, and Johnnie would eat, talk, tell stories and laugh as they ate dinner. During her junior and senior years as she became more frustrated with her father's lack of communication and involvement in her life, J.C. would start off with 'do you remember when Johnnie ...?' Immediately,

Evelyn would reach out and touch her arm, give her a sorrowful look, and shake her head back and forth. A couple of times J.C. continued until her father said, "Young lady go to your room!"

Well, Evelyn was not here to give updates, nor was she here to protect him from those stories. J.C. wondered what would happen if tonight she said, 'remember when?' Instead, she decided for her first evening back she would revert to the nightly update, which had become her pattern since her mother's death. "Nadine says 'Hi'. I stopped to see her after picking up some groceries at Al's today. The old town of Stuart looks the same; I did not recognize any new businesses on Main Street. We had coffee and cookies. Nadine looks great for seventy-seven. I hope someday she will tell me her secret for staying young. She really does not look like she is in her seventies. I bought whole wheat bread instead of that white bread you have been eating. I think it's better for your heart and diabetes. If you decide that you don't like it let me know. I just think it is important to eat as healthy as we can. Oh, Nadine and I will probably start going through mom's clothes, jewelry, and personal items here soon. Are you OK with that?"

After what seemed like a ten-minute pause, Will said, "Sure." No emotion, no eye contact; just sure.

As soon as Will finished eating, he stood up and walked into the living room, turned on the floor lamp behind his chair, picked up his Bible, and sat down to read. J.C. cleared the table and returned items to the kitchen. She washed and dried the dishes and put everything away. She turned off the lights in the kitchen and dining room and walked into the living room. Will did not look up from his reading. She walked towards his chair and said, "I am headed up for the night, Dad." No response.

J.C. took her computer out and plugged it in. She was glad for her hot spot mobile modem that IBM allowed her to keep. Without it, there would be no internet connection at the farm. She quickly breezed through a handful of emails. Outside of work, J.C. had very few contacts so not much to keep up on now that she was outside the IBM circle. She did keep in touch with a couple of women that she had worked with for years. Both married with multiple children that kept them busy outside of work, so she never developed a social connection with them, but they enjoyed coffee and stories at work. Once she had looked at her emails she decided to unpack.

Heading back into the dressing room she opened her suitcases and began putting jeans, slacks, and sweaters in the cubical holes along the wall. She put her underwear and t-shirts in the built-in drawers and hung up a few dressier items on the rail. Taking the shoes out of the bottom of her suitcase, she placed them on the floor under the hanging rod. After thirty minutes, she was done and wondered what to do with the remainder of her evening. She knew her dad only had an antenna on the top of the house – so watching TV was not going to be very exciting. It was 8:00 p.m.; was she going to go to bed that early? She walked into the study and looked through the books on the shelf. These were from her high school era and nothing caught her interest now. She should have planned better she thought. On her weekend trips to the farm this past year ... she worked. Now without work to fill the quiet hours, what was she going to do?

J.C. walked into her bedroom and switched on the light. After walking one complete circle around the room, she laid down on the bed and looked up at the ceiling for a moment and then her head slowly turned to the left and stared at Johnnie's door. It had been forty years since Johnnie died but tonight it seemed like yesterday. That night when her father drove home from Des Moines and picked her up at Nadine's, she knew from the look on his face that Johnnie was not coming home even before he told Nadine what the doctors had told him and Evelyn earlier that day. "There is nothing more they can do. The leukemia will kill him within a day or two. Evelyn will stay with him until it is over." Her father's voice was strong and controlled as she replayed that conversation in her head from Nadine's living room almost forty years earlier. The car ride home was silent. It was 9:30 p.m. when they pulled into the farm that night. Once inside the house, Will said, "Jacquelyn, go to the bathroom and get yourself ready for bed. Make sure you brush your teeth and hurry off to bed. You have school tomorrow and it's past your bedtime." His face was emotionless, and his stern words kept her from asking any questions. At ten years old, she did what her father said and headed upstairs. When she got to her room, Will was closing the door between their two rooms, a door that had stayed closed, except for a couple of occasions in high school when she snuck in there–until tonight. J.C. rose slowly and walked across her room to the door.

Chapter 4

*T*he room was completely dark. The two south windows of this room were covered by curtains that had been drawn for many years. The overhead light did not come on when J.C. flipped the switch, so the only light coming in was through the door from her bedroom. It smelled old and musty. When she was younger, she knew that her mother would spend time in there during the days when J.C. was at school. Sometimes J.C. would put things in front of the door just to check if they had been moved when she got home. It was a stupid game, but she was only a child. That first few weeks after her mother came home from the hospital the house was filled with people. Every day when J.C. got off the bus, a neighbor, someone from church, friends from town, or people that she didn't know were there sitting at the kitchen table with her mother drinking coffee or tea and talking quietly. Nadine was there almost every day for weeks it seemed. Dinners at night were made by someone else and silence became the norm. It was months before talking during dinner resumed.

J.C. could still remember that first conversation. She almost choked on her chicken when Evelyn started to speak.

"I think we should take Jacquelyn to Marie Price in Greenfield to start baton twirling lessons. They start at 5:00 p.m. and last forty-five minutes, two times a month." Jacquelyn was excited. She had gotten a baton for her birthday that year and loved playing in the front yard, but to learn real routines would be great. She knew a couple of girls in the sixth grade who took lessons and showed off some of the things they learned at recess. Even tonight, walking back through her memories J.C. did not know what response Will gave; but the following week she went with Evelyn and started baton lessons that lasted until her junior year in high school.

J.C. walked over to the child-sized bed and picked up the teddy bear. It was dusty. She moved it into the light and could see the green eyes. Johnnie had green eyes. He was so full of life and nothing seemed to scare him except maybe thunderstorms. Jacquelyn was four when Johnnie was born. He was like a precious doll that sometimes her mother would let her feed.

As a toddler he followed Will everywhere around the farm. He loved the animals, the mud, the tractors, the pickup, and just being in his father's shadow. During the summer when the big thunderstorms would hit, Johnnie would call out from his room at night. "Jac Que Lyn"–he always pronounced her name in three distinct syllables. "Jac Que Lyn, do you hear that noise? I think something is breaking in heaven." If the thunder would crack close to the house, Johnnie would come running and hop into bed with Jacquelyn. She did not mind. Sometimes the big cracks even scared her. At the age of five, Johnnie started riding the bus with Jacquelyn to school. She was his big sister, and no one was more protective than she was. Life was perfect. In the evening after dinner the entire family would be in the living room playing games or reading. Sometimes she read to the whole family and once she even remembered Johnnie trying to read a story that he was learning at school. In the summers between school years, Johnnie spent his days in the barnyard or fields with Will and

CHAPTER 4

Jacquelyn spent time in the garden and house with Evelyn. They were the picture-perfect Midwest Iowa farm family.

Then in the fall when it was time for school to start, Evelyn took Jacquelyn and Johnnie to the doctor for a checkup and their shots. Jacquelyn hated shots but Johnnie was so brave when it was time for his tetanus shot, he did not even cry. The first day of school the bus came and off they went; Johnnie to first grade and Jacquelyn to fifth grade. This year Johnnie knew some kids on the bus and sat with them and Jacquelyn sat with her friend Monica. A couple of weeks into the school year Evelyn sent Jacquelyn to the bus alone. Johnnie needs to go back to the doctor is all that Jacquelyn knew. The next day Johnnie was back on the bus and things were normal again.

It wasn't long until Jacquelyn could tell that things were changing at home. One night, Will went upstairs and brought Johnnie's bed down and placed it at the foot of the bed in her parents' bedroom. Jacquelyn was sent up to bed on her own that night and Johnnie got to sleep downstairs. More and more days came when Johnnie stayed home and did not go to school with Jacquelyn. One day Nadine came to school and took Jacquelyn to her house instead of having her ride the bus home. It must have been a Friday because she stayed the night with Nadine. They got up the next morning and went to the restaurant on Main Street for pancakes. Jacquelyn was having a great time with Nadine when her parents arrived to pick her up. Evelyn came to the house and told Jacquelyn to get her things. Nadine and Evelyn did not have coffee or even talk that day. When they got to the car, Jacquelyn saw Johnnie and she knew he was really sick. His eyes were not bright green anymore. They were surrounded by dark red circles and purple bags. His hair was almost gone, and his bones were starting to stick out of his skin. It had been a while since she and Johnnie had played together. Most of the time when she got home from school he was sleeping. He was happy to finally see her. She moved over next to him in the car and held his hand in hers. Inside she felt sad but did not understand why.

J.C. recalled it was years after Johnnie's death that Evelyn finally explained to her what had happened. The doctor discovered that Johnnie had leukemia when they went in for their school physical and shots. Will and Evelyn tried to find doctors that understood this disease but in 1958 few doctors knew how to treat leukemia.

J.C. took the teddy bear back to her room with her, flipped the light switch off and closed the door.

Chapter 5

*T*he sun started to peek through the curtains around 7:00 a.m. J.C. was shocked that she had slept that long. Her normal routine was up at 5:30 a.m. and down to the gym in her building for a forty-five-minute workout before showering, breakfast, and then off to Frederick's for her first cup of coffee. She could smell coffee and knew that her father was already making breakfast. She put on her robe and headed downstairs. The living room was dark, but she could see into her parents' bedroom. It was neat and tidy. The bed was already made. She had not paid attention to that yesterday but was surprised at what a good housekeeper her father really was. Now that she was thinking about it, these past eleven months, he had done a great job of keeping everything clean and in pristine condition just like her mother did all those years.

"Good Morning, Dad." J.C. smiled as she entered the kitchen to find her father leaning over the stove making eggs and sausage. No reply.

She headed straight to the coffee pot and poured herself a cup, then opened the refrigerator and pulled out a grapefruit that she purchased yesterday. She walked across the room to the cabinet and took out the oatmeal. She poured half a cup into a cereal bowl, added water, and put it in the microwave to cook. J.C. smiled as she recalled giving this microwave to her mother for Christmas. Evelyn enjoyed cooking, and the microwave added some new options to her already supreme menus. J.C. took her coffee and grapefruit into the dining room and placed them on the table before returning to retrieve her oatmeal. "Dad, I am planning on cleaning out Johnnie's room today." After a long pause and no response, she took her oatmeal and walked back into the dining room.

As Will finished preparing his breakfast, he turned on the radio to hear the morning livestock markets report. J.C. remembered waking up every day to KMA radio out of Red Oak, Iowa, telling the prices of feeder cattle, fat hogs, chickens, and sheep. Wow, some things never change, she thought. Breakfast ended with Will taking his dishes to the kitchen sink and J.C. calling out to him, "Dad, I will take care of those when I do mine."

Will turned and walked into the mudroom and was gone.

J.C. thought back to the warning that Nadine had given her yesterday. "Take time to get to know his situation before making drastic changes." What did she mean by that? Drastic... what is drastic with forty years of things staying the same? The room that she had surveyed in the dark last night, looked the same as the day Will had carried that small bed back up there and closed the door. At some point her mother had probably washed the bedding, curtains, and a few of Johnnie's things, but by the level of musty smell she experienced last night that had not happened in some time either. She was washing dishes by the time she realized her mental tangent had gone on for a while. She finished the dishes and went upstairs to retrieve her overnight bag and clothes before returning to the bathroom for a shower. J.C. was just finishing putting on some mascara when she heard a knock on the dining room door. J.C. opened the door to find

CHAPTER 5

Vince Martin standing on the front porch. "Dad is outside somewhere." J.C. blurted without even a hi or hello.

"I actually came for some advice from you, J.C." Vince's smile caused J.C. to step back and suck in her breath.

"Oh, sorry, I thought you were here because of the cow again. Come in." She stepped back further and opened the door wider. Vince leaned down and unbuckled the side of his boots and stepped out of them.

"Would you like some coffee?" J.C. asked.

"Just a half a cup, I am headed to vaccinate 100 head of feeder pigs at Earl Jones' place. It will be a while before I am back at the clinic." Vince smiled again. J.C. stepped into the kitchen to grab a cup from the cupboard and reached inside the bathroom to retrieve hers, filling them both before returning to the dining room. She reached across the table to hand Vince a cup and motioned for him to sit down.

"What kind of advice could you possibly need from me?" J.C. looked quizzically at Vince.

"Prom shopping!" He drew in a big breath. "Kelsey, my seventeen-year-old daughter is ready for her first prom and I *hate* shopping. I have taken her into West Des Moines a couple of times to the malls, but it is just not my thing and prom, well I think, is a pretty big deal for teenage girls." Vince wrinkled up his nose and eyes trying to get some sympathy.

"Oh, sorry, Vince but I am not experienced in that field at all!" J.C. said in a very direct voice. "I do not have children and all my prom, homecoming, spring fling, and all other dresses were made by my mother. You might need to talk to one of Kelsey's friends' mothers. I am sure one of them would not mind helping you, or even take Kelsey along with them when they take their daughters shopping."

"Well," Vince drew in a long deep breath. "Here's the deal," another long deep breath. "Kelsey does not want anyone to see her dress before prom – again a phenomenon that I do not understand. Her closest friends' mothers are women that I know, would probably not be able to keep their mouths

STOP

shut about their own daughters' dresses; let alone mine. And Kelsey thinks she can just do this on her own. I have no clue as to how much a prom dress should cost." He sighed deeply. "Any advice you can offer will be helpful." Vince looked down into his lap and then shot a sympathetic look at J.C.

J.C. thought for a few moments as she sipped her coffee.

"OK, I know some moms in Des Moines that have daughters about the same age. I will call them. Also, my neighbor who is watering my plants and picking up my mail just recently raised her granddaughter through her high school years. I am sure Doris might have some ideas. I will make some calls." J.C. saw relief coming back into Vince's face as she spoke.

Vince took his last sip of coffee and set his mug down. "My cell number is 742-9224; the office is another pool of gossips so please do not leave a message there. I may not answer when you call, but I will appreciate any information and help you can give me." He slipped his boots back on and J.C. held the door as he stepped out on the porch and was gone.

J.C. stood at the dining room door and wondered what raising a child would have been like. She had never even wanted children. Work was her life. Children brought risks and heartache that she experienced in her own childhood. Vince was so genuinely concerned about getting this prom process right and making sure that Kelsey's dreams of having a dress that no one saw, was honored. Even if it meant sacrificing his own comfort to make that happen. Wow, that must be what fatherly love was. J.C. would not know what that was like. She stepped into the kitchen and left Vince's cup in the sink, refreshed her cup of coffee and headed upstairs to start the task of cleaning Johnnie's room.

As she hit the top of the stairs, she went into her own dressing room and grabbed the hamper. Opening the door to Johnnie's room she remembered that the light bulb was burnt out. She pulled the two curtains open and let the sunlight from the south windows in. Setting her cup of coffee on the dresser, she headed back down to the kitchen to find a new light bulb. When she walked into the kitchen, Will was standing there. He looked at her and then the cup in the sink. Without thinking, she said, "Oh, Vince Martin stopped by to ask me for some advice about his daughter. Where do you keep the light bulbs?" Will pointed to the top of the cupboard over the stove. "Thanks, the light is out in Johnnie's room," she stated.

"I know," Will responded.

J.C. froze in place with her hand above her head reaching for the light bulb. She was too short to pull it down. Will reached over the top and handed her a box that had bulbs in it. "You will need two for that ceiling light," he said.

Still frozen, J.C. just stood holding the box as Will stepped back and she heard the kitchen door close behind him. Will had been in Johnnie's room! When? How long ago? Why did he not change the light bulbs? She envisioned him sitting there in the dark. Her chest tightened. She was immediately sad thinking of her father alone in the room upstairs–in the dark. J.C. took a couple of deep breaths and walked slowly back to Johnnie's room.

The light fixture was in the center of the ceiling. She needed something to stand on. She walked back to her study and took the chair from her desk. She slowly stepped up on the chair and twisted the hardware on the bottom of the light fixture and released it into her hand. She brought it down and put it between her feet on the chair. Reaching back up, J.C. unscrewed the light bulbs and put them in the light fixture between her feet and replaced them with the two new bulbs. She decided the light fixture needed to be cleaned, which meant another trip to the kitchen. She laid the light fixture and bulbs on the top of the dresser and opened the drawers. She might as well pull the clothes out that needed to go to the laundry room and save a trip downstairs. At least all the up and down would be a pseudo replacement workout for her normal gym time she thought. The clothes she pulled out were small little boys' briefs, T-shirts, pajamas, shirts, and jeans. She dropped them in the hamper. When the drawers were empty, she pulled the bed cover and sheets off the bed and put them in the hamper also. Finally, with a full hamper she placed the light fixture and old bulbs on top and headed downstairs.

In the mudroom she started a load of clothes. Between the washer and dryer was a folded step stool. She pulled that out and returned to the kitchen. She was able to return the half-used box of light bulbs back to their original spot and took the stool with her upstairs. It would be much safer than her desk chair to replace the freshly washed light fixture.

With bright lights and windows open, the dust on the floor looked like light fur. Frustrated, J.C. headed back to the mudroom to get the vacuum. An educated woman with all the business experience in the world was struggling to organize a day of cleaning. This was starting to annoy her. She drew in a deep breath and grabbed the bucket and hand mop while she was in the mudroom. She filled the bucket with hot water and added Lysol from under the kitchen sink. She found a couple of small hand towels that looked like they had been used for cleaning and stuffed them in the back pockets of her jeans. One last look under the sink brought out the bottle of Windex to clean the windows. Now, how would she maneuver all these items up the stairs? No wonder her mom, at seventy-plus years of age, did not spend time cleaning the second floor. She clutched the mop handle in the same hand as the vacuum, hooked the Windex to the side of the water bucket and smiled at her ability to solve her problem. She slowly climbed the stairs to avoid spilling water or dropping the vacuum and finally was back in Johnnie's room to clean. As she washed the south windows, she watched Will move slowly from lot to lot and building to building with feed buckets and pitchforks of hay. He moved well for a seventy-five-year-old man. His posture was still straight which confirmed her mother's theory that carrying five gallon buckets of feed and water all those years will give you great posture.

As she finished the second window, she found herself reminiscing about that last summer when Johnnie was six and followed Will everywhere. How did that not drive her father nuts? Having Johnnie always in the way, asking question after question and never getting a break. As much as she loved her little brother, he was a big nuisance at times. She could not remember her father ever sending Johnnie back to the house or away when Will was doing something more difficult. He might sit him on the top of the fence at the corral when they were working cattle or have him stand at his side on the tractor when he was driving out in the field, but day in and day out Johnnie was Will's shadow. It had to be hard when Johnnie got sick. Will's dreams of training his son, farming with his son, and someday turning over the farm to his son like his parents had done, must have been very difficult to accept when Johnnie died. Had Will ever felt like Vince does about Kelsey? A chill ran through J.C. as she remembered those nights in the living room after dinner. 'Tickle Fights!' How had she forgotten about 'Tickle Fights'? At least that is what Will called them. Her dad would get down on all fours and she would hop on his back. Her mother would get down on all fours and Johnnie would get on her back. They would chase each other around the living room tickling Jacquelyn and Johnnie until one of them fell off. Whoever stayed on the longest was the winner. Evelyn loved to tickle Will too. Sometimes Will would laugh so hard, and collapse and they (Evelyn and Johnnie) would win by default. Where had that memory been all these years? Today it was so clear, and she even could hear Will's laughter in her mind. The sun was streaming in the windows, but J.C. was chilled to the bone. She quickly vacuumed the floor and ran the mop over it to collect the remaining dust from the old wood floor. Before leaving the room, she walked back to the window and looked down. Will was nowhere in sight.

J.C. collected all her cleaning supplies and returned to the first floor in the same manner she came up. Slowly edging her way down the narrow stairs with her hands full, hoping not to spill the bucket of dirty water.

Chapter 6

Entering the mudroom, J.C. pulled the clothes out of the washing machine, placed them in the dryer, and started a second load. She put the vacuum, mop, bucket, and stool away and headed into the kitchen to make some lunch. Yesterday's trip to the grocery store opened up more options for today's lunch. She decided to make tomato soup and a grilled cheese sandwich. She didn't know when and if Will would come in for lunch, but she made enough soup for two and could easily whip up another sandwich if he did. The soup was finished in the microwave just as the kitchen door opened and Will came inside. "I made tomato soup and grilled cheese for lunch." No response.

J.C. set the table for two and finished the sandwiches while Will was in the bathroom. They sat down together for lunch and J.C. started with the morning's report. "Vince's daughter wants to buy a prom dress that none of her friends see before prom night. Vince is not much of a shopper, so I am going to call some of the women I used to work with to find out where they should go and what prom dresses cost these days. You know mom made all of mine and since I don't have a daughter, I really couldn't even begin to guess what one costs." Long pause as J.C. took a few bites of her sandwich and sipped some soup. "I pulled out all the old clothes in Johnnie's room and I'm running them through the washer to freshen them up. I was thinking I will call Nadine and see if they still ship clothes to a mission overseas from her church. These are so dated, no one here will be able to use them." J.C. caught herself as she recalled some of her memories from earlier in the morning and wondered how painful this might be for her father, knowing that the last memories of his son would be leaving the house. Did he go up and look at Johnnie's clothes from time to time? Did he just sit in the room and remember the fun and laughter that Johnnie brought to their lives for those brief six years? Seeing Vince's compassion to please his daughter this morning and recalling the 'Tickle Fights' memories, J.C. found some compassion for her father that she never remembered feeling before.

"Dad, do you not want me to take Johnnie's things to Nadine's church?" J.C.'s words almost caught in her throat.

After what seemed like an eternity, he replied, "That's fine." Will stood and took his dishes to the sink in the kitchen and walked out the door into the mudroom.

J.C. sat at the dining room table for a long time, staring across the table where Johnnie once sat, grinning and bursting with life. He was a miniature Will. She imagined that Will must have looked just like Johnnie when he was a boy with blond hair, bright eyes, and strong physique. At the age of six, Johnnie knew more about farming than many adults. He and Will carried on conversations about cows, hay, crops and all the facets of farm life. What a devastation that must have been when Johnnie was gone. But was J.C. *chopped liver* because she was a girl? Why had Will stopped loving her when Johnnie died? With the old memories creeping back in, J.C. remembered more than the 'Tickle Fights'; sitting on her dad's lap in his chair as he helped her sound out words in a book when she was Johnnie's age, teaching her how to tie her shoes, taking her on tractor rides around the farm. Will had been a compassionate father before Johnnie died. How had her mom been able to bounce back but Will had not? Her cell phone rang jolting her back to reality.

"Hello, this is J.C., can I help you?" She was still in customer service mode when she answered her phone.

"J.C., this is Doris. Your mail is heavy this week and I think you might have a few bills. Do you want to give me a forwarding address?" The older lady on the other end was always eager to help J.C. out whenever she traveled or was away from her condo for a period of time.

"Doris, I was going to call you tonight," J.C. said with a smile. "The mail is fine. I will be coming back to Des Moines before any of those bills need to be paid; so just put them on my counter in the kitchen and I will grab them. The reason I was going to call you was to ask about prom dress shopping. I have a friend out here that is a widower with a teenage daughter. He needs some guidance on where to go and how much to spend on prom dresses." J.C. felt confident that Doris would have a few suggestions for Vince.

"Well, I never took my granddaughter to the malls. Those stores sell the same or similar dresses to all the girls that come in. You could show up and be dressed just like someone else. I like the trunk shows," Doris said sternly.

"Trunk Shows? What are those?" J.C. inquired.

"They are designers that bring gowns into a hotel or convention room and sell them out of large clothing trunks," Doris said.

"I don't think my friend is looking for a designer dress for his daughter. Pretty sure that was his concern with the second question about a reasonable price." J.C. pushed back.

"Well, actually the dresses we found at the trunk shows were much more reasonable than the malls. I think since they did not have shipping fees and store mark-up, they were cheaper. Both of my granddaughter's prom dresses were close to $100. One slightly over that but nowhere near the

$500 to $600 some of her friends spent," Doris said with a punch of confidence.

"OK, well that sounds like something he might be interested in knowing more about. Where and when are these trunk shows?" J. C. asked.

"This time of year, they are usually at the larger hotels or convention centers on Saturdays and Sundays. These designers come in for just a couple of weekends during prom season and that is your only chance to see their gowns. If you are interested, you better check it out soon. They are usually done before early March." Doris showed some intensity in her voice.

"Last question, where can I find out about these?" J.C. felt the urgency to move quickly on this idea.

"The Des Moines Register sometimes runs an ad for them or you could go on the internet and see if there are any scheduled in Des Moines," Doris replied.

"OK, thanks so much, Doris. I will inquire on the internet and pass on this idea to my friend. I will call you when I am headed back to Des Moines. Thanks so much for taking care of my place while I am away. Good-bye." J.C. switched her phone over to the internet.

She typed in Prom Dress Trunk Shows. Talesse' Designs at Adventureland Inn popped up. The date was this coming Saturday only. Wow! Thank you, Doris, she thought. J.C. read the website and looked through a few pictures that were posted. This was exactly what Vince needed. No mall, lower prices, unique dresses, and the help of the designer's staff to make sure the fit was perfect. She copied the website and forwarded it to the cell number he had left her earlier that day.

Next, she called Nadine. "Hello, Nadine. It's J.C. I have been cleaning Johnnie's room today and washed all his clothes. Does your church still ship clothing to missions in foreign countries?" she asked.

"Yes." Nadine's voice had some hesitation.

CHAPTER 6

"Good, I will bring these in the next time I head to town and you can donate them to your church," J.C. replied.

"Does Will know what you're up to?" Nadine inquired.

"Yes, I told him at dinner last night and again at lunch today. He said '*Fine!*'" J.C. emphasized the fine! "What are you up to tomorrow? I was thinking we could start on Mom's stuff." J.C. was in her 'let's get things done mode' and wanted Nadine to jump on her bandwagon.

"Tomorrow won't work for me," Nadine replied.

"Oh, well what is a good day?" J.C. shot back.

"Let's look at Monday or Tuesday next week," Nadine suggested.

Boy, that slows down the getting-things-done-quickly mode that J.C. was in, but she agreed, "OK."

"What else have you been up to?" Nadine asked.

"Not much, there is not much to do. I guess the big excitement of my day was finding out some information about prom dresses," J.C. shared.

"Tell me more, this sounds interesting." Nadine's interest picked up.

"Well, Vince Martin stopped over this morning and asked me to give him some advice on shopping for his daughter, Kelsey's prom dress. You know Mom made all my dresses for high school dances and I have no personal experience, so I tried to send him to some local moms. He was not interested in that route at all. Seems he knows what a gossip center the Stuart community is. I agreed to use some of my contacts in Des Moines and Doris. You remember my neighbor that you and mom met when you came to see my condo, right?" J.C. took a breath.

"Yes," Nadine replied.

"Well, Doris raised her granddaughter through her high school years and there are these trunk shows where designers come to town with literally trunks full of dresses and sell them at a hotel. There is a show this weekend at

35

Adventureland Inn, so I passed that information on to Vince." With a big sigh J.C. took a deep breath.

"Well, that did not take long." Nadine was smiling into the phone and J.C. could tell from her tone that Nadine was up to something.

"What is that supposed to mean?" J.C. shot back.

"Vince Martin stopping by to see you the first week you are home." Nadine was still smiling thinking she was super insightful.

"Funny!" J.C. said sarcastically. "He knew I was here because he was giving a cow a shot the day I got here. And he thought since I was an accomplished businesswoman, I might know a thing or two about shopping."

"Whatever you say," Nadine responded. "Sorry got to run to make my hair appointment. I will call you the first of the week and we can decide which day works best to go through Evelyn's things."

"OK, good-bye." J.C. hung up the phone and went to check on the laundry.

Chapter 7

J.C. finished dinner preparation of chicken fried steak with mashed potatoes. This had been one of her father's favorite meals that Evelyn made. J.C. was certain that her potatoes were not as fluffy, and the steak might be a little tough but at least she attempted to make a nice dinner for her dad. Her cell phone rang, and she looked around a few seconds before locating it on the corner of the dining room table. She was shocked to see Vince Martin's name on the screen. She had only added his number that morning. "Hello, Vince," J.C. said.

"Hello, J.C. I cannot thank you enough for getting me this information so quickly. Am I calling at a bad time?" Vince asked.

"No, dad has not come in for dinner yet," J.C. replied.

"Well, do you know if there will be another show like this in the next couple of weeks?" Vince inquired.

"No, why?" J.C. asked.

"Well, this weekend I am on call, so I cannot take Kelsey and as much as she thinks she is ready to do this on her own... I just do not want to send her to a hotel by herself with my credit card. She was so excited when we looked at the website after school today. I know she will be disappointed if we can't find another show like this, or I guess we can resort to going to the mall like everyone else." Vince's voice dropped, and J.C. could tell he was trying to convince himself more than her.

"I could take her," came out of J.C.'s mouth before her mind had time to even think of what to say. She was offering to take a teenager dress shopping for a very important event in her life, and J.C. knew less about dress shopping than Vince did. Her heart started to race. "I have to pick up some mail and swap out some clothes, so I was going to head back to the city this weekend anyway." J.C. stopped herself and drew in a deep breath and held the phone away from her body looking at it with surprise.

"J.C. that is extremely generous; are you sure you wouldn't mind? Kelsey will be thrilled to get the opportunity to go to this trunk show." Vince's voice was filled with excitement.

J.C. took another deep breath before pulling the phone back to her ear. "Not a problem at all." She had committed now, and her heart raced even faster.

"You are a lifesaver! I do not know how to thank you for doing this for me, J.C." Vince was in full genuine nice mode.

"I don't know about the lifesaving part. Remember, I have less experience shopping with a teenage daughter than you do. You will need to give me some guidelines. And, when you run this idea by Kelsey, she may shoot it down. So, let's not get too excited." J.C. saw her way out. Maybe Kelsey would not want a total stranger taking her to such a meaningful appointment.

"I'll talk to Kelsey and call you tomorrow. Thanks again, J.C. Good night." Vince hung up.

J.C. was still standing at the corner of the dining room table when Will came through the kitchen door. He stepped immediately into the bathroom and she heard the shower come on. J.C. began setting the table and putting the rest of the evening meal together. Her mind was not thinking about what she was doing; instead, she had made a commitment to take a seventeen-year-old shopping. She felt nervous and a little scared. A couple of the women she worked with had told horror stories of having to walk behind their daughters at the mall, getting yelled at when things did not fit right and many tears during shopping excursions. At those discussions during coffee, J.C. always congratulated herself that she had been wise enough not to get herself into that situation. Some of these moms seemed completely miserable. Now, she was putting herself into a situation that she knew nothing about. This girl had just lost her mother, her emotions could be very high and what's more she could really disappoint Vince. Why did that matter? Now she was starting an argument in her mind and just had to toss her head side to side to clear it all out. She was a professional that dealt with every type of personality over the years and would not be baffled by a teenager.

Will came out of the bathroom and walked through the dining room to his bedroom. She pulled the steaks out of the oven and sat down at the table. Will quickly returned, sat down, bowed his head, and silently prayed. J.C. just stared at him. Dinner was completely silent. She had given the update at lunch and he would have no interest in the latest developments. Will finished eating, took his plate to the kitchen and placed it in the sink. J.C. finished eating as she sat alone in silence. She cleared the table, washed, and dried the dishes, put the leftovers away and straightened up the kitchen. Before heading upstairs, she brushed her teeth, took off her make-up and walked slowly through the living room. "Good night, Dad," J.C. said. No response.

Once upstairs, J.C. put on her P.J.'s and laid out some workout clothes. She would set an alarm and head into town to work out at the middle school early the next morning. A hard workout would feel good and maybe clear some of the crazy thoughts that were starting to build up in her mind. It was still early so she sat down at the desk and checked emails. Only two from former colleagues. One with a question about work and the second just checking to see what she had been up to. She quickly replied to both. Next, she pulled up Talesse' Designs. The company was thirty-five years old. Talesse' was the mother of three daughters and they all worked together creating designs and making dresses in their New York studio. No two dresses alike! No chance of someone else showing up in a dress just like yours, J.C. thought. Approximately twenty years ago they started taking their designs throughout the United States by doing these trunk shows. Prom dresses, wedding dresses, cocktail and holiday themes seem to be their lines of business. Saturday was their first Midwest show. They were testing the market with a one day stop in Des Moines. The show was split between prom and wedding designs. Attendees were encouraged to come early to complete the registration process and sizing. J.C. drilled down on sizing. Really! They must measure each patron so that no one wastes time trying on dresses that wouldn't fit. That's impressive, J.C. thought to herself. Once the runway portion was completed, you would be called by your registration number and using a selection card that you marked during the show, an attendant pulls the gowns for patrons to try on. You and your chaperone (mother, in most cases) were sent to a room and the dresses were brought to you. Each patron could try on up to ten dresses. If you did not select one, you could get a second card but had to return to the viewing area to mark additional dresses while someone else was in the dressing rooms. Wow! This is quite the event. If nothing else, J.C. was a little excited just to see the production.

She smiled as the thought crossed her mind, that Vince might have gone there totally unprepared if he was not on call this weekend. When he called tomorrow, she would recommend that they leave around 7:00 a.m. on Saturday. Oh, no, what if Kelsey was one of those teens that sleeps till noon she thought? The early bird gets the best dress would be the summary of her research that she would pass along.

J.C. leaned back in her chair and her mind drifted to her own high school proms. She stood up and walked over to the bookshelf to pull out her photo albums. The high school one contained the pictures she was remembering. As she began to flip through them, she gulped at how awful her hair looked; dark brown curls dropping down from the top of her head. How ridiculous was that style? The first dress was a bright red satin. It had long sleeves and a small V-neck. No waist, slightly fitted and draped to the floor. It did make her look taller and the shine of the material reflected a nice glow on her face. Her necklace was a string of pearls that belonged to her mom. J.C. remembered thinking the night of prom that she looked elegant as she admired herself in the dressing room before heading downstairs to meet Jim Powell who was her date their junior year. Jim brought a wrist corsage of red roses and white carnations which was a perfect accent to her dress. The picture of her and Jim made her look even better. He was a very handsome athletic type, and they did make a nice-looking couple.

She flipped forward a few more pages and found her senior year pictures. The hair was slightly better. The sides were pulled to the top of her head and she only had curls flowing down the back; most of her long hair was straight. The light-yellow dress was much frillier. The ruffles started around the shoulders and were three layers deep to the bustline. It had an empire waistline and an A-line skirt. She again wore her mother's pearl necklace but added some teardrop earrings. I think those I borrowed from Nadine, J.C. thought to herself. Dick Thomas was her date that year; he was not as handsome as Jim, but they had more fun she recalled. She smiled as she put the book back on the shelf and headed into bed.

Chapter 8

*T*he alarm on J.C.'s phone made her jump. It had been over two weeks since she had set an alarm and this morning, she could hear the cold wind blowing fiercely outside her window. Maybe she should just roll over and pull the covers over her head. It was only 5:30 a.m.; she might wake up her dad. Who in this small town would be at the gym at this hour she wondered? If she thought long enough there would eventually be an excuse to stay in bed. She pushed the covers back and walked to the dressing room. As she came down the stairs, she was surprised to see her father seated in his chair with the floor lamp on. Reading his Bible! Had he gone to bed? Did the man ever sleep? "Good Morning Dad, I am headed into town to work out." J.C. laid out her plan as she headed out the front door. The wind was blowing, and the air was extremely cold as she ran to the Lexus which she had remotely started from her bedroom earlier. "Ah!" she sighed as she settled into her warm car. "I know if this car did not have remote start, I would still be under those warm blankets upstairs," J.C. said out loud even though no one could hear her.

The middle school was full of people at 5:55 a.m. J.C. did not look around. She set her gym bag on the bleachers and started to stretch. Once she felt her muscles loosen up, she began to jog around the outside of the gym on the indoor track. She tried hard to stay focused and not look around too much. She was not wanting to draw attention or stop to get caught up with some ancient friend from her past. It was on her second lap that her plan was failed. Someone jogged up alongside of her and said, "I could not believe my eyes when you walked in this morning." J.C. turned her head and right beside her was Jim Powell. At least she thought it has to be Jim. His eyes, smile and face seemed to fit but that out of shape and overweight body looked nothing like the athletic build he had maintained all through high school. "Hi, Jim." J.C. smiled.

"What brings you out on such a cold morning?" he asked.

"Just needed to get some exercise," J.C. responded.

"Doesn't look to me like you need much of that. My gosh, J.C. you look as great as you did on the softball mound your senior year in high school. You haven't changed one bit and are just as gorgeous as ever," Jim gushed.

J.C. quickly remembered why she and Jim never developed much of a relationship in high school. Jim was a lady's man then and by the sounds of things this morning that had not changed. Her local friends had kept her updated over the years about his multiple marriages. Which this morning, she could not recall if he was currently in one or not. "What's new with you, Jim?" J.C. asked to stop his unnecessary dribble.

"Recently divorced and trying to get the old gut under control." Jim grinned as if he was making progress.

"Well, don't let me keep you from your normal workout. I just need to loosen up and then see if one of those bikes open up." J.C. tried to give the hint that she was not looking for a workout partner. There were a couple of older men who lived in her condo building that always were looking for companionship while they worked out. She avoided them too and was hopeful Jim would take the hint. He did not!

"So, home for a visit?" Jim inquired.

"Yes." J.C. was not going to give out any more information than was required. She started to run a little faster hoping that Jim might get tired and lag behind. He surprisingly was able to match her pace.

"Well, if you have some free time while you are home, we should get together and catch up." Jim smiled.

"Oh, it looks like one of the bikes is free … see you, Jim." J.C. turned and cut across the gym at an angle to make sure she was next on the exercise bike. Jim waved and continued to run laps. J.C. spent thirty minutes on the bike and made sure she saw Jim head to the locker room before moving over to do free weights.

It was exactly 7:00 a.m. when J.C. picked up her last round of weights and began reps. As she pulled up two 25 lb. weights, Jim was directly in front of her. He had showered, dressed, and somehow come up from behind her. She almost dropped the weights in mid-air. "Jim, you startled me!" J.C. gasped for air.

"Oh, sorry, just wanted to say how great it was to see you. Stop by the office when you are done here, and we can set up a time to get together. I am still up on Main Street." Jim smiled big and turned.

"Wait." J.C. breathed in deep to catch her breath. "Jim, I am really busy and just came into town this morning because I have been away from the gym for over a week. I need to get back out to the farm today. Sorry, not sure when I will have time to get together." J.C. was relieved that she had stopped him and hoped he got the message that she was not planning on stopping today or any day.

Jim looked disappointed. "Well, you know where to find me." He turned and walked out of the gym.

J.C. heaved a sigh of relief and dropped the weights and herself right behind them to the floor. It had felt good to work out, but the risk of bumping into Jim each morning would be a deterrent. She grabbed her bag and headed into the locker room to shower.

Chapter 9

Will had finished breakfast and was outside when J.C. got back home that morning. She poured herself a cup of coffee and sipped on it while she waited for her whole wheat toast to pop up. As she studied the contents of the refrigerator, she grabbed a carton of yogurt to go with her toast. J.C. had just sat down at the dining room table when her phone rang. It was Vince Martin.

"Good morning, Vince," J.C. said with a smile on her face.

"J.C., am I calling too early?" Vince asked.

"No, I just got back from the middle school. I went in there to work out this morning," J.C. informed him.

"Well, you are ambitious." Vince chuckled. "Kelsey was over the moon excited last night when I told her you were going to Des Moines on Saturday and would take her to the trunk show."

"Really, I wondered how she would feel about a total stranger ..." J.C. stopped as she could not think how to finish the sentence without sounding like she was trying to get out of her obligation.

"Stranger!" Vince laughed, "Kelsey has never met anyone that she considers a stranger, which was one of my concerns about her going by herself. Secondly, I have not allowed her to drive in Des Moines alone yet. Plus, the thought of her going into a hotel with a bunch of unknown people that might be looking to take advantage of a young teenager was giving me heartburn." Vince paused. "Kelsey and I both know that this is a big favor you are doing for us, which is why Kelsey suggested that we have you over for dinner on Friday night so the two of you could meet prior to your shopping spree." Vince paused again.

J.C. sat straight up in her chair and drew in a deep breath. "You want me to come for dinner tomorrow night?" she asked. That is what he said. Why are you repeating that back to him? Just trying to buy time in case I can come up with a logical excuse. Do I want an excuse? Her mind was racing before J.C. caught herself and realized she did not hear what Vince had said.

"What? I'm sorry; I got distracted," J.C. admitted.

"Kelsey thought it might be a nice gesture to have you over for dinner since you were doing us such a big favor. Also, that would give you both a chance to get to know one another before Saturday morning," Vince repeated nicely.

"Oh, sure," J.C. responded. "Speaking of Saturday morning we will need to leave kind of early. I did some more research online last night and they recommend you get there early to register before the style show starts." J.C. was passing along the warning of 'early bird gets the best dress' theme she had picked up from the website.

"Great, we kind of thought the same thing last night as we researched their website a little more thoroughly," Vince said.

Vince looking at the same website J.C. had been on last night. What dad does that? "What time were you thinking?" Vince asked.

"The doors open at 8:00 a.m. so we need to leave no later than 7:00 a.m., or maybe even 6:45 a.m., if Kelsey is up by that time?" J.C. could hear hesitation in her voice as she suggested the time.

CHAPTER 9

"Kelsey will be ready by 5:00 a.m. probably, but you ladies can finalize that at dinner tomorrow night. Will 6:30 p.m. work for you?" Vince asked J.C., to confirm she was accepting their invitation.

"6:30 p.m. is fine." J.C. exhaled.

"Great, we will see you tomorrow night. You remember where my parents' farm is, right?" Vince asked.

"Sure, go to Morgan's corner north of the church, turn right and go three miles east." J.C. could distinctly remember this bus stop. Vince had two older sisters that were the prettiest girls on the bus when she first started riding. They were always so nice to the younger kids and on special occasions even gave them candy canes, apples, or handmade cards. She loved watching them walk to the bus as they were always pristinely dressed and carried their books like they were movie stars. Vince followed close behind them. His mother must have taught him to be a gentleman when he was a toddler.

Wow, another walk down memory lane was interrupted, when Vince said, "OK, see you tomorrow. Goodbye, J.C."

"Bye," was all she could squeak out.

The cup of coffee in front of her reminded her of where and who she was. J.C. had not accepted an invitation to dinner in over five years. Life had been complicated at one point with men and at the age of forty-five, she told her mother she was done. No more relationships! Evelyn had said to her, "the right guy has just not come along yet, honey. When he does, you won't know what hit you." Well, Evelyn had not been the greatest at picking men, so J.C. had brushed off those comments as soon as she heard them. She was not looking for a relationship and this was definitely not that. A neighbor needed help and she offered that since he had to work this weekend. She found herself in a mental argument as she finished her toast and yogurt. Vince was such a nice guy, but his greatest concern was making his daughter happy in the absence of her mother. This was just the neighborly thing to do.

J.C. picked up her dishes and placed them in the kitchen sink. It was 9:00 a.m. Her task today was to wash the curtains in her bedroom and Johnnie's. She grabbed the stool out of the mudroom and headed upstairs. Returning to Johnnie's room where she had left the door open from yesterday, J.C. recognized the scent of Lysol as she walked in. It smelled clean rather than musty. J.C. placed the stool in front of the first window and examined the hooks that held the curtains on the rod. It was a simple hook, and she was able to lift them off each pleat until the curtain fell limp in her arms. Dust sifted through the air and made her sneeze. It had been years since these had seen soap and water, she thought. She moved to the second window and did the same. As she went back through the door between the two rooms, she noticed the corner of a box underneath Johnnie's bed. She quickly removed the two curtains from her room and leaving the stool upstairs, hurried down to the mudroom and put the curtains in the washer. She set the dial on warm water, added some gentle detergent, and headed back upstairs.

Re-entering Johnnie's room, she knelt at the bottom of the small bed and pulled out the box. It was covered in dust. She pulled it towards her on the floor and slowly opened the flaps on top. The first thing she saw were Johnnie's kindergarten pictures smiling up at her. She knew immediately that was what they were. She remembered them both showing each other their school pictures on the bus before they got home. Now, after all this time she realized she did not have one picture of Johnnie. She never thought to ask her mother for one when she was growing up. Until today, she did not remember any pictures of him. Her senior picture was still hanging on the living room wall downstairs. She asked herself–*Was there ever a picture of Johnnie anywhere in the house while she was growing up?* No, her mind answered.

Under the pictures were some school papers, math, penmanship, art, and workbooks. As she sifted through the box she wondered if this was what her mother did when she would come into Johnnie's room while she was at school. J.C. stopped and recalled the conversation with Will in the kitchen the day before. He knew the light bulbs were burnt out – so he was not looking at these. Did he even know they were there? Did he want to know they were there? J.C. picked the box up, took it downstairs and set it on the end of the dining room table. She poured herself another cup of coffee. Slowly she sorted through the box again. Taking time to really look at each item, she tried to remember Johnnie on the bus, and anything that would bring back memories of what these forty-year-old papers meant to this family.

The kitchen door opened, and Will came in for lunch. J.C. sucked in her breath as she looked at the clock on the wall and realized it was 12:15 p.m. and she had not prepared anything. "Dad, I am sorry, I got caught up…" She stopped herself before she blurted out what she was doing. "I can make you a sandwich or soup really quick." J.C. wanted to hide the box, but it was all spread out on the table. Will glanced into the dining room and turned towards the refrigerator. He opened the door and took out the leftovers from dinner the night before. Placing a piece of steak and some potatoes on a plate, he set them in the microwave. While the microwave reheated his meal, Will went into the bathroom. When he came out, he stood at the kitchen counter and ate his lunch. Within ten minutes, he was finished and back out the door before J.C. had a chance to collect all the contents and stack them back into the box. She heard the door close and knew that Will recognized the items immediately. A chill ran through her body and a tear fell down her cheek. J.C. carried the box back upstairs and put it next to her desk in the study. She did not know what she would do with the items inside, but she would not leave them out where Will would have to see them again.

J.C. was not hungry and skipped lunch. The curtains finished drying and as she pulled them out of the dryer, she decided to iron them before rehanging them in the bedrooms. The ironing board was hanging on the back of the mudroom door. J.C. lifted it down and set it in the walk space of the mudroom. She looked around to see where the iron might be. Finally, she found it in the small cupboard next to the washer. J.C. plugged it in and hoped that it would heat up. It did. As she completed each panel, J.C. carried them in and draped them over the dining room chairs. She ironed four sets of curtains and her back ached. How in the world did women of her mother's generation stand and iron clothes all day long? J.C. was relieved when she finally finished. She carried the clean pressed curtains back upstairs and rehung them on the windows in Johnnie's room. She realized that her windows needed washing before putting her curtains back up. She headed downstairs and grabbed the Windex and rags that she used the previous day. While she was down there, she decided to put the ironing board and iron away, so they would not be in Will's way if he came back in. Just as she was finishing, Will came to the back door and waited while she hung the ironing board up. When she had finished, he came in, took off his boots and walked through the kitchen into the dining room and picked up the phone.

J.C. watched from the kitchen as her father dialed the phone. "John, it is Will Mason. I have about thirty head of fat hogs that I need to sell in the next week to ten days. What kind of price can you give me? That sounds a little lower than the average that KMA has reported this past week. OK, call me back. Yes, I will wait by the phone." Will sounded gruff on the phone and sat down at the dining room table to wait for the return call. J.C. handed him a cup of coffee. He did not look up or say a word. She walked through the living room with her rags and Windex and went back upstairs.

Climbing the stairs, J.C. thought he really does have control of his business. No one is going to take advantage of Will. He keeps up with the market trends and won't settle for less than the top market price. She began cleaning her south windows and heard the phone ring below her. "OK, that sounds more like it. I will bring a load of thirty in tomorrow morning." J.C.

CHAPTER 9

could hear Will through the floor register. Then she heard the kitchen door and watched her father walk across the driveway and into the barnyard. When the curtains were back up, J.C. decided to change her clothes and head outside to see if she could help Will separate the hogs and prepare for his delivery the following morning.

It had been years since J.C. had been in the barnyard. Approximately eight years ago, Will had gotten sick and Evelyn called J.C. to come home. The doctors finally determined that Will had diabetes and with medication and some changes to his diet, he got back on his feet quickly. But there was about two weeks in which Evelyn did all the chores and took care of everything outside. J.C. took some days off work and helped for four or five days.

Her mother's coveralls hung on a hook in the mudroom. J.C. pulled them on over her jeans and sweatshirt and put her boots on, opened the back door and headed to the hog barn. She found her mother's work gloves in the pockets of the coveralls. When she opened the door, the hog smell almost took her breath away. She held her nose for a minute before entering the barn. It had been years since she was in there. Will was in one corner moving gates.

J.C. walked over to him. "Dad, what can I do to help?" Will looked at J.C. Her heart skipped a beat, and her mouth went dry. Her father had not looked into her eyes in such a long time it was almost shocking. Her breath caught in her chest. The next moment, she realized they were in the hog barn! J.C. shook off her daze as Will motioned for her to pick up the other end of the gate. She helped him bring four more gates from the corner of the barn to build a temporary pen in the center aisle. The hogs were loud and squealing constantly. She had forgotten how much she disliked this part of farming. When they finished building the temporary pen, Will stepped into a full pen of hogs, and using his sorting cane he started moving one hog at a time out of the pen. When he got close to the corner, he waved his hand at J.C. and she knew that meant to open the gate just enough that only that pig could get through. This process continued for almost two hours. A couple of times she allowed more than one through and then Will would step into the newly made pen and find the hog he did not want to sell and bring it back to the gate. J.C. would swing it the other way and the pig would re-enter the bigger feeding pen. When thirty head of hogs were in the temporary holding pen, Will locked the corner gate of the pen that the hogs were sorted from. He walked through the group of hogs he had selected and ran his hand over their backs and pressed into their spine to confirm these were fat enough to go to market. Then he poured feed into some round feed troughs that he had placed in the temporary pen.

Will walked out of the barn and J.C. stood for a moment wondering if they were done. No, thank you – nothing at all, she thought. How does he possibly do this by himself? It had taken over two hours with her help. If he was there alone it would have taken him all day. As she was standing there trying to determine if he really did do all this alone, the barn door opened. Will pushed the sliding door open and walked back to his tractor that was attached to a loading shoot. He backed the tractor into the barn and eased the shoot right up to the corner of the gates on the opposite side of where J.C. was standing. Sure, she thought to herself. He needs that shoot in place so that tomorrow morning, he can walk these hogs into the trailer and take them to town. J.C. could see that her father had things under control and headed back to the house. She was starving since she skipped lunch and she wanted to get through with her shower before he came into the house. After removing the coveralls and boots in the mudroom, J.C. grabbed an apple and ran upstairs to get her robe. She immediately returned to take a shower, wash her hair, and put on clean clothes before starting dinner.

Chapter 10

*F*riday morning, J.C. rose to her 5:30 a.m. alarm again. She was not headed back to the middle school, but instead planned on helping Will load the hogs. She pulled on her dirty jeans and sweatshirt from yesterday and headed down to breakfast. Will was still seated in his chair with his Bible in his lap. She did not speak and walked quietly past into the dark dining room and kitchen. She flipped on the kitchen light and pulled out a skillet, cracked three eggs, and whipped them into a fluff adding some fresh onion and bacon bits to make scrambled eggs. While those finished, she put two pieces of whole wheat bread in the toaster, poured some orange juice into two glasses, and started the coffee. The sausage patties were precooked so she tossed a couple of those in the microwave for Will. When Will came into the kitchen J.C. said, "I got this today, Dad." He filled a cup of coffee, turned on the radio, and headed to the dining room table.

J.C. fixed him a plate with eggs, sausage and toast and set it on the table in front of him. She returned to the kitchen and prepared a separate plate of eggs and toast for herself. She reached in the refrigerator and grabbed another yogurt. As soon as the morning livestock report was over, Will finished his coffee, took his dishes to the kitchen, and headed into the mudroom. J.C. knew that it would take approximately thirty minutes for him to hay and feed the other animals before he would be ready to start the loading process. She was certain that this was something he normally did on his own, but today she was committed to helping him.

She cleaned up the kitchen, then took a roast out of the freezer and placed it in an old crock pot her mother kept on the top of the kitchen cupboards. Since she was not going to be around tonight for dinner, she wanted to make sure she left something for Will. As she finished seasoning the meat, she thought to herself, he has been feeding himself these past eleven months; he would have been just fine if she was not there. She thought back to her comments earlier that week about Nadine staying so young. Will also did not let his seventy-five years of age slow him down much.

J.C. put the coveralls back on, put on her boots and pulled on work gloves before stepping out into the cold morning air. The light in the eastern sky indicated that the sun was about to pop over the pasture's ridge. She stood for a few moments just taking in the early morning on the farm. As a child she enjoyed getting up early and being outside as soon as possible. When she was young, her mother raised chickens and Jacquelyn helped gather the eggs and feed the hens before breakfast each morning. Her mother stopped raising chickens once J.C. was gone, so she could have the flexibility to come and stay at J.C.'s from time to time and do things together.

J.C. walked slowly to the hog barn and opened the door. Will was still filling the feeders in the three pens of hogs that were not going to town today. She watched him carefully move between the feed tank and the pens balancing five-gallon buckets of feed in each hand. His motion was perfect as he made three more trips after she came into the barn. Will turned and saw J.C. watching him and he motioned towards the rubber pans that he had hung on the wall the day prior. J.C. grabbed the pans and put them into the temporary pen just as Will arrived with two buckets of feed. The pigs quickly ate all the feed; J.C. grabbed the rubber pans and walked to the opposite side and held them until Will was there with two more buckets. She dropped, he poured, and the hogs consumed in a matter of a few minutes.

Will left the two buckets next to the feed tank, walked through the door, and was gone. J.C. knew he was headed out to get the pickup and trailer. She hung the feed pans back on the wall and slowly walked along side of the other pig pens. She estimated two-hundred feeder pigs still left in the barn. Will no longer farrowed his own pigs. He bought smaller pigs from neighbors and fed them out for market. The big east door of the barn opened and J.C. saw Will walking to the pickup, so he could back the trailer into the entrance and up to the loading shoot. She walked toward the loading shoot knowing it would be helpful if she could motion to him how close he was coming to it. She positioned herself in the sight line of his left pickup mirror and waited as he slowly backed into the barn. J.C. raised her right hand and began slowly motioning that he could continue to back in. When Will was about two feet away, she held her palm up to stop. He immediately stopped. She held up both hands showing him the twenty-four inches left to reach his destination. Will took his foot off the brake and slowly eased backwards. At less than five inches, J.C. gave him the sign again to stop and held up both hands five inches apart. Will released the brake and the trailer rolled up against the loading shoot.

Will locked the pickup brakes and turned off the ignition. He walked back to the trailer and lifted the overhead gate with the pulley. J.C. stepped back out of the way as Will slowly adjusted the jack under the loading shoot so that the top of the shoot was level with the trailer gate. Once everything was set, Will stepped into the temporary pen with his sorting cane and began herding the hogs up the shoot. J.C. stood back and watched as her father did something he had done hundreds of times before with ease and confidence. Will followed the last hog up the shoot and released the overhead gate on the trailer. He crawled down the side of the shoot and walked to the front of the pickup. He stepped inside, started the ignition, released the brake, and slowly pulled out of the barn. J.C. followed the trailer until it cleared the east door and then waved to her father that she was closing it.

J.C. looked at the temporary pen and remembered how they constructed it the day before. She walked over to the toolbox underneath the hanging feed pans and pulled out a pair of pliers. She returned to the pen and twisted the wire to release the first gate. She continued until all the holding wires were released. She began dragging gates behind her to the corner until all the gates were back where Will stored them in the corner. She knew when her dad got home, he would park the trailer and bring the skid steer down to pull the posts up and store them also. When she dropped the pliers back in the toolbox, she smiled that her help had successfully worked up a good sweat and she saved her dad a couple hours of work.

J.C. was just taking off her coveralls when the pickup and trailer pulled back into the driveway. She hoped Will would be pleased with his surprise. She also thought about how all her colleagues at 'big blue' would never believe her if she told them what she had just done.

Will came in for lunch about an hour later. J.C. had made potato soup out of the leftovers in the refrigerator and set a bowl of soup in front of Will just as he said, "Thanks." He did not look up or say anything more... just thanks! J.C. smiled.

The lunch report began as soon as J.C. set her bowl of soup on the table. "Dad, I am going over to Vince Martin's tonight for dinner. He wants me to get to know his daughter, Kelsey, before I take her into Des Moines tomorrow. I need to go pick up my mail and she needs someone to take her to look for prom dresses. Vince is on call, so he cannot go. I started a roast in the slow cooker this morning and you can make some sandwiches out of that for tonight and tomorrow. I think we will leave pretty early in the morning and I am not sure how late we will be tomorrow night." J.C. took a breath and sipped some soup.

"Vince Martin is a good man." Will made a single statement.

J.C.'s head shot up and she looked to see if her father was looking at her. No, his head was bent over his bowl – but he had engaged in the current topic! "Yes, Vince is a good man and good father. He just wants to make sure that his daughter is safe and happy," J.C. explained.

The rest of the day was spent on J.C. getting ready for dinner with Vince and his daughter. She showered after lunch, dried her hair, and flattened it with her flat iron. In her dressing room, she flipped through all the clothes she had brought with her. J.C. again wondered why she brought so many workout clothes. Jeans and a sweater were the obvious selection but of the ones she brought, none of them seemed to be right for tonight. Selecting the right jeans was a start. She pulled out her dark blue, Gap brand jeans that she would tuck into her brown boots. Half done. She held up each sweater and shook her head that none of them were right. Hanging next to one of the dresses she had brought, was a blue and white striped button-down blouse. She held that up. OK, that would do with the jeans she thought. She sat down in front of the mirror to do her makeup. J.C. never wore much makeup. Mascara, eye liner under her eyes and a little toner on her cheeks was her normal style. Today she tried a couple of shades of eye shadow and wiped them both off immediately.

She wondered if Vince's daughter Kelsey was into makeup and current style trends. Would she have weird streaks of color in her hair and piercings? J.C. stopped herself. It did not matter what Kelsey's style was. J.C. just needed to stick to what worked for her; she found she was the most confident when she was true to herself.

Chapter 11

*A*t 6:00 p.m., J.C. headed downstairs. Will had not come in from outside. She checked the roast. It was done. She turned the crockpot on low and set the table with one plate and silverware. She looked in the downstairs bathroom mirror one more time. The lighting there was not nearly as good as in her dressing room upstairs, but she was still pleased with what she saw. She had her brown boots and down jacket with her when she came downstairs. She sat down and slipped on her boots. Putting on her jacket, she looked over her shoulder, for what ...? She did not know and then headed out the door to Vince's.

Her car clock said 6:25 p.m. when she pulled into the driveway of what had to be Vince Martin's place. It just looked so different. The big square house that was like her own parents was gone. A new ranch style house with a long deck on the front sat in its place. The barn had been resided with metal sheeting; and the grain bins that were along the driveway were all gone. She looked over her shoulder at the corner and confirmed this had to be the right place. She turned off her car and got out. J.C. walked up to the deck and rang the doorbell. Vince immediately opened the door.

"Wow, right on time; that is pretty rare for most women," Vince said with a big smile.

"My mother was a stickler for being on time and it has always been my Achilles' heel. People at work made fun of me for always being the first person to every meeting." J.C. explained her punctuality.

"Nothing wrong with that, please come in," Vince said welcoming her into his home.

Vince's home was comfortable and beautifully decorated. The kitchen was off to her left and opened to the great room she was standing in. A large stone fireplace covered the wall to her right. "Vince, this is beautiful, I almost thought I was at the wrong place. I didn't know you had torn down your parents' farmhouse and built a new home." J.C. spoke as she slipped out of her coat that Vince was taking as he walked back towards the kitchen. He hung it on a decorative hook at the end of the kitchen counter.

"Well, we lived in town when we first moved back but after my mother passed away, we decided we really wanted to live here on the farm. Teri, my wife, was not too excited about that draughty old farmhouse, so she designed and decorated this place for us. She studied interior design at Iowa State and after designing this house for us she started her own business. Kelsey had gotten older, and Teri needed something to keep her busy." Vince was very open and seemed comfortable sharing this information with J.C.

"Well, she was very talented. This is beautiful and has an immediate feeling of warmth when you walk in." J.C. complimented a woman she had never even met.

"Teri would have loved to hear that. She enjoyed entertaining and always wanted people to feel comfortable the minute they walked in. Kelsey, come out here. I want you to meet my friend, J.C. Mason." Vince raised his voice to get his daughter's attention.

"One minute, Dad, I am finishing my hair," Kelsey called back.

J.C. turned and smiled at Vince as she touched her own hair. They both chuckled.

"What can I get you to drink? Soda, iced tea, coffee?" Vince asked.

"A coffee would be great," J.C. responded.

Vince lit up when Kelsey walked into the room. J.C. turned to be introduced. "Kelsey, this is J.C. Mason. We went to high school and college together," Vince said as Kelsey walked toward J.C.

Kelsey was beautiful. She had long blonde hair, big blue eyes, the perfect complexion, stood five feet three inches tall and weighed about 100 lbs. She had Vince's smile. Her mother must have had the blonde hair and blue eyes, but her dad had given her the smile, her most attractive feature. "Hello, I am Kelsey Jo or K.J. as some of my high school friends call me," Kelsey said with that big smile still filling the room.

"Well, K.J., it is nice to meet you," J.C. said back returning the smile. "I got my nickname, J.C., in high school also!" They both giggled a little.

"So, you and my dad went to high school together? I cannot wait to hear some stories about his dorky days!" Kelsey said looking at her father as her eyes lit up.

"Sorry to disappoint you, but your father was nowhere close to dorky in high school. He was more of what we called 'hunky' in my day." J.C. blushed a little as the word 'hunky' came out of her mouth.

Kelsey burst into laughter. "My dad a hunk? You've got to be kidding! He is so straight and strict no one would ever believe that he wasn't a big *nerd* in high school." Kelsey was still laughing.

"Star football player, star basketball player, star track and baseball athlete. Smartest kid in his class. Homecoming King and Prom King. No one would have ever used the "*nerd*" word to describe your father. In fact, the word most associated with him was *nice*. Your father was an all-around *nice guy*." J. C. took in a big breath and continued. "*But* we did not really

CHAPTER 11

move in the same circles back then. He was a senior and I was a freshman, so I am only relaying what others said about him." J.C. felt compelled to dismiss a myth that they might have been friends in the past.

"All right ladies, enough about me," Vince said. "Tonight was planned so the two of you can get to know one another. The topic of Vince Martin is off the table for the night."

"Did you know my mom at Iowa State?" Kelsey's inquisitions were not going to stop anytime soon J.C. thought.

"No, I never met your mom. I rarely saw your dad while I was at Iowa State," J.C. admitted.

"Really, you never saw him in the four years you were there?" Kelsey seemed surprised.

"It is a big campus, and your dad was in the Veterinary School on the southeast side and my classes were mostly in the far northwest corner. So, we were on the opposite sides of campus. I would have been a freshman when your dad was finishing his senior year of undergraduate and then he started into the Veterinary School, so our paths never crossed." J.C. again making sure that Kelsey was clear on the relationship.

"Well, that is not completely true," Vince interjected.

J.C.'s head spun around towards the kitchen where Vince was standing and shot him a quizzical look.

"I saw J.C. every weekend there was a home football game and a few home basketball games when she was the halftime entertainment." Vince smiled from ear to ear knowing that this news was catching J.C. off guard.

Her face blushed and her heart started to race. What was he saying? He, along with thousands of others, watched her baton twirling routines with the marching band as they performed at home athletic events. He was confirming that he knew that was her. He must have kept track of the fact that she came to Iowa State and she performed with the band. Her name was not announced or publicized in the program booklets. She was still blushing when she gathered her composure. "Ok, you got me. Your dad and thousands of other fans watched me perform as a twirler with the marching band." J.C. was looking right at Vince as she spoke, and he was grinning from ear to ear.

"You performed at the games. *Wow!* That's a big deal. We have gone to a few football games at Iowa State, and I cannot believe that you were out there in front of all those fans. I would be so scared to do something like that." Kelsey was truly impressed with J.C.'s courage.

J.C. nodded and accepted the compliment politely.

"Kelsey, you can start setting the table while I take the steaks off the grill," Vince instructed his daughter.

"What can I do?" J.C. asked.

"Nothing, you are our guest," Vince said with a wink as he stepped out on the deck to retrieve the steaks.

J.C. followed Kelsey into the kitchen and helped anyway. They took plates out of the cupboard and placed them on the table in front of the fireplace. Kelsey brought over some glasses and silverware, handing the glasses over to J.C. to put at each place setting. As Kelsey poured water into each glass she asked, "J.C. do you have a family?"

J.C. was not ready for that question. Family had always been her parents. Now there was just her and her father. But she knew that was not what Kelsey meant. "No, I never got married or had children." J.C. made a statement of fact.

"Didn't you want to have a family?" Kelsey asked as Vince was reentering the house.

"Kelsey, that's a little too personal," Vince said in a stern and strict voice as he stepped back in from the deck.

"No, it's all right," J.C. responded after a deep breath. "I guess I just got so caught up in my career that I did not make time for a family. I moved from place to place and it would have been hard for a family to always have to follow me around the United States with each move that I made for the company." J.C. knew that was not all factual but at least it sounded like she was not as cold hearted towards this topic as her life had actually been. J.C. decided to stop playing defense and go on the offense for the remainder of the night. A sales tool that she learned early in her career. "Kelsey, what activities are you involved in at school?" she asked. J.C. was good at this and could play the 'what about you game' all night if she had to.

"Well, I am a cheerleader, in theater, chorus, and honors programs. I am on the Prom committee; it's so much fun. Our prom is April 13th and we are planning a 'Rain Theme'; which was my idea. We found a D.J. that brings a rain wall with him so all night it will sound like falling water in the gym. I am so excited about tomorrow." Vince motioned for them to sit down at the table and held his finger up to show Kelsey it was time to stop talking. Vince and Kelsey both bowed their heads and Vince prayed "Thank you God for the food, great health and our special guest that has so graciously agreed to help us out this weekend. Bless this food to our bodies. Amen." J.C. was stunned. She did not have time to react to her surprise. Vince immediately apologized when he lifted his head. "J.C., I am sorry, I should have asked you if you were OK with us saying grace. That was rude of me to assume." He was genuinely apologizing to her for doing something he had every right to do in his own home.

"No," she spoke directly, "it is perfectly fine; this is your home where you should do whatever you feel is appropriate." J.C.'s stomach churned, and she felt her temperature rising slightly. To clear the awkwardness in the air she turned the conversation back to Kelsey. "Do you have a specific dress style or color in mind for tomorrow?"

"I have been looking online for over a month and there are so many gorgeous dresses out there. I just hope I can find one that will be awesome! Not even close to what anyone else will have," she said with so much excitement in her voice.

"One that covers from here to here!" Vince said holding one hand up to his chin and leaning down with the other to touch his toes.

"Dad!" Kelsey protested. "My dad thinks I am going to buy some sleazy dress that shows too much skin. I am not that kind of girl, Dad! Besides, I want to look elegant and mature."

Vince smiled but J.C. could see a slight bit of worry in his eyes. She smiled back and winked hoping to let him know she got the message and said, "Say no to the dress that shows too much skin!" He winked back.

"How is your steak?" he asked J.C.

"Great, did you raise this meat? It is so tender," J.C. replied.

"Yes, I like grass fed meat rather than feedlot meat." Vince smiled, "Is it done enough? Some people like it red in the center, but with grass fed beef you can keep it tender even when it is a little more done."

"I like my meat done, so this is perfect. I usually will not order beef in a restaurant because I cannot eat meat if it still has a red center." J.C. was being herself and completely honest about how she liked her meat cooked. She smiled at Vince and he returned her smile.

"I like hamburgers more than steak," Kelsey complained. "Dad thought tonight was more of a steak night, but I would have preferred a great big hamburger and fries."

"I am sure your dad makes a great hamburger too." J.C. complimented the chef. "These green beans and rice are just as good as the steak. Did you take cooking classes while you were at Iowa State?" she asked Vince.

"No, I really learned to cook from my mom and two older sisters. Since I was the youngest, my mom protected me a little more than she should have. I spent a lot of time in the kitchen with the three of them when my dad probably thought I needed to be outside helping him more." Vince shared his opinion on his parents' style of raising him. No wonder he was the perfect gentleman and nice guy... he had spent all those hours with his two perfect sisters J.C. thought.

"Do you have any brothers or sisters?" Kelsey asked.

Oh, no, J.C. had let her guard down and was back on defense. "No, I had a little brother, but he died when I was ten years old." J.C. cleared her throat which must have made Vince think she was struggling with the questions.

"Who is ready for dessert?" Vince jumped up from the table and headed back to the kitchen.

"Not me, Dad, I will probably have popcorn at the movie, and I am trying on prom dresses tomorrow!" Kelsey's voice was filled with excitement.

"Oh, one little piece of peanut butter pie will not keep a dress from fitting," he ribbed Kelsey.

"I will eat two pieces when I get home tomorrow with the perfect dress," she said as she picked up her plate and glass and carried them to the kitchen. Kelsey rinsed her dishes and placed them in the dishwasher. "So, J.C. what time do I need to be ready in the morning? Also do you want me to come to your father's place or will you pick me up here?" Kelsey was preparing to leave the conversation which made J.C. a little tense.

"I was thinking we should probably leave here by 6:45 a.m. so we get to Adventureland before 8:00 a.m. I will come by and pick you up here. Does that schedule work for you, Kelsey?" J.C. wanted to make sure this teenage girl was on board with the plan.

"Sure, I will be up and ready," Kelsey said with confidence. She exited the great room and went back through the archway to the back part of the house.

Vince returned to the table with two plates of pie. He set one at J.C.'s plate and the other directly in front of his own. "Thanks again for doing this. She is so excited." Vince was looking directly at J.C. with the sincerest look in his eyes.

"Like I said, I am headed into Des Moines anyway. She is a really nice young lady, Vince. You and your wife can be proud of a wonderful daughter you are raising." J.C. knew what she had experienced so far was much different than the spoiled brat stories the women at work had shared.

"Thank you. Teri deserves most of the credit. She spent all of the development years with Kelsey while I was building a

practice, raising livestock, and taking care of my mom's farm."
Vince paused as Kelsey reentered the room.

"Dad, we are going to Greenfield to the movies, and I should be home by 10:00 p.m.," Kelsey reported. Again, impressing J.C. with the level of communication between this father and daughter.

"Watch out for deer," Vince cautioned as Kelsey closed the door to the deck behind her.

Vince and J.C. sat in silence for a moment, neither one knowing what the other one was thinking. J.C.'s mind still reeling with the idea that she never had this kind of conversation with her father; no discussion, no back and forth, no input, nothing. Vince was wondering how to politely apologize for Kelsey asking about family and siblings.

Vince spoke first. "J.C., I am so sorry that Kelsey brought up Johnnie. I should have told her ahead of time not to ask about your siblings." He showed great concern in his face as he spoke.

"Vince, it is OK. It has been forty years. I really was not bothered by any of her questions. She is a normal teenager that is inquisitive around new people. I am amazed at the open relationship you have with your daughter. In the short time I have been here, you and Kelsey had more conversation than I have had with my father in over forty years." J.C.'s voice carried sadness as she admitted to herself that she wanted more from her father.

"J.C., I am sorry to hear that. Will is a complex man," Vince replied.

Complex! Is that what people around the neighborhood and town think of her father? No, he is cold-hearted, emotionless, self-centered, and *old*! J.C. thought. She was distracted as Vince was asking her if she was done with her plate. "Sorry, yes, it was delicious." J.C. spoke with slight embarrassment.

J.C. pulled her pie in front of her just as Vince brought her a fresh cup of coffee. "I hope you like the pie. It was one of

Teri's simple recipes. One cup of peanut butter, one container of cool whip, mixed and pressed into a premade cookie crust. Kelsey always adds the crumbled Reese's Peanut Butter Cups on top for 'splash'!" Vince explained the dessert.

"It tastes amazing! I am no chef, so you could have told me you spent days preparing this and I would not know the difference." They both laughed.

"So, what are you doing back at the farm; if I am not being too pushy to ask?" Vince cautiously questioned.

"Well, my dad is seventy-five years old, has a bad heart and diabetes so someone needs to make some decisions about what to do next. I promised my mom I would take care of the legal and financial side of things once she was gone. It has been eleven months now and this opportunity to take a break from work came up, so here I am trying to assess what needs to be done and where dad should go next." There it was in a nutshell, J.C. thought.

"Will seems pretty able bodied and mentally on top of his game anytime I am around him," Vince stated.

"I know, in fact just yesterday I realized how much he is able to do on his own. He sold thirty head of hogs today. He would have sorted and loaded them completely on his own if I was not there," J.C. admitted. "He has just lived in this silent cocoon for so long I worry that there might be something seriously wrong with him and he would never tell anyone."

Vince picked up their pie plates and started to clear the rest of the items from the table. J.C. immediately started to help him. They moved the dishes, platters, glasses, and silverware back to the sink. J.C. rinsed each item and put them in the dishwasher, just as she had seen Kelsey do earlier. Once the table was cleared, Vince picked up his coffee cup and invited J.C. to join him in the living room in front of the fireplace.

"I can start a fire if you like," Vince asked.

"Oh, I should be going soon. Early morning tomorrow." They both chuckled.

"Finish your coffee at least," Vince suggested.

"OK." J.C. sat down on the corner of the couch and Vince took one of the easy chairs next to the fireplace.

"Will is not much of a social body in the neighborhood but everyone knows him and understands that he is all business." Vince restarted the conversation.

"He definitely is all business. I just need to know what will happen to his business when he is gone. I am not a farmer and do not plan on staying around here. So, I just need to put things into a legal format so that everything will be taken care of. I have a little time now with this retirement package but sooner or later, I will take a new job and chances are it will not be in Iowa." J.C. laid out the same explanation she had given to Nadine earlier in the week.

"I understand; this is not your future. It's just sad to think that everything Will has worked his whole life for, will someday belong to someone else." Vince looked away as if thinking about someone other than Will.

"Well, I better get home and rested. I have no idea what I am in for tomorrow. I told you I am not a mother or a shopper. Consider me the driver only. I probably should have you sign a disclaimer that I am in no way responsible for the dress that is selected." J.C. smiled at Vince.

"I got a non-verbal commitment earlier tonight with your wink that the dress will be modest, right?" Vince was starting to laugh knowing he was kidding J.C.

She burst out laughing. "Non-verbal wink. I will keep that one in my back pocket in case I need that someday in contract negotiations."

Vince took her cup to the kitchen and returned with her jacket. He held it as she slipped her arms in.

"Thanks again, J.C. He reached around to his pocket and pulled out his wallet. Here is my credit card. Kelsey is a signer on the account, but I would prefer you carry the card. I may be out on a call in the morning, so wanted to give this to you tonight." Vince handed over the card.

"Price? Does Kelsey have a price range you want her to stay within?" J.C. asked.

"When we looked at the website it appears most of the prom dresses are around $200. I would say that is the top end, but I will make that clear to Kelsey. You do not need to worry about that." Vince was confident that his daughter would honor his restrictions.

J.C. walked out onto the deck and looked over her shoulder. "Thanks for dinner. Good night, Vince."

As she moved towards her car, she wished she had hit the remote start before she put on her coat. It was only six miles. She would be fine for the five minutes it took her to drive home. As she drove home, her mind centered on how nice Vince Martin was and his relationship with his daughter. She kept replaying the level of conversations that took place between the two of them and how different that was from her teenage years with her own father.

J.C. walked into the dark dining room and left her brown boots on the mat. She unzipped her jacket and left it on one of the dining room chairs as she went into the bathroom. Looking into the mirrors, she stopped and admired her skin's glow. Was it just this light or had something happened to make her skin look this good tonight? She brushed her teeth, removed her makeup, and prepared for bed. Coming out of the bathroom J.C. grabbed her jacket and walked into the living room. Her father was seated in his chair and reading his Bible.

"Good night, Dad," J.C. said softly as she walked by. No response.

Chapter 12

*T*he 5:30 a.m. alarm was getting J.C. back into her normal schedule. She went downstairs to take a quick shower. To no surprise, Will was sitting in his chair with his Bible in his lap. She did not speak and walked quietly to the bathroom. When J.C. was done with her shower, Will was standing at the stove preparing his breakfast. She said, "Good Morning, Dad." No response.

J.C. returned to her dressing room and pulled out a pair of light blue jeans and one of the sweaters she had passed over the night before. She put on some mascara, no eye liner, and just a slight brush of bronzer on her cheeks.

Heading back downstairs, she grabbed one of the suitcases and threw in half of the workout clothes she had brought with her. She almost forgot part of her excuse to go to Des Moines was to bring back more clothes she needed. She set the suitcase next to the front door and headed into the kitchen.

Just as she was surveying her options for breakfast, Will moved into the dining room, and sat down to eat. J.C. made some toast, took a grapefruit and yogurt from the refrigerator, and joined Will at the table. "I will be gone most of the day to Des Moines with Vince Martin's daughter. Not sure how long

CHAPTER 12

this prom dress shopping will take. I need to stop at my condo to pick up my mail and swap out some clothes. I think we will be back before dinner, but I can't guarantee it." J.C. thought how different this was than the back-and-forth routine she had witnessed the night before.

Will stood up and took his dishes to the sink. He washed them and set them on the drainer to dry. J.C. did not speak up and tell him she would do them this time. Instead, she just watched him take care of it on his own. Will turned and walked towards her and then went into the living room. J.C. was surprised as she had expected him to head out and start chores. Instead, he reemerged carrying the sheets from his bedroom to the mudroom. J.C. could hear the washer start as she finished her breakfast. Wow, she thought to herself. This is how he keeps everything as pristine as Evelyn had left it.

After cleaning up her breakfast dishes she looked through the cupboards for a travel coffee mug. She was about ready to give up when she spotted one in the cupboard over the refrigerator. She went out to the mudroom and retrieved the stool. Yes! Her mother still had the travel mug that she would send home with her. J.C. rinsed it out and put the stool back out in the mudroom. She filled the mug with coffee and hit the remote start on her car. Walking through the living room, she needed to grab her coat from upstairs. Why hadn't her parents ever added a coat closet behind the front door? It would have been like a telephone booth since that is where the land line was. She smiled thinking about a telephone/closet booth. She quickly retrieved her coat, put her boots on, picked up her suitcase, grabbed her coffee, and headed out to her car.

She pulled into Vince's driveway at 6:42 a.m. and before she decided whether to get out and go to the door, it opened and out rushed Kelsey waving and saying something over her shoulder. She ran to the car and opened the passenger side and slipped into the seat next to J.C. She looked bright and chipper for a teenage girl before 7:00 a.m. on a Saturday. She

71

had a bottle of water with her and asked permission to drink it in J.C.'s car.

"Sure," J.C. said as she pointed to the beverage holders. J.C. took a sip of coffee before backing out of the driveway.

They were not even three miles down the road when Kelsey started with the questions, "What was your prom like?" was her opener.

"It was nice. It was more focused on the banquet portion and less on the dance back then," J.C. acknowledged.

"What was your prom dress like?" Kelsey asked.

J.C. was glad she had refreshed her memory a few nights earlier. "My junior year, I wore a red satin dress with long sleeves. My senior year, a sleeveless yellow ruffled dress," J.C. answered.

"Where did you buy your dresses?" Kelsey was going to fill the drive with one-hundred questions J.C. thought.

"My mom made both of my dresses. Back then most girls wore homemade dresses. It was not common for anyone to buy a dress for school dances." J.C. thought how times had changed.

"Really, I cannot imagine wearing homemade clothes," Kelsey stated.

"It was just different; most mothers sewed and even some of their daughters were talented seamstresses in my high school." J.C. remembered.

"I do not know anyone that can sew," Kelsey stated.

They turned onto Interstate 80 and were heading east towards Des Moines when the morning sky was showing signs of sunrise. J.C. took this opportunity to change the subject. "I think we are going to see a beautiful sunrise while we drive into Des Moines this morning," she stated.

"I love sunrises and sunsets," Kelsey said. "Sometimes I just set my alarm on Saturday, so I can get up and watch the sunrise. It reminds me of my mom. She loved to watch the sun rise."

A lump caught in J.C.'s throat as she heard those words. She also loved to watch the sun come up on the farm. Probably one of her only treasures left now that her mother was gone.

"Kelsey, I am sorry that your mom is not here today to go with you. I lost my mom when I was forty-nine years old, and it was hard. I am sure this has been a very difficult year for you," J.C. spoke softly and with compassion in her voice.

"I do miss my mom a lot, but I know that she is in heaven. Also, I have really gotten a lot closer to my dad these past few months. We are helping each other deal with mom being gone." Kelsey sounded extremely mature.

During the next few miles, neither one of them spoke. They were both lost in their own thoughts. J.C.'s mind had caught on the statement 'she is in heaven'. Of course, she knew what that meant and as a child believed that all good people went to heaven and all bad people go to hell. J.C. could not imagine making that statement with such certainty about her own mother, who was a saint to put up with Will. It was more than that. Kelsey's voice had a peacefulness when she spoke those words. It truly comforted her to know that her mother was in heaven.

J.C. decided it was not good to let the silence go on too long. "Kelsey, you tell me where and what you need my help with today. Your father gave me his credit card last night and if you like I can sit off to the side until you are finished..." J.C. stopped to collect her thoughts before going on.

"No way. I want you to be with me the entire time. I need your help. J.C., I am not the kind of girl that needs to be told I look great in everything. If some of these dresses are 'dogs' I expect you to tell me straight up." Kelsey's tone was strong and directive.

J.C. laughed and said "Dogs? Is that what you call a bad one? We used to refer to them as a 'Granny Sack'!" She laughed at the memories of her friends making fun of dresses they thought were old fashioned or too modest during her high school years.

"Granny Sack, I love that. OK, do not tell me I look good in a 'Granny Sack today'!" Kelsey was laughing right along with J.C.

"After looking at their website, I am excited to see what this is all about. Since I've never gone through the purchase process during my prom days and didn't have a daughter to do this with, I am curious to see what this will be like," J.C. admitted.

"Great," Kelsey replied. "J.C., can I ask you something about my dad?"

"Well, that depends. I really do not know your dad all that well," J.C. admitted.

"That's why I want to know why you are doing this for us?" Kelsey asked sincerely. "If you are not friends with my dad, and did not know my mom, why would you offer to take me prom dress shopping?"

J.C. drew in a deep breath and surprised herself with the words that came out of her mouth. "I kind of owe your dad a favor. It was on the bus right after my little brother died and some kids were making fun of me. Not about my brother, but I started to cry, and your dad came from the back of the bus and bopped those kids on the head and told them to cut it out. It was the silliest thing. They were singing this rhyme about two love birds sitting in a tree kissing and had matched me up with a kid who was kind of a bully. Normally, that kind of thing did not get to me, but I was confused with everything that was going on at home, so I guess my emotions were a little raw. I never forgot his kindness. Your dad was exactly what I told you last night–the ultimate nice guy!" J.C. realized for the first time since seeing Vince on the farm last week, that she had always admired him and looked up to him. Vince was nice, and she did owe him. "When he told me that he was on call today, I just thought I could do something nice for him to return the favor."

"OK, I guess that makes sense. He said pretty much the same thing about you. You were never one of those girls chasing after him at the sporting events, you were not a gossip, you were very respectful of your parents and teachers and you had a classy way about you that he could trust to help me pick out a dress that he would approve of." Kelsey smiled at J.C. confirming that she agreed with her father.

J.C. could not respond to that. Vince was aware of her in high school. She was a lowly freshman when he was a senior star.

"It must have been really sad losing your brother when you were that young. I never had a brother or sister. My mom told me once that she was lucky to get pregnant and have me. J.C., do you still miss him?" Kelsey was so sincere; J.C. knew she had to come up with an answer.

"Well, over the years I tried to forget how much fun we had as kids. I did not have pictures to remind me. Rarely did my parents and I talk about him, so it got easier to stop thinking about him at all. One of the things I did this week was clean out his room at our farmhouse. I saw his picture and some of his things from school and yes, I miss him. I really miss him. His name was Johnnie." J.C.'s voice cracked as she said his name.

For some reason Nadine popped into J.C.'s mind. She thought of all those times her mother and Nadine talked. A chill ran down her back. They were just entering the West Des Moines city limits. It would take approximately fifteen minutes to get to Adventureland Inn on the east side of town. It was exactly 7:30 a.m. so they were right on schedule.

"I think we are going to be there around 7:45 a.m. and hopefully the line for registration will not be too long," J.C. commented.

"Hope not," Kelsey agreed. "I should tell you that I am not a very patient person. Standing in lines with me drove my mom nuts with all my fidgeting." She smiled at J.C.

J.C. pulled her Lexus up to the front row parking lane in front of the Adventureland Inn. They simultaneously looked at each other and said, "Let's do this!" Laughing out loud they both exited the car into the cold wintery morning and hurried inside the hotel.

Chapter 13

*I*nside the door of the hotel lobby were large signs directing patrons for the Talesse' Designs Show to go to the atrium that surrounded the swimming pool. J.C. and Kelsey followed the hallway around to the open atrium. It had been transformed with a beautiful stage that had three runways shooting out in different directions. The longest runway went over the swimming pool with an exit staircase on the back.

"Wow!" was the first thing out of Kelsey's mouth. "This is awesome!"

J.C. scanned the room looking for the registration area. She spotted it in the opposite corner of where they were standing. She gently grabbed Kelsey's elbow and headed in that direction. The line was already formed and appeared to be seventy-plus patrons deep. When they got closer, she could see there were two roped lines; one for wedding dresses and one for prom dresses. The prom dress line had approximately thirty people in it already. They smiled at each other knowing that their chances of getting through paperwork and measurements could potentially be done before the style show started. Kelsey was not kidding about her impatience waiting in line. She talked non-stop and pointed to everything she saw.

At 8:10 a.m. they were next. A sales associate handed them a clipboard and rushed through the instructions of completing the three forms attached. Once that step was finished, they would turn in the paperwork at the counter and then proceed to one of the rooms where a large sign–"Measurements"–was posted on the door.

They stepped out of line and stopped at a small table to complete their forms. The first one was a legal disclaimer that said you would not duplicate, replicate, or copy the dress without being liable of legal action from the designer. Kelsey looked at J.C. who had seen plenty of legal documents in her life to know this was boilerplate language. Plus, Kelsey had already confessed she was not a seamstress so J.C. said, "Yes, you can sign that." Kelsey pointed to the language below her signature. If she was not eighteen, her legal guardian was required to sign on the line below her. J.C. turned the paper around and signed her name as legal guardian.

The next form was regarding photographs and had similar boilerplate language and signature requirements. They repeated the signature lines and moved on to the last form.

All sales are final! All alterations were the patron's responsibility! And finally, any damage that occurs during the fitting process is the responsibility of the legal guardian or individual trying on the dresses if they are of legal age. If you do not sign this form, you will not be allowed into the fitting area following the show. Kelsey looked concerned. "What's the matter?" J.C. asked.

"What if I accidently tear something or the zipper breaks?" Kelsey understood that there were consequences.

"You won't!" J.C. said with the utmost confidence; all the while hoping this teenage girl that she barely knew, was as conscientious as her first impression of her had been.

They signed the final form, walked to the counter with large smiles on their faces and were given a number. "Wait behind this red line until they call you to one of the measurement rooms," the girl at the counter instructed them.

"Do you want to go in by yourself?" J.C. quietly asked.

"No, I think you should come in with me," Kelsey nervously replied.

"OK," J.C. agreed.

The measurement process was quick and painless. Two associates worked as a team to measure Kelsey. First, they measured her back starting at her right shoulder to the floor and then repeating that on the left side. They moved to the bottom of her spine and measured from there to the floor. Coming around to the front they measured her right shoulder to the floor and again the left shoulder to the floor. Next, they placed the tape between her breasts and measured from there to the floor. Moving to each shoulder they measured to her wrists on both sides. They took a bust measurement and a waist measurement. Next, they measured the hips and around her thighs. Each time they pulled the tape back, that measurement went on an eight by ten card that was already completed with her name, address, and cell number that was taken from the forms that they had just filled in. Once all the measurements were taken, they handed the card to Kelsey and instructed them to go out and help themselves to some refreshments before the show started at 9:00 a.m.

"That was fast!" Kelsey said as they walked out the door in less than three minutes.

"Sure was," J.C. confirmed.

Again, sizing up the venue, J.C. took Kelsey's elbow and lead them around to a buffet that had juice, coffee, water, fruit, yogurt, and tiny muffins. They both filled a small plate and looked around at the seating in front of the stage.

J.C. advised that they step back and watch for a bit before taking a seat. Her experience had taught her that sometimes you can get an edge if you study the people in charge. She just needed to assess who was in charge of this venue. Kelsey was busy watching the lines of people and enjoying her snack, so

J.C. intently studied the people close to the stage, working in the background, and the sound team. After fifteen minutes, she had seen and overheard enough conversations to pick a spot. She asked Kelsey, "Will you need to use the restroom before the show starts?"

"Yes, that is probably a good idea." Kelsey smiled appreciating the intuitive manner of her guardian.

They disposed of their cups and plates and headed back towards the lobby where they had passed the restrooms. There was a line, but it was moving quickly. When they finished there, J.C. lead them back into the atrium to find their seats.

"Where do you think we should sit?" Kelsey asked.

"Follow me." J.C. led the way around the first runway that came directly out from the stage. She maneuvered them around a cluster of girls that were holding court between the first runway and the second one. The second runway was the one that extended over the swimming pool and was longer than the first one. J.C. worked through a few smaller groups until they were where the two runways met. One headed straight out the front and the second one came over the pool. She was certain that the models would walk in front of these two chairs at least three times before exiting and their final walk, in front of these chairs was the longest runway. Other females were still milling around when the announcement was made over the sound system that the show was about to start and people should take their seats.

J.C. looked at the card in Kelsey's lap. It had ten lines on it. She reached in her purse and pulled out a pen. "Kelsey, do you want to write down the dresses or would you like me to do that?" J.C. asked quietly.

"I don't know," Kelsey said honestly. "I am afraid I might get caught up in the show and not get all the numbers I want. Would you mind writing them down for me?"

"You just say 'that one' whenever you see something you like," J.C. instructed.

"What if there is more than ten that I like?" Kelsey was starting to show a little concern.

"No problem. I will list the numbers on the back with a small description and when the show is over, we will narrow it down to the top ten. Is that OK?" J.C. was a master of details.

Kelsey smiled as the lights came up and the music started. The first segment of the show were bridal gowns which gave them a chance to see how fast the flow was going to be. J.C. quickly noticed the type of styles that caught Kelsey's eye which would be a great advantage when the prom dresses came out. Twenty minutes later, the prom dresses started coming out. J.C. was right; this corner spot was perfect. Kelsey got to see a dress for approximately two minutes, versus some girls who were only seeing them for about thirty seconds. During the first segment of the show, Kelsey selected seven dresses that she liked. There was a ten-minute intermission which gave them a chance to discuss what she had seen so far. The second half of the show was fifteen minutes of prom dresses. This series of dresses was more elaborate than the first group. Kelsey really liked some of these dresses and selected nine from this group. J.C. was glad when the prom dress portion was over. It was harder than she thought it would be, to capture enough information so that Kelsey could hopefully eliminate a few. Especially when two of the dresses she liked in the second segment were back-to-back on the runway.

As the second bridal dress portion was going on in front of them, they put their heads down and started quietly discussing the dresses on their list. Kelsey eliminated a couple of dresses from the very beginning of the show almost immediately. They were down to fourteen and needed to eliminate four more before their number was called for fitting. The show ended with a finale that brought back the designers' favorites for this year's collection. Five of the dresses on Kelsey's list were in the finale. She eliminated one after seeing it again. She was convinced that the other four in the finale were dresses that she would like to try. J.C. moved those to the front of the card.

The announcer explained how the fitting process would work. They had five fitting rooms for prom and five fitting rooms for bridal. Each girl would be called in the order of her card number. They looked down. Kelsey's number was fifteen. As dresses were purchased, those numbers would be posted on the electronic screen at the back of the main stage and should be removed from your card before entering the fitting area. J.C. knew they would be in the third round of girls to be fitted so their chance of getting one of Kelsey's choices was pretty good. The old 'early bird gets the dress theory' had paid off. She smiled to herself.

They got up and walked back to get some water. While they were waiting, J.C. explained to Kelsey that the final dresses for elimination may not matter.

"Kelsey, you have the numbers for thirteen dresses and some of those may already be gone when you go in, so I recommend that you wait until we hear them call number twelve for fitting to make any other changes to your card." J.C. walked Kelsey through the logic of how this process would work.

Kelsey shook her head in agreement and sighed. J.C. recognized that Kelsey was showing some signs of being overwhelmed. Maybe the mall really is an easier option for teenage girls she thought.

It took about twenty minutes before they heard, *"Number twelve, please report to the fitting area."* J.C. led Kelsey through the mob toward the front of the stage, and they began comparing numbers. J.C. had been right. Two of Kelsey's choices were already gone.

"Number thirteen and number fourteen, please report to the fitting area." J.C. felt a knot in her stomach. "Kelsey, let's walk over by the racks and jot down a couple more numbers on the back of our card," J.C. advised.

They hurried over to the racks that lined the runways and Kelsey selected three more dresses that she could try on.

"Number fifteen, please report to the fitting area." They looked at each other with a little fear in their faces and proceeded to

the roped off area. A stern man reviewed their card and then motioned for a sales associate to come meet them.

"Hello, my name is Mary. What is your name?" Mary spoke directly to Kelsey.

"Kelsey," Kelsey responded.

They were all walking briskly to a room as Mary continued to ask questions. "How old are you, Kelsey?"

"Seventeen," Kelsey replied.

"Where do you live?" Mary asked.

"On a farm about fifty miles from here," Kelsey answered.

"You do not look like a farm girl. Here is our room." Mary handed Kelsey's card to another attendant who immediately disappeared.

Once in the room, the door was locked behind them. Mary started explaining in detail what would happen in the next few minutes. "Jolie, her attendant would go and retrieve those dresses that Kelsey had selected. If any of them were more than three sizes larger than Kelsey's measurements, they would not be brought in for the fitting. Of the remaining dresses brought to the fitting room, she would be allowed to try them on and determine which, if any, of them she wanted. Whatever dress she selected would be paid for before she left that room, and it was her responsibility to make any alterations to it if it did not fit. Do you understand, Kelsey?"

Kelsey meekly replied, "Yes."

"Are you the mother?" Mary asked.

"No, I'm her guardian," J.C. replied without thinking. "I have a question, "Why do you limit it to three sizes?"

"Any more alterations would destroy the design of the dress," Mary said sternly.

Next, Mary pointed to a box next to the door. The lid stood open and there was a padlock dangling from it. "You will need to put your phones and purses in this box now!" Mary said sternly.

"Why?" Kelsey asked.

CHAPTER 13

"Because you already signed agreements that you would not photograph or copy any of these designs and while I am out of the room this is our guarantee that it does not happen." Mary nodded toward the box.

Both Kelsey and J.C. obediently walked to the box and put their purses into the box. J.C. pulled her phone out of her coat pocket and laid it in as well. Kelsey spoke up and said, "My phone is in my purse."

There was a knock on the door and Jolie entered carrying an armful of dresses. "Well, you are a lucky girl; it looks like seven of your choices are still available and within the range of your size. I will step outside the door while you try them on." Looking directly at J.C., Mary said, "You have twenty minutes."

As the door clicked shut, they both burst into laughter. "Wow," J.C. said as she walked to the rack holding the dresses, "they sure have a direct approach, don't they?" Kelsey was still laughing as she nodded and started to undress.

The first dress J.C. handed her was a light yellow silky fitted style and was slightly too big, but she could tell as soon as Kelsey looked in the mirror, this was not the one. Kelsey quickly stepped out of it and J.C. handed her a deep sea-green dress. It really looked great against Kelsey's skin and hair. Next came a red and white combination that was very cute and fun on such a tiny figure. J.C. thought maybe this unique dress would be the one. The royal blue was a favorite for J.C.; it had a few rhinestones scattered over the bodice. Next, she handed Kelsey a bright fuchsia dress that fit high on the collarbone in the front and cut in a V down the back; it also had a few rhinestones scattered over the bodice. The tangerine dress was fun with lots of ruffles around the neck and hemline. J.C. had saved the white and silver dress for last. As Kelsey slipped into it, J.C. was surprised at how mature it made her look. The white chiffon dropped beautifully from the waist to create a graceful skirt. The bodice was designed with chiffon and satin vertical pleats that created a perfect V from her shoulders to Kelsey's waist. At the waist was a combination of faux pearls and rhinestones that accented Kelsey's figure. This dress was possibly one size too big. They had six minutes left.

"OK!" J.C. said. "What dresses do you want eliminated?" Kelsey pointed to the yellow, red, and white, sea-green, and tangerine. J.C. quickly moved them to the end of the rack. "Is there anything you want to try on again?" she asked quietly.

Kelsey stood for a moment and then said, "The pinkish-purple one." J.C. handed her the dress.

Kelsey slipped into it and walked up close to the mirror, twirled around a couple of times, and said, "This is it!" She had a big smile on her face.

J.C. looked at the price tag; it was $179. Perfect, she thought. She smiled and said, "Kelsey you look beautiful in that color and I think your dad will love the style."

They pushed the other two dresses to the end of the rack and Kelsey put her clothes back on while J.C. notified Mary that they were ready to make a purchase.

Mary entered the room and unlocked the box that held their purses and phones. She began completing the order form. Jolie placed the dress in a long dress bag, zipped it up and placed a card in the front pocket of the bag. She explained to J.C. that the card would provide the necessary instructions for alterations. Jolie took the remaining dresses with her and was gone.

"OK, all I need is a credit card and signature," Mary said. J.C. reached in her purse and pulled out Vince's credit card and handed it to Mary. She ran it through her credit card scanner on her iPad and turned the iPad around for a signature. Kelsey stepped up and signed the iPad and put her cell phone number in to receive a receipt. Kelsey took the dress from the end of the rack and they walked through the maze of people back through the atrium, lobby and out the front door of the Adventureland Inn. J.C. opened her back door, and they laid the dress across the back seat. When they were seated in the car, they looked at each other and burst out laughing.

CHAPTER 13

"I cannot believe that!" Kelsey said through her belts of laughter. "I never imagined anything like that in my whole life."

"Me either," said J.C. It was 11:00 a.m. "Kelsey, I have been in some tough negotiations throughout my career and this pressure today was as intense as any of them. You handled yourself so well and made quick, decisive choices better than most of my colleagues at work."

"First, I had no idea if I was picking dresses that I really liked. When you said I had more than ten, then I worried what if I eliminated one that I should try. Next I was scared that Mary was going to yell at me if I did not make a decision soon enough." Kelsey admitted it had been stressful. "But I know I have the right dress, and this was really fun! Thank you for helping me." She smiled as J.C. started the car.

"What made you pick that one?" J.C. asked hesitantly.

"Remember when we were driving in this morning and watching the sunrise?" Kelsey asked J.C.

"Yes," J.C. responded.

"Well, that was the color of the sunrise and I knew that both my mom and me could see it this morning, so I told myself that I would pick a dress that matched that pinkish-purple color." Kelsey smiled sweetly as she looked over her shoulder into the backseat.

A chill ran down J.C.'s spine. They drove in silence for a few minutes.

J.C. broke the silence, "Are you hungry? We can stop at Zombie Burger if you want before going to my condo." J.C. remembered Kelsey's comments about hamburgers the night before.

"Zombie Burger! That sounds fun! Yes, I am starving!" Kelsey's excitement filled the car.

Chapter 14

*W*hen they pulled into the parking garage underneath The Plaza downtown Kelsey asked, "Is this where you live?"

"Yes," said J.C.

"Wow, you really do live downtown!" Kelsey exclaimed.

When they took the elevator to the twenty-fifth floor and stepped out, Kelsey's eyes were wide open. J.C. knocked on Doris' door first. After a few minutes, an elderly lady opened the door. "Hello, Doris. This is my friend, Kelsey. Her father is the guy I told you about on the phone that needed help finding a prom dress," J.C. explained her companion.

"Come in, come in." The elderly lady welcomed them inside.

"I just wanted to say hello," explained J.C. "Everything OK next door?"

"It sure is! Your mail is on the counter and I just watered the plants yesterday," Doris replied. "Well, are you girls shopping today?"

J.C. and Kelsey looked at each other and grinned. "It's not like any shopping I have ever experienced in my life, Doris.

But yes, we took your advice and went to a trunk show. Kelsey wanted to thank you in person for giving us such a great tip."

"Yes, thank you so much. I found the perfect dress and it was really a lot of fun once I got past all those rude people telling us what not to do!" Kelsey giggled a little.

"Well, where is the dress?" Doris asked. "It has been years since I got to go to one of those trunk shows, and I am curious to see what kind of gowns they are showing these days."

Kelsey looked at J.C. and they both smiled. "OK," J.C. said. "I will run down and get it." She headed back to her car, leaving Doris and Kelsey to get to know one another.

Five minutes later the door opened, and J.C. entered with the long bag containing the dress. She started to unzip it, but Doris interrupted her.

"Honey, do you mind putting it on? This old lady does not get much excitement these days and I would love to see a pretty little girl in her gown." Doris' eyes were lighting up as she spoke.

"Sure," Kelsey said as Doris pointed to a door off the living room that she could go in to try the dress on.

Doris caught J.C. up on the gossip from the condominium while Kelsey changed. When Kelsey walked back into the living room, J.C. caught her breath. The lights in the hotel room had not done this dress justice; or maybe it was the rushing nerves that kept her from seeing how perfect this dress looked on Kelsey.

"Absolutely gorgeous!" Doris exclaimed throwing her hands up in the air. Kelsey gave a really big smile.

"Gorgeous is right," J.C. echoed.

"It looks like a perfect fit, too," Doris said. Kelsey spun around a couple of times and J.C. concentrated on the shoulders, waist, and length.

"It might be a little long, but you will need to wait until you find some shoes," J.C. advised.

"Something strappy with rhinestones," Doris suggested. "Wait, I think Melody left a pair of prom shoes in that closet of the room you were just in." She walked slowly past Kelsey and disappeared into the bedroom.

Kelsey could see herself in the big mirror over the bookcase. She smiled and turned a couple more times. "I still do not believe I found the perfect dress today," she said directly to J.C.

Doris reemerged with a shoe box. "I am not sure what shoe size you wear. I think these are six-and-a-half."

Kelsey opened the box to see a beautiful pair of silver sandals that crisscrossed over the toes with rhinestones. She pulled one out and slipped her right foot into it. Immediately her head shot up and her eyes met Doris' confirming it fit. She quickly pulled out the second one and slipped it on. Standing up straight she pushed her shoulders up and back.

J.C. looked, and the hem of the dress was one inch off the floor. "How do they feel?" she asked Kelsey.

"They feel good," Kelsey replied.

Doris smiled and said, "They are yours. Melody left them here and I am sure her feet will never fit in them again." She looked at J.C. and said, "She has gained quite a bit of weight these past couple of years."

"Doris, are you sure?" Kelsey asked.

"They are yours, dear. I think they match the stones on the bodice perfectly." Doris was smiling and proud that she had contributed to the beautiful results in front of her.

"Well, my dad would want me to pay for these. How much do you want for them?" Kelsey spoke in a professional, almost business tone.

"They are yours and I will not take a dime for them," Doris said sternly. J.C. shook her head at Kelsey letting her know that Doris would not give in.

"Thank you so much, Doris, not only for the shoes but also for getting us the information about the show today. I would not have either the dress or the shoes without your help." Kelsey walked over and gave Doris a little hug. She turned and went back to the bedroom to change.

"Doris, you are too sweet," J.C. said when Kelsey was gone.

"Made my day just to see that pretty little thing in her dress. She is such a mature girl for a teenager," Doris complimented.

"Yes, she is. Her parents have trained her well," J.C. confirmed and changed the subject. "I will take those bills and get them paid. It will probably be a couple of weeks before I am back in town to pick up my mail again. Doris, it might take a month or two out there; are you sure you want to keep checking on things for me? I can make other arrangements."

"Oh, honey, it is no bother. What else do I have to do? I know that you need to get things taken care of for your father. Such a shame that your mom went first." Doris' words trailed off.

"Doris, thanks again," Kelsey said as she returned from the bedroom. "My dad is going to be relieved that I got my dress and shoes all taken care of today." She had a big smile on her face.

"OK, Doris, see you next time I am in town," J.C. said as they stepped into the hallway. J.C. took about ten steps to her right and unlocked a door that looked just like Doris'.

"Here is my place," she said to Kelsey.

"Wow, this is awesome," Kelsey exclaimed. Unlike Doris' place, J.C.'s was decorated with modern décor and was very classy. "My mom would have loved to decorate a condo in Des Moines. She loved looking at pictures of these places and talked about someday being a designer for the 'rich and famous.'"

"Well, I am not the rich and famous; and could probably use a few tips from someone like your mom. My mom also liked to decorate and helped me find most of the items in my condo. Oh, Kelsey, I just remembered that I left my suitcase in the trunk of my car. Why don't you call your dad and let him know that we should be on the road in about thirty minutes and home before 3:00 p.m. I will be right back." J.C. hurried out the door to the elevator and back to the garage.

J.C. was frustrated that her organizational skills were really slipping since she left her corporate job and made her second trip back from the garage. "Kelsey, did you get a hold of your dad?" she asked when she returned.

"No, he must be on a call. I left a message to say that we had some exciting things to show him when we get there around 3:00 p.m." Kelsey reported.

J.C. hustled back into her condo and headed down a hallway to the master suite. "Kelsey, you can come back here if you like," she said over her shoulder. Kelsey followed J.C. into her bedroom.

"J.C., this is beautiful. Your bed looks so comfortable, I would never get out of it." Kelsey was looking at an oak headboard that was six feet taller than the bed. The duvet was a light grey over a rich cream bedspread and bed skirt. A mixture of colorful pillows and shams against the headboard gave it an elegant look. Kelsey watched J.C. in her walk-in closet that was perfect in every way. Clothes were hung by color sections, types, and lengths. It reminded her of pictures her mom would show her from time to time in magazines. Kelsey's closet was a 'hot mess'! "You really have a classy place, J.C.," Kelsey said with genuine sincerity.

"I enjoy living here. It was close to my work and downtown has lots of fun things to do nearby. My favorite is the farmers market in the summer. See that street down there?" J.C. came out of the closet and pointed down to Court Ave. "On Saturday mornings that is jammed from the river to the courthouse with vendors. I love to grab a cup of coffee and wander from one end to the other. People watch, pick up some fresh fruits and vegetables, and maybe some bread or rolls." She stopped herself before rambling on too much.

"Really, I would love that! Kelsey exclaimed. "Someday I would love to live in a place just like this!"

"OK, I think I have what I need here," J.C. said as she took a medium sized suitcase back out into the living room. "Do you want some water or a soda for the ride back?"

"A water would be great," Kelsey said.

It was 3:10 p.m. when J.C. pulled into the driveway at Vince's farm. Kelsey jumped out of the car and opened the back door. She reached in and pulled out the long bag that held the prize prom dress.

J.C. turned off the ignition and got out of the car also. She reached in the back and pulled out the shoe box. Kelsey was walking on her tip toes holding the dress bag over her head out of the snow slush and mud. When they got to the deck, the door opened, and Vince greeted them. "Hello, ladies, I see you had a successful day!" His voice was filled with excitement and relief.

"Dad, it was great, but a little scary too!" Kelsey blurted out. She kicked her shoes off on the rug inside the door and threw her coat on the couch. Reaching back towards J.C., she took the box out of J.C.'s hand and headed through the archway and out of sight.

J.C. stopped on the rug and retrieved the credit card from her purse. She handed it to Vince and took in a deep breath.

"How will I ever repay you for this?" Vince asked.

"Oh, we are even. This is my way of paying you back for that awful day on the bus." J.C. looked down at her feet.

"What day on the bus?" Vince asked.

"When the kids were making fun of me and Jerry Dickson and you made them stop. We are even now." J.C. sighed, "Besides, I really had fun. She is such a great girl, Vince. You can be proud of how mature she is. She really handles pressure well, too."

"Pressure?" Vince asked.

"Dad, look!" Kelsey was standing in the middle of the archway just beyond the living room.

Vince's face lit up like it was Christmas morning and he was five years old again, J.C. thought. He was beaming from ear to ear. His eyes were dancing, and he was completely speechless.

"Dad, what do you think?" Kelsey pushed him for his approval.

Vince stood and took it in for another minute or two. "Kelsey, you are the most beautiful thing I have seen since my wedding day, when I saw your mom for the first time in her wedding dress."

J.C. blushed and her heart started to race. She felt uncomfortable and out of place in such a private moment. Vince took a few steps away from J.C. at the door and towards Kelsey. J.C.'s mind raced for words that would announce her exit. Maybe they would not even notice if she did not say anything and just left.

Kelsey began to twirl around like she had at Doris' condo, and her smile matched Vince's. They both looked into each other's faces confirming their mutual approval of what they were seeing.

"Well, Kelsey, thank you for letting me be your guardian today. I had better get home and make some dinner for my dad." J.C. had her hand on the door and was turning the knob.

"Wait," Kelsey gushed!

J.C. stopped. Kelsey rushed over to her and hugged her tightly. "Thank you, J.C., I will never forget today. It was so much fun. You were not my guardian; you were my guardian angel today." She hugged J.C. again and then released her.

J.C.'s stomach jumped up into her throat; she smiled and nodded at Vince before leaving.

J.C. pulled into the farm driveway and just sat in her car for a few minutes. It was 3:45 p.m. and Will would still be doing chores. She turned off the ignition and she imagined Kelsey relaying the entire day's experiences to her father. The intense designer staff, the show, the decisions, the paperwork, the purse lock up, the time limits and how she knew this was the perfect dress. Then she would tell him about the fun lunch and meeting Doris. Yes, Doris–this wonderful grandmother who gave her the shoes. Finally, how J.C.'s condo was better than any pictures her mother had ever shown them in the design magazines. J.C. opened the car door, stepped out into the wintery blustering winds, and walked to the house.

She opened the dining room door and stood motionless. Six miles away, a father and daughter were sharing hugs, smiles, laughter, and joy that J.C. had never seen before. This old house was cold, empty, and just being here made her sad. She needed to call Nadine and get things moving for next week. Once she showed Will that she meant business with all the personal items, maybe it would be easier to talk to him about the land and assets. J.C. walked upstairs to leave her coat and purse before returning to the kitchen to make dinner.

Chapter 15

*I*t was Sunday afternoon. J.C. pulled out her mother's recipe box and made cinnamon rolls. The dough was not quite as fluffy as Evelyn's, but close enough. On Monday morning, she popped them in the oven when she came downstairs. Will was outside for the day even before J.C. had showered. She put her wet hair in a ponytail and started pulling her mother's clothes out of the old chifforobe, that stood behind her parents' bedroom door. She put the clothes into the hamper and started the first load of laundry.

Nadine arrived at 9:30 a.m. She wanted to start with coffee as soon as she walked in. She could smell the fresh rolls. "Something smells great! Are those cinnamon rolls?" she asked.

"Yes, I thought we might need a coffee break a little later," J.C. stated.

"I need coffee right now, and rolls are best when they are warm. So, bring me one of those too," Nadine instructed. Nadine likes her sweets J.C. thought.

J.C. poured Nadine a cup of coffee and cut the corner out of the pan of rolls, taking it to Nadine who was waiting at the dining room table. Nadine smiled up at J.C. as she set it down in front of her.

J.C. returned to the kitchen and brought one in for herself along with her cup of coffee.

"What's new?" Nadine asked.

"Nothing new here," J.C. stated.

"Did Vince get his daughter a prom dress?" Nadine had not forgotten; much to J.C.'s dismay.

"No, I helped Kelsey get a prom dress on Saturday." J.C. made a statement.

Nadine looked up from her roll. "You did what with who?" she shot back.

"Calm down, Nadine, it was no big deal. I was going to Des Moines to pick up bills and swap out clothes. So, I took Vince's daughter, Kelsey, with me to Des Moines on Saturday. We went to a trunk show that Doris told me about. Kelsey found a dress that she liked. We stopped by the condo and saw Doris, who gave Kelsey a pair of shoes that matched her dress and we were home by 3:00 p.m." J.C. heaved a sigh after giving Nadine the full report.

Nadine was shaking her head, rolling her eyes, and laughing all at the same time. "You can fool a fool, but I am no *fool*! There is a whole lot more to this story than what I just heard!"

J.C. got up and walked to the mudroom to put the clothes into the dryer and start a second load. When she returned, she headed directly into the living room and grabbed two bags of clothes that she had left there earlier. "Here are Johnnie's things that I told you about last week. They have all been laundered and are ready for your mission boxes." J.C. walked to the front door and left them on the mat. "I found a box of Johnnie's school papers and some pictures under his bed when I cleaned out his room," J.C. said as she returned to her coffee across the table from Nadine.

"Really, what pictures? Nadine asked.

"Just his school pictures from kindergarten. Those were the only photographs. The rest were pictures he had drawn or school papers that he brought home. Not sure what to do with them. Will has been up in Johnnie's room." J.C. was not sure why she shared that with Nadine.

Nadine responded, "So, this is his house and Johnnie's room is not off limits to him, is it?"

"Well, it just surprised me, I guess. He has never spoken his name and I did not even remember that we had pictures of Johnnie. He was definitely unsettled when he came in for lunch last week and I had them spread out on the table," J.C. admitted.

"You did what?" Nadine snapped.

"I did not mean to upset him, but there was no good place upstairs to go through them, so I brought the box down here and lost track of time. He came in for lunch and I had everything spread out on the table," J.C. responded apologetically.

"Girl, ... you will be the one that gives that man a heart attack, Nadine cautioned.

"OK, it's over and I put the box back up in my study, so he does not have to see it. Let's get started on mom's things. I am already washing the clothes that were hanging in that old chifforobe. I still need to take things out of the chest of drawers and closet." J.C. stood up and took their plates to the kitchen sink. "You need more coffee, Nadine?" she called over her shoulder.

"Just a little bit to warm it up," Nadine responded.

J.C. returned with the pot and filled up both cups. "Where did that old chifforobe come from anyway?" J.C. asked.

"It belonged to Will's mother and maybe her mother before her. You are not planning on getting rid of that are you?" Nadine inquired sternly.

"Well, after today it will be empty so not much use for it here. I emptied Johnnie's dresser and stripped his bed. I should probably call an antique dealer to have them come give me a bid for all these old things." J.C. was very businesslike in her approach.

"You better talk to Will before you get someone in here to sell off his personal property." Nadine was sterner than she had been earlier. J.C. nodded at Nadine to pacify her.

"Why don't you bring out the items you want me to sort, and I will sit here on the couch and go through them." Nadine positioned herself in the center of the couch in the living room, "I am not real comfortable going into Will's bedroom." She heaved a sigh as she settled onto the couch.

J.C. disappeared into the bedroom and came out carrying a small jewelry box. "Here is mom's jewelry, you said there were a couple of pieces you wanted. Go through it and take what you want." J.C. was almost demanding in her tone.

Nadine gently opened the box and laid items out on the cushion next to her. J.C. vanished again back into the bedroom. She returned with a metal box. "This was on the shelf in the closet underneath the stairs. It looks like most of dad's clothes are in there. I do not think I have ever seen this box before." She sat down on the end of the couch and opened the lid.

The first things that J.C. saw were four or five small pictures. They were pictures of small children, but she did not recognize them. One picture caught her eye though. Three little boys sitting in a row on the front porch of this house. The smallest boy looked just like Johnnie. But it could not be Johnnie. The clothes were much older in style. The porch floorboards were wider and some of them were broken on the ends. "Nadine, do you know who these boys are?" J.C. asked abruptly.

Nadine glanced up from her jewelry box and said, "That is your dad and his brothers."

J.C. was sure Nadine said brothers, but her dad was an only child. "Nadine, my dad did not have any brothers. He was an only child." J.C. could not believe that Nadine who was born and raised in Stuart, lived here her whole life and was only two years older than Will, would not know that.

"Will had two older brothers. John was in my class at school and Jack was a year older than us." Nadine closed the jewelry box and looked up at J.C. "Honey, didn't anyone ever tell you about Will's two brothers?"

J.C.'s heart was racing. She clutched the picture in her hand and stared at the face that could have been Johnnie's, sitting on the porch just outside the door in front of where she currently sat. "My dad had two brothers?" J.C. could not understand how this information had escaped her fifty years of life.

Nadine gathered the jewelry that was spread on the cushion next to her and laid it back in the jewelry box. She patted the cushion indicating that J.C. should sit down next to her.

"It was winter and many children at our school got sick with scarlet fever that year. Jack and John, both got it bad. Will was not in school yet, so I do not know if they kept him away from the other two boys when they got the fever. Mrs. Mason also got sick and at one point everyone expected her to die also. John died first and a couple of days later, Jack died. Both boys are buried in the same grave at the Fairview Church just a mile up the road. I think about ten children and a couple of adults from this area died that winter.

Mrs. Mason finally got better but she was always sickly after that. She kept Will out of school for another whole year. He was well over six years old when he finally started. I think she just could not bring herself to risk losing her baby boy. When he turned eighteen, he was drafted, I think. Mrs. Mason wanted him to apply for a waiver since he was their only son, and she was sick. Will would not. He felt it was his duty to fight. So, he went to Germany with the troops in World War II. When he came home, Mrs. Mason threw the biggest lawn party I have ever been to. That was the party where I brought Evelyn with me. The first time she laid eyes on William Mason she was head over heels." Nadine took a breath and could see that J.C. had not kept up with her story. Her eyes were glazed as she stared at the picture in her lap.

"Honey, it was a long time ago. I just barely remember John and Jack from church and school." Nadine tried to reassure J.C. that it was all OK.

"Nadine, we were named after them, Jacquelyn and Johnnie. Dad named us after his two brothers. If they meant enough to him to name us after them, why didn't he tell us about them?" J.C.'s breath was short and choppy.

"Will is a complicated man and talking about things like this was never something he did well. Your mother knew that more than anyone else." Nadine was not sure what J.C. wanted her to say.

"Will had only been home nine months when his mother died. Some people said she hung on just to see him come home from the war. It wasn't much more than a couple months when Will's dad died of a heart attack in the barnyard, and Will was all alone. Will struggled and if Evelyn had not been persistent who knows what would have happened to him." Nadine tried to speak more cheerfully and lighten the mood.

"I feel sick," J.C. said, pulling her dad's dog tags out of the metal box and holding them up in front of her. Then she put them back in the box, placed the pictures back on top, and closed the lid. Standing up, she walked back into the bedroom and laid the metal box on the shelf in the closet over Will's clothes.

"Nadine, I do not think I can do this today," J.C. said as she came out of the bedroom.

"Honey, sit down. Let me get you some more coffee. I will check on the clothes in the mudroom." Nadine disappeared, and J.C. just stared at the porch door in front of her. Her mind was frozen on that picture. Why had her mother not told her? Why had Nadine not told her? How many times had she been to the cemetery as a child and not wondered why there was a small stone cross next to her grandparent's grave and never asked why? Johnnie and her mother were buried on the other side of Will's parents and Will's plot was there waiting for him.

Nadine returned with a load of clean clothes and began sorting and folding them on the couch next to J.C. "I remember your mom wearing this Iowa State sweatshirt when we would come to Ames to watch your halftime shows. I have one just like this. We looked ridiculous sitting in the stands like twins each time we came. Evelyn loved to come to those games and watch you perform." Nadine was trying to distract J.C. but it was not working.

"Nadine, why didn't mom or you ever tell me about dad's brothers?" J.C. quietly asked.

"Oh, honey, since your mom's childhood was ..." Nadine's voice trailed off as she searched for the right words.

"Nadine, I know my mom was an orphan who was left at a church when she was seven months old and was raised at an orphanage until she was eighteen, and then went off to teachers' college. She received her certification and came to Stuart to teach. She never found her parents or any information that would help her find where her life started. She had a note that was pinned to her blanket with 'Evelyn Caine' written on it. She wanted to make sure that the 'Caine' name was a part of us and that is why Johnnie and I both had Caine as our middle name. If she thought it was important for us to know that, why didn't she think I should know that my dad had an older brother named Jack that I was named after and Johnnie for his other brother?" J.C. was indignant and she wanted answers.

Nadine sat down next to J.C. "Well," she drew in a deep breath, "for two years after his father died, Will was exactly like he is right now. He farmed, he kept to himself, and spoke to no one. Evelyn would come out here every Saturday when she was not teaching and clean, cook, decorate, and garden. I kept telling her it was no use. He may be handsome and smart, but Will was a loner and did not want or need anyone else in his life. Evelyn would say, 'No, I am the loner! I have no one else, so I am going to take care of Will. You have George, and your brothers and parents. I have never had a family and now Will does not have a family; so, I will take care of him until he tells me to stop." Nadine sipped her coffee and looked into J.C.'s eyes to confirm she was following. J.C. nodded.

"One day our mutual friend, Everett Nelson, stopped by and talked to Will. Everett had grown up near here, been in

Germany with Will, and knew more about the Mason family than most of us. He told us what he said to Will, 'You better make an honest woman out of Evelyn or she is going to lose her job at the school and there is not another soul on this earth that will take care of you like she has.' Two weeks later at one of their Saturday lunches, Evelyn said Will handed her his mother's diamond ring and asked her if she wanted to get married. They were married two months later. I was her maid of honor and Everett was Will's best man. Will slowly started to come to church and into town with Evelyn and when she was obviously pregnant, he hardly let her out of his sight. When you were born, Evelyn stopped teaching and stayed home to take care of you. She was so happy, and Will was a proud father." Nadine stopped and let this sink in to J.C.

"I know this story. Mom told me how long she came around before dad finally proposed. I still do not know what that has to do with not telling me about his brothers." J.C. was relentless to find out why.

"Evelyn and I talked about everything but this subject. I have to believe at some point Will made it very plain that this topic was a closed chapter in his life and Evelyn respected that; even to the point of not talking to you or me about it," Nadine said with confidence. "Over the years when she was searching for her family, it was very painful not to know why her parents did not want her, why her grandparents did not look for her, why if she had siblings, they did not try and find her. That pain was very deep and hard for Evelyn to bear at times. I believe that she respected Will's pain about his brothers in a similar fashion." Nadine did make sense and if Evelyn had never talked to her about Will's brothers, then maybe she was right. They, Evelyn and Will, must have made a pact not to discuss their painful pasts.

"J.C., they were happy, and you two children were all either one of them ever wanted. Johnnie's death was the hardest thing I have ever experienced in my lifetime. When George was killed, I was sad and knew that the love of my life was gone.

I was never going to find someone like him that made me laugh and feel loved the way he did. But, when I sat with your mom at the hospital and then here at this house after Johnnie was gone, I felt such deep grief, I could not imagine how either one of them could possibly go on. Losing a child that was so full of life one day and then in a matter of months was gone, had to be life shattering. Those are far more complex emotions than losing an adult that has an accident and is taken. They both had to watch Johnnie deteriorate knowing that they could not stop it from happening. Will just could not do it one more time." Nadine hung her head and sat quietly next to J.C.

J.C.'s heart hurt. Her chest was tight and the sad feeling she had in the backseat of the car sitting next to Johnnie, forty years ago was washing over her with such power that she leaned sideways and buried her head into Nadine's chest and sobbed.

They both jumped when the kitchen door opened. J.C. quickly looked at the clock. It was 12:30 p.m. Nadine motioned for J.C. to head upstairs. Nadine stood up and walked to the kitchen.

Through the floor register, J.C. could hear Nadine updating Will on the mornings' events of cleaning drawers, jewelry, and doing laundry. J.C. could hear Will making himself something to eat and she knew he was probably hurrying to get back outside as soon as possible. When she heard the kitchen door, she looked out of her bedroom window and saw Will walking back to the barnyard.

J.C. headed downstairs and was greeted by Nadine who had made two sandwiches and was waiting for her at the dining room table.

Chapter 16

*A*t 2:30 p.m., all the clothes were cleaned, sorted, and packed in bags for Goodwill. A small tote sat off to one side of the pile that Nadine would take home to keep for herself. J.C. was putting on her jacket and shoes to help Nadine carry the bags to the car when someone knocked on the door behind her. She quickly turned and opened the dining room door.

A delivery man was standing on the front porch holding a beautiful bouquet of roses. J.C. blushed. She accepted the bouquet and turned to face Nadine.

Nadine was grinning and there was no chance she would leave until she knew who they were from.

J.C. set the bouquet on the dining room table and slowly opened the small card sticking up out of the bouquet. 'Thanks so much. Kelsey and Vince,' read the message.

"Vince?" Nadine asked.

"Kelsey and Vince," J.C. confirmed.

"I am no fool!" Nadine laughed hard. "Those are really beautiful."

"Yes," J.C. commented. "That was very thoughtful of them to send me flowers for helping Kelsey."

"Thoughtful." Nadine laughed again.

"Nadine," J.C. spoke very sternly, "Not one word about these to anyone in town. Vince does not appreciate being part of the gossip mill."

"My lips are sealed!" Nadine's eyes were still dancing with joy.

J.C. opened the door and grabbed the two bags of Johnnie's clothes. Nadine carried her tote bag and J.C. made sure that Nadine did not slip as they headed down to Nadine's car. When Nadine had pulled away, J.C. returned and brought the remaining bags of her mother's items and set them on the back seat of her car. She would take them to Goodwill in Greenfield.

She returned to the kitchen and laid out some chicken breasts to thaw for dinner. J.C. took a couple of items she had kept from her mother's closet and headed upstairs. She sat down at her desk and looked at the box on the floor next to her. She opened one flap and took out a picture of Johnnie. She set it up against her computer screen as a conversation began in her mind. "Johnnie, you were named after your Uncle John who was dad's older brother. He died in childhood just like you did. Dad was younger than you when both his brothers died. I know it doesn't matter to you, but I just wanted to tell you. Not sure why no one told us before. I miss you, Johnnie. I wish I could have experienced growing up with a brother and really wish you were here now to help me decide what to do about dad."

J.C. opened the gold heart locket she had kept from her mother's jewelry box and there was her face and Johnnie's looking up at her. She smiled as she remembered how many times her mother had worn it around her neck. J.C. pulled it over her head and let it fall around her own neck. "I will keep you right next to my heart, Johnnie," she thought.

"J.C.!" Will's voice shot up through the register.

"I am upstairs, Dad." J.C. jumped up from her chair and headed downstairs. She rounded the dining room table and saw Will standing in the kitchen doorway with a worried look on his face.

"I got the silage wagon stuck. Can you come pull me out?" Will was looking directly at J.C.

"Sure, just let me change my clothes and I'll be right there." J.C. was already turned around and headed back upstairs to put on her chore jeans and sweatshirt. Coming back to the mudroom she put on the coveralls and boots before hurrying out the door.

When J.C. got outside, Will had already backed his pickup up to the tractor and wagon and connected a tow chain to the two of them. "I will pull, if you can just steer the tractor?" he asked.

"Sure," J.C. said as she crawled onto the tractor.

Will was already in the pickup and had shifted into four-wheel drive. He pulled forward and the chain was tight between the two vehicles. J.C. clasped the steering wheel, pushed in the clutch, and put the tractor into gear. The tractor jerked forward a couple of feet. The motor in the pickup revved and then the tractor slowly followed the pickup back onto the rock driveway leading out of the lots. Will stopped the pickup, stepped out of the truck, unhitched the tractor, and drove the pickup out of the lot. J.C. sat for a moment and then decided she should follow him. Looking over her shoulder she confirmed that the silage trough was full and the cows were eating. She let out the clutch and followed her dad around the barnyard and back to the machine shed where the tractor and wagon would stay parked until tomorrow, when it was time to feed again. She eased through the side door that was standing open and parked the wagon in its normal spot and was considering getting down when Will came in.

"Thanks, J.C., I just got caught in the mud. You did not have to bring the rig back here. I could have done that." He almost had a smile on his face.

"No problem, Dad. I am glad I was here to help you. Who do you call when you are here alone?" J.C. asked.

Will hesitated before answering. "Usually, Vince Martin stops by when I get in a bind."

"He just stops by?" J.C. wanted clarification.

Will nodded. J.C. shook her head. "Is there anything else I can do to help, Dad? I'm already in my chore clothes and finished with my project inside for today."

"I could use a hand." Will turned and J.C. followed him. As he left the machine shed, he picked up a small toolbox and headed towards the corral. When Will reached the corral, he set the toolbox down in front of a section where the top board was broken. He lifted the broken piece back up in place and motioned for J.C. to hold it in place. He opened the toolbox and took out a hammer and some long nails. He drove two nails into the broken plank against a post on the opposite side. After reattaching that board, he pulled up the second half and J.C. held it as he repeated the process to reaffix that one as well. "Thanks," Will said as he put his tools away and walked toward the machine shed. J.C. knew that meant she was done.

When J.C. got back to the house, she opened a can of cream of chicken soup and poured it over the two chicken breasts in a casserole dish, added some salt and pepper and put it in the oven. Opening the freezer, she saw that she had green beans she could make a little later in the microwave. She pulled out some potatoes, peeled and sliced three of them into another casserole dish, added some milk, salt and pepper and finished off with shredded cheese then put it in the oven with the chicken.

Walking into the dining room, she sat at the table staring at the bouquet of roses. Her mind started to wonder as she tried to remember the last time she had received a bouquet of flowers. It had been years. She walked into the living room and opened the antique secretary desk to look for thank you notes. In the second drawer she found a package of thank you cards. She sat down and wrote, "Dear Kelsey and Vince, what a surprise to receive such a beautiful bouquet of roses today. It has been years since I have been surprised with such a lovely gift. You are both so thoughtful and I enjoy all my memories from Saturday. Kelsey, thank you for allowing me to be a part of this special event in your life. Your friend, J.C. Mason."

She returned to the kitchen and continued her preparation of dinner. Will came through the door at exactly 6:00 p.m. He followed his nightly routine and sat at the head of the table by 6:30 p.m. J.C. had placed the chicken breasts, potatoes, and green beans on the table. Will bowed his head and prayed before serving himself. J.C. sat frozen not knowing what there was to discuss since Nadine had already updated Will on Evelyn's items that they had taken care of that day. "Dad, what do you want me to do with the furniture that you do not need? I have cleaned out Johnnie's room and now the chifforobe in your room is empty. Those items should probably be appraised by an antique dealer before they are sold." J.C. was very matter of fact in requesting his input.

Will did not look up, he did not clear his throat, he did not gesture. Minutes passed before even the slightest sound of the furnace relighting was heard. "Who are the flowers from?" Will finally spoke.

J.C. was taken aback by her father's complete avoidance of her question or was it his interest in the flowers which she doubted. "Kelsey and Vince sent them as a thank you for helping her find a prom dress. Really unnecessary but a nice gesture."

The remainder of the dinner was silent until Will got up to take his dishes to the kitchen. "J.C., thanks again for pulling me out of the mud. I will call in the morning and order a load of gravel to spread in front of that feeding trough." He set his dishes in the sink and went into the living room.

J.C. completed her nightly routine. She put the leftovers away, washed, dried, and put the dishes away. She stopped in the bathroom to get ready for bed. As she walked into the living room, she stopped and studied her father who was seated in his chair reading his Bible. Why didn't he answer her question about the furniture? Just then she heard her cell phone ringing upstairs. "Good night, Dad," she said as she headed up the stairs. No response.

As she entered the study, her phone was still ringing. "Hello, J.C.," Vince greeted her as she grabbed her phone off the desk. "Am I calling at a bad time?"

"No," J.C. responded.

"I need to get your friend Doris' name and address so that I can properly thank her for the shoes that she gave Kelsey. I also feel bad that I have not called before now to tell you how much it meant to me when you took Kelsey to Des Moines. She has talked about nothing else since then. I have heard every last detail at least three times. And, the dress is perfect, J.C. It looks like it was made for her and definitely falls within my modesty guidelines." Vince's voice carried his gratitude clearly.

"Well, first I need to thank you for that beautiful bouquet of roses that showed up here today. Vince, that was not necessary, but they are definitely beautiful and add some fresh aroma to this old house." J.C. was smiling as she remembered her excitement as she opened the door earlier for the delivery man.

"So glad you like them. It was Kelsey's idea to get the multicolored bouquet. She said it was for all the different colored dresses that she tried on." Vince laughed recalling his conversation with his daughter.

"Tell Kelsey I appreciate the thought. Vince, you have one very special daughter. I was amazed at how decisive and mature she was in making her choice. It was a pretty intense setting and there were a few meltdowns going on around us. But Kelsey, she kept her cool and focused on her plan. I do wish you could have seen her in a couple of gowns that she did not select. There was a white and silver one that was gorgeous and made her look twenty-five. I know that is probably not what a father of a seventeen-year-old daughter wants to hear; just know that someday your little girl is going to be a very beautiful young lady." J.C. was relaxed and leaned back on her couch upstairs as she settled into her conversation with Vince.

"You are right, the last thing I need to think about before prom is how my daughter could possibly look twenty-five already. Thanks for that mental picture!" Vince was laughing as he kidded J.C. "I was wondering if we could tempt you with another dinner invitation this week? Kelsey is getting ready for her performance in '*Over the Rainbow*', the spring musical production, and wanted your opinion on a couple of things."

J.C. was not expecting that and hesitated before answering. "What night were you thinking about?" J.C. bought a little time.

"Saturday night if you are free. Friday is a home basketball game and I usually go and watch Kelsey cheer," Vince responded.

Of course, she was free Saturday night; why was she hesitating? J.C. took in a deep breath and said, "Sure, but this time you have to let me bring something. Can I bring the dessert?" she asked.

"Sure," Vince replied, "well, I better let you go, I do not want to consume your entire evening." Vince's tone almost sounded like a question.

"Wait, Vince, I have a question for you." J.C. really wanted to know about her father's relationship with Vince. "My dad got stuck in the mud today and I had to help him get the tractor and wagon pulled out. When I asked him what he would have done if I wasn't here, he indicated that you usually come by and help him out of those kinds of situations."

"Yes, I guess I have, more-so in the last couple of years. Once your Mom was sick and then after she passed away, there have been a few times when he needed help and I was there." Vince did not seem like he was saying anything out of the ordinary.

"So, does he call and ask you to come over?" J.C. inquired.

"No, it just seems like I stop by at the right time." Vince again made it sound like that was normal.

"So, my dad needs help, and you magically stop and lend a hand?" J.C. was starting to sound like an inquisition.

"Well, I like to think it is more of a God thing than magic," Vince said softly.

J.C. sucked in her breath. Did he just say, 'a God thing'? "Oh!" was all she could say in response.

"Before I let you go, can I get Doris' address?" Vince gently reminded J.C. why he had called.

"Oh, sure. It is Doris Buck, 300 Walnut Street, #2502 The Plaza, Des Moines, IA 50309. She will be overjoyed to receive anything and is the kind of person that expects nothing." J.C. wanted Vince to know the kind of person Doris really was.

"Thanks. OK, we'll see you Saturday. Does 6:00 p.m. work for you?" Vince asked.

"6:00 p.m. will be fine." J.C. sat in total silence as her head spun in so many different directions.

Did Vince really say that God sent him to help Will? He must have been joking and she missed the sarcasm in his voice.

Did her father really avoid her question tonight about the furniture? What would have happened if she had asked the question that she really wanted an answer to; why he had never told her about his brothers?

J.C. pulled her afghan up over her legs and stared across the room at Johnnie's picture. The more she looked at the young innocent face, the more her mind was perplexed about one thing–God! Her father was seated below her in the living room clutching a Bible. Meaning he must believe in God. Kelsey confidently stated that her mother was with God. J.C. wanted to believe that last night in the hospital room with her mother and father, as Evelyn took her final breath, that she was going to a better place. Was that heaven? But wait. Why would God take Johnnie when he was so full of life? And that same God also took two other small children from her grandmother and her father. Vince, the nicest guy in the world, did not deserve to have his wife taken when he still needed her help raising Kelsey. Kelsey did not deserve to lose her mother. Nadine was barely thirty when George was killed. How does a God like that take so many people that are loved and needed and turn around to send Vince each time Will is in trouble? J.C. reached up and held the locket hanging around her neck in her hand. Knowing that her mother had done that a million times before, it brought comfort to her racing mind.

J.C. got up and went into her dressing room to change into her pajamas. She looked down the stairs and noticed the light behind her father's chair was already turned off. She realized he'd be going into the bedroom tonight without Evelyn's things in there. She was sad. Would he open the chifforobe and stare at the emptiness? Would he look for her jewelry box? What if he noticed that the metal box had been moved off the shelf? Would he wonder if she knew about his brothers? Would he care?

J.C. walked into Johnnie's room. The emptiness was haunting. She slowly lowered herself down on the mattress of his bed. She pulled her knees up to her chest, clutched the locket again in her right hand, and sobbed. She was a loner, just like Evelyn had been when she came to take care of Will. What good was it that she knew who her father was? He did not want her. Her brother and mother were gone. She did not have anyone to love like Vince and Kelsey had each other. She had not made friends over the years like Nadine and Evelyn. She was totally alone.

Chapter 17

*S*aturday began just like the rest of the days of the week on the farm. J.C. was awakened to the sound of a loud truck in the driveway. She had fallen back into her habit of sleeping in since the workout option was too dangerous. She got out of bed and looked out her south window. The quarry truck was there with the load of gravel. She watched as Will led the driver through the gates and into the lot where he needed the gravel. The dump truck lifted and began to spread gravel along the south side of the feeding trough. Once the load was empty, the driver followed Will back through each gate to the driveway and was gone. J.C. watched Will walk to the machine shed and re-emerge with the skid-steer. It had a blade across the front of it. He maneuvered through each lot getting on and off the skid-steer three times, before he was in the lot where the gravel had just been dumped. He closed the last gate behind him and slowly started to push the rock up tight to the feeding trough. He was unaware that he was being studied. J.C. mentally confirmed that he did not act like he was seventy-five years old. He was very capable of taking care of his business.

CHAPTER 17

J.C. made her way downstairs and poured a cup of coffee. She was not even sure what she wanted for breakfast. The past week had been a blur. Just going through the motions of making meals, doing some cleaning, dropping off items at Goodwill, and picking up groceries. Meals with her father had become totally silent again.

A knock at the front door startled her. She walked to the door in her robe and was surprised to see Kelsey standing there. "Kelsey, what are you doing here?" J.C. blurted out almost sounding rude.

"I am sorry, did I come at a bad time?" Kelsey's genuine tone surprised J.C.

"No, I am just getting a slow start today." J.C. felt embarrassed that she was still in her pj's at 8:30 a.m. "Come in." J.C. tried to sound more welcoming.

"Thanks, I needed to talk to an adult and thought maybe you could give me some advice." Kelsey looked hopeful at J.C.

"I can try. Can I get you something to drink?" J.C. had been taught to be a good hostess even in her worst moments.

"A glass of milk would be great." Kelsey smiled. She was taking off her boots and unzipping her jacket when J.C. came back in the dining room.

"I made some cinnamon rolls earlier this week and I was just about to warm one up for myself; would you like one?" J.C. asked.

"That sounds great. We had practice early this morning for our musical and I grabbed a banana on my way out the door. Still a little hungry I guess," Kelsey admitted.

J.C. took the rolls out of the refrigerator and placed two in the microwave to warm them. She stepped into the bathroom and pulled her hair into a ponytail before returning to the dining room with the rolls.

"Are these the flowers my dad sent you?" Kelsey asked.

"Those are the flowers from you and your dad!" J.C. commented. "He said you selected the multi-colored roses because of the different colored dresses you tried on."

"Yes, I guess I did tell him not to send the standard red roses. That is kind of boring and I thought something with more color would be fun. He called me from the florist on Monday morning and said they had these different colors and I said that reminded me of all those prom dresses that we saw." Kelsey smiled thinking she was letting J.C. in on a little secret. "These rolls are awesome! Did you make them from scratch?" Kelsey was quickly devouring hers.

"Yes, I am glad they still taste OK. I baked them on Monday," J.C. admitted. "My mother could make them much better than I do."

"J.C., I kind of have a boy problem," Kelsey said as she took another bite.

Jumping right in, J.C. thought, "What's the problem?"

"Two guys asked me to prom." Kelsey looked at J.C. scrunching up her nose.

"Which one asked first?" J.C. was sure there was an easy solution to this teenage problem.

"I do not know," Kelsey replied, "I was talking to some friends at lunch and Jason came up and wanted to talk to me. So, we walked away from the group and he asked if anyone had asked me to prom yet. I said no. So, he asked if I would like to go with him. I said, yes. When I got back to my friends, I told them what Jason wanted and my girlfriend Becca said, 'Oh no! I just put a note in your locker from Zack.' I really wanted Zack to ask me." She looked perplexed.

Really, it is not even 9 a.m. on Saturday morning and this teenage girl thinks I have the answer to this! J.C. took in two large gulps of coffee. "Well, Kelsey, what do you think your dad would tell you to do?" Good, safe answer J.C. thought.

"He would say to honor my word. I know that I agreed to go with Jason, but I did not know that Zack would ask me at the same time. If I had known that Zack was leaving that note in my locker I would have never said yes to Jason." J.C. thought Kelsey wanted her to say it was OK to back out of her commitment to Jason and go with Zack.

"Kelsey, you know I am no expert when it comes to these kinds of situations. You seem close to your dad. Why don't you ask him what he thinks?" J.C. really did not want to give parenting advice.

"Well, my dad doesn't really like Jason's dad. He is kind of a ladies' man around town. Jason is really not like that and my dad does not know Jason like I do. So that is why I came to ask you." Kelsey was very sincere.

J.C. really did not want to get in the middle of something that she felt was outside her role as a friend, even thinking of herself as a friend was a stretch in her mind. "Who is his dad?" she asked buying some time.

"Jim Powell," Kelsey responded.

Well of course, thought J.C. "I knew Jim back in high school. In fact, I went to my first prom with Jim." Why was she sharing that information with Kelsey; maybe to buy more time she thought?

"Really? You went to prom with Mr. Powell? I cannot believe that!" Kelsey said with a big exclamation in her voice.

"Do you want to see the pictures?" J.C. asked before thinking: why am I getting drawn into this high school drama? At least showing Kelsey the pictures kept her from having to give advice. "Come with me upstairs, I have some photo albums with some old pictures in them."

Kelsey dutifully followed J.C. upstairs. J.C. turned the corner at the top of the stairs and walked into her study. Kelsey hesitated and peeked in the dressing room. "Wow, this is an awesome closet," she shouted from behind J.C.

"Yes, it was a gift from my mom on my sixteenth birthday. She had been working on it for a few weeks while I was at school. The original door was locked because it had been storage for most of my childhood, so I didn't know that she had a carpenter coming in while I was at school. That afternoon when I got home and ran up the stairs, the door was gone and 'presto, I had my own dressing room'. It was a pretty awesome gift for a sixteen-year-old back then." J.C.

recalled the excitement she had felt reaching that top stair, as if it were yesterday.

"That would be an awesome gift anytime." Kelsey was standing in the study taking it all in when J.C. handed her the photo album.

"These dresses are going to look like 'granny sacks', or 'dogs' as you call them compared to what we just experienced at the Talesse' Design Show." J.C. started to laugh even before Kelsey could see them.

"J.C., you looked great. Jason looks just like his dad did. Wow! The hair is different but everything else is the same." Kelsey was studying the picture carefully. "Mr. Powell does not look anything like that now!"

"I know," J.C. agreed before thinking about what she had just said, "I bumped into him one morning last week at the middle school gym; a little out of shape!"

"You could say that, but he acts like he still looks like this. I think that is what gets to my dad. He struts around town and dates so many different women. I know Jason doesn't like that his dad is like that and I feel sorry for him. I really hope he does not turn out like his dad. J.C., I think I know what I need to do." Kelsey slowly closed the photo album and handed it back to J.C.

"Good," J.C. said with a sigh.

"I am going to tell Zack that I already said yes to Jason," Kelsey said looking down at the floor.

J.C. motioned for Kelsey to sit down on the couch. "Kelsey, when I was your age, I thought that going to prom with the most popular boy in school was all any girl could hope for. Our proms were much different, however, than they are today. Ours started with a formal dinner in the lunchroom served by parents dressed up in their Sunday best, and girls in our homemade dresses, and boys in their Sunday suits. The lights were turned down and we had candles on the tables. Students gave speeches and a local band played soft music during dinner. When dinner was over, we went into the gym decorated with streamers and played records for a couple of hours before everyone went back home, and prom was over. Mostly we stood around in our small groups of friends and felt embarrassed and awkward. If I remember right, Jim danced with me two maybe three times, but spent most of the night moving from girl-to-girl dancing with as many as he could. I actually rode home with my mom after she helped clean up the lunchroom. I never had another date with Jim after that. I hope you are right that Jason is different but if he is not, you will move on and maybe next year Zack will have enough courage to ask you face to face." J.C. smiled realizing that moment had really not defined her life either.

"I know and I really do think that Jason is different than his dad. Would you be OK with me telling my dad at dinner tonight when you are there?" Kelsey looked helpless at J.C.

"Really, you want me to be the buffer? You think he will hold back his opinion if I am there?" J.C. was smiling knowing that any teenager probably doesn't want to disappoint their parent or hear their opinions at times like these.

"I don't know, but maybe if he knew that you went to prom with Mr. Powell and turned out this great, he will not think it is such a big deal if I go with Jason." Kelsey wrinkled her nose and smiled.

"I guess I can throw myself on the fire if your dad goes crazy." J.C. was full out laughing at just the thought of Vince (Mr. Nice Guy) losing his temper over something as innocent as this.

"Thanks, J.C. can I see the rest of your house?" Kelsey was curious.

J.C. led Kelsey through the study into her bedroom walking to the windows to show her the rest of the farm from there. As they turned around, Kelsey moved to the door that looked inside Johnnie's room.

"Was this your brother's room?" she asked softly.

"Yes, you can go in. There is really nothing but furniture left in there," J.C. said as she stepped through the door behind Kelsey. "Is that a picture of him on your computer in the other room?" Kelsey inquired.

"Yes, that was him in kindergarten. He was too sick for school pictures in first grade so that is the only one I have." J.C. paused. "Except ..." she opened the locket around her neck and showed Kelsey the baby faces in her mother's locket.

"He sure was cute. I always wondered what it would have been like to have a brother or sister," Kelsey said almost to the air and not truly directed toward J.C.

"It was great. Sometimes when storms would come, he would get scared, run into my room, and jump under the covers. I loved feeling like I was not afraid of the storm and could protect him." J.C. turned and walked back into her own room. "Kelsey, I wonder too what it would have been like to grow up with a brother. My life changed when Johnnie died." J.C. put her hand over her mouth subconsciously to stop herself from saying anything more. This was a teenage girl she had almost poured out her heart to. J.C. Mason did not share those thoughts with *anyone*! Moving quickly J.C. walked through the study and back downstairs.

As they returned to the dining room, Kelsey picked up her glass and saucer and headed to the kitchen. "I will take care of those," J.C. said, taking them from Kelsey.

"OK, thanks for the cinnamon roll and the talk. I will see you tonight for dinner. What are you bringing for dessert? You know my dad is a chocoholic!" Kelsey said giggling.

"Really, I did not know that, but I picked up everything I need to make my mom's sour cream chocolate cake this week when I bought groceries ... so chocolate it is!" J.C. smiled right back at Kelsey.

Chapter 18

J.C. arrived in Vince's driveway at 6:03 p.m. She opened the passenger door and carefully lifted the cake carrier from the floor of the front seat. She walked carefully across the driveway and up on the deck just as Vince opened the door with a big smile. J.C. gently handed the cake carrier to Vince who set it on the counter and spun back around to hold her coat as she slipped out of it. J.C. wore a soft yellow sweater and blue jeans with a pair of ankle boots. She quickly stepped out of her boots and straightened her hair over her shoulders. Her mother's gold locket hung around her neck.

"It smells amazing in here," J.C. opened the conversation.

"Well, I hope you like pork chops; I grilled them earlier and just put them in the oven to make sure they are cooked all the way through. Kelsey made some scalloped potatoes this afternoon that are almost ready. Would you like a glass of wine before dinner?" Vince asked.

"Yes, that would be great." J.C. smiled and let out a small sigh.

"Bad day?" Vince picked up on her sigh.

"No, more like a strange week." J.C. caught herself. Why would she say something that would invite more inquiries?

"J.C.," Kelsey said from behind her.

"Hello, Kelsey." J.C. turned and smiled to see the vibrant Kelsey bouncing through the archway and into the great room.

"Dad, thanks for making a fire. It just makes things cozier, don't you think, J.C.?" Kelsey winked.

J.C. was on edge knowing that at some point the Jason topic would be introduced and she needed to be on her toes. Her business background had taught her that having the inside scoop was always better than being blindsided. Vince might not appreciate being ganged up on. She accepted her glass of wine from Vince.

"It is a favorite of mine. I hope you like Pinot," Vince said.

"As a matter of fact, Pinot is my favorite as well," J.C. confidently responded.

The table had already been set before J.C. arrived, and as Kelsey came out from the kitchen with her glass of milk, she motioned for J.C. to sit down. Vince was beginning to bring the food from the oven.

"So, Kelsey, tell me about the play," J.C. inquired.

"Well, 'Over the Rainbow' is a musical about dreams. I play a maiden who wishes to meet a prince that she has dreamed about. You will have to come see it if you want to know if my wish comes true. After dinner I will show you the three costumes I have to wear. One is a long night gown for the dreaming portion. The next one is a granny sack," Kelsey giggled at J.C. "that I wear for my gardening and housework, and the final costume is a formal party dress that I hope to wear to a ball and meet my prince. These costumes came with the script to our drama teacher in a box. They are really not that great. We can add to them, but it has to be done in a way that can easily be removed because when we are done, they are shipped on to the next school."

Vince sat down at the end of the table between Kelsey and J.C. He bowed his head and asked God's blessing over the food, their conversation and friendship. J.C. was better prepared for it this time and bowed her head and said "Amen" when Vince and Kelsey did.

"When is your play?" J.C. asked.

"It is two weeks from tonight and then a matinee on Sunday afternoon," Kelsey said.

"I will see if my mom's friend, Nadine, would like to come with me. Where can I buy tickets?" J.C. inquired.

"You can get them at the door right before the show," Vince responded, "that is really nice of you, J.C."

"I love plays and besides, I want to see if Kelsey is any kind of an actress!" J.C. chided.

"Oh, I can act," Kelsey shot back, "Oscar level performance is what you are going to see." They all three broke out laughing.

"How is your pork chop, I hope they are not too dry?" Vince asked.

"Mine is perfect," J.C. said with a smile.

"Dad," Kelsey opened with a soft voice, "I got asked to the prom this week."

"OK, well it's nice to know we have someone to escort the prettiest girl to the prom, isn't it J.C.?" Vince proudly smiled at Kelsey.

J.C. kept silent.

"Well, it's kind of funny but two boys asked me at the same time." Kelsey was beginning to lay out her case.

"Not surprising!" Vince had another proud papa moment.

Kelsey sighed big. "Jason Powell," J.C. watched Vince's jawbone tighten, "asked me right after lunch and then when I got to my locker, Zack had put a note in there." Kelsey took a bite of her potatoes.

A few moments of silence passed. "So, who did you say yes to?" Vince asked.

"Jason," Kelsey replied. Another minute passed before Kelsey continued. "Jason did not know that Zack was going to ask me and when he said, 'has anyone else asked you?' I did not know that Zack was going to ask me too, so I said, 'yes' to Jason." Kelsey was talking really fast.

"I see." Vince paused. "Kelsey, can we trust Jason?" Vince's voice was the sternest tone J.C. had ever heard out of him.

"Dad, Jason is not like his dad. He lives with his mom full time and he is so quiet. Not pushy at all like his father. He has always been nice to me. I don't know of any other girls that he has asked out before." Kelsey was a little calmer as she pleaded her case. "Dad, you know that I have had a crush on Zack for over a year and if he had asked me first, I know we would not be having this conversation. But I also know that God would not want me to judge Jason based on hearsay about his dad. I really did want to go with Zack, but it just would not be right to do that to Jason, right?"

J.C. caught her breath with Kelsey's last comment. She was pulling out all the stops to convince her dad that she was doing the right thing. What dad could argue with God? She was *good*! Future contract negotiator ... J.C. thought.

Vince chewed his meat and did not say anything for a few minutes. Kelsey looked across the table with an innocent smile at J.C.

"Kelsey, I will need to sleep on this one. We can talk about it again tomorrow." Vince closed that topic with a big nail in the coffin approach.

"J.C., what did you do to keep yourself busy this week?" Vince moved the attention back to her.

This was one week she really did not want to talk about. "More cleaning, sorting, and taking things to Goodwill and church missions," J.C. reported.

"J.C. has an awesome dressing room, Dad. You should take a look at it to get some ideas on how to remodel my puny little closet." Kelsey seemed to bounce back from the previous conversation pretty quickly, J.C. thought.

"I am sure J.C.'s condo is nice all the way around," Vince commented.

"No, Dad, at her dad's farmhouse. She has a full dressing room like a movie star and her own study lounge next to her bedroom." Kelsey had let the cat out of the bag and J.C.'s heart started to race.

Vince stopped eating and looked at J.C. and then back at Kelsey. "When were you at Mr. Mason's farm?" Vince asked quizzically.

"Today, after practice. I stopped over to talk to J.C. about my prom problem. Did you know that she went to her first prom with Jim Powell?" Kelsey was on a roll and J.C. felt like she was being served up as the main course. How could she let this happen? She was a skilled salesperson that should always anticipate the next chess move. Vince was going to explode and tell her to mind her own business. He had every right...

"J.C.," Vince said for the second time, "so you went to prom with the infamous Jim Powell or Jim "Prowl" as the guys in the locker room referred to him?" Vince surprisingly was smiling and did not show any signs of anger.

"Yes," J.C. responded almost shamefully.

"Dad, J.C. looked awesome, and Mr. Powell looked just like Jason does right now. It was kind of weird seeing Mr. Powell looking so athletic when he is so out of shape now." Kelsey did not seem to notice that J.C. was still on edge and worried that at any moment she would have to justify her earlier actions.

"He wasn't a very nice date. He danced with other girls instead of J.C. and her mother had to bring her home." Kelsey continued to lay J.C. out like a well-prepared turkey at Thanksgiving.

"Old Jim lives up to his reputation yet again," Vince said.

"Vince, I am not a parent, and prom today is totally different than when you and I were in high school, so I have no room to give advice." J.C. took in a deep breath and thought maybe this would be a great time to grab her coat, get in her car, and head back to Des Moines. Yes, get as far away from this situation as possible. "So, I did not give Kelsey any advice earlier today. She really arrived at her decision completely on her own once she had time to talk it through. I have to admire her for thinking about Jason's feelings over and above her own. Not many girls her age could be that mature. She genuinely wants to do the right thing and maybe Jason is more like his mom than his dad." J.C. stopped herself and was prepared to exit as soon as Vince showed her the door.

Vince looked very concerned. "J.C., I hope you did not misunderstand my decision to delay this conversation. I thought we were being inconsiderate having such a personal conversation in front of you. Little did I know that the two of you had already worked this out without the insights of my great wisdom?" Vince laughed. "I agree. Kelsey is doing the right thing and I am proud that she puts others ahead of her own feelings." He reached over and patted his daughter's shoulder. Kelsey smiled back at Vince.

J.C. was completely perplexed. Her own relationship had not prepared her in any way to communicate with her father like this. The stories that women at work shared seemed more like spoiled rotten brats who intimidated their parents, and none of that was what she was experiencing here.

They had all finished eating when Vince announced, "I am going to clean up while the two of you head back to Kelsey's room and try on those costumes before we have dessert in front of the fire." Kelsey and J.C. both smiled and headed through the archway into the back part of the house.

Kelsey's room was at the end of the hallway directly behind the kitchen. She had a nice size room, her own bath, and a small walk-in closet. "This is nice!" J.C. said looking around.

"It is not a full second floor of a house, but you are right. It is all I need." Kelsey smiled. "OK," she held up a flannel night gown. "This is the first one and I guess I am OK with it. I like the blue and yellow flowers anyway. I was thinking I would wear a yellow ribbon in my hair and maybe some yellow bootie socks. What do you think?"

"Sounds cute to me," J.C. said.

"This is the 'granny sack' that I really do not like. It is just so plain," Kelsey complained. The light blue Chambray dress was very simple.

"What if you added an apron? Did your mom have any aprons?" J.C. asked.

"I think so. Dad ...!" Kelsey started to yell from her room to get Vince's attention.

"Let me go ask," J.C. offered. "Can you slip that one on so we can get a better idea what it is going to look like?" J.C. headed down the hall and back to the kitchen.

"Vince, did Teri have any aprons?" J.C. inquired as she reentered the kitchen.

Vince smiled and motioned with his hand to a drawer at the end of the counter, next to the bookshelf full of cookbooks. "If she did, they would be in there," he said.

J.C. pulled out the drawer and found the jackpot of aprons. Just then Kelsey came bounding around the corner in the Chambray dress. "Did you find one?" she asked.

"Oh, no!" J.C. said with a big smile "I found the mother-load!" They all burst out laughing.

J.C. held them up to Kelsey one by one. Vince would give a thumb's up if he liked it. J.C. would say not bad on some, and one of them Kelsey pushed back and said, "That is a real dog! Dad, you should take it to the shop for a grease rag. No one will ever want that ugly thing." After looking through the entire drawer, they laid three aside. Kelsey tried each one on again. Two of them went over her head covering the bodice and the front of her skirt. The last one was a red and white gingham checked pattern that tied around the waist and just covered the skirt. Kelsey picked that one.

"I bet some of these belonged to your Grandmother Andrews," Vince said. "When you talk to her next time, you will have to ask. Have you invited them to the play?"

"No, it is a long drive from Ankeny. Do you really think they will want to come?" Kelsey asked.

"Well, they might come to the Sunday matinee. They wouldn't have to travel after dark that way," Vince said.

"OK, I will call them." Kelsey relented. "J.C., come back here with me. You have to see the horrible party dress."

They returned to Kelsey's room and she stepped into the closet to change. When she came out, J.C. gasped and said, "Dog!" before catching herself. "I am sorry, do you like it?" She tried to recover.

"No, it is awful! I hate the color and it is too big on me. I really have no idea what to do to make it better. I just want to ask Mr. Hempen if I can wear something else." Kelsey stepped in front of her mirror and wrinkled her nose. J.C. moved around behind her. She pulled the dark orange satin dress in tight around Kelsey's waist. "Do you have any pins?"

Kelsey went back in her closet and came out with two safety pins. J.C. pinned the dress, so it fit tighter. "Can I look in your closet?" J.C. asked.

"Sure, what are you looking for?" Kelsey replied.

"Maybe a lace top or sundress that you can put over the top of this to tone it down a little." J.C. was hoping that something in there might give her an idea. They tried a few options but none of them really made much of a difference. "I think your idea of talking to Mr. Hempen and asking if he will let you wear something else might be best," J.C. suggested.

"What about your red prom dress?" Kelsey asked. "Do you still have it?"

J.C. was taken aback, "Yes, it is in the corner of my closet over at the farm. I think it will be a little long and maybe too wide in the shoulders. I guess we could see if Nadine would alter it for you, if it is OK with your drama teacher." J.C. felt a strange warm feeling thinking that Kelsey had just asked to borrow her thirty-three-year-old prom dress. This would have made Evelyn happy she thought, as she smiled to herself.

"I am going to ask him first thing on Monday," Kelsey said, turning to have J.C. release her from this 'dog' dress she was in.

"Kelsey if you want to, on the blue dress we could add some red buttons down the front and if you wear a red ribbon in your hair that might make the outfit a little more colorful," J.C. suggested.

"I like that idea. I will stop at the Ben Franklin and pick up some buttons after school on Monday. You will have to show me how to sew them on," Kelsey said.

"No, Nadine will have to show us!" J.C. smiled.

They hung up the costumes and headed back out to the kitchen to find Vince. "Well, what is the verdict?" he asked.

"I really like the apron idea and J.C. said we can add some buttons to the blue dress to make it look even better. The orange dress is a dog; and I mean D-O-G. I cannot wear that. I am going to ask Mr. Hempen if I can wear J.C.'s prom dress for the scenes at the end of the play. I think he will be fine with that. The dresses are not that much different." Kelsey was practicing her speech for Mr. Hempen, J.C. could tell.

"Will J.C.'s dress fit?" He looked at J.C. and then at Kelsey.

"It will have to be shortened and maybe taken in a little. My mom's friend Nadine, is a skilled seamstress and can make the alterations if the drama teacher agrees." J.C. smiled at Kelsey.

"Thanks, J.C. You have come to our rescue once again in this teenage world of wardrobe drama!" Vince was smiling at J.C. and she felt her face begin to warm.

"Who wants dessert?" J.C. asked.

Kelsey said giggling, "Dad is trying to drop a couple of pounds, so I think he should pass."

"OK." J.C. took the bait smiling. "I will just cut two large pieces of my mom's sour cream chocolate cake for the two of us then."

"Now, wait a minute, you two." Vince began to defend his male territory that was seemingly getting smaller as the night wore on. "I worked hard today and cleaned the kitchen while the two of you played dress-up. I think I have earned my piece of what sounds like will soon be my new favorite dessert." He laughed as he patted his mid-section indicating he was not too fat.

J.C. opened the cake carrier as Kelsey brought her three dessert plates. Kelsey showed J.C. how big a piece she wanted with her fingers. "Are you sure you only want that much?" J.C. asked.

"Prom dress! Musical! and my cheer skirt will all thank me for not eating more than that." Kelsey took her piece and headed over next to the fireplace.

J.C. cut a two-inch slice for Vince and laid it sideways on a plate. He was pouring coffee for them. "Kelsey, do you want more milk?" he asked.

"No, I just want to savor every last crumb of this cake. J.C., this is amazing. I think this is the best cake I have ever eaten." Kelsey seemed very sincere as she licked her lips after each bite.

"Thanks. I cannot take credit for that. It was mom's recipe. I am just good at following directions." J.C. was humble in her response.

Vince and J.C. joined Kelsey in front of the fire. Vince on one end of the couch and J.C. on the other.

"Kelsey was right; this is probably the moistest cake I have ever had. Is the frosting homemade too?" Vince was licking his lips with each bite to catch all the crumbs.

"Yes, my mother's fudge frosting was another one of her signature recipes." J.C. blushed a little.

"Definitely my new favorite dessert," Vince proclaimed.

"Thank you, both." J.C. accepted the compliments.

"J.C., that was off the charts one of the best desserts ever. Only one thing could have made it better." Kelsey paused for effect. "Homemade ice cream!" She stood up and headed to the kitchen where she rinsed her plate and fork and placed them in the dishwasher. "I really should work on my history paper a little bit tonight. We have cheer practice tomorrow afternoon and I do not want to leave it 'til tomorrow night. J.C., thanks for your advice on my costumes. I think I am really going to like the blue dress once we fix it up a little." Kelsey was standing in the archway of the great room.

"You are welcome. Just let me know what your drama teacher says about switching dresses. If he is OK with that, I can meet you at Nadine's some afternoon after school, so she can make the alterations." J.C. smiled at Kelsey before she walked away.

"J.C., I meant what I said earlier. We really do appreciate your help with this. Teri took care of all of this for Kelsey, and I am such a fish out of water," Vince admitted.

"What about your sisters? I would have thought that Kelsey might have wanted one of them to help her with her prom dress. Or maybe her grandmother? Do Teri's parents spend much time with Kelsey?" J.C. hoped she was not getting too personal.

"Oh, my sisters would love to help out with Kelsey, but Nancy lives in Washington D.C. Her husband works for the USDA and they have three children all older than Kelsey. Two are in college and one is a senior in high school. Caroline lives in St Louis. She is divorced and raising two boys on her own. Her sons are two and three years older than Kelsey. If I had called either one of them, they both would have flown home to take Kelsey shopping. Not a week goes by that they do not ask how she is, what I need, and if they can come take care of us. Caroline considered moving here right after Teri's death, but I said that was not fair to her boys. They have grown up in St. Louis. All their friends and dad are there. I knew that we would be OK eventually. Kelsey has more of my personality and can take things in her stride pretty well. Teri was a wonderful wife and mother, but her creative side meant that she worried more and took things to heart more than Kelsey and I do. As far as Teri's parents, we see them less and less. I think that Kelsey reminds them of what they lost. I still want them to spend time with her and that is why I remind her from time to time to call and include them in her life. Margaret and Teri never went shopping together in all the years we were married, so Margaret would be the last person I would ask to help Kelsey. Sorry for the long explanation, but you asked for it," Vince said smiling. He stood up and reached for J.C.'s dessert plate. He took the dishes to the kitchen.

J.C.'s mind was starting to run away with her again. What would that be like to have a family? Yes, family, a group of people who cared about you, wanted to help you, communicated with you regularly about what was going on in your life. She felt emptiness inside and really missed Johnnie. When she realized she was lost in her thoughts and pulled herself back to the present, Vince was standing in front of her with a glass of wine. "Are you OK?" Vince asked gently, "you look very sad."

"Oh, I am fine." J.C. quickly put her emotions in check. "Thanks for the wine."

Vince sat back down on the couch. This time closer to the center than the opposite end. They were both facing the fire which created a relaxed feeling in the room.

"Vince, can I ask you some questions about my father?" J.C. felt safe with Vince and Kelsey. They had been extremely open with her. Maybe Vince could help her find the answers to some of her *why's* about Will.

"Sure," Vince responded quickly.

"Did you know that he had two brothers?" J.C. opened cautiously with some newly discovered facts.

"No, where do they live?" Vince asked.

"They don't. They both died of scarlet fever when they were children. They were older than my dad. He was just four years old when they died." J.C. looked into her wine glass and spoke quietly and slowly as she opened up about the topic that had been bothering her.

"J.C., I am sorry. I guess I just assumed Will had been an only child. No one around here that I know has ever talked about them." Vince was very compassionate.

"I just found out this week." J.C. paused and hesitated before telling Vince her whole story. "My mom's friend Nadine came to help me clean out my mother's things, and while we were doing that, I found this old box with some of my father's items in it. Dog tags, old army IDs, high school graduation picture, and then there were a few pictures of three little boys. One of them was taken on the front porch of my parents' farmhouse. So, I asked Nadine who the other two boys were with my dad. She said they were his brothers, Jack and John. Vince, it completely blew my mind that my dad had two brothers that my parents had never mentioned; but worse than that, Johnnie and I were named after them." She hesitated before going on.

Vince reached over and squeezed her hand and then let go.

"Nadine said about ten children and a couple of adults died that winter from the disease. My grandmother got really sick, and they expected her to die, but she didn't. The rest of her life she was weak and sickly. My dad was all she had left, and she did not even let him start school until he was over six years old. Nadine was in school with one of my uncles and also knew them from church. She does not think it is a big deal that my parents kept this from me. I could understand if it was just my dad, but my mom told me everything. She was an orphan and always wanted to know her parents, grandparents, and siblings, if she had any. I really cannot stop wondering why she never brought this up to me. If she agreed to name me after one of them, why would she not tell me about it?" J.C. heaved a big sigh and it felt good to tell someone what she had spent the last week thinking about.

"No wonder you said you had a strange week. J.C., I would not begin to know what to tell you. Your mother was one of the most generous and kind women I've ever met. She always thanked me for coming to help Will when the livestock needed tending. When I first came home, before I was married, she would leave fresh cookies, bread, or a casserole in my truck almost every time I was at your farm. Teri really liked her too. Evelyn went out of her way to welcome Teri and help her get acquainted after we got married. They were on some committees together at church and at the library. Teri wondered how your mother could be so outgoing and your father barely left the farm. I never gave that much thought... must be a guy thing." Vince smiled, hoping he could break the sad expression on J.C.'s face.

"I am sure it is no surprise that I am not close to my dad. When I see you and Kelsey, I wonder what it would be like to talk to my dad about everything. My father cannot even communicate with me about the most benign topics. We have lived in a silent world since Johnnie died." J.C.'s throat was tight, and she could feel her emotions coming to the surface. This topic, and wine was not a good combination. "Vince, I think the wine is doing the talking. I should probably go before I say too much." J. C. started to get up from the couch.

Vince reached over and gently pulled her back down. "J.C., finish your wine. We do not have to talk about anything you don't want to. But, when you do need or want to talk, I will be here to listen." Vince's smile almost made J.C. cry. No man had ever treated her with this kind of tenderness.

"I will change the subject," Vince said abruptly. "Kelsey's birthday is coming up in May and I wanted to get tickets to a play in Des Moines. I thought I would take her and one of her friends into the city for dinner and a show. She will be eighteen and I want to do something special for her. I have looked on the Civic Center website and there are a couple of plays coming right around that time. Would you mind telling me which one you think she would enjoy more?" Vince was calmly changing the atmosphere and bringing J.C. back to an even keel.

"Which plays were you thinking about?" J.C. asked.

"'Hairspray' or 'Phantom of the Opera'?" Vince asked.

CHAPTER 18

"Well, '*Hairspray*' is a comedy that I am sure she would enjoy. '*Phantom*' is beautiful and very memorable. I used to have season tickets to the Civic Center. My mother and I saw '*Phantom*' the first time it came to Des Moines. It is a beautiful opera and if Kelsey likes musicals, she will really appreciate the music." J.C. finished her wine and smiled at Vince.

"'*Phantom*' it is. Thanks, I know less about opera than I do about shopping. I thought you would be better suited to advise me on this, than anyone else I know. I am beginning to think we need to hire you as a family consultant." Vince laughed as he stood, took her empty glass and his, and headed back to the kitchen.

Chapter 19

*M*onday afternoon, J.C.'s phone rang at 3:30 p.m. "J.C., it is Kelsey. Mr. Hempen said 'yes!' I can use your dress. Can you bring it in for him to see sometime this week? We do not have much time since dress rehearsal is only eleven days away." Kelsey sounded like she was in a hurry.

"Why don't I bring it over to your house tonight and you can take it with you tomorrow. If he approves, I will meet you tomorrow after school at Nadine's for a fitting, that is, if Nadine can fit us into her busy social calendar," J.C. said sarcastically. Nadine had one hair appointment each week and everything else could be changed with a single call from J.C.

"J.C., you are the best. I should be home around 5:00 p.m. Is that a good time for you to come over?" Kelsey asked.

"Perfect, I will see you at 5:00 p.m." J.C. hung up the phone and walked into her dressing room to pull out the red prom dress. Her mother had put it into a sealed hanging bag with moth balls. J.C. wanted to air it out before taking it to Kelsey. She removed the dress and left the bag in the dressing room. She walked downstairs and out to the front porch. She hooked the hanger through the support chain for the porch swing and let the red dress gently toss in the breeze.

"Nadine, its J.C.," she started out slowly on the phone. "I need a favor. You remember my red satin prom dress that mom made? I am going to give that to Kelsey to wear for her school musical. It will need some alterations and I was wondering if you would do those for her?"

"You still have that old dress? I thought that Evelyn would have thrown that out years ago." Nadine spoke with some surprise in her voice.

"We talked about getting rid of my high school dresses that she made for dances and my early baton performance outfits, but each time the subject came up, we hung them back in the closet for another year or two. I am kind of glad now that they are still here. I think Mom would be proud to know that her handiwork was going to become part of a high school musical." J.C. spoke with soft pride in her voice.

"Nadine, would you like to go to Kelsey's musical with me in a couple of weeks? They have a Saturday evening performance and a Sunday matinee." J.C. was hopeful that Nadine would say yes.

"Well, I usually go with Louise and Marge, but I guess we can let you tag along." Nadine laughed into the phone.

J.C. was not surprised that Nadine's circle of friends had been attending these types of events. Evelyn would have joined them if she was still alive. "Thanks, Nadine. I appreciate being included in your social circle," J.C. replied.

"You had better get prepared for the inquisition. These women will not go easy on you like I have over the Vince situation." Nadine was chuckling as she spoke.

"Vince situation!" J.C. spoke quickly and with a slight anger in her tone. "Nadine, I have told you there is *no* Vince situation. I am helping out a neighbor. Now, can we get back to my original question? Will you make the alterations that Kelsey needs done to my old dress?"

"Of course, I will; I am just trying to get under your skin about Vince, and I have to say I'm pretty proud of myself for doing that! When does she need it altered? I think that play is coming up next week, isn't it?" Nadine sounded more sensible, J.C. thought.

"I was hoping that we could stop over tomorrow after Kelsey is done with school. Will you be home between 3:30 p.m. and 5:00 p.m.?" J.C. asked.

"Yes. I will have to pull out my machine and oil some of the gears. I bet it has been five years since I used that old thing. If it doesn't work, you may need to bring Evelyn's over," Nadine responded.

"Thanks, Nadine. Just let me know tomorrow if I need to bring Mom's machine in." J.C. hesitated. "Second thought... I will just bring it with me. It is not going to get any more use here, so if you do not want it, I can donate it to your mission group." J.C. decided that was one more thing that needed to be moved out of this old house.

"J.C., if you are coming tomorrow anyway, would you mind coming a little earlier, so you and I can talk before Kelsey gets out of school?" Nadine sounded serious for some reason.

"Sure," J.C. replied, "Is everything alright?" She asked.

"Yes, I just have something we need to talk about. See you tomorrow." Nadine hung up.

J.C. felt a little unsettled with Nadine's abruptness. Nadine had such an easy-going personality this was out of character for her. She mulled over their conversation again in her mind as she walked out to the front porch and brought the red satin dress back inside. Returning upstairs she dumped the old moth balls into the trash and placed the dress back in the hanging bag.

Now, where was Evelyn's sewing machine? She started in the mudroom. It was not in any of the cupboards out there. J.C. came back through the house to her parents' bedroom. She pushed her way through the hanging clothes in the closet under the staircase and with the limited light, saw the sewing machine on the floor next to a couple of old suitcases. She pulled it towards herself and out into the light. It was a portable sewing machine that Evelyn would set on the dining room table whenever she was making one of J.C.'s costumes or dresses. She pulled on the handle and realized it was heavier than it looked. J.C. carried it out to the dining room and left it by the front door.

Her phone rang, and she saw Doris' number on the screen. "Hello, Doris, what is going on?"

"I got the most beautiful bouquet of flowers from that farmer friend of yours," Doris reported. "He did not need to do that. Those shoes should have gone to Goodwill years ago. I am just glad I got to see that pretty little girl in her dress and the shoes matched it perfectly." J.C. could tell that Doris was starved for someone to talk to. "Your mail is pretty light, lots of junk mail. Mr. Beener died last week; he lived down on the fifth floor. I did not go to the memorial. I guess I really did not know him all that well. Just read his obituary in the paper."

"Doris," J.C. interrupted her. "I am so glad you got the bouquet of flowers. Vince and Kelsey really appreciated your tip on the trunk show and the shoes were a special touch that they also really appreciated. I was just headed out the door. I have to meet someone at 5:00 p.m. Can I call you later tonight to chat and catch up?"

"Sure, honey, sorry to interrupt. We can talk more later." Doris hung up.

J.C. stepped into the bathroom and put on some mascara and blush before running upstairs to grab her coat and the dress to take to Kelsey. J.C. pulled into Vince's driveway at 5:01 p.m. Kelsey was just getting out of her car and waved at J.C. They met on the deck and headed inside.

"Can I try it on?" Kelsey asked.

"Sure," J.C. responded.

Kelsey kicked off her boots inside the door and dropped her bags on the couch. "Would you like some water or coffee?" Kelsey asked.

"Just a glass of water," J.C. replied.

Kelsey hurried into the kitchen and pulled two glasses out of the cupboard and filled them with water. As she handed one to J.C. she said, "go ahead and take off your coat and shoes... we can go back to my room and see what this is going to look like." Kelsey was gathering her backpack and other bags that she had left on the couch and headed towards the archway.

J.C. did as she was instructed and followed Kelsey back to her bedroom. Kelsey quickly took off her jeans and shirt as J.C. unzipped the bag. "I know it is going to be really long on you and I think the bodice might be a little oversized also," J.C. cautioned.

She held the dress over Kelsey's head and let it fall down over the teenager. When Kelsey's head popped out, she was facing the mirror on her closet door. Her face lit up with a huge smile. "J.C., this is so much better than that 'orange dog', don't you think?" Kelsey was looking for confirmation from J.C.

"Yes, this color is much better for you and I think this style is a little classier also," J.C. added.

Kelsey stood for a moment admiring herself in the mirror and then without any warning asked, "J.C., I know you said that you were too busy for a family, but did you ever have a serious boyfriend?" Kelsey had some hesitation in her voice.

J.C. drew in a deep breath. "Yes, I was engaged once but that did not work out," J.C. said.

"Why didn't you get married?" Kelsey continued with the questions.

"We planned to, but I got transferred back to Chicago and he was still in Dallas. Six months of trying to make things work long distance showed us we were not meant to be." J.C. felt oddly relieved hearing those words come out of her mouth. She had spent years feeling guilty about Roger and now there was confidence in her voice as she honestly admitted that they had not been right for each other all along.

"Was that the only real boyfriend you had?" Kelsey's inquisition continued.

"He was the most serious I had. The only one that I even considered marrying," J.C. said. "I had a lot of friends right out of college that were just dates. Some of them lasted a few months, but none of them were husband material." She giggled a little thinking about 'what is husband material'?

"What does husband material mean?" Kelsey asked.

J.C. burst out laughing, "I was just thinking that exact same thing. It is like you read my mind. You know, I am not sure what husband material is; but I do know it is not something you have to worry about for a long time!" She was laughing at herself for using a term that Evelyn had used with her many times.

"What is going on in here?" Vince asked as he stepped into the doorway of Kelsey's room.

J.C. jumped, and her face flushed hoping Vince had not overheard their conversation. "Dad, I did not think you were home," Kelsey said.

"I wasn't, but when I drove in and saw J.C.'s car in the driveway, I knew we must have a fashion crisis going on again." He smiled at both of them.

"Dad, what do you think? This is J.C.'s prom dress. We are going to alter it for my final costume in the play." This was Kelsey's way of updating her dad on what was going on.

"I think the dress and the girl are both beautiful!" Vince said.

The ultimate nice guy lives on, J.C. thought. "My mom's friend, Nadine is going to look at it tomorrow and make the alterations," J.C. informed Vince.

"Is that Nadine Crawford?" Vince asked. "She was my mother's second cousin."

"Really, Nadine is a relative of yours?" J.C. shot a quizzical look at Vince.

"Distant relative. I do not think that they were ever very close," Vince admitted. "You know that in a small community like this everyone is related somehow."

J.C. thought about that for a moment; maybe everyone but her. She was related to her father, who was the last living relative of his family and her mother was deceased without any known relatives either. "I guess you are right," she said sheepishly thinking 'except me'.

"Dad, can you give us some privacy?" Kelsey asked.

"Well, sure." Vince smiled and disappeared.

J.C. lifted the dress back over Kelsey's head and placed it back in the garment bag. She laid it on Kelsey's bed. "I better get back home," she said to Kelsey.

"Thanks, J.C. Sorry if I was too nosy earlier. I just wondered why you never had a family of your own." Kelsey spoke softly and sincere.

"It is OK. I know that most people of my age have a family." J.C. started to walk out of Kelsey's room.

Kelsey stopped her and gave her a hug. J.C. was not certain what to do but after a moment she hugged Kelsey back. As she walked down the hallway she thought, Kelsey must really miss her mother, especially now getting ready for all this stuff at school and prom. It is sad that at her age, she is facing this without that female influence in her life. As she walked to the front door, J.C. did not see Vince anywhere. She stepped into her boots and slipped her coat back on. What if Kelsey was looking to her for that? A shiver went down her spine as she opened the door and stepped out on the deck. She surveyed the barnyard and saw Vince's back as he was pouring feed into the calves' bunk. J.C. walked slowly to her car, started the engine, and backed out onto the gravel road.

Chapter 20

*T*he pork roast that J.C. had put in the crock pot before leaving earlier was the first aroma she smelled when she entered the dining room. She looked at her mother's sewing machine on the floor and decided to take it to her car now. She opened the front door again and, squatting down picked up the heavy case that contained the portable sewing machine and walked to her car. She steadied the machine against the side of the trunk while opening the back door. She gently sat the machine on the backseat of the car, closed the door and heaved a sigh. "That is heavy," she said to herself. As J.C. walked back to the house, she scanned the barnyard for sight of her father. No Will in sight.

It was 6:15 p.m. and most days he would be in the shower by now. She headed back to the house to finish preparing for dinner. J.C. was surprised when she walked through the living room to take her coat and purse upstairs, to see Will sitting on the couch. The TV was on low and he was watching the news.

She rushed up the stairs and dropped her stuff in the dressing room. As she returned through the living room she said, "It will take me about twenty to thirty minutes to finish up dinner, Dad. I had to run a quick errand. I will hurry," J.C. sputtered over her shoulder as she went back into the kitchen.

She grabbed some leftover cheesy potatoes and put them in the microwave. She took out a head of lettuce and chopped up a third of it to make a tossed salad with a green pepper and tomato. While the potatoes were warming up, she set the table. It was 6:30 p.m. when she stuck her head back in the living room. "Dad, dinner is on the table," J.C. said, out of breath.

Dinner started with the usual prayer and silence but after a few minutes J.C. began the nightly update routine. "Kelsey, Vince Martin's daughter, is going to use my red prom dress that mom made for me during my junior year for her play next week. I took that over to Vince's so she can take it to school for her drama teacher to approve it. Tomorrow, I will meet her at Nadine's so it can be shortened, and the bodice taken in to fit better." J.C. paused and drew in a deep breath. "I did not know that Nadine was related to Vince Martin's mother. Nadine wants me to come early so I will go in right after lunch to see what she needs to talk about." J.C. took another deep breath.

"J.C., can you help me sort off a couple of hogs in the morning? I have two that have a rupture and need some attention," Will asked quietly.

J.C. almost choked on her bite of pork. "Sure, Dad. What time do you want to do that?" she asked.

"It would be best to do it first thing before I feed them. I built a holding pen today, so if you could come out when you are done with breakfast that would work," Will said, still not looking up but speaking slowly and quietly into his plate.

"All right, I will be down at the barn before 7:00 a.m.," J.C. said. That concluded their conversation for the remainder of the meal.

Will stood when he was done eating, took his dishes to the kitchen, and walked back into the living room. J.C. heard him switch on the light behind his chair and knew he was reading his Bible.

When the kitchen was put back in order after her hurried dinner preparation, J.C. went into the bathroom to prepare for bed. As she brushed her teeth she looked into her own eyes in the mirror and mentally asked, "did I really see my dad watching the T.V. earlier and did he ask me for help at dinner?" She finished up in the bathroom and went upstairs to her study.

Before it got too late, she wanted to call Doris back. She dialed her number. "Hello, Doris, I am sorry that I was in a rush earlier. I had to make a delivery," she explained.

"Oh, honey, I know you are busy out there. No need to apologize to me. I just thought you would want to know the news about Mr. Beener. Did you know him? I know he liked to work out in the gym downstairs..."

J.C.'s mind started to wander. Yes, she knew Beener. He was a kind of creepy old fart that really did not work out. Just hung out down there to check out any female that was working out. Some of the elderly women that came down even commented that they thought he was a 'dirty old man'. J.C. thought he was probably harmless but occasionally, she would catch him staring at her while she was working out. He was old, and his wife had been dead for ten-plus years so not surprising. He had to be older than Will she thought. Will was looking younger since she had been back. Maybe he was getting a more balanced diet since she had been home to grocery shop and cook for him. She still could not believe that he was watching TV. Tomorrow she would ask him why he did not do that more. It seemed odd that in the past twelve months this was the first time she had ever observed him doing that. Maybe he was coming out of his shell a bit. Something was changing because he was asking for her help every so often.

"My ladies circle has tickets to go see 'Hairspray' at the Civic Center this spring. I really do not know if I will like that sort of thing, but it is an outing. We are getting tired of just trying new restaurants and so we are going to try some things at the Civic Center and Playhouse. One member suggested we do a concert at the Arena. I said no! That music is just way too loud." J.C. tuned back in to catch up on what Doris was talking about. Her phone buzzed, and she saw that Vince was trying to call her.

"Doris, I have another call coming in. I think I will try and make it into Des Moines sometime in the next week or so. I will call you before I come. Take care of yourself." J.C. was trying to wrap up her call quickly.

"Did you tell Kelsey and her father that I really appreciated the flowers?" Doris asked.

"No, but I will. Talk to you soon," J.C. said.

"OK, goodbye." Doris hung up.

J.C. quickly accepted the incoming call.

"J.C., am I calling at a bad time?" Vince asked.

"No, we have finished dinner, I am upstairs in the study, dad is downstairs reading his Bible; everything is the normal boring evening over here," J.C. said lightheartedly.

"I just wanted to thank you for allowing Kelsey to use your dress. That is very generous of you," Vince said sincerely.

"Speaking of generosity, I was just on the phone with Doris, and she wanted me to pass along her appreciation for the bouquet of flowers you sent her. As far as the old prom dress, it would have ended up in the burn pile or Goodwill over the next few weeks as I clean out the rest of this old house," J.C. said.

"J.C., that is the other reason I called," Vince hesitated before he went on. "Is it your intention to try and convince Will to move off the farm sometime soon? I know this is none of my business, but I do not think that Will is ready to stop farming. He is only seventy-five and many men like him actively farm into their nineties. I see more and more of them each year." Vince's tone was somber, yet he spoke gently into the phone.

J.C. did not know how to respond. She had learned to respect Vince these past three weeks, but he was right about one thing. It really was none of his business. She did not want to point that out and sound rude, but ...

"Will called the office this afternoon and made an appointment for me to come look at a couple of hogs that have ruptured tomorrow afternoon. I just wanted to talk to you tonight before I did that. If your plan is to have things wrapped up in two or three months, I will recommend that he sell them and not waste his money on a vet bill to repair them. Will has always been good to me and I want to be fair." Vince was silent.

J.C. sat for a moment before responding. "Vince, honestly, I do not know what to do. You're right. I came here to convince dad it was time to stop farming and move into a place where someone could monitor his diet and medications. I have not looked at any of those places yet. My first instinct was to gauge how he was doing. Surprising to me, he is doing pretty well. I have helped him with a couple of tasks but for the most part he manages all the farm work on his own and if I was not here, I can tell he manages the housework fine also. I am not sure about his bookwork and finances. I have not even found where he keeps his records. My time so far has been spent on removing Johnnie's and Mom's things from the house which I am sure bothers him, but he does not say so. If he would just talk to me, I could get a better sense of what to do." J.C. stopped talking.

"How much time do you have?" Vince asked. "When do you plan on going back to work?"

"I am fine financially. I got a nice package from IBM, so I am not under any pressure to hurry back and find another job right away. It's just that I know long term, I cannot take over this farm and he has no one else, so we need to come up with a plan that works if something happens tomorrow or ten years from now. I just wish I could talk to him the way you talk to Kelsey." J.C. truly wished in her heart that the father she knew at the age of ten was still her father today.

"Well, I do not want to pry and like I said the other night, I am here to listen whenever you want to talk. J.C., you answered my question about tomorrow. Depending on the size of those pigs, we can probably make the repairs, get them fattened up and to market before too long. Please forgive me if I overstepped our friendship in any way by asking too many questions." Vince's tone was so respectful and genuine.

Neither one of them said anything for a while but it was obvious neither one wanted to say goodbye. "Will asked me to help him sort those hogs off in the morning." J.C. spoke first. "I can tell that something is changing. When I came back from your house today, he was watching the news on TV. I have never seen him do that before. He gets all his news from the radio in the house, his shop or pickup. If he had turned up the volume, I probably would have thought we had a prowler when I got home." She giggled a little.

"Really, Will does not watch TV?" Vince asked.

"No, Will reads his Bible morning and night, takes care of his chores, farms the ground during planting and harvest season. He buys feeder pigs and cattle and sells them once they get market ready. That is what Will does!" J.C. said somewhat sarcastically.

"It's a good life," Vince responded. "Farming, I mean, is a good life."

"Could you do it without talking to anyone?" J.C. asked.

"Probably not, but I have a different personality than Will." Vince sensed J.C. agreed with him.

"You think so? I thought I was watching two skilled actors talking, the first time I witnessed you and Kelsey. I have never had that much conversation with my dad in fifty years and could not imagine some of the topics that you both maneuver through so easily," J.C. spoke with admiration.

"Well, we have our rough moments too," Vince assured her.

"But I bet you also talk when the moments are rough, right?" J.C. asked.

"We try to," Vince responded.

"Well, I sat in a hospital room across my mother's death bed and could not get one word out of my dad. When she took her final breath, I walked out into the hallway at 1:30 a.m. and waved for a nurse to come in. She took down the time and pulled the sheet over my mother. We both walked in silence to the garage. I said, 'Dad, you need to come to my condo and sleep before you drive home.' He followed me to the condo, parked his car, and we took the elevator to the twenty-fifth floor in silence. I showed him the guest room and I went into my bedroom. When I got up the next morning, he was gone. Not one word! Even the following day at the funeral home, he just sat there as I answered every question and made every decision. When he pulled out his checkbook to write the check, I wanted to tear his head off." J.C.'s voice was trembling, and Vince was completely silent on the other end of the line. "He had no input whatsoever and it was just another business transaction to him!" Tears were starting to roll down J.C.'s cheeks and she took in a deep breath.

"J.C., I am sorry, I am sure it was more than a business transaction to Will. He is a very unique man and showing emotion or talking about it must be very difficult for him." Vince tried to help with some reassuring thoughts.

"Do not defend him." J.C. shot back. "She did everything for him when he was like this after his father's death and again when Johnnie died; she stayed and took care of him. I will never understand why!" J.C. was done. There was no way Vince could understand and she really did not blame him. He was just trying to be nice ... but she could not handle *nice* right now. "I have to go," she choked as she hung up the phone.

J.C. sat in silence in the upstairs of the old farmhouse and sobbed. All alone with no one to understand or explain why.

Will was not a monster. He had always given Evelyn and J.C. what they needed financially and more. The baton twirling lessons, the band trips, vacations, remodeling projects, and a car when she learned to drive, Evelyn's new cars when she needed them, food, shelter, etc. He must have cared for them a little to be willing to always let Evelyn buy whatever she wanted or needed. Evelyn never spent money wildly but there were extra things that she did for J.C. that other girls did not get to do.

Once Evelyn planned a two-day trip to Kansas City for just the two of them before J.C.'s freshman year of high school. They drove to Kansas City and stayed in a beautiful hotel, ate at wonderful restaurants, and shopped for school clothes. While they were there, they toured the art museum, history museum and zoo.

When J.C. was at Iowa State, Evelyn had season tickets for the football games so she and Nadine could come to watch J.C. perform. The year the football team went to a bowl game in Florida, Evelyn and Nadine were there. Once J.C. started working, Evelyn came to Des Moines, Dallas, and Chicago on a regular basis to visit her daughter. Since Evelyn had not worked after J.C. was born it was obvious that Will was providing the funds for all this. J.C.'s mind tried to understand. Her mother was a good teacher and could have divorced Will and taken care of them on her own. Evelyn loved Will, J.C. knew that; but even when you love someone there must be limits as to how much you give without receiving a lot in return.

J.C. got off her couch and walked into the dressing room to get ready for bed. She looked in the mirror at her tearstained face. Something in the mirror caught her attention. She saw the resemblance of her mother's face. The next thought took her breath away. In all her life she had never seen her mother cry.

Chapter 21

J.C.'s alarm startled her awake the next morning. She immediately got up and put on her chore clothes. I really need to wash these when I come back in today, she thought to herself. Heading downstairs, Will was just getting up from his chair and laying his Bible on the stand next to it. It sent a chill down J.C.'s spine as her mind shot back to the evening before.

"Good morning, Dad," J.C. said softly. No response.

J.C. headed into the kitchen first and started making the coffee. Will was right behind her and turned on the radio to KMA. He pulled out a skillet and started making eggs. She stayed out of his way and just grabbed some yogurt and a grapefruit from the refrigerator. She also dropped a piece of bread into the toaster. While the coffee was brewing, and her toast was finishing up; she went into the bathroom and brushed her teeth. When the toast came up, she buttered it and carried her food into the dining room. She returned for a cup of coffee and then started to eat. J.C. contemplated how she could change the situation between her and Will. What if she just pelted him with questions like Kelsey did to her sometimes. Would he remain silent, or answer some just to make her stop? She played a couple of scenarios over in her mind. J.C. was so caught up in thought she hardly noticed when Will joined her at the table. They both ate in silence.

Will headed outside first, and J.C. cleaned up the dishes and put the kitchen back in order. She went back upstairs and took her phone off the charger. She typed in a simple text. 'Vince, I am sorry. J.C.' She wished she could explain why but she did not have an explanation that even she could understand; so, she just said she was sorry.

She headed back downstairs and into the mudroom to put on her overalls, boots, and gloves before heading out the door to the hog barn. Will had completed the gate moving process and built a small pen in the center driveway of the barn. The pigs were in two separate pens, so Will started in the first one and herded the pig to the corner where J.C. unlocked the gate and let the pig walk into the center of the barn. Will followed the animal and kept tapping its nose to get it to the free-standing pen. Once the first pig was in that pen, Will fastened the corner gate and they repeated the process for the second one. It took them less than thirty minutes to move these two animals out of their feeding pens and into the holding pen. Will waved towards J.C. when he locked the gate the second time, letting her know she was free to go.

J.C. returned to the house and took a shower. When she was finished getting ready for her day, she started a load of laundry. While the laundry was going, J.C. ran the vacuum through the downstairs and dusted the living room and dining room. She made a list of groceries that she would pick up while she was in town. At 11:00 a.m. she started some cheese and potato soup for lunch. Will came in at 11:45 a.m. and they ate in almost silence. "I am going into Nadine's this afternoon and will stop at Al's for groceries before I come home. Is there anything you would like?" J.C. asked Will.

"No," was Will's response.

CHAPTER 21

After lunch, J.C. headed into Stuart. She looked at the clock on the dash of her car and decided she had a few extra minutes. She pulled in and parked in front of Ken Barr's office. She really hoped that Jim Powell who shared a law office with her father's attorney, would be out for a long lunch. She opened the door and spoke to a young receptionist. "Is Ken in?" J.C. inquired.

"He just got back from lunch. Who should I say is here to see him?" A very professional response from such a young-looking person, J.C. thought.

"Jacquelyn Mason," J.C. said.

The receptionist disappeared and within moments J.C. heard a voice, "Jacquelyn, come on in. It has been years since I saw you. Well, I guess I saw you about a year ago at your mother's funeral, but we really didn't get a chance to talk..." Ken was a talker and J.C. knew she would have to use her sales skills to get the information she needed without having to listen to Ken's life story.

"Great to see you again, Ken," J.C. said as she stepped into his office and shook his hand. He waved for the receptionist to leave and she closed the door behind her.

"What brings you to the great town of Stuart and into my office this afternoon?" Ken asked.

"As you said my mother has passed, my father is not getting any younger and I need to get some documents drawn up to make sure my father's affairs are in order before anything happens to him." Short and to the point J.C. thought.

Ken looked a little taken aback and then asked J.C. a question she was not expecting. "What makes you think your father's affairs are not in order?"

"Ken, to my knowledge my parents did not have a will when my mother died. I have been away from the farm for over thirty years. My father is aging, and I just want to get some paperwork started before something happens to him," J.C. replied.

"Jacquelyn, I am your father's attorney and bound by the law not to discuss his affairs with anyone else. I am sure as a businesswoman, you understand that." Ken stopped and looked directly into J.C.'s eyes.

At first J.C. was not certain how to respond. Ken had handled the purchase of farmland for her father, completed his taxes annually and at least once did a search for Evelyn who tried to find her birth parents when J.C. was in high school. Was there something she was missing? "Ken, I am not asking for you to disclose anything. I am asking you to help draft a will, trust, power of attorney and those types of documents so that things are taken care of in the manner that my father wants them to be when he passes away," J.C. stated clearly.

"Jacquelyn, you need to talk to your father; maybe the two of you should come back in together," Ken advised.

J.C. was confused. Why was Ken being so evasive and unwilling to help her? She could go to an attorney in Des Moines, but they would not have the knowledge and background that Ken had about her parents' affairs. "Thanks for your time," J.C. said as she stood up and headed for the door.

"Jacquelyn, just talk to Will," Ken said one more time.

J.C. walked out of his office into the reception area and out the front door. Jim Powell was just getting out of his car and headed toward the front door. "J.C.," he yelled.

J.C. waved and got in her car quickly before he could say anymore. She started the car and immediately backed out. She was mad and confused. If Ken knew her father at all, he would know Will was not the type of person you can just 'talk to'. She drove over to Nadine's house and was still mad when she knocked on the door.

"Hello, come in," Nadine greeted her as she stepped inside.

"Would you like some coffee?" Nadine asked.

"I would prefer a glass of wine, but it is probably too early in the day to start that!" J.C. said sarcastically.

"What has got you so wound up?" Nadine asked.

"Ken Barr," J.C. responded. "I stopped in there to see what type of documents we needed to get started and he refused to talk to me. He said I needed to talk to Will and bring him back in with me." J.C. gulped her first swig of coffee.

"Well, I am no attorney, but that doesn't sound too far out of line." Nadine tried to calm J.C. down.

"Nadine, I do not know what Will's intentions are and really have no desire to have any influence over them. If he wants to leave his assets in a trust for an organization, I would be just fine with that. I do not want his money! I just do not want the government to take more than their fair share of it. Or, if he becomes incapacitated and needs financial support for end-of-life care, I promised mom I would make sure that was taken care of. I am just about ready to get in my car, drive to Des Moines, and call IBM to see if that job in New York has been filled yet." J.C. was exasperated.

"Calm down, calm down," Nadine said. "Ken is doing his job and protecting his client. You have no idea what discussions have taken place between Will and Ken. Even though you are Will's daughter, Ken has no authority to discuss that with you without Will's permission. You came here with a mission in mind to wrap this up like one of your business contracts, J.C. Will is not one of your clients, prospects, or a contract that you can blow into town and sell a product or idea to. He is your father and whether you like the man or not it is more complicated than what you thought." Nadine stopped and let that settle in.

Neither one of them spoke for a while. J.C. had never seen this side of Nadine. She had always been laid back, funny and supportive of Evelyn and J.C. for as long as J.C. could remember. It was beginning to look like everyone in this town was defending Will. Why did he need defending? Maybe she should just hit the road and never look back. J.C. took another sip of coffee. She did not look at Nadine. She just sat there.

"J.C., I am worried about you," Nadine said very directly. "You seem to be very off-balance since you came back this time. Jumping in so quickly to help Vince and his daughter and pushing to make all these changes at the farm. What is really driving you?"

"Helping Vince?" J.C. was getting madder by the moment. "What is so off-balance with my helping Vince and Kelsey? I thought that was the neighborly thing to do out here in the country." She set her cup down hard and contemplated leaving right then.

"It is normal for those of us that have spent our whole lives in a rural community to do that. You, however, have not looked back since the day you drove off the farm and headed to Iowa State. I cannot remember one time where you did something like this for a stranger. Vince is recently widowed and seeing you so out of character concerns me that you might be getting too involved for your own good." Nadine had said her piece on that subject.

"So, this is what you wanted me to come in early for? To give me the 'be careful speech'? Do not fall for this nice guy! Well, Nadine, I know that Vince is not interested in me like that. He has a daughter to raise, and she is the one and only thing on his mind. I see that every time I am around them. I cannot believe that fathers and daughters can have that kind of relationship." She was on a roll and about to give Nadine a real piece of her mind.

"Stop, stop that is not why I wanted you to come in early or what I wanted to talk about. I am sorry if I over-stepped my bounds on the subject of Vince. I remember how hard you fell for Roger after his divorce when he was not looking for another wife right away. J.C., I do not want you to be hurt like that again. But I asked you to come in today to talk about Evelyn and Will. You know that she was my closest friend and we shared everything. Evelyn loved Will more than anything on this earth. She hurt every day knowing that she could not remove the pain he felt when Johnnie died.

She thought that he somehow compared that to his brothers. That was the extent of our conversation about his brothers. I always thought that might be the reason she would not talk about them either. She did not want Will to be hurt any more than he already was. What I do know is that she worked tirelessly to bring Will back to reality for your sake, not hers. She kept him updated on every detail that went on in your life: Every song that was played in the band that you marched to. Every softball pitch that you threw. Every class you were in at high school and college. Every picture from every vacation the two of you took. When you got the offer from IBM, she researched the company and told Will all about it. She poured all her efforts into loving the two of you. Maybe because she never had anyone that loved her growing up. I don't know. I just know that she loved him and you. If you have any respect for your mother — slow down. Take some time to try and get to know the man inside Will Mason. He is your father." Nadine reached over and squeezed J.C.'s hand that was laying limp in her lap.

Tears rolling down her cheeks, she finally picked up her chin and looked at Nadine. "Why didn't I ever see my mom cry?" J.C. asked.

Nadine hesitated, "Because she never thought she had a reason to cry. Like I just told you, she loved two things more than her own life, you and Will. She cried when Johnnie was sick and at his passing; never in front of Will or you, though. She made sure you were at school and Will was outside when she would go into Johnnie's room and hold his things to her chest and weep. I came over a few times and found her up there. Once she accepted that Johnnie was in God's hands, she was done mourning for herself and got on with life. She wanted to make sure you had a happy childhood and opportunities to do things that she never got to do as a child. Every day she enjoyed being your mother and watching you grow up. Do you want to know why Vince and Kelsey are so special to you?" Nadine paused, and waited for J.C. to acknowledge that she wanted to know what Nadine was about to say. "Because you are reminded of your relationship with Evelyn."

Nadine was right! She was drawn to two people that were living out the life that she had with her own mother. Evelyn had treated her just like Vince was acting with Kelsey. After Johnnie died, Evelyn made sure that J.C. was her first priority. "Nadine, why could I not see that, but you could?" J.C. sputtered through her tears.

Nadine said nothing. She stood up and refilled their coffee cups and handed J.C. a tissue. They sat in silence for a while.

"Nadine, I do not know what to do. If Will did not talk to Mom, how am I ever going to break through?" J.C spoke softly and with sincere concern.

"I do not know honey, but I think a little bit of time will help. Just slow down, watch and learn," Nadine advised.

Nadine's words did not make a lot of sense, but J.C. was willing to try anything at this point. "When I got home yesterday, he was watching the news on TV," J.C. informed Nadine.

"Really, I did not think that Will ever watched TV. Evelyn said that he would stay at the kitchen table and read if she watched a show after dinner," Nadine commented.

"I know, that is what happened when I was home and watched TV with her." J.C. was still trying to figure out what had caused this change in behavior the night before.

"Well, we better get stuff out so that we are ready when Kelsey gets here," Nadine cautioned.

"Right, let me check my face in your bathroom. Do you need mom's sewing machine? It is in the back of my car. That thing weighs a ton, so I did not bring it in when I got here." J.C. was talking from the bathroom.

"Mine is working fine, but if you do not want it, I will have you drop it off at Mable's. Hers died a couple of weeks ago and I told her not to buy a new one," Nadine shot back.

Chapter 22

*O*n Wednesday morning, J.C.'s alarm went off at 6:00 a.m. She jumped out of bed and dashed into the dressing room to put on her chore clothes. After dressing, she headed downstairs and saw that Will was still in his chair with his Bible on his lap.

"I will start some breakfast for us, Dad," J.C. said as she passed through the living room. In the kitchen, she immediately scrambled some eggs, took out some bacon, and put that in another skillet. While those were cooking on the stove, she started the coffee and toast. It took about twenty minutes before J.C. had breakfast ready and on the table. Will came out of the living room and sat down at the head of the table, bowed his head, and prayed. J.C. bowed her head also; she did not pray but instead talked to her mother in her mind. 'Mom, please help me. You know that I am struggling to understand this man. Help me to see what you saw in him.' When J.C. lifted her head, Will was looking at her. She smiled and took her first bite of food.

They both finished their breakfast in silence. Will stood first and left his dishes in the sink on his way out the door. J.C. enjoyed her coffee and then cleaned up the kitchen. She brushed her teeth and tied her hair up on the back of her head. She stepped out into the mudroom and pulled on her coveralls, boots, and gloves before heading outside. J.C. walked slowly around the barnyard. She surveyed the lots and livestock. They all seemed to be in good condition. She headed down to the hog barn and found Will scraping the hog pen floors. He used a big blade on the end of a pole and pushed the manure off into a long pit on the south end of the barn. She walked over and looked at the two hogs in the holding pen in the middle driveway. They would be there for about a week allowing their sutures to heal from the work that Vince had completed the day before to repair their ruptures. J.C. watched while Will finished the first pen and headed outside where he hooked up the 'honey wagon' to the drain on the east end of the pit and sucked the manure into the wagon. While he was doing that, J.C. grabbed the blade and began cleaning the second pen. They continued to work in tandem until all the floors were cleaned and Will had spread the manure over the cornstalks on the south forty of the farm. J.C. cleaned the blade and rinsed off her boots carefully before leaving the hog confinement building. Will pulled the 'honey wagon' back into the machine shed and came out with the silage wagon attached.

J.C. followed on foot over to the silage pit and helped Will back up to the entrance using the universal farm hand signals. Once Will was in position he got off the tractor and came around to start loading the silage into the wagon. He used another tractor that had a large end loader bucket on the front to lift silage and dump into the wagon. J.C. watched in amazement thinking that he did this every day without any help at all. His motions were so routine, she wondered if he even had to think about what he was doing. After sixty-plus years of doing this, it had to be so habitual that he could probably do it in his sleep. When the wagon was full, he parked the tractor and scoop back inside the silage pit and crawled up on the tractor attached to the silage wagon. Will drove around the barnyard until he was at the east gate of the feed lot for the feeder cattle. J.C. had taken a shortcut across the barnyard and was there ready with the gate open for him. Will drove through the gate and past the concrete feeding troughs. The cows knew the tractor meant silage was about to be poured and they lined the entire trough. Will turned the tractor around at the opposite end of the trough and slowly inched the tractor along the south side of the feed trough along the new gravel. He released the spout on the silage wagon and silage filled the trough as he made his way across the lot. When he reached the east end, J.C. watched him leave and head back to the machine shed. She closed the gate and locked it. Retracing her steps across the barnyard, she headed into the house. Her stomach told her it was nearing lunchtime.

J.C. had turkey sandwiches and some beef stew on the table when Will came in. He washed up and sat down in his normal spot, bowed his head, and prayed. When he lifted his head, he spoke. "Thanks, J.C. for your help this morning."

"No problem, Dad. I plan on helping you out as much as I can while I am here," she said with a smile. Will did not look up or respond in any way.

When Will had finished his lunch, he put his dishes in the sink and went into his bedroom. When he returned, he went into the bathroom and J.C. heard the shower come on. Will showered and came out in a pair of dress slacks and a long-sleeved dress shirt. He took his jeans and work shirt back to his bedroom. When he returned the second time, he had on dress shoes and a wool jacket that Evelyn had given him for Christmas a few years earlier. He walked out the front door. J.C. watched him walk across the lawn to the driveway and open the door to the small wooden garage. Within minutes her mother's car backed out of the driveway and onto the paved road. The car turned south. He was not going to Stuart, J.C. thought. Where would Will be going in the middle of the day?

She cleaned up the kitchen and jumped in the shower, the entire time thinking of multiple scenarios in her head of what would draw Will away from the farm in the middle of the day in dress clothes. While J.C. was upstairs dressing after her shower, she checked her email. A message from her old boss popped up. 'J.C., we would like you to complete a review of the Northwest Region, similar to what you presented for the Midwest. We think there is substantial savings there also. If I send you the reports, can you give me an estimate of savings? We can pay you a consulting fee of $25,000. Your knowledge and expertise are unmatched to any outside contractor that we could find. We would need this done in the next forty-five days. Please call if you have questions.' J.C. sat at her desk and re-read the message. IBM needed to make major cuts in all their markets to keep their pricing competitive, so this message was not a total surprise. The $25,000 fee was cheap compared to what a national consulting firm would charge. It did surprise her, however, that it came so quickly after she had handed them the savings from the Midwest region.

J.C. picked up her phone and called John. "John, this is J.C. Yes, I read your email. I think that is something I can do. You just want me to run numbers and projections; no travel or site evaluations, right?"

John confirmed what J.C. was thinking. "If you send the data to me, I will look at it and confirm in writing that I can meet that deadline. No, it is all right. I am happy to help you with this analysis and I will call if I have any questions once I get into it." J.C. hung up the phone and felt a slight rush. It was good to feel needed again. This project would be a nice distraction from the emotional stress of these past few weeks.

J.C. sat for a few minutes not really thinking about anything until she heard the front door open. She recognized Will's footsteps crossing the dining room and living room. He had been gone less than two hours. Where had he gone? J.C. stayed upstairs until she heard him close the door of the mudroom.

The next two days J.C. followed the same routine: 6:00 a.m. wake up, making breakfast, helping out around the farm in the morning, and focusing on housework in the afternoon. Later in the week the files came in from John. That night J.C.

stayed up late going over them. Her mind loved being engaged again with something that challenged her. She pulled up the old numbers from her Midwest projections and copied the format, cleared out her old numbers and began to fill in the Northwest results. She looked at the time on the computer and saw it was 3:00 a.m.. *What!* She thought, if I am going to be up at 6:00 a.m., I have to stop.

The alarm at 6:00 a.m. was painful. J.C. crawled to the dressing room and put on her chore clothes, stumbled down the stairs, and into the kitchen. Will was already in the kitchen making breakfast. "I got this today," he said as he handed her a cup of coffee. J.C. gladly took it and headed into the dining room and plopped down at the table.

Will brought her a plate of eggs, sausage, and toast. He sat down in his normal spot and bowed his head. When he lifted his head, he said. "A late night?"

"How did you know?" J.C. asked.

"Light comes down through the floor register," Will responded.

"Oh, yeah, I forgot. You can see that reflection in your room. I'm sorry; I hope it didn't keep you awake. I got a project from my old boss at IBM. They want me to complete a similar analysis for the Northwest Region that I did for the Midwest. I got into it and did not realize how late it was getting." J.C. yawned.

"I can handle the chores this morning. You better go back to bed and get more rest," Will said.

J.C. felt her temperature raise slightly as her face flushed; was that concern her father was expressing? "I will be fine but may need a second cup of coffee to keep me going this morning." She smiled at her father who was looking down at his plate and did not respond.

Will headed outside, and J.C. had a second cup of coffee before cleaning the kitchen and getting herself ready for the morning outside. As she stepped out of the mudroom, Vince pulled into the driveway. J.C.'s stomach skipped. She was embarrassed at how she had cut him off on the phone the prior week. She texted him that she was sorry but got no response.

"Good morning, J.C.," Vince said with a smile.

"Good morning," J.C. responded.

"Is Will OK?" Vince asked.

"Yes, why?" J.C. inquired.

"Your attire gives the impression you are ready to do some heavy-duty work." Vince justified his inquiry.

"I am. I have been helping dad out with the chores this week. Trying to get an assessment, watching and learning." J.C. stopped herself. She was not making sense to herself and knew it must sound even odder to Vince. "What are you doing here?" she asked.

"Checking on those two hogs I repaired earlier this week. How are they?" Vince asked but not expecting J.C. to really know.

"I think their sutures have healed nicely," J.C. responded. They were both walking toward the hog confinement building. When they arrived, Vince opened the door and held it for J.C.

Will was inside already cleaning pens and came over to Vince when they came in. "J.C. said those hogs are healing up nicely," Vince said. "Do you think they are ready to go back into their normal pens?" Vince asked.

"Yeah, they are fine," Will said as he and Vince walked toward the center holding pen. J.C. stayed back.

Vince stepped into the pen and rubbed his hand over the first pig's lower belly. He nodded towards Will and then repeated the same process with the second pig. "I agree. These guys have come along pretty quickly. Do you want me to help move them back?" Vince asked.

"I can do that," J.C. spoke up from behind the two men. Vince looked at Will. Will nodded affirming that J.C. was correct.

"Well, OK then." Vince shot J.C. a surprised look and smiled. He stepped out of the pen and walked over to the water hydrant to wash off his boots. Will returned to scraping the first pen. Vince walked toward J.C. and she escorted him to the door. When they were outside the barn J.C. said, "Vince I am so sorry about my actions the other night. I had no reason to be that rude to you." J.C. was trying to make up for her sudden hang up on the phone.

"You were not rude," Vince said. "J.C., you were upset and like I said, I am here to listen; not judge, or give advice–unless asked for it. I know you need some space to make whatever decisions you are working through." Vince paused and looked intently at J.C. "You look really tired. Are you getting enough sleep?" Vince could not help himself from being the eternal nice guy, J.C. thought.

"I am fine. I got a project from IBM yesterday and stayed up way too late last night looking at some figures. I will take a nap this afternoon and be just fine," J.C. said.

"Good." Vince gave a big smile. "Farmer by day and executive by night!" He broke into laughter at his own joke.

"I know." J.C. was laughing along with him. "No one I know would believe it if they saw me right now. This is a long way from my navy suit and pumps!"

They stood in the cold and laughed for a minute or two. "Well, I better get going. My schedule is pretty full today," Vince said. "Take care of yourself, J.C." Vince continued to smile as he walked away.

J.C. turned and re-entered the hog building. Will was already out on the tractor and unloading the first round of manure. J.C. picked up the blade and started into her morning routine. Today the work seemed to go much quicker. Her mind toggled between the projections she had seen last night and her moments of laughter with Vince outside the barn.

When the floors were clean, J.C. and Will moved the two pigs back to their respective pens and then dismantled the holding pen before heading out to give the cows their silage. While J.C. walked up to the cow lot, she caught herself reliving a conversation she had with Nadine. I am not going to become a farmer, was the consensus of that discussion. Yet here she was walking through the barnyard looking like the one thing she said she would never be. What exactly had Nadine meant last week when she said watch, learn, and listen? Why had J.C. repeated that to Vince earlier? As she recalled what she had seen this week, it confirmed that both Vince and Nadine had been right. Will was still capable of doing his own farming and it did not appear that he had any desire to stop soon. It lightened his load when she came out to help him, but he obviously was getting it done when she was not there to help. J.C. had not found anything new to learn about the farm business and since Will barely spoke, the listening part was non-existent. Will pulled up to the gate that J.C. opened into the feed lot. He distributed the silage and headed back out the gate. He stopped in the gate and looked down at J.C. "Can you follow me to the machine shed?" he asked.

J.C. looked up and nodded, affirming her agreement. She closed and locked the gate and walked behind the tractor and wagon to the machine shed. After Will had parked them in their standard place, he turned off the tractor and dismounted. Again, J.C. watched in amazement of how agile he was. Will walked to the corner in the machine shed. J.C. followed him. He opened the door and held it for his daughter to walk through.

She was surprised at what she saw inside. A desk, two chairs, file cabinets, a bookcase full of binders, a lamp, coffeepot, and papers. It looked like the study at her condo minus the couch and TV. "J.C., please sit down." Will motioned for her to take a chair at the side of his desk. Will pulled down two notebooks, full of logs, that he had on the bookshelf on the other side of his desk. He laid them open for J.C. to look at. The logs were handwritten dates and numbers in columns. "Can you help me put these in a format that could be sorted automatically?" Will asked.

"Dad, are these production reports for your livestock?" J.C. asked.

"Yes, when I buy an animal, I put them in this log with a number, price, add number of days they are on feed, vaccinations or medications, and sale price. If I could get this in a more automated form, I think I could do a better job of managing my costs." Will looked at J.C. with a question in his eyes.

"Dad, we can definitely automate these journals. Do these numbers represent the current livestock that's on the farm?" J.C. inquired.

"Yes," Will said confidently.

"Can I take these to the house and start putting them in my computer?" J.C. asked.

"Sure." Will handed her the two notebooks.

"When I get the data loaded, we will look at what criteria you want sorted out and then decide if you really need to collect all this information going forward," J.C. responded with enthusiasm in her voice.

"Thanks," Will said. J.C. knew that was her cue to leave. She took another look around Will's office before leaving. As she stepped out the door, she wondered why her mother had never mentioned that Will had an office in the machine shed.

J.C. set the notebooks on the washer while she took off her overalls and boots. Entering the house, she laid them on the dining room table while she washed up. Coming out of the bathroom, she opened the cupboard to see what options she had for a quick lunch. Grabbing a can of tuna, she mixed up some tuna salad and made a couple of sandwiches. She also made a tossed salad. Will had not come inside yet so she ran the notebooks upstairs. She flipped through one again and was amazed at the details her father had kept on each animal. She was sure that the shelves full of notebooks in his office were all identical to the two she had.

J.C. heard the kitchen door and knew that Will had come in for lunch. She hurried downstairs and finished putting items on the table. Will washed up and sat down, bowed his head to pray and when he lifted his head, J.C. was setting a bowl of salad and a side plate with a sandwich in front of him. She returned to the kitchen to get her own. While she was in the kitchen the house phone rang. Will stood and went to the phone. "Hello," Will answered. "Oh, I am sorry to hear that. I just visited him on Tuesday at the hospital. Really, OK, I will be there. Thanks for calling." Will returned to the table.

"Who was that on the phone?" J.C. asked.

"It was Ronald Nelson. His father, Everett, passed away this morning." Will sat in his chair, his head resting on his chest.

"Dad, I am sorry. I know he was a friend to you and mom for many years. When is the funeral?" J.C. asked.

"Next Monday," Will replied.

J.C. sat in silence with her father. Her mind put the puzzle together with this new information. On Tuesday, when Will had left after lunch, he had gone into Greenfield to the Adair County Hospital to visit the one person that she knew was his friend. She felt sad for him. She had wanted to ask him some questions about the livestock logs over lunch but decided to let him have some time to remember Everett.

After lunch Will headed back outside. J.C.'s phone rang almost the minute Will was out the door. It was Nadine. "J.C., its Nadine."

"Hello, Nadine. I was planning on calling you this afternoon," J.C. replied.

"I wanted to give you a heads up that Everett Nelson passed away," Nadine said.

"Too late. Ronald, his son, called dad while he was in the house for lunch," J.C. reported.

"Oh, no. Is Will OK?" Nadine asked.

"How am I supposed to know that?" J.C. inquired.

"Well, I am worried that this might be another blow for Will. I cannot think of another friend he has in this community. Except Vince Martin, I guess." Nadine was talking to herself more than J.C.

J.C.'s head was spinning. She wanted to talk to Nadine about the IBM project, the office, notebooks, and some perceived changes in Will's behavior and now all the focus was on Everett. She abruptly started in, "Nadine, I have been doing what you suggested, taking time, watching, listening, and helping out. Before this Everett news hit, I thought I was seeing some progress in Will," J.C. reported.

"Really, like what?" Nadine asked.

"Did you know that Will has an office in his machine shed?" J.C. inquired.

"No," Nadine responded. "What kind of office?"

"One just like mine in Des Moines. A desk, chairs, bookshelves, the whole works," J.C. reported.

"Well, I'll be," Nadine replied.

"He invited me in after we finished chores this morning and gave me two notebooks that he wants me to convert to spreadsheets for him on my computer. Livestock production reports. He knows I was up late last night working on some analysis for IBM and maybe that gave him the idea that I could do this for him. I don't know but it seems pretty crazy don't you think?" J.C. took a breath.

"Crazy, let's start at the beginning. Did I hear you say that you were helping with chores?" Nadine asked.

"Yes. I took your advice and started getting up every day at 6:00 a.m. to help clean hog floors and feed cows," J.C. reported proudly.

"What happened to the big city girl that had no interest in becoming a farmer?" Nadine chided.

"I was a farm girl long before I was a big city girl and still know my way around the barnyard." J.C. pushed back.

"So, you and Will sat down in his secret office and talked about livestock." Nadine laughed into the phone.

"Oh, Nadine, you make it sound so simple." J.C. scoffed at Nadine's simple summation of what she thought was a major breakthrough in her morning.

"What did you say about IBM? Are you back working for them?" Nadine had a way of keeping you off-balance no matter what subject matter the conversation was currently on.

"John, my old boss, emailed and asked me to prepare some projections for the Northwest Region similar to what I did in the Midwest. I was working on those late last night and Will saw my light on upstairs through the register. When I told him the type of work I was doing for IBM, I guess that made him think I might be able to do some analysis on his manual reports also," J.C. informed Nadine. Drawing in a deep breath J.C. said, "Nadine, remember I said I was going to call you?"

"Oh, yes, what about?" Nadine replied.

"I thought I would go into Des Moines for a couple of days and work on these IBM reports and wanted to know if you would like to go with me. I could work much faster with my desk computer and laptop side by side. You could spend some time with Doris, maybe take her out to lunch and shopping. You and I could catch a movie and have dinner one night. I just thought it might be a nice break for both of us." J.C. laid out her plan.

"When were you planning this little get away?" Nadine's interest was piqued.

"Originally, I thought we could go on Monday after seeing Kelsey's play Sunday afternoon, but now that is Everett's funeral. I think I should probably stay and help out at the farm that day, so maybe we could push it back to Wednesday next week," J.C. suggested.

"Yes, I will need to be here for that funeral on Monday too. Then I get my hair done on Tuesdays. So, Wednesday would be best for me. It has been a while since I took a couple of days to relax in the big city. Count me in." Nadine was smiling as she confirmed the plan.

Chapter 23

J.C. pulled into Nadine's driveway at 1:30 p.m. on Sunday afternoon. Nadine popped out the front door and into J.C.'s car. "The girls are going to meet us at the school," Nadine announced as she fastened her seat belt. J.C. knew that the girls were the other women in town that went to social events with Nadine.

"Great, we get tickets at the door, right?" J.C. asked.

"Sure do. I think we have been going to this spring show for over fifty years now. Evelyn loved these performances. She would especially like this fairy tale theme and one of her special dresses being a part of it." Nadine smiled at J.C. who returned the smile. J.C. felt a warm sensation in her chest thinking about her mother right then.

J.C. parked the car across the street from the gymnasium and they walked into the crowd standing at the doors. Nadine immediately spotted her friends as they made their way through the crowd. They wanted to all be together when they purchased their tickets. Not that it matters since it was open seating, but it seemed important to Nadine and her friends, J.C. thought. Within minutes they had tickets and walked inside the gym. The curtains on the stage were closed and covered with stars, rain drops, and vines. J.C. looked around and smiled at a few familiar faces. Unfortunately, one of them was Jim Powell who was making a beeline for her. Nadine and the ladies were scoping out chairs toward the front when Jim reached J.C.

Touching her elbow, Jim said, "J.C. I am so sorry I was tied up the other day when you were in the office. I checked with the receptionist when I got inside, and she said you had been there to see Ken. I hope he was able to take care of whatever you needed. If not, I would be more than happy to go over any legal matters you might need help with." Jim finally stopped to catch a breath.

"No, I am good. Ken has been our family attorney for years and I got all the information I needed." J.C. wanted to close that book before it got opened any further. Although she was still confused and frustrated over her meeting with Ken, she was not about to show her concern to Jim Powell.

"What brings you to this afternoon's matinee?" Jim inquired.

"Well, Jim, I provided one of the costumes for the production. You might recognize my red prom dress from our junior year prom." J.C. was almost beaming knowing that Jim would have no idea what she wore to prom, and even more surprised at how after all this time it would end up on the stage today.

As she could see Jim trying to think of something to say, J.C. continued, "Ladies, have you picked our spot yet? Jim, sorry I need to stay with Nadine and her group. We will have to catch up later." J.C. casually turned and gently pushed Nadine down the aisle away from Jim.

The ladies had spotted some seats in the third row on the left-hand side and filed into the row and sat down. J.C. was on the aisle seat and when she sat down, she looked to her right and there sat Vince Martin smiling at her. "Well, good afternoon Ms. Mason," Vince said with a big smile.

"Vince, how are you?" J.C. responded.

"J.C., these are Teri's parents, Margaret and John Andrews." Vince turned towards the couple seated next to him, smiled, and said, "Margaret and John, this is J.C. Mason, the woman that helped Kelsey with her prom dress and loaned her the red dress for this show."

J.C. stood and walked across the aisle. She bent down and shook hands with the Andrews. "I never had the honor of meeting your daughter, but I have seen her handiwork in the home she decorated and the daughter she raised. Both are beautiful!" They both smiled back at her and nodded in agreement. The lights flickered indicating that the show would start soon. J.C. excused herself and stepped back across the aisle to her seat. As she sat down, the lights were dimming. She looked back at Vince who was smiling at her. She returned the smile.

The show was broken down into three short stories. The first was a modern-day "Galileo" who wished upon the stars to achieve his dreams. The second was Kelsey's piece which was the modern-day "Cinderella" story, which ended with her getting the prince that just happened to be played by Jason Powell. J.C. was extremely impressed with the vocal talents of both Kelsey and Jason. Their first duet 'Somewhere out There' was equivalent to performances at the Des Moines Playhouse. When they sang 'I Pledge My Love' as their finale with Kelsey in J.C.'s red satin dress, it was as good as some Broadway plays that J.C. had seen in New York. The crowd gave them a standing ovation for their final song. J.C. could hardly sit still for the final story which was a very modern "Jack and the Beanstalk" story about an architect that built skyscrapers to capture his dreams. When the show ended, and the entire cast came back on stage for the final curtain call, J.C. had butterflies in her stomach. She was so excited to tell Kelsey what a perfect performance she had given. Why was she so nervous, J.C. asked herself?

It seemed like an hour before Kelsey came out to see them, still wearing the red satin dress. Margaret and John handed her a bouquet of yellow roses and Vince handed her a single red rose. J.C. was embarrassed that she had not thought to bring flowers. She really was losing her sales intuition. This was obviously one of those occasions where flowers were appropriate. She and Nadine stood back to let Kelsey talk with her grandparents and father first. When she had thanked them for the flowers a second time and conversations were lagging, Vince indicated that she needed to acknowledge Nadine and J.C.

Kelsey stepped over in front of the two women and spun in a complete circle. "What do you think? I love the way this dress makes me feel." She was smiling from ear to ear.

"You look like a princess in that dress my dear." Nadine spoke first. "I bet you had one sharp seamstress make it fit you like a glove!" Vince nodded over Kelsey's back. Kelsey stepped up and hugged Nadine, holding her bouquet of flowers behind Nadine's back.

"Kelsey, you look amazing in that old dress; but your voice is so beautiful I thought I was sitting in a Broadway theater in New York City." J.C. gushed out her compliment.

"Really?" Kelsey stepped back and looked at J.C. to measure if the compliment was true. "I think today was my strongest vocal performance, but I do not think that I am that great," she humbly replied.

"'*I Pledge My Love*' was breathtaking and sent chills up my spine," J.C. stressed.

Grandpa Andrews nodded his head in agreement. "Kelsey, she is right, you were as good as anyone your grandmother and I have heard sing at the Civic Center," he said smiling, as he paid his granddaughter the compliment.

"Thank you for inviting me; this will be a treasured memory-you in my dress and singing that song," J.C. said.

Nadine nudged J.C. and stepped back to indicate they were leaving. Smiling towards Vince and the Andrews, they headed down the aisle towards the door. The crowd had thinned as only parents and special friends waited for cast members to come out. J.C. and Nadine walked up on a group that seemed to be a family circled around another student. They tried to go around and came face to face with Jim Powell. "What a show! *And*, what a dress, J.C. I'm glad you told me to watch for that!" Jim said with too much enthusiasm in his voice. J.C. just smiled and tried to keep on moving. Just then she recognized the young man who had played the prince, Jim's son, Jason. "Jason, I wanted to tell you how much I enjoyed your performance today. You have an exceptional voice," J.C. complimented the young man.

The young man looked startled at the stranger in front of him. His eyes moved towards Nadine who he obviously recognized. "This is J.C. Mason, Evelyn Mason's daughter. She went to high school with your father." Nadine filled in the blanks that the young man was trying to pull together.

Jason smiled, "Thank you, Ms. Mason, that is very kind of you to say."

"You will have a big future with that voice if you decide to use it." J.C. smiled and kept moving past Jim with Nadine right on her heels.

They exited the building and headed towards J.C.'s car. J.C. could hear sounds of footsteps behind them and was afraid to look in fear that Jim was close behind. When she unlocked her car and started to get inside, she could feel the touch of a hand on her waist.

"J.C., thank you so much," gushed Kelsey who threw herself into J.C.'s chest as she turned into Kelsey's hug. "I think my performance was the best today because you were here!" J.C. felt her temperature rise. She returned the hug and stood holding Kelsey for another minute before noticing Vince and her grandparents coming up behind Kelsey. J.C. gently released her hug and Kelsey stepped back and looked up into J.C.'s face.

"Can I keep the dress?" Kelsey asked.

"Of course!" J.C. exclaimed. She got into her car and smiled towards Vince and the Andrews as she closed her door. Her heart was racing, her face was flush, and she was experiencing a very uneasy feeling in her stomach. The car started, and J.C. pulled away from the curb.

"Well, that family has got their hooks into you, girl," Nadine said without any warning.

"Hooks, what do you mean?" J.C. shot back almost defensively.

"I told you the other day that I was worried you were pushing it too fast and maybe would be hurt again. I think I was wrong. They are coming after you and bowling you over. They have hit you so hard that you did not see it coming." Nadine was chuckling to herself.

"Nadine," J.C. said sternly. "I have no idea what you are saying and none of that makes any sense at all."

"It will, I am no one's fool!" Nadine was still chuckling. "Are you going to the funeral and luncheon tomorrow?" In perfect Nadine fashion, she had changed the subject on J.C. before she had a chance to digest the last bombshell that was dropped.

"Well, I guess I don't know. Dad needs to be there, so I will see if I need to stay at the farm and cover the chores." J.C. was almost talking out loud to herself confirming that she needed to check with Will.

"Well, you can just come for lunch even if you cannot make the funeral. It is at the Fairview Church in the basement. I am bringing my chicken and noodles over homemade mashed potatoes. You do not want to miss that." Nadine was bragging, knowing that her reputation for this dish was well known throughout the community.

"I will call you in the morning to let you know for sure," J.C. said as she pulled into Nadine's driveway to drop her off.

"See you tomorrow," Nadine said as she stepped out of the car.

J.C. shook her head as she knew that Nadine expected her to come to the luncheon even if she was not able to make the funeral. Evelyn's mothering style was much gentler than Nadine's surrogate style had been these past few months.

Chapter 24

J.C. began the dinner preparation as soon as she got home. She fried some hamburger and opened a can of tomato paste, adding in some brown sugar and seasoning to make sloppy joes. She peeled two large potatoes and sliced them thin. It was 6:30 p.m. when Will came through the kitchen door that evening. While he was taking his shower, J.C. fried the potatoes and finished the sloppy joes. It had been years since she enjoyed this meal. Comfort food is what some people would call this. Definitely not what she normally ate but tonight she was feeling kind of strange, and some old-fashioned farm fried potatoes and sloppy joes seemed appropriate.

Will sat down just as J.C. finished placing the items on the table. He bowed his head and prayed. J.C. filled their glasses with milk and sat down and waited for Will. When he raised his head, she passed him the fried potatoes. He helped himself and passed them back. She then handed him a bun followed by the dish with the hamburger mix for a sloppy joe. Will made his own sandwich and began eating.

"Dad, what can I do in the morning to make chores go as quickly as possible for you? I know you want to be at the funeral home early." J.C. was trying to sound helpful but not pushy.

"I already scraped the floors in the hog building and loaded the silage wagon this afternoon. I will be fine in the morning," Will said.

"Dad, you did not need to do that. I can do more if you let me." J.C. directing her concern with how much extra work he had completed while she had gone to the play.

"It's OK, the funeral is at 10:00 a.m., and the pallbearers just need to be there by 9:45 a.m.," Will added.

J.C. realized for the first time that her father was a pallbearer. She sat and let that information sink in. He would sit through the service, help carry the casket of his friend to a hearse and follow it to the grave, carry the casket to the open gravesite and help lower it into the ground. As her mind walked through the steps, her chest felt heavy. Who had done that for Will's brothers? Who had done that for Johnnie? She tried hard but could not remember Johnnie's funeral. The only one that she could recall was her mother's that had taken place less than a year ago.

In the middle of her mental inquiry, Will asked J.C., "Are you planning on going to the funeral?"

J.C.'s head snapped up startled, and she drew in a deep breath, "I really had not decided. I did not know Everett Nelson or his family. I just remember Mom talking about him over dinner a few times. I know that he was your friend when you and mom met. Nadine thinks I should come for the luncheon, but I told her I needed to see if there were things here that required my attention." J.C. stopped; she could tell she was rambling to cover her shock that Will was continuing the conversation.

"You should come to the luncheon. Vince and Nadine will be there," Will stated.

"Are you sure there are not things that I should be doing here? J.C. confirmed.

"No, it will be fine," Will said.

"OK, I will come to the luncheon." J.C. smiled at Will. He did not smile, but just looked into J.C.'s eyes again that made her feel flush. Will again lowered his head.

"Dad," J.C. said meekly "why did you not tell me I was named after your older brother, Jack?"

Will's head shot up; his eyes were full of fear. He stood and walked into the living room. J.C. heard him turn on the light. She knew he was retreating to his Bible. She was confused, angry, sad, and most importantly felt completely alone in a place she should be calling home. She sat in silence looking at his plate that was half eaten and then back at her plate. Her appetite was gone. The comfort food was not comforting at all. After a few minutes, she rose and took everything back to the kitchen, put the leftovers away, cleaned up the kitchen and got ready for bed.

Will was sitting in his chair with his head lowered over the Bible in his lap. J.C. walked slowly through the living room. When she was directly behind his chair, she softly said, "Dad, I am sorry."

J.C. threw herself on her couch in the study and cried herself to sleep. She did not wake to an alarm the next morning but woke suddenly with a sharp pain in her neck. She unfolded herself from the couch and looked at the clock on her desk. It was 8:10 a.m. How could she have slept that long in such an uncomfortable position? She sat on the couch in her wrinkled clothes and stared at Johnnie. Her chest felt so heavy that she thought this must be what it feels like to have a heart attack. She was in good health and her most recent physical did not indicate anything was wrong. Could stress cause a sudden heart attack? Her mind was playing tricks on her. She just needed to get in the shower and on with her day. She pulled herself off the couch and walked to her bedroom window.

She could see Will just finishing emptying the silage for the feeder cattle. She knew that he was nearing the end of the chores and would be in shortly to take his shower and head to town. She darted downstairs, brushed her teeth, made a piece of toast and a cup of coffee. J.C. was back upstairs in her study when she heard Will come in. She just wanted to avoid him until after the funeral. She felt bad about the timing of her question. Why did she pick last night to ask him that question knowing that today he would bury his last known friend? Was that insensitive of her? Nadine was right; she was definitely not herself since she moved home. Going back to Des Moines this week would be a welcome break from this nightmare. Just a few days ago she had thought they were making progress but last night was more than she could bear.

J.C. heard the front door close shortly after 9:00 a.m. She knew that Will was headed to the funeral home in Stuart. She grabbed her stuff and headed down to the shower. She relaxed and took an extra-long one. She took her time to dry and fix her hair. J.C. carefully put on her make-up and gave herself an extra look before heading upstairs to dress. When she walked into her dressing room, she looked at the two dresses she had brought. Thank goodness one was navy. She pulled out a pair of panty hose and smiled as she put them on. It had been months since she had worn panty hose. She put on a slip and then pulled the navy-blue double-breasted coat dress off the hanger. This was a power dress that she wore on more than one occasion to close a deal for IBM. Today was not a deal closer but this outfit gave her confidence and she needed that today.

Around 11:15 a.m., J.C. headed out the door and up the road towards the Fairview Church. It was a small single-story country church that had been there throughout her childhood. She pulled into the north parking lot where half a dozen cars were parked and noticed that Nadine's was one of them. The women who were preparing the lunch were already there. She sat for a few minutes before deciding to go in and volunteer to help serve the lunch.

Once inside the church, J.C. made her way to the basement. She noticed they had added a lift chair to the stairway, making it accessible to a person with a disability, she thought. Even little Fairview Church must keep compliant with the law. She stepped through the doorway at the bottom of the stairs and surveyed the group of women in the kitchen. Most of them were friends of her mother. Nadine caught her eye and flashed a big smile.

J.C. walked toward the kitchen and Nadine stepped out to greet her. "This is not a corporate luncheon; aren't you a little overdressed?" Nadine inquired.

"I had two dresses and this one seemed the most appropriate." J.C. surveyed the ladies in the kitchen who were all in polyester pant suits, including Nadine.

"You're fine," Nadine said with a big smile.

"What can I do to help?" J.C. asked.

"Follow me." Nadine turned and walked back into the kitchen. "Ladies you all remember Jacquelyn Mason, Evelyn's daughter." Heads nodded and most of them said 'hello' simultaneously.

"Hello, ladies, I am here to work so give me a job to do." J.C. smiled as she slowly canvassed the room.

"You can fill the relish trays if you want and set them on the tables," Marge Johnson said.

J.C. immediately started opening jars of pickles, olives, beets, carrots, celery, and radishes, and filled four trays. When the trays were filled, she carried them out of the kitchen and set them in the center of serving tables. The women continued their discussion around what a nice service it was. How many years since Everett's wife died? Did all the children make it back? Which cousins and other relatives were spotted at the service? J.C. thought to herself what this conversation would be like for Will's funeral. Short and... she wanted to say sweet but stopped herself. Her next thought was about her own funeral. She was certain that by the time she passed away, Will, Nadine and Doris would all be gone so no need for a funeral, burial, or luncheon. She had contemplated when her mother died, to go ahead and prearrange for her cremation. Standing in the basement of the Fairview Church, it seemed like that was the most sensible thing to do. J.C.'s mind got stuck on one thought. What happens when no one shows up to pick up the ashes? She was frozen, holding the last relish tray when a voice interrupted her thoughts.

"You look very nice today." Vince's compliment brought her back to reality.

"Thank you, I hear it was a nice service." Taking a deep breath, J.C. commented as she noticed people streaming through the door and headed toward the table. She set the last relish tray down and stepped back away from the food.

Vince followed her, "Yes it was very nice. Everett was just a good farmer, great neighbor, and family man. I never heard anyone say a bad word about him."

"How many children did he have?" J.C. asked.

"Two sons and a daughter. His oldest son passed away a few years ago. I do not remember what caused his death. Ronald and Marie are both here with their families. You know that Ronald lives in Greenfield and works for the Adair County Bank. Marie and her family are from Indiana; I'm not sure what they do. I can introduce you if you would like," Vince offered.

"*No*, they do not need to meet another stranger today that they will never see again. I better get back to the kitchen." J.C. turned abruptly and left Vince. She did not fit in here. He probably knew every person in the room and could mingle with his gracious demeanor. It was nice of him to offer but she would much rather hide in the kitchen. Most of the ladies were out mingling and so J.C. busied herself with cleanup from the relish containers. She noticed that the lemonade was going fast, so she mixed up another pitcher and swapped those out. Just as she was headed back to the kitchen, she spotted Will. She nodded and smiled at him. No response. A chill ran down her spine thinking back to their previous night's conversation. Not that she would call that a conversation!

CHAPTER 24

"Hey, come fill a plate and eat with us," Nadine coaxed J.C., poking her head around the kitchen door.

"I am fine, not really that hungry," J.C. said, slightly a lie. She was starting to feel some hunger pangs since her incomplete dinner the night before and very light breakfast this morning.

"My chicken, noodles and potatoes will be gone soon if you do not get out here," Nadine chided.

J.C. shook her head at Nadine and continued to put things away in the kitchen. As she stuck her head in the refrigerator to pull out more carrots and celery, she did not notice someone had come into the kitchen. "Would you please join me for lunch?" Vince invited.

"Oh, I was not planning on eating," J.C. said as she stood up holding two bags of vegetables.

"OK, then I guess I won't either," Vince replied.

They stood looking at each other for a minute. "OK, you guilted me into it!" J.C. said.

She quickly washed the vegetables and replenished the relish trays before joining Vince. They were the last two people to go through the line. The rest of the room was caught up in chatter when they finished filling their plates and took seats at the far corner of the basement, just beyond where most of the pallbearers were seated.

"The ladies in this community really know how to cook," Vince opened the conversation. "These meals remind me of my mother and yours. Both were great cooks and always serving their community."

"Yes, I know. Mom never missed an opportunity to make a casserole when someone was in need. She really did enjoy cooking. I kind of forgot that. Thanks Vince. You are always so nice with your compliments," J.C. responded.

"You are not so bad yourself. We just finished that chocolate cake you baked. I kept it in the refrigerator to keep it moist. You didn't happen to bring one, did you?" Vince raised his eyebrows and smiled as he asked.

"No." J.C. smiled. "I am kind of embarrassed that I did not bring anything today. Not that there is a shortage of food but as I said, my mom would never have come empty-handed to a luncheon like this."

As they quietly ate, J.C. noticed Will standing up and nodding to some of the other pallbearers as he left the group. He stopped on his way to the kitchen and shook hands with Ronald. Will left his plate in the kitchen and without talking to anyone, he was out the door and gone. J.C. let out a big sigh.

"Are you OK?" Vince asked.

"Yes, just a little uncomfortable around my dad I guess," J.C. admitted.

Vince reached across the table and gently touched her forearm. Chills ran down J.C.'s spine and her face flushed. Just then Jim Powell pulled the chair out next to J.C. and plopped down. "I did not expect to see you here today," Jim announced looking directly at J.C. and ignoring Vince.

"Everett was a good friend to my parents," J.C. responded quietly.

"Miss seeing you at the gym in the mornings. Have you stopped working out?" Jim leaned closer to J.C.

"No, just conflicts with chore time," J.C. replied.

Jim let out a big laugh and tried to lean even closer. J.C. immediately stood up and said, "Thanks Vince, for keeping me company during lunch. I better get back to the kitchen and help with the cleanup. Nice to see you, Jim." She quickly made her way to the kitchen.

Jim engaged Vince as soon as she left the table and J.C. knew that Vince could handle Jim without Jim even realizing he was being handled.

"So, I see you decided to eat after all," Nadine starting in on J.C. immediately, when she got back to the kitchen.

"Nadine, please." J.C. looked at Nadine with a pleading look in her eyes and picked up a dish towel and began drying dishes. "I had forgotten how good your chicken and noodles were. I would have gone back for seconds but you were right;

they were almost gone." J.C.'s sales skills had come in handy to turn the conversation before any of the other women picked up on it in the kitchen.

"Always a favorite at these meals!" Nadine said with pride. She turned and followed Marge Johnson back out to bring in more empty dishes.

Donna Johnson, Marge's sister-in-law, was washing dishes. "J.C. how long have you been back?" she asked.

"About a month," J.C. replied.

"Do you still work for IBM?" Donna kept the conversation going.

"Yes, on a consulting basis," J.C. responded.

"That's nice," Donna replied.

"How is your family?" J.C. inquired.

"They are fine; I have seven grandchildren now ..."

J.C. watched the final few people leave the basement. Vince walked out with Everett's daughter and J.C. was sure he would help her load flowers into her car or do whatever nice gesture was needed to comfort her at this time.

"My oldest son lives in Denver and his two children are both in college there." As J.C. tuned back in, she was glad that she could pick up right where she left off. Donna and J.C. continued their small talk until all the dishes were washed, dried, and returned to the church's cupboard or packed into the ladies' baskets that had brought food.

"What time are you picking me up on Wednesday?" Nadine asked, as she pulled on her coat.

"Is 10:00 a.m. OK?" J.C. asked, "I want to help with the morning chores before we leave."

"10:00 a.m. is perfect. Does Doris know we are coming?" Nadine inquired.

"No, I will call her later today or tomorrow," J.C. said.

The women bid multiple good-byes and wished each other hope that the next one of these luncheons would not be for one of them. J.C. could see that conversation might last hours, so she quietly stepped out of the kitchen and vanished up the stairs. At the top of the stairs were multiple green plants and flowers that were left as a thank you gesture from the family to the women in the kitchen. It was a tradition that had been there since J.C. was a child. Martin had given some remarks at the beginning of the lunch and confirmed that the ladies who had worked tirelessly to put on such a wonderful lunch should all take a plant or flower when they left. J.C. walked out the door without anything. Her mind confirmed that is another tradition that will end with Will. No one would send flowers at her death; no lunch would be served, and no one would even show up to pick up her ashes. She would instruct the funeral home to discard them once the cremation was completed.

Chapter 25

J.C. worked on Will's files the rest of the day.
She was starting to see some patterns emerge regarding
feed consumption to weight gain. At 4:00 p.m., she stopped
and went downstairs to contemplate dinner. She pulled
canned beef from the cupboard and poured it into a large
saucepan on the stove. She peeled potatoes, carrots and
onions and added them to the pan and turned the heat on
low. She would come back and check on it in an hour.

When J.C. was back upstairs, she pulled out her overnight
bag and began packing for her short trip to Des Moines.
She started to feel anxious as she packed. She was looking
forward to a break from the farm and excited about getting
into the IBM project; so, where was her anxiety coming from,
she asked herself?

She returned to the study and sat back down focusing
on the livestock files she was creating for Will. She would
probably complete her input tomorrow. She wished she
had a printer so that she could show Will the reports and
discuss some sorting options. J.C. had started a list of items
that she wanted to bring back from Des Moines. She added
a small wireless printer. She could pick that up when she

took Nadine shopping. It would be nice to have a printer here at the farm she thought. J.C. saved her files and closed her computer down for the night. She looked at her phone attached to the charger. I will call Doris in the morning.

J.C. returned to the kitchen and pulled out her mother's Betty Crocker Cookbook. The edges were ragged, and a few pages had been torn, but she knew exactly where to find the Baking Powder Biscuit recipe on page fifty-seven. She stirred the beef stew again and then pulled all the ingredients out of the cupboards for her biscuits. J.C. quickly mixed up the ingredients and dropped the biscuits onto the cookie tray. It was 6:00 p.m. and Will would be coming through the door any minute for dinner.

J.C. continued to stir the stew. The biscuits came out of the oven at 6:20 p.m. and then she turned the stove off. It was taking Will a little longer since he was gone for three hours out of the middle of his day she thought.

At 6:45 p.m., J.C. noticed that the anxiety she had felt earlier upstairs was back. Her stomach was starting to tighten and so was her chest. She watched the clock. It slowly moved from 6:45 p.m. to 6:50 p.m. J.C. stood up and walked to the mudroom. She pulled on her boots and Carhartt jacket. She stepped outside into the dark night air. Turning around she stepped back into the mudroom and scanned the shelves for a flashlight. Opening the cupboard door over the dryer, she found one. J.C. opened the door and was again outside in the cold night air. She started toward the cattle lots, her eyes darting in every direction. Everything there seemed normal. She headed to the machine shed. Once inside she flipped on the overhead lights and scanned each piece of machinery. Walking slowly, looking in every direction, she was finally at Will's office door. She opened that door and flipped on the light. No Will. Her heart was starting to beat faster. She turned off the light and closed his office door. Briskly walking back through the machine shed, she flipped the light switch off as she exited the building and headed towards the hog barn.

Opening the door to the hog barn, she flashed her light around the side of the door. Finally, she saw the switch and hurried to turn on the overhead lights. When J.C. turned around, she saw Will, lying face down in the center driveway. She rushed to him and bent down to see if he was breathing. "Dad! Are you OK?" she cried. J.C. quickly placed her two fingers on the side of his throat and could feel his heart beat. "Dad!" she yelled as she bent closer towards his face and turned him on his side. Will's eyes were slightly open but were not focusing. J.C. crouched in front of Will's limp body and rolled him onto his back. His eyes looked glazed. "Dad, Dad, Dad!" J.C. continued to yell. She felt his pulse on his wrist and listened to his chest. "My phone!" she yelled to no one that could hear her. "I should have brought my phone with me," she said to Will, knowing that he may not even know she was there. Her mind was racing. She did not want to leave him to go get a phone but what else could she do? J.C. leaned close to her father's face. "Dad, I am going to..." J.C.'s entire body shot off the ground as she felt a hand on her shoulder. She was upright and spinning to see what and who had touched her back.

"Vince?!? Where did you, how did you know? Dad!" Words were coming out of J.C.'s mouth but her mind was not able to process what had occurred. Vince gently stroked her arm and then knelt next to Will's body. "Will, do you have any of your Nitroglycerin pills on you?" No response. "Will, I am going to check your pockets for pills," Vince said calmly. He immediately started to reach into Will's overall pockets. After pulling an empty hand out of the third pocket, he looked up at J.C. and said, "Go to the house and find his Nitroglycerin pills." J.C. bounded out of the barn, up the hill, through the mudroom and into the bathroom. She opened the medicine cabinet over the bathroom sink and grabbed the first medicine bottle she saw. She read the label Welchol for diabetes. "No," she shouted. She grabbed a second bottle–Nitroglycerin. "*Yes!*" She spun around and ran through the mudroom, down the hill and back into the hog barn. Vince was still bent over Will's body. She rushed over to them and opened the bottle, dropping one small pill into Vince's open hand. Vince gently opened Will's mouth and lifted his tongue, placing the pill under it. J.C. closed the lid on the bottle and put the bottle in her inside coat pocket. She looked at Vince with worry in her eyes. "It is going to be all right," Vince said quietly.

A single tear rolled out of Will's left eye. J.C. bent down and whispered in his ear, "Dad, I am here." It seemed like an eternity but was only minutes when Will's eyes focused, and he tried to lift his head.

"Will, rest here for a few minutes and then we will get you to the house," Vince spoke calmly.

J.C.'s body was shaking, and she could not take her eyes off her father's face as it started to change from grey to pink again. He blinked his eyes to stop the tears while trying to raise one arm. Vince continued to speak quietly to Will that he needed to rest until the Nitro had a chance to work. Out of the corner of her eye, she could see that Vince's attention was distracted by something over Will's body. J.C. looked and followed his gaze.

A large hog was caught in the corner panel of the gate next to the waterer. It's head and front quarter was stuck, and it could not get loose. The high pitch squealing finally resonated with J.C. She started to stand, but Vince grabbed her arm. "Stay here with Will. Keep him flat and quiet for another ten minutes. I will see what I can do." He walked toward the trapped hog.

J.C. returned her attention to Will. His eyes were focused on her face. His cheeks were flushed with color. He continued to try and raise his right arm. He was sweating profusely. J.C. gently held it on the ground. Will tried to speak but all that came out was a few weak breaths. "Dad, just rest." J.C.

CHAPTER 25

tried to speak softly and as calmly as Vince had; but the panic was obvious in her voice. She glanced up to check on Vince. He was pushing on the hog's head. She returned her attention to Will.

"Jacquelyn," gently came across Will's lips. J.C. froze, holding her dad's arm and staring into his eyes. "Jacquelyn, ... I ... am ... so ... sorry. Please ... forgive ... me." Will's chest pushed hard as he struggled to get those words out.

Tears streamed down her face and her hands began to quiver as J.C. heard those words, and they sank into her heart. She dropped her head onto her father's chest and wept. Vince's hand on her back caused her to gently sit back up and wipe her face. "How are you feeling, Will?" Vince asked.

"Thanks," Will said quietly looking into Vince's face. "Did you get that hog loose?"

"No, I am going to need some help with that; but I will take care of that later. Did you try to get it free?" Vince asked.

"Yes, I tried to pull it out and I think I overexerted myself. My heart started to race. So, I stepped out of the pen and then everything just went black," Will admitted in a weakened voice to Vince.

Vince was shaking his head, "Will, you should have called."

"I know, I thought if I just give her one good tug then maybe she would be free," Will explained.

J.C. had collected her emotions but could not believe that these two men were concerned about a hog when her father obviously needed medical attention. "Dad, we need to get you to the hospital. Vince, can I use your phone to call the ambulance?" J.C. had gained some composure and was ready to take charge of things.

"J.C., I am not going to the hospital like this," Will spoke firmly. "Help me to the house so I can clean up. I will call the heart doctor in the morning and make an appointment to go see him. He only comes to Greenfield a couple of times per month anyway."

"Dad, you are not waiting to see a doctor that only comes to town a couple of times a month when you have just had what could be a heart attack." J.C. was just as stern in her response.

"Let's get Will to the house," Vince said calmly.

Collectively they all agreed. Vince bent down and put his arm under Will's left side and J.C. did the same on the right. They helped Will stand up and steadied him on his feet. The three of them walked slowly out of the barn and started up the hill.

"Where do you keep your hack saw?" Vince asked as they were walking.

"It is in the machine shed in the toolbox. If we go there, I can show you," Will offered.

"No, you are going to the house. I will find it on my own," Vince stated.

At the mudroom door, Will stepped out of his boots. Inside the door, J.C. unsnapped his overalls and then pushed them off his shoulders until they dropped to the floor. Opening the door to the kitchen, J.C. lead the three of them inside to a chair at the dining room table. They lowered Will onto the chair, and he rested his head in his hands on the dining room table and took in some deep breaths.

J.C. returned to the kitchen and brought back a glass of water.

"Thanks," Will said softly.

"Can I have that flashlight in your back pocket?" Vince asked J.C. She immediately handed it to him. "I will get the hacksaw and go free that hog. Do you have a spare gate that I can tie up to that corner for the night, Will?"

"They are in the corner next to the grain storage bins," J.C. said to Vince as he was headed back out the kitchen door.

J.C. pulled a chair up next to her dad who was rubbing his head. "Dad, please let me drive you to Des Moines tonight so that you can be examined by a heart specialist," she pleaded.

"J.C., I will be fine waiting to see Dr. Wilson. He has all my files and knows my case. This is not the first time this has happened," Will admitted.

"Dad, how many of these have you had?" J.C. spoke quickly and sternly.

"A couple, one about four years ago and one in the year before your mother passed away." Will was still breathing heavily and the pain in his head was making it harder to concentrate. "Can I lay down for a little bit?" he asked.

J.C. helped Will get to his feet and held his arm as he walked into the living room and then into his bedroom. He turned slowly and sat on the edge of the bed. J.C. guided his body down onto two pillows that she propped behind his head. Then she reached down and lifted his legs one at a time onto the bed.

"Thanks, it usually takes a while for the pounding in my head to stop after I take that Nitroglycerin," Will stated.

J.C. stood and looked at her father's body stretched out on his bed. The man she had watched these past few weeks and convinced herself that he was capable of handling his own affairs, was limp and weak. J.C. still had her chore jacket and boots on. "Dad, I am going to go hang up my chore clothes; I will be right back to check on you," J.C. spoke softly as she left her father's bedroom.

J.C. hung up her father's overalls first, opened the back door, and pulled his boots inside. She unzipped her jacket and hung it up. Immediately she pulled it off the hook and reached inside the pocket to get the bottle before returning it to the medicine cabinet. She picked up her father's glass of water and returned to his bedroom. He seemed to be calmer. "Dad, do you need another drink of water?" J.C. asked.

"No," Will said softly.

J.C. heard the kitchen door and knew that Vince had come back in. She left her father and met Vince in the dining room. "How is Will?" Vince asked.

"He is resting on his bed," J.C. replied. She stood staring at Vince with Will's water glass in her hand.

"Did he drink much water?" Vince asked.

Using her fingers, J.C. showed him on the glass, "About this much."

"Well, we should let him rest for about thirty minutes and see how his head is feeling. How are you doing?" Vince looked into J.C.'s eyes as he asked the question.

"I do not know!" J.C. exclaimed, not meaning to let so much emotion come out with her answer.

"Sit down, can I get you something?" Vince asked.

J.C. sat down at the dining room table as she shook her head 'no' to Vince's question. "I am going to get myself some water if that is OK? Vince asked as he washed up at the kitchen sink.

"Sure," J.C. replied. "How is the hog?" she asked when Vince sat down at the table.

"It's OK, I just cut the one post out of the corner gate, so it could get free and then pulled a small gate out of the pile and wired it up, so another hog can't do that. It happens more than you think. The hogs start pushing one another around the waterer and one gets punched into a spot that normally they would not fit through. At least this one was not injured in the process," Vince explained.

J.C. was not really listening to Vince's explanation. "Vince, why did you stop by tonight?" J.C. looked up into Vince's eyes to make sure she could read his response.

Vince did not answer right away. Finally, he drew in a deep breath and said,

"Kelsey was at a study group tonight for a history exam. After eating dinner alone, I remember how nice lunch was and just hopped in the car. I know I should have called. When I got here and saw the lights on in the house, but no one answered the door, I opened it and smelled fresh food. The table was set but it was obvious no one had eaten, so I started looking for you guys." Vince did not look away as he explained.

J.C. could not respond. She just stared at Vince; she was afraid he was going to say it was another 'God Moment'.

Vince smiled at her and said, "I guess God must have nudged me to come by."

J.C.'s eyes widened. He said it! God sent him! That was crazy. Every time Will was in trouble or needed something, God sends Vince? J.C. sat in total silence until she heard Vince speak.

"We should probably decide what needs to happen with Will now." J.C. stood up and started into the living room.

Vince followed J.C. back to her father's bedroom. "Dad, can you sit up and drink some water?" J.C. coaxed.

Will slowly opened his eyes. It took him a couple of blinks to clear his vision. "Vince, how is the hog?" Will asked softly.

"It is fine, how are you doing?" Vince responded.

"Better. My head does not hurt as much. I will take some of that water, J.C." Will reached for the glass in his daughter's hand.

"You really need to be checked out by a heart specialist," Vince said, "If you want, J.C. and I can drive you into Des Moines to an emergency room tonight."

"No, no, I will be fine waiting until Dr. Wilson comes to Greenfield in the next week or two," Will stated.

"I cannot let you do that, Will," Vince said. "You needed medical attention when I got here tonight and even though I am an animal doctor, I know the Hippocratic Oath and feel obliged to get you that attention."

Will looked down and shook his head. "You are not going to let this go, are you?" Will questioned.

"No. I know that Evelyn pleaded with you the last time this happened to get checked out immediately and you refused. You need a full scan of your heart and arteries. Will, you could have a blockage and the next time you exert yourself it could kill you." Vince calmly explained the importance of medical attention.

"OK. J.C. do you want me to go?" Will was asking for her input.

"Yes, Dad! I want you to find out what is going on," J.C. spoke sincerely to her father.

"OK," Will said defeated.

J.C. rushed upstairs to get the bag that she had started to pack earlier in the day, threw her laptop in her bag with her father's notebooks, and grabbed her purse. Coming back downstairs, she stopped in Will's room and packed a small bag of his things. Finally stopping in the bathroom, she added toiletries to their two bags. Vince took the bags out to his car. J.C. put the stew in the refrigerator and the biscuits into a Tupperware container. Within minutes, they had Will loaded in Vince's car. Vince called Kelsey to let her know that he would not be home when she got there but he would see her in the morning.

During the ride to Des Moines, Will went over the chores schedule with Vince. "It will be OK. I have a couple of high school boys that come and help me when I get tied up. I will call them in the morning and get them out there to help me." Vince reassured Will that everything would be taken care of.

They arrived at Mercy Hospital in downtown Des Moines at 9:00 p.m. The emergency room desk clerk took down some initial information and sent them back to an examination room. Within minutes, the ER doctor was in the room. He listened to Will's chest, ordered bloodwork, chest X-ray, ultrasound of the heart and an angiogram. While the tests were being done, Vince went to find coffee for J.C. and himself. J.C. stayed in the exam room with her father. Her mind began to replay the events of the evening. Finding Will on the ground in the hog building, Vince showing up, Will saying he was sorry. J.C. stopped her mental replay. Will had said to her he was sorry. Sorry! She had waited forty years to hear that word and tonight he told her he was sorry.

CHAPTER 25

She felt different. Then Vince saying God nudged him. Her mind was swirling, and the room started to move also. She really needed to sit down. Her legs were wobbling as the room started to spin faster. Vince caught her as she stumbled towards the chair against the wall.

"J.C. are you OK?" Vince spoke directly and with concern in his voice.

"Just a little light-headed," she admitted. Vince handed her the coffee, and she took a few sips. "Better," J.C. said as she took some deep breaths and her head cleared.

It was almost 1:00 a.m. when the ER doctor returned to report that they had found some damage. He would admit Will into the hospital and a surgeon would come by in the morning to discuss surgery. The nurses came into prep Will for transfer up to the heart floor.

J.C. followed Vince back to his car to get their bags. "Vince, thank you for helping me get dad in here tonight. I do not think I could have convinced him without your support. Thanks for organizing the chores for us also. Let me know how much you pay these guys, and I will write them a check." J.C. took the bags out of Vince's trunk.

"J.C., I will be back down tomorrow after work. If there is anything you need me to bring, just call. Make sure you get some rest," Vince said as he crawled into the driver's seat of his car.

Chapter 26

*I*t was 2:15 a.m. when Will was finally settled into a room and all the paperwork was completed. J.C. thanked the nurses and was preparing to call a taxi to take her to the condo. As she pulled her phone out, Will said, "wait, there are some things I need to say before you leave tonight."

J.C. stopped and looked directly at her father. "Dad, we can talk later. We are both exhausted and you need some sleep. It looks like you will have surgery sometime tomorrow and I want you to get some rest before hand."

"No," Will said sternly. "I have waited too long, and I need to tell you some things before you leave here tonight." He patted the side of the bed indicating that J.C. should sit down.

J.C. set the bags down, drew in a deep breath, and sat on the edge of her father's hospital bed.

"When I was four years old, my father carried my bed downstairs one night and placed it at the end of his bed. He told me I was going to sleep in there with him for a few nights. Next, he bundled me up in all the clothes I owned and took me outside with him. I realized after a few days that I had not seen my mother or either one of my two brothers for some time. I asked my dad where they were and if I could see them. He told me they were sick, and I could not see them until they got well. Occasionally I would hear my brothers crying upstairs when I was in the house. I even tried to go up there a few times, but the stairway door was locked. For the next few weeks, I went everywhere with my dad. I was only four years old, and he was my dad, so I did whatever he said, and the weeks passed by. Finally, we came in for lunch one day in late spring and my mom was sitting at the dining room table. I was afraid of her. I had not seen her in months, and she did not even look like my mom. She was older, thinner, and sickly. She said weakly 'William, come in here so I can take a look at how much my boy has grown.' My father pushed my back and I walked cautiously towards her. She cried when I got up close and then we both cried. She did not touch me or reach for me. I just stood there crying and not really understanding why I was crying. After lunch, I went back outside with dad. Mom slept in the room with us that night and every night thereafter. It was summertime I think, when dad announced one night it was time for me to go back upstairs. He carried my bed up the stairs and back into my room. When he came back down, he took my hand, walked me upstairs and I knew they were gone. No one told me. I just saw how different Jack's and John's rooms looked and I knew they had left and were not coming back. I cried myself to sleep that night and for a few nights after that; not sure why I was crying. But I was overwhelmed with the idea that my brothers were gone, and I would never see them again.

I think I was twelve when I finally asked my mother what happened. She told me they had scarlet fever and died within two days of each other. She moved upstairs to take care of them. While I was outside with dad, she came down and washed their clothes, towels, and bedding in lye soap. She would make chicken broth and take it up to them. Doctors came and went, the mortician came and went, and different ladies from the community came and went, all without my knowledge. She said she was protecting me, and she was happy that she had. When my brothers died, she brought all their clothes, bedding, and towels down and burnt them in the garden one day while dad and I were in town. She was so weak herself by the time Jack and John were gone. She stayed upstairs and dad would bring her broth and clean clothes after I went to sleep each night. She told me she wanted to die most days but when my father would tell her how I was doing, she used every bit of strength she had to get well so she could see me again." Will paused.

"My dad and I did everything together. I knew every inch of the farm and every animal on it. I knew how to drive a tractor before I started school. I could hold baby pigs when he castrated them when I was only five years old. I cooked and cleaned right alongside him. We did everything." Will had not taken his eyes off J.C.'s face since he started talking.

He drew in a deep breath and started in again, "I started school when I was six years old and did not know any different. As I progressed through school, I heard the stories of how many children died of scarlet fever that winter. These matched with the story my mother finally told me. When I wasn't at school I was farming with my dad. I loved farming and being able to help my dad is all I ever wanted to do. As I grew older, we would listen to the radio at night. I began to understand that there was a war going on and many young men from America were joining the armed forces, so they could protect America. I decided in my junior year of high school that I was going. I was already eighteen and like many of the boys in school ahead of me that had already gone, I decided to go. One day when I rode into town with dad, I walked to the enlistment office on Main Street and signed my papers. When we got back home, I announced at dinner that night what I had done. My mother cried and cried. She begged me to go back and tell them I could not serve because I was an only son and they needed me on the farm. She said to tell them she was sick and dying and they would not make me go. I was stubborn and went anyway." Will paused again.

"Basic training was hard, but I expected it to be. I met Max from New York City and Richard from Alabama and we became inseparable friends. While in basic training, we made great plans for when we got back from the war. I was going to New York City to visit Max, to Alabama to visit Richard's family, and they were both coming to the farm. We took a huge ship across the ocean and landed in France where they put us on trains that carried us into Germany. We were in full-fledged combat within hours of landing. It was overwhelming at times, but I was with Max and Richard and we had convinced ourselves we were invincible. Because I was so tall, Max and Richard always wanted me to follow them. I would look over their heads and watch for signs of danger. I got really good at picking up the slightest movement or something that looked out of place. It became a game to find the hidden danger before it found us. Except one day I was looking up and around the sides of the road we were marching on as Richard stepped on a buried land mine. His body shot up in the air in front of me and exploded into a million pieces. Within seconds, Max's did the same. I fell to the ground and blacked out. It was days later in a Berlin hospital that I found out a piece of shrapnel hit my forehead and knocked me out. I also had pieces of shrapnel in my left shoulder and a small piece had gotten caught in my leg." Will took a few deep breaths and studied J.C.'s face that was intent on hearing his every word.

"It was in Berlin that I met Everett and we became friends. I found out that he grew up south of Greenfield on a farm. We had lived within twenty miles of each other back in Iowa. Everett and I were the same age, but he had finished school before enlisting. He worked in the central office and handled all the payroll paperwork for the soldiers. Everett was really good with numbers. I was assigned there to work after my injuries. My job was logistics; making arrangements for bodies that were being sent home. I hated my job and Everett started to train me on other duties around the office so I could get promoted out of that position. It took about eight weeks until something else opened up and I got moved off the logistics desk. What a relief!

Everett and I spent most of our time off base together. Neither one of us were that adventurous so we stuck together. We did a little sightseeing but did not venture too far into the German countryside. He had a girlfriend back home that wrote to him each week and he shared her letters. I shared mine from my mother and we kept up on what was going on back home. The war ended, and Everett's rank allowed him to ship home immediately. We committed to keeping in touch once we were both back in the States. I had to serve out my enlistment time and came home eight months later. Everett and Vivian were married within weeks of me coming home. They bought a farm just three miles south of my parents and started their family immediately. Everett really did not like farming and soon took a job in town keeping books by day and trying to farm at night." Will sighed deeply before continuing.

"My mother seemed to be about the same when I got home. The day I arrived home, the yard was full of people. Dad had replaced the old porch while I was gone, and it was covered with tables of food that all the neighbors brought in. People played yard games and I think there was even some live music. I was happy to be home. Evelyn came with Nadine that day. She was very outgoing and nice to everyone that Nadine introduced her to. I knew she was a new teacher at the school, but I was way too shy to talk to her that day. It seemed like my life was just beginning and I could not wait to get back into farming. I spent my war pay on the forty acres that laid behind my father's ground and we were right back where we had always been since I was four years old." Will hesitated.

"It wasn't more than a couple of months that my mom's health really changed. She did not get out of bed. Dad fed her, bathed her, and changed the bedding when he was not able to get her up and outside to the outhouse. So, we tore out a wall in the kitchen and had a plumber come from Greenfield to put in an indoor toilet and bathtub. When that was completed, my mom seemed to get stronger for a few weeks. She spent a lot of time soaking in the tub and we were glad that she was getting stronger. One night we came in for dinner and realized she had gotten in the tub after lunch and was still there. Dad went in and when he came out, he called the doctor. The doctor came that night and it was a couple days later he came back, and she was dead. 'Her lungs just gave out,' he said when he walked into the dining room where dad and I sat at the table. We buried her next to my brothers at the Fairview Cemetery.

I did not know when my brothers were buried but that day, I heard many stories over lunch as people recalled the day my dad stood alone because my mother was too weak to come. Jack and John were buried together in the same coffin and a single white granite cross was placed at their gravesite. My father used the cross as a marker until my mother was strong enough to pick out a headstone. She never did. I have no memory of where I was that day, but I am certain I was not there," Will said sadly, but continued,

"Dad and I had worked side by side for so long. Now that I was back, we could do anything that needed to be done. We harvested a good crop that fall. Evelyn started stopping by on Saturday or Sunday to drop off food for us. My dad took a liking to her straight away and encouraged me to spend some time with her. I did not know how to ask a girl out. She talked more to dad than me when she came over.

One afternoon, dad sent me to town to pick up supplies. When I got back it seemed like he had not finished any of the feeding that normally would have been done in the afternoon. I found his body face down behind the corn crib.

The doctor said it must have been a heart attack. I am not sure what I did for the next few weeks. I guess I just went through the motions. At night I had horrible nightmares about my brothers, the war, and seeing my dad's lifeless body. I barely got any sleep. I worked harder on the farm, kept house, and then Evelyn would come. In the spring she asked if she could use my mother's garden spot. She rented a room from someone in town and did not have a place to grow anything. I said sure.

I do not know how long that went on, but I do remember the day Everett came by and said that I needed to make an honest woman out of her, or the school board would fire her. Some gossip was going around town about us that was not appropriate for a schoolteacher. So, I proposed. Still to this day I do not know why she said yes. J.C., she was my angel sent from heaven." Will smiled gently as those words crossed his lips. J.C. felt her emotions being torn but held everything inside. She stoically continued to study her father as he spoke.

Will did not speak for a few minutes and J.C. knew he was exhausted, "Dad, you need to rest; we can talk more tomorrow." J.C. started to stand.

Will reached for her hand and she let him hold it, "No, I really need to tell you this," he said.

"When you were born, I thought the curse was broken. Finally, whatever God was punishing me for was over. I saw your face on this tiny perfect body and melted. I had always been afraid to let myself really fall in love with Evelyn; never really felt worthy of her. When I saw her in that hospital bed holding the most precious baby girl in the world, I was so overjoyed. She could see in my eyes that I had changed. For the first time in my life, I was truly happy. I knew she was too. Her past had been so painful and mine was not much better, but together we had made the most beautiful thing in this world and that was you. Jacquelyn, I loved you at that moment and every moment since. I wish I could undo all the pain I have caused you." Will's face was covered in tears. J.C.'s emotions exploded and her face matched Will's.

"Dad, I know, I know," was all J.C. could say. After a few minutes of silence J.C. asked Will, "My name, Dad. Was I named after your brother Jack?"

Will drew in a deep breath and swallowed hard, "Yes, that was Evelyn's doing. I was not in favor of that at all. She convinced me that we could carry Jack and her family forward in your name. We were home from the hospital for almost a week before she finally wore me down. She said no one needs to know; it can be our special secret. I drove back into the courthouse in Greenfield and had your birth certificate issued. That night at dinner she was so happy, dancing around the dining room table holding you and that certificate up in the air singing Jacquelyn Caine Mason over and over. Our lives were perfect! You grew into a beautiful little girl. Bright and well mannered. A perfect little angel just like your mother, Evelyn."

"When Evelyn told me that she was pregnant again, I was excited and wanted a son in the worst way. Someone who would be at my side and loved farming as much as I did. Johnnie was all that and more. I knew when he was born what his name would be, and Evelyn winked at me as soon as the doctor said, 'it's a boy'! Johnnie Caine Mason brought even more joy and laughter to our home than my heart could hold. Each day I got up and thanked God for the three people that made my life so rich and full." Will stopped, and tears flowed down his face like a small river running off his jawbone, onto the pillow.

"Dad, I know you could not bear the loss of Johnnie. I know it was too hard for you." J.C. leaned forward to hug her father, but he pushed her back. J.C. felt a chill run down her back. "Dad?"

"Jacquelyn, I had to protect you just like my mother protected me. Separation." A cold chill went through the room. Will's voice was brutally cold. "It was so hard to walk out of that hospital and leave Evelyn there holding Johnnie through his final breaths; then to come home and see your face full of questions. I knew what I had to do. Push and pull myself out of the lives of the two people that I had left to love. If I loved them like I had my brothers, mother, Max, Richard, Dad and Johnnie; they were going to die. It was obvious that I was the curse that brought death time and time again." Will lay limp in the hospital bed. A nurse came in to take vitals and asked if there was anything she could do. J.C. just shook her head.

When the nurse was gone J.C. stood up and bent over her father and kissed his forehead. "I will be back in the morning to talk to the surgeon. Do you need something to help you sleep?" Will shook his head no. His eyes were closed but tears still ran down his face onto the pillow.

J.C. picked up her two bags and walked out of her father's hospital room. She pulled out her cell phone and called a cab to take her to the condo. It was 4:00 a.m.

Chapter 27

At 8:00 a.m. with a shower and less than three hours of sleep, J.C. was back at the hospital waiting in her father's room for the doctors to make their rounds. Will was resting comfortably. She had called Nadine to update her on the change of plans and Will's situation. Nadine wanted to come to Des Moines and sit with J.C. for the day. J.C. had said, "no, let's wait until after surgery." She did not share with Nadine any more details from the previous evening.

At 9:15 a.m., Dr. Milton from Iowa Heart Center came into the room. "Good morning, I am Dr. Milton. I have reviewed the test from last night's ER doctor and agree that you need to have an angioplasty procedure to insert stents in your heart. We normally would do a stress test first but based on the oral information collected from the doctor who brought you in, I think your heart has been stressed extensively in the past forty-eight hours."

"Do either of you have any questions?" Dr. Milton looked at J.C.

"Yes, how long will the surgery take, and will you check all the valves while you are in there?" J.C. asked.

"Each surgery is unique so there is no timeline that I can give you. We will check the entire heart during surgery to ensure that everything else is normal," Dr. Milton replied.

"When do you plan on doing it?" Will asked.

"I will go back to my office now and let the schedulers talk to the hospital surgery staff. Your nurse will let you know as soon as an operating room and team has been reserved. It will be later today or tomorrow most likely. Mr. Mason, you should rest as much as possible prior to the surgery. They will continue to keep you hydrated with IVs but no solid food until after surgery. Are you experiencing any chest pains now?" Dr. Milton asked.

"No," Will said.

"That is good, I will see you when they bring you down for surgery." Changing his focus to J.C. he said, "I will come out and give you an update when I have finished his procedure. The nurses will show you where to wait outside the operating room." And with that Dr. Milton turned and left the room.

For the next two hours, J.C. sat and watched Will's chest move up and down as he slept. She replayed in her mind their conversation from the night before. She had so many questions. She had so many emotions. She needed more time with Will. She had waited forty years to talk to him.

The nurse came in with a tech at 11:45 a.m. "They have scheduled your surgery for 1:30 p.m. this afternoon, Mr. Mason. We are going to begin your prep work up here. The transporter is on their way up." She brought Will out of his slumber by taking his vitals and the tech began drawing blood.

J.C. organized her books and papers back into her day bag so that she would be ready to follow the transporter. She knew this routine all too well from the months she had spent bringing her mother here for treatments.

Surgery began right on schedule at 1:30 p.m. J.C. sat in the small waiting room with two other people and tried to focus on the same book she was reading earlier. The overhead TV was on some annoying game show. She got up and went in search of coffee. While she was looking around the area for the coffee station her phone buzzed, and she saw that a text from Vince had come in. She found the coffee and poured a cup as she read his text.

'How are you doing? How is Will? Surgery yet?'

J.C. walked back to the waiting area and replied, 'Tired. Will got a few hours of sleep between 4:00 a.m. and 12:00 p.m. Surgery started at 1:30 p.m.'

'Plan to be there by 6 p.m.,' was Vince's reply.

The afternoon was long and the clock on the wall was a constant reminder of how slow time was passing. When J.C. could not keep her mind on her book any longer, she walked over to the end table and flipped through the magazines. None of them looked interesting. She started to walk away when she noticed on the back corner of the stand was a Gideon Bible. She reached for it, pulled her hand back and then reached down and picked it up.

When she was resettled in her spot, she took a sip of coffee and then opened the Bible. It fell open to Hebrews, chapter 4. Her eyes read verse 3 first. 'Those who don't believe in me will never get in.' She closed the Bible. She was not going to heaven! A sharp thought dashed through her brain. She had stopped believing in anything other than the life she was living long ago; when life ended, she expected to be made into dust through her own plan of cremation. So why did these words bother her? She believed that there was nothing after this life anyway so what if this Bible said that if she did not believe in God, she could not enter heaven's gate. Was it because so many people believed in heaven? Evelyn had taken her to Sunday school and youth groups; she even went to a Bible camp one summer, but once she went to college, she only attended church when she was with her mother. As a child she was certain her dad did not believe in a God, but she had to admit now it was confusing knowing how much time he spent reading the Bible. Vince and Kelsey obviously believed in heaven. They had both made statements about

Teri being in heaven with so much confidence that she knew they were certain of this belief.

What did she believe? What if her mother really existed in some form in the afterlife? She drew in a deep breath and let her mind go. OK, if her mom was a spiritual being then Johnnie also would be in this afterlife realm. A warm feeling went through her chest. Right now, her mother could be dancing through the meadows of flowers playing tag with Johnnie. J.C. almost hoped that could be the case. But then that would mean God did exist which would also mean God took people from earth to heaven without consideration of the impact on those left behind. A bolt of anger shot through her thinking that God made a conscious decision to destroy Johnnie's body with leukemia, a disease that not only killed Johnnie but destroyed her family. Johnnie had everything to live for. Evelyn? What about tiny little Evelyn being left at seven months of age never knowing who her parents were; never, never finding them. And finally, Vince and Kelsey losing the woman they loved. Their lives instantly changed because God decided to take her life in a car accident. No, that is not possible. The God that J.C. learned about in Sunday school was kind and loving. She immediately recalled pictures of a shepherd carrying sheep and a gentle man with long hair holding children on his knee. Those images were just to make you feel good and grow up to be nice she thought.

J.C. checked the clock; it was 2:15 p.m. She took a sip of coffee; it was cold. She returned the Bible to the table and walked around the corner to get a fresh cup of coffee.

When J.C. returned to her seat, her mind re-engaged where it had left off. Children are told these stories so they obey their parents, do not lie, steal, curse or do any of those bad things that good moral people think are right. Church and Sunday school classes are just a way to make people more manageable when they grow up. In college she met a few coeds who had never gone to church and were extremely loose with their morals. So, it just makes sense that if you teach people to pattern their lives after this Jesus guy who was perfect and if they continue with those patterns into adulthood, the world will be a better place. For the most part J.C. had followed those patterns. She had been kind, tried not to lie too much, did not steal, murder, or sleep around. So, why wasn't she good enough? J.C. took another sip of coffee. She was fine; her life philosophy was just fine. When her life was over, it was over!

Her stomach started to contract. Her heart started to beat a little faster. Her mind was jumping from end-of-life thoughts to that verse she had read in the Bible. 'Those who do not believe will never get in.' J.C. felt clammy and cold; shivers ran down her spine; and she was starting to feel a little panicky. She slowly sipped her coffee and kept her eyes glued to the clock. 2:35 p.m.–really! Could this day move any slower she thought? Just then her phone buzzed in her pocket.

"Hello?" J.C. said quietly.

"How are things goings?" Nadine asked.

"I do not know. The surgery started at 1:30 p.m. and no one has come out to talk to me yet," J.C. said anxiously.

"Well, if they started at 1:30 p.m. it will be a few hours." Nadine spoke as if she was an authority on the subject. "When Marge's husband had by-pass surgery, they were in there for six hours. I hope you have a good book."

"Really, Nadine! Can it really take that long?" J.C. said sharply. "Besides the doctor did not say anything about bypass."

"OK, it just depends on how much damage there is and how many stents they put in." Nadine sounded a little less authoritarian.

"The surgeon said two stents would be all that were needed," J.C. confirmed what she remembered Dr. Milton saying that morning.

"Yes, but when they start checking around, they might find...," Nadine stopped mid-sentence to keep from adding to J.C.'s anxiety. "Honey, I wish you would let me come down there, I could leave now and be there before dark."

"No, it does not make any sense for two people to sit here staring at a clock on the wall that does not move!" J.C. expressed her frustrations. "Besides, Vince will be here in a couple of hours."

"Vince, why is he coming?" Nadine asked inquisitively.

Oh, no. J.C. could not believe that she had let that slip out with Nadine on the phone; now she had no choice but to tell her. "Vince came by the farm last night and helped me bring Will into Des Moines. Before you get too excited Nadine, just listen. It was a miracle that he did because when I went out looking for dad, I did not take my phone with me. I found Will face down in the center of the hog building and was trying to decide if I should leave him and run to the house and get my phone when Vince walked in and knew exactly what to do. He sent me to the house to get the Nytro pills and kept dad's head up, so he could breathe until the Nytro took effect. Then together we got Will to the house. After the Nytro had slowed his heart down to a normal pace, it was Vince that convinced dad to come into Des Moines."

"Well, that's good. I was wondering how you managed to get him in your car and down there by yourself. That Vince is such a nice guy." Nadine paused, "So he is coming back down tonight?"

"Yes, he hired some high school guys to help him with dad's chores for the next few days. Yes, Nadine, Vince is the ultimate Nice Guy!" J.C. sighed watching the clock move to 3:00 p.m.

"Honey, I am glad that Vince is coming back to check on you; you need some support. I think I will come down tomorrow. Do not try and talk me out of it ... I am coming! Call me when he gets out of surgery." Nadine spoke to J.C. like she was her mother.

"Thanks, Nadine. Yes, it will be great to see you tomorrow. Make sure you wait and come late enough that you miss the morning rush. Will won't be up too early anyway or ready for any company." J.C. returned the daughter-like compassion hoping that Nadine would not be stressed out with city driving.

"OK, I will call you before I leave." Nadine hung up.

It was 5:45 p.m. when Vince texted that he was in the parking lot. 'Just parked the car. Where are you?'

'Still waiting outside the operating room on the first floor. When you get in the lobby follow the signs to the chapel. Turn right past the chapel and follow the signs to surgery. I will watch for you.'

Within minutes, Vince was there. He had a gentle smile on his face. J.C. returned a tired smile. She pointed toward the coffee pot and Vince poured a cup for himself and followed J.C. back into the waiting area. She was the only person left there. An hour earlier the other people who were waiting got called back to visit with the doctor.

"Long day?" Vince asked. He pulled out a zip lock bag of granola bars. "Kelsey sent these."

J.C. nodded. "I cannot believe it takes this long to put in two stents." J.C. was worried, and Vince could see it in her face and hear it in her voice. Seeing the bars, she realized she was a little hungry and took one out and started to eat it.

"I am sure they go slow to make sure everything is perfect." Vince tried to instill some confidence.

Just then the door opened, and Dr. Milton stepped out. He looked around and not seeing anyone else in the area walked over and sat in the chair next to J.C. "First of all, your father is fine. His heart is very strong. The damage was not as bad as the scope indicated. We did find a small tear in one valve. It looked new and probably occurred during the recent stress on his heart. I have repaired the tear and inserted stents. We did experience some blood pressure issues during surgery which caused us to slow down and stabilize him a couple of times. He is a very strong man for seventy-five. I expect a good recovery, but he must rest for at least six weeks.

No strenuous activities. His heart needs to heal completely. Do you understand?"

J.C. nodded that she did. "Can I see him?"

"Not yet, they are moving him into recovery. They will come get you in about forty-five minutes. I will be back in the morning to see him." Dr. Milton smiled and stood up. He shook J.C.'s hand and Vince's although he was never introduced to him.

J.C. collapsed back into her seat. Vince sat down next to her. "Will is going to be OK. The doctor said he is very strong for his age."

"I know." J.C.'s emotions and mind were all over the place. She was trying to reconcile all her feelings over the past twenty-four hours. "It will be nice when we can finally see him," she said softly to Vince.

Just before 7:00 p.m., the door opened again and a large man in scrubs announced into the open air, "Family for William Mason." J.C. and Vince rose together and followed him down a hallway and behind a curtain where Will lay completely flat on a gurney. His color was light grey and J.C.'s mind shot back to the last time she looked at her mother. Will looked dead just like Evelyn had that final time before they pulled the sheet over her face.

J.C. bent down and kissed Will's forehead. "Dad, I am here," she whispered. J.C. and Vince stood in silence for about ten minutes before Will's eyes started to focus on them.

"Jacquelyn, I am sorry. I am so sorry." Will could barely get the words out. "Please forgive me, Jacquelyn."

"Dad, just rest; we can talk later. Right now, you need to rest." J.C. said softly.

"You were my little princess. I loved you most of all." Will's voice was gradually getting stronger. "I loved Evelyn because she was my guardian angel; and Johnnie because he was the son that reminded me of how I was there for my dad all those years. But you, Jacquelyn, you were special, so delicate and so strong. You were beautiful, graceful, and smart. I loved watching you dance around the yard with your baton working each week on a new routine. You do not know this, but I was at all your home softball games. I parked out behind the equipment shed and watched from my pickup window. Remember that game against Adair-Casey. No Hitter! I was so proud of you; I thought my heart would burst right out of my chest. You should have gotten a softball scholarship instead of a band scholarship. Oh well, band was fine, and Evelyn and Nadine sure enjoyed coming to watch you perform at the ISU games. Jacquelyn, can you ever forgive me?" Will was looking right into J.C.'s eyes as rambling thoughts were pouring out of him.

"Dad," J.C. sighed "rest!" Her emotions were so raw she wanted to yell at the top of her lungs and at the same time throw her arms around his neck, but instead she held it together in front of Vince and the attending nurse. J.C. also knew that the anesthetic was giving Will the courage to say things that he may not even mean.

"Will, J.C. is right, you really need to rest. The doctor said your blood pressure was a little erratic during surgery. We are going to stay here with you but try and rest so that they can move you back up to a normal room." Vince's voice was calm.

J.C. stood frozen at the side of the gurney looking into her father's eyes.

Chapter 28

*D*r. Milton and Dr. Wilson came into Will's room at 7:45 a.m. and woke him up. J.C. had been there for about fifteen minutes. "Well, Mr. Mason, you finally gave in and let someone take a look inside that chest of yours," Dr. Wilson said. "Hello, I am your father's cardiologist." Dr. Wilson extended his hand toward J.C.

"Nice to meet you," J.C. responded. "How long have you taken care of my father?"

"Over ten years now. I am also with Iowa Heart Center and rotate out to the county hospitals a couple of times each month. Your mother brought him into Adair County Hospital one day with chest pains and we have been monitoring him ever since. I wanted to do a scope then, and again after his last episode, but Will is pretty stubborn." Dr. Wilson smiled at Will when he made that comment.

"Well, now what does he need?" J.C. stood with her back straight and looked directly at both doctors.

Dr. Milton was listening to Will's chest after reviewing his chart. "It looks like you had a good night. Today they will introduce some soft foods and get you upright a few times to see how your pressure holds up. Tomorrow we will get you on your feet if today goes well and then some physical therapy before you go home. It is mostly rest for six weeks, Mr. Mason. At your age you cannot afford to push this too fast. Do what we say, and you should have a great recovery." Dr. Milton nodded at Dr. Wilson to take over.

"Will, this is not up for discussion. You will not be able to farm at all until I say so. Do you have a plan for someone to take care of things for you?" Dr. Wilson asked.

J.C. answered before Will could. "I will make sure that everything is taken care of at the farm, and he does not leave the house until you give him permission."

Dr. Wilson looked puzzled at J.C.

"I have been home for over a month and know the chore routine; currently we have hired some additional help to take care of daily chores and we'll hire contractors for spring work if needed. I will make sure he honors the plan." She did not look at Will but at both doctors to confirm her commitment to keeping Will on task.

"Great," said Dr. Wilson. "Will, I will stop in each day until you are released. Dr. Milton was responsible for the surgery, but I will take it from here."

Will shook hands with Dr. Milton. "Thank you," he said with a smile.

"You are welcome; take care of yourself and do exactly what these two people tell you to do," he said with a wave of his hand at Dr. Wilson and J.C.

"Doesn't sound like I am going to have a choice," Will said.

"I will see you tomorrow," Dr. Wilson said as both doctors turned and left the room.

The nurse came in as the doctors were leaving and started her morning routine. She checked his bandage, took his blood pressure, temperature, uncovered his feet to check his circulation and then started in. "Do you feel like eating something? You can have some broth or Jell-O to start with."

Will hesitated and said, "Jell-O, orange, please."

"Have you taken your diabetes medications in the past two days?" was her next question.

"No," Will looked to J.C. to confirm. "No, he hasn't," J.C. confirmed.

"We will restart those meds today. You will also get a shot to avoid blood clots each day you are here. No getting out of bed today. Call us for the urinal or bed pan. If you behave today, tomorrow we can get you up for those things. A physical therapist will be in today to walk you through the exercises that you'll start soon. Your body needs rest, so try and sleep as much as possible these next couple of days. Buzz the nurses' station if you have questions or need something. I will be back in with your meds." With those instructions, the nurse turned and left Will's room.

Nadine walked into Will's hospital room at 10:00 a.m. on Thursday. "How are you doing?" she said to the open air as she entered the room.

Both J.C. and Will spoke at the same time. "Tired," J.C. said. "Good," Will said.

Nadine was a little taken aback that Will spoke so readily to her. She focused on him. "Will, you know this is serious stuff. The heart is not something you can push too far. You gave us all a scare," she said as she patted the back of his hand that lay on the side of his hospital bed.

"Of course, you are tired, dear," she said as she walked over to J.C. She patted her shoulder and asked, "Where is the coffee in this place? I will go and get us some."

"I will walk downstairs with you and let dad rest. They really want him to get as much rest as possible these next couple of days," J.C. said standing up and motioning for Nadine to head towards the door. "Dad, rest, we will be back to check on you later."

Nadine spun around and was out in the hallway before she could even say goodbye to Will. "Well, I guess we know who is in charge here!" she said sarcastically to J.C.

CHAPTER 28

J.C. did not respond. She just walked to the elevator and pushed the down arrow. "Nadine, let's get some coffee so we can talk."

A new Starbuck's Coffee shop had just opened in the lobby of Mercy Hospital, so J.C. led them around the corner from the elevators. She purchased two cups of coffee and looked at Nadine, "Do you want a pastry or cookie?"

"Sure." Nadine smiled.

J.C. pointed at two items in the case and added those to her bill before handing over her credit card for payment. Once she had the coffee and pastries, she led Nadine to a table next to the windows.

Nadine took off her coat and draped it over the chair where she had set her purse down. Slowly looking around, she sat down and situated herself into a comfortable position. J.C. did the same.

"How was your drive in?" J.C. inquired.

"Easy," Nadine replied taking her first sip of coffee.

"Good, I am glad you waited until the traffic was lighter," J.C. commented.

"Lighter? Des Moines traffic is always heavy!" Nadine shot back.

"You would understand lighter if you had to drive into downtown at 7:30 a.m. on a workday," J.C. said confidently.

"How is Will doing?" Nadine asked.

"Pretty well." J.C. took a sip of coffee and a deep breath. "Like I said last night, the surgeon was impressed with how strong his heart was for seventy-five years of age. He is in good physical shape. Both doctors think he can make a full recovery if he lets those stents heal completely before trying to do too much."

"What are you going to do about the farm work?" Nadine asked.

"Manage it," J.C. said quickly.

"How are you going to manage it? You cannot do all that yourself," Nadine cautioned.

"I know. Vince said there is a young vet on their staff that is a farm kid from up north. He is not married and thinks he might be interested in helping out with the animals. I can interview some local farmers that do custom field work to plant the crops and put on fertilizer this spring. Nadine, I really can manage this for a couple of months," J.C. said with the utmost confidence. "I have been helping out with chores and can probably do most of the daily work myself."

"Really, are you planning on sticking around that long?" Nadine asked.

"I already told you that I am not pressed for money and have more than twenty months left on my severance package from IBM. I will manage!" J.C. wanted Nadine to know that was not the biggest concern she had right now.

"OK?" Nadine hesitated to say anything more; she studied J.C.'s face that looked like it was about to explode.

J.C. and Nadine sat in silence sipping their coffee, eating their pastries, and studying each other.

"I really think he looks good for five hours of surgery." Nadine finally broke the silence.

"Yes," J.C. responded but her mind seemed somewhere else. Just then her phone rang. "Hello."

"Jacquelyn, this is Ken Barr. I heard at coffee this morning that Will had a heart attack and is in Mercy Hospital in Des Moines. Is that correct?" he asked solemnly.

"Yes, Ken, that is true. Will had surgery yesterday and is doing well," J.C. responded.

"Great, that is good to hear, Jacquelyn. Did you and Will ever talk about what you and I did a couple of weeks ago?" Ken asked.

"No, Ken. You and I did not talk about anything as you remember," J.C. said sharply.

Ken paused before responding. "Jacquelyn, ask Will if he needs me to come down. If he does, I can be there tomorrow in the afternoon. You can reach me at this number." Ken hung up.

J.C. pulled her phone away from her ear and looked at it confused.

"What did Ken want?" Nadine asked.

"He wants to know if dad needs to talk to him," J.C. said with some confusion in her voice. "That man is strange."

"Which man?" Nadine asked.

"Both, Will and Ken!" J.C. said sarcastically. "We better head back upstairs and check on Will." J.C. picked up their trash and carried it to a trash can next to the counter. She returned and picked up her cup of coffee and they both walked to the elevators.

When they got to Will's room, he was sitting up in bed. He smiled at them as they walked in the door.

"Wow, how does it feel to be upright?" Nadine asked.

"Great," Will said with gusto, "I plan on working my way out of here in the next day or two."

"Dad, remember what the surgeon said? Six weeks if you do everything according to the book," J.C. reminded her father. "Ken Barr called me this morning. He had heard that you were here. He wants to know if you need to see him," J.C. asked.

"No, I am not dying! Tell him I will give him a call when I am back home," Will said firmly.

"OK," J.C. said. They visited with Will for a few minutes and when the nurses came in, J.C. suggested, "Nadine, let's head over to the condo and maybe catch some lunch with Doris. Dad, I will be back later today to check on you."

Nadine and J.C. walked down the hallway to the elevators. "Where are you parked?" J.C. asked.

"I am just inside that little parking ramp on the first floor." Nadine pointed to the east as they were walking out of the elevator.

They walked in silence to Nadine's car.

Chapter 29

*I*t was Friday at 8:30 a.m. when Dr. Wilson told Will how well things were going. "I am going to release you today. Will, you are surprising all the staff here on how well you are recovering. J.C. has agreed to take you to her place in Des Moines for the next week so you can get back and forth to physical therapy. I will see you in my office a week from today, and we will discuss your return to the farm at that time."

Will smiled, "Thanks, Doc. I won't let you down. I will be ready to head back to the farm next week. You can tell those therapists to crank it up a notch or two. I think I can do more than they are giving me right now."

"Will, take it slow. Remember, you are seventy-five, and your body will take more time than you think to heal on the inside, even when the outside looks good." Turning his head, Dr. Wilson said, "J.C., I am counting on you to keep him under control."

"I will," J.C. responded.

It took two hours for the nurses to go through all the paperwork, follow-up instructions, and prescriptions. J.C. called Nadine at 10:30 a.m. and asked her to come to the hospital and pick them up. They met Nadine at the front door at 10:50 a.m. and loaded Will into her car.

When they got back to the condo, Will opened the back-seat door, and stood up before either J.C. or Nadine were out of the vehicle. "Dad, slow down! Just rest there a minute while I get your bags and then you can lean on me as we walk to the elevator." J.C. was very stern in her instructions.

Will shook his head. He was not used to being dependent on someone else.

When they were inside J.C.'s condo, Nadine brought her bags out of the guest room. "I already washed the sheets, and they are in the dryer," she said.

"Thanks, Nadine. You did not need to do that." J.C. appreciated these past few days of Nadine's company. The night before, they had discussed that Nadine would head back to Stuart today.

"I put a roast in the oven first thing this morning with some potatoes and carrots. They should be ready around noon," Nadine commented.

"Aren't you staying for lunch before you drive home?" J.C. inquired.

"No, that is not a good plan. If I eat lunch, I will be too tired to drive this afternoon. I am heading out now and will be home in time to have lunch there. Will, you do exactly what the doctors and J.C. say, and I will see you as soon as you get back to the farm." Nadine pulled her jacket on.

"Nadine, thank you so much for all your help this week," J.C. said.

"Thanks, Nadine," Will also said.

After Nadine left, J.C. took Will's things into the guest room. She got the sheets out of the dryer and made the bed again. Will was seated next to her front window, looking down at the street below when she came back into the living room. "Sure is busy down there," Will said.

"Yes, it is. Dad, I will finish getting lunch ready and then you better lay down and rest for a little while," J.C. said.

"Do you have one of those walking machines in your building, like the one in the therapy center at the hospital?" Will asked.

"Yes," J.C. said with some hesitation in her voice. "Why, Dad?"

"I would like to get some exercise each day, and not just on the days when we are scheduled to go back to the hospital for physical therapy. I have been on it the last two days and it makes sense that if I continue to do that, I will get my strength back sooner." Will was beginning to make his plan.

"We will see after your nap," J.C. said cautiously.

During lunch, J.C. informed Will that Vince and Kelsey would be coming down for dinner that night and bringing her car in from the farm. J.C. was grateful that she would have her own transportation again, especially now that Nadine left with her car. "Since they are coming tonight, I am going to walk down to the market and get some groceries while you rest. Is there anything that you would like me to pick up while I am out?" J.C. asked.

"Some ice cream sounds really good," Will said with enthusiasm in his voice.

J.C. smiled, "What flavor do you like?"

"Neapolitan!" Will said.

A chill went down J.C.'s spine. She had forgotten that Neapolitan ice cream had been Johnnie's and Will's favorite while she and Evelyn liked French Vanilla. "Neapolitan, it is!" she said with a smile.

J.C.'s walk to the small grocery store downtown would normally take her thirty minutes round trip in her former rushed life. Today, she took her time. J.C. stopped at Fredrick's and got a cup of coffee in the skywalk and then she stopped at Boesen Florists and purchased a bouquet of flowers before ending up at the market. First, she went to the freezer section and scanned to make sure they had Neapolitan ice cream. None. They had various kinds of gelato along with frozen yogurts but no Neapolitan. She stopped and texted Kelsey who she knew would be getting out of school at any moment and hoped she could do her a quick favor. 'Kelsey, need a favor. Can you bring a box of Neapolitan ice cream from Al's tonight?' Thx. J.C. J.C. continued to pick up the other items she needed for dinner. When she was checking out, her phone buzzed. 'Sure! Kelsey'.

It was a cool afternoon, but J.C. decided to walk back on the street instead of using the skywalk. It was only four blocks and it felt good to get some fresh air.

When J.C. got back to the condo, Will was still sleeping. She knew it would be hard for him to slow down, but Dr. Wilson was right. His body needed to heal on the inside and that meant rest.

J.C. found a vase and put the flowers in the center of her table. She prepared her chicken ingredients and placed them in the oven to bake. Next J.C. mixed up the pie crust for her chicken pot pie. She wanted Vince and Kelsey to know how much she appreciated all their support this week, so she pulled out her recipes and started the sour cream chocolate cake that would go nicely with the ice cream that Kelsey was picking up for her.

Around 3:00 p.m., Will came out of the guest room. "Something smells pretty good out here," he said smiling.

J.C. looked up and was happy to see he looked rested. "How was your nap?" she asked.

"Good, I pulled the blinds down and closed the door, so it was pretty dark in there. You know us old farmers can't sleep when the sun is shining." Will chuckled.

"Can I get you some coffee or water?" J.C. asked.

"Coffee sounds good but let me get it. You keep working on whatever you're making." Will walked around the island and poured himself a cup of coffee. Once he had filled his cup, he sat down on one of the bar stools across the island from where J.C. was making her cake.

"Ken Barr calls me almost every day to check on you, Dad," J.C. informed Will.

"I'm sorry he is such a pest. I am sure he wants to finalize some things for Everett's place," Will said.

J.C. looked at Will with confusion in her face. "Why is Ken talking to you about Everett's farm?" she asked.

Will took a sip of coffee and leaned forward towards J.C. "It's not Everett's farm. I own it and Ronald and Marie probably want to sell Everett's assets, so Ken just wants to make sure the legal work is current." Will leaned back on the stool and took another sip of coffee.

"Dad, why do you own Everett's farm?" J.C. was still confused.

"Everett was never a farmer. He worked in town during the day and tried to farm at night but couldn't make that work, so FHA was going to foreclose on him. He came to me and we decided that I would buy the land, farm it and he kept a lifetime lease on the building site. Vivian was worried about what people would think, so this way no one needed to know. After Vivian died, Everett told Ronald and Marie. They had both left home by then and neither one of them wanted to farm so they were thankful that their parents had been able to live there without any of the neighborhood gossip. It made your mother really proud that we were able to help them out when they were struggling," Will explained without any emotion or pride in his voice.

J.C. was moved at the humility and compassion her father had shown to his friend. "Dad, that is amazing. How many years ago was that?" J.C. asked.

"About forty-five years ago," Will stated.

J.C. dropped the spoon into the mixing bowl. "Dad, you have worked his land and kept his secret for forty-five years?" she gasped.

"Everett took care of me during the war," Will stated firmly. "I was struggling after Max and Richard died; that's when the nightmares started up again. Some guys were getting discharged because they could not hold it together. I really hated the logistics desk and Everett knew that work added to my nightmares. He trained me to type and do higher level office work to get me off that desk. I owed him and this seemed like the right thing to do. Evelyn had just given birth to Johnnie. We thought maybe someday that could be Johnnie's place..." Will's voice trailed off and his eyes saddened.

J.C. stood frozen at her kitchen island. This was a side of Will that she had never seen. She was getting to know Will, and it felt like meeting a stranger for the first time.

Chapter 30

'We are parked on Third Street at the east side of your building. I am first, with Kelsey right behind me.' It was a text from Vince at 6:00 p.m.

'Press 2510 into the code pad and pull into the garage. I will meet you down on Parking Level two.' J.C. texted back.

"Dad, Vince and Kelsey are here. I am going down to show them where to park. We will be right back," J.C. said over her shoulder as she headed out the door. When the elevator opened on Parking Level two, she saw her car and Vince's car waiting on the side of the driveway. J.C. walked out and waved toward her car to follow her. She walked forward about six stalls and motioned for Vince to pull in. Next, she waved for Kelsey to follow her further down that side of the garage to the end where there were visitor spaces. Kelsey parked Vince's car and jumped out. "J.C., it is so good to see you. Are you doing OK?" she asked.

"Sure," J.C. responded not expecting Kelsey to be so concerned. Kelsey was walking to the back of the car and J.C. followed her. She opened the trunk; inside was a cooler. Kelsey leaned in and pulled out a bag with the ice cream. "Thank you so much; this is my dad's favorite," J.C. stated.

CHAPTER 30

"That's funny, it is my grandpa's too." Kelsey laughed.

"Well, let's get your dad and go upstairs," J.C. said.

They walked back to where Vince had parked J.C.'s car and he handed her the keys. "Thanks, Vince, I can't thank you enough for all the help this week. This is really over the top bringing my car in tonight."

"I loved it," Kelsey said. "This is my first time driving alone into Des Moines. Dad let me drive with him a couple of times to the mall on the west side but never downtown and by myself," she said gleefully.

"I owe you both!" J.C. smiled as they reached the elevator and headed back upstairs to her condo.

When they reached the twenty-fifth floor, Vince asked, "Which door is Doris'?"

"This one," J.C. said pointing to the one next to hers.

Vince knocked on the door. They waited as Doris slowly opened the door. "Hello, Doris, I am Vince Martin, Kelsey's dad. I just wanted to thank you again for helping us find the perfect prom dress and giving Kelsey those shoes. Will you please let me pay you for the shoes?" Vince asked.

"Well, I'll be. It is so nice to see you again Kelsey and meet your father. No, absolutely not, you cannot pay for those old things. Like I told J.C. they were on their way to Goodwill or the trash, so I am glad that this lovely little lady could use them," Doris exclaimed.

"They brought my car back from the farm." J.C. gave Doris an explanation for the interruption.

"Well, that is so nice of you to help out my friend this week. She has had a busy week," Doris said.

"Yes, I have, and they have really done more than anyone could ask at the farm and now here. We better get in and check on Will. Doris, I will talk to you tomorrow." J.C. knew that Doris could talk for hours if she did not keep things moving.

"OK, it was so nice to meet you, Mr. Martin," Doris said as she closed her door.

"Will, you are looking good," Vince said as he walked into J.C.'s condo.

"Feeling good too," Will said.

"Will, this is my daughter, Kelsey. She is a junior at Stuart High School," Vince said motioning for Kelsey to shake Will's hand.

"So nice to meet you, Mr. Mason," Kelsey said.

"Just Will." He shook her hand and smiled at Kelsey.

J.C. had the table prepared and began bringing the food from the kitchen into the dining area.

"How are the chores going? Did you find those feed logs I told you were in my office?" Will asked.

"Sure did, things are going well. Josh Davidson, the young vet that came out with me last fall when we worked on those steers is helping me with your chores. He is a farm kid from northeast Iowa and knows what he is doing. The younger guys I mentioned had track practice after school, so it works best to have Josh help me at your place. I will need to order feed this week. Does the elevator deliver a premix for the hogs?" Vince asked.

"Yes, you can see the ticket in my desk drawer from last month and just have them send the same order out," Will said. "I grind that into the corn from the grain bins and fill the feed bin in the corner of the hog barn."

"OK, we can wait on selling that first lot until you get home. I think they will still be under the weight limit for another two to three weeks." Vince and Will were fully engaged in chore discussions.

Kelsey was helping J.C. bring the food to the table and quietly updating J.C. on her life. "Jason and I are talking more since the play. He is really easy to talk to and I am getting excited about prom," Kelsey shared with J.C.

"That is great. You will have a lot of fun. Do you plan on getting your hair or nails done that day?" J.C. asked.

CHAPTER 30

"I do not know. Some girls are going all out, like coming to Des Moines to spas and all. I think that is ridiculous," Kelsey said.

"I agree, but if you just want to get a manicure/pedicure, I could see if my nail salon has an opening that day," J.C. offered.

"Thanks, I will think about it," Kelsey said.

"I think everything is ready if you guys are ready to eat," J.C. announced over the dining room table, directing her comments towards Vince and Will.

Everyone took a seat at the table. "Vince would you please say grace for us?" J.C. asked.

"Dear Father in Heaven we thank you for the healing power we see working in Will. We thank you for helping Kelsey drive safely through rush hour traffic today. We thank you for our new friendship with J.C. and this wonderful meal that she has prepared for us tonight. Please pour out your blessings on her for this bountiful meal. Amen." Vince lifted his head and smiled at J.C.

"Oh, Kelsey, I was not thinking about you driving in rush hour traffic today. Were you nervous?" J.C. asked.

"Not at all. I just kept one eye on the bumper of your car and the other eye in the rear-view mirror." Kelsey crossed her eyes and made a funny face. They all burst out laughing... even Will.

"It is good experience for her to start driving in the city. A year from now she will be headed off to college and needs to get some experience driving on her own," Vince said.

Dinner went well with just casual small talk about the news from Stuart and J.C.'s condo that Vince was seeing for the first time. When the main course was finished, J.C. picked up plates and headed back to the kitchen to prepare the dessert.

"I have cake and ice cream," she announced from the counter.

"Sour cream chocolate?" Vince said with a question in his tone.

"Yes, sorry Kelsey, no homemade ice cream; but Dad, Kelsey brought Neapolitan from Al's and I picked up some chocolate gelato at the market today. Dad, I already know you want Neapolitan; Vince and Kelsey what is your preference?" J.C. asked.

"Chocolate on chocolate sounds perfect for me," Vince said.

"Same here!" Kelsey said.

J.C. sliced the cake and placed four pieces on dessert plates and then added scoops of ice cream and gelato on the side.

J.C. poured coffee for Will, Vince and herself and brought Kelsey a glass of milk. They all enjoyed their dessert with very little conversation. "This is even better than the last one," Kelsey said licking her lips after her last bite. "You are going to have to teach me how to make this."

"It tastes just like Evelyn's," Will said softly. "You definitely got your mother's gift for baking."

J.C. blushed and felt awkward not being used to receiving a compliment from her father. She started clearing the table and put things away. Vince immediately stood and began helping her.

Will finished his coffee and went to the chair next to the window. "Kelsey, look at all these people on the street tonight." Will called Kelsey over to the window.

"Wow, they are coming from every direction and going into the Civic Center." Kelsey looked to the corner marquee to see what was playing. "It says Billy Joel, who is that?" she asked.

"He was a popular singer back in the 1970s," Will said. "I am certain you would not know any of his music and it's probably why so many people look like they are your dad's age." He laughed.

"Dinner was delicious." Vince complimented J.C. again.

"Thanks, just a small down payment towards what I am now indebted to you for. Thanks for getting Josh started with the chores. Once we get back to the farm, I think I can handle the day-to-day stuff. May need a hand every once in a while, when it is time to sell or sort livestock. How does he want to be paid? Weekly? Bi-monthly?" J.C. wanted to make sure that Vince was not paying him.

"He is fine working that out once you get there. I did not make any financial arrangements. Just told him you were a fair businesswoman and would take care of him," Vince said with a big smile.

"Thanks, and my car! I cannot tell you what it meant to me that you and Kelsey would bring that in. In fact, I am going to box up this cake and send that and the chocolate gelato home with you. Dad is not supposed to eat a lot of sweets and I do not need them." J.C. pulled out a large square Tupperware container and placed the cake in it. She left it on the corner of the island. "You have a cooler, so we will take some ice down and pack it so you can take the gelato home with you."

"I am not going to say no to my favorite dessert," Vince said with a big smile. "Kelsey, it is almost 8:00 p.m. We need to head back home, so you can be up and ready for show choir in the morning."

"OK. J.C., can I show my dad your bedroom before we go?" Kelsey asked.

"Kelsey Martin! Where are your manners? That is not something you ask when you are a guest in someone's home." Vince spoke in a stern tone to his daughter.

"Vince, it is fine." J.C. said immediately. "Here it is, right down this hallway." They all followed J.C. back to the bedroom.

"Very nice," Vince said.

"Look at the bathroom and closet." Kelsey coached. "Don't these look like the pictures Mom showed us from all her decorating magazines?"

"Yes," Vince said with a soft smile. They all stood and admired the spacious and classic decorated room. J.C. realized as they were standing there in silence, that Will had also followed them.

"Well, good night, Will. Continue to do what you are doing, and I agree you will be back home in a few days," Vince said. "J.C., call if you think of anything else you need or want us to check on at the farm."

"Thanks for the great dinner," Kelsey said.

"Wait," J.C. said picking up the container with the cake. "Take this." She handed the cake to Kelsey. Turning back to the refrigerator, she pulled out the container of gelato and put it in a plastic grocery bag and then dumped ice into the bag. She handed the bag to Vince.

"Wow, we get the cake and gelato!" Kelsey was smiling from ear to ear.

"Enjoy!" J.C. said.

Chapter 31

On Saturday, J.C. got up at 6:30 a.m. and put on her workout clothes. She was excited that she had been able to work out regularly this past week while she was back home. When she entered the living room, Will asked, "can I join you?"

"Sure," J.C. responded tentatively.

"I want to try out that treadmill like the therapist puts me on at the hospital," Will said as they headed out the door to the elevator.

"OK," J.C. responded with surprise in her voice.

J.C. was pleased to see that they had the facility all to themselves. She showed Will how to set the controls on the treadmill and then started on the elliptical herself. The news was on the TV, but J.C. did not change it. She kept an eye on Will to make sure he was not pushing too hard. He seemed to be going at a steady pace.

After their workout, J.C. prepared a light breakfast and they sat down to eat. J.C. noticed her stomach was a little nervous. Her mind raced to think of something they had just seen on the news that she could open the conversation with.

"Vince Martin is such a nice guy," Will said before J.C. had a chance to speak.

"The ultimate nice guy," J.C. replied.

"I do not know where I would be without his help with the chores right now. I have met this new vet, Josh, once. He seems to be a trustworthy sort of guy. I will feel better once we are back there and can see for myself how he is handling things," Will said with caution in his voice.

"Agree, but I trust Vince would not have him involved if he didn't have confidence in him," J.C. reassured Will.

"Dad, if you are going to continue working out, maybe we should go and buy some tennis shoes and sweatpants today." J.C. had finally thought of a topic.

"OK. I noticed my dress shoes are too slick for the treadmill, so I kick them off and walk in my socks. Why do I need sweatpants? My jeans are comfortable enough?" Will said with a question in his voice.

"Yes, I noticed you were walking in your socks, which is not good on your feet. So, we will get you some walking shoes." J.C. smiled before she continued. "And Dad, you will not believe how comfortable sweatpants are. I know you have lived in jeans your whole life but once you lounge in loose fitting sweatpants, you may never want to wear jeans again." J.C. was laughing as she finished.

"Well, I can tell you right now, I am not going to be seen in town in those things. I have seen plenty of men much younger than me in town in them and they look ridiculous!" Will stated firmly.

"OK, well there are all sorts of options; some classier than others." J.C. was still giggling a little thinking of Will in workout clothes. She got up and freshened both of their coffees.

As she was returning to the table, Will asked, "J.C. do you think I have that PTSD?"

"What? Where did you get that idea?" J.C. stopped and stared at Will.

"Everett and I talked about it a few times and then last week, I watched a segment on the news about it. I am not trying to make an excuse for how I have acted all these years, but maybe there is something to this." Will's head was bowed over his breakfast and his voice gradually got lower.

J.C. sat down and waited before she responded. Her mind started to race through the definition of post-traumatic stress disorder–extreme trauma from a terrifying event or ordeal that a person has experienced or witnessed, especially one that is life-threatening or causes physical harm leaving a person feeling fear and helplessness. Will definitely had experiences that would qualify. "Dad, I guess it is possible with the loss of your brothers at a young age, your army friends, your own injury during the war and then your parents dying might be categorized as PTSD. I am sure the loss of Johnnie brought a huge sense of helplessness, too. Do you want to talk to the doctor about this?" J.C. was gently trying to identify where Will was headed with this question.

"No, I just wondered what you thought," Will said quietly. "I really do not think a shrink could fix me now?" Will's voice trailed off as if he was thinking of something more but did not say it.

J.C. did not know how to respond. "Dad, I just want you to get better both physically and mentally." She had said it! Her father struggled with some mental demons; were they categorized as PTSD or something else? She was not sure; but something had kept Will from living and loving her and Evelyn for the past forty years.

Will sat in silence and sipped his coffee for a few minutes.

When Will started to speak, the walls seemed to close in, and the air got heavier. "J.C., I started to tell you at the hospital how much I regretted these past forty years. I truly believed that God was punishing me for something that I had done. I spent hours searching the Bible hoping to find answers that would bring everything back to normal." Will paused. "It wasn't until I lay face down in the hog barn begging God not to take me, that I realized God was not punishing me. I was! As my heart was pumping and sweat was pouring off my body, the first Bible verse came to my mind; 'My flesh and my heart failed: but God is the strength of my heart, and my portion forever'. Psalms 73:26, 'I felt such a peace come over me as if someone was watching over me'. Next came Psalms 37:24, 'though he falls, he shall not be utterly cast down: for the Lord upheld him with his hand'. Finally, Jeremiah 30:17, 'For I will restore health unto thee, and I will heal thee of thy wounds, saith the Lord'." Will looked deep into J.C.'s eyes that were wide with confusion. "I wanted to be able to explain everything to you. I wanted to say I was sorry. I wanted to tell you how much I loved you. I wanted to make things right between us. I prayed for this chance to explain."

J.C. was frozen in her chair. She did not say a word but stared straight into Will's eyes.

"I started having nightmares when my brothers were crying upstairs. I wondered when I would get sick and have to go upstairs. I did not like to go to sleep because I knew the nightmares would come. After my mother got better, they stopped for a while. But when Max and Richard were blown up, I had more nightmares. When the war was over, and I came home they lessened but were not completely gone. After both my parents died, they came back almost every night. Everett thought I should come into Des Moines to the Veterans Hospital and be evaluated. I thought they would think I was crazy and lock me up, so I just ignored them. Evelyn came along and they got better. You and Johnnie were born, and they were gone. But when Johnnie got sick, they came back. After a few months, Evelyn taught me some Bible verses that she said helped comfort her, so I tried it. Soon the only way I could get to sleep at night was reciting Bible verses." Will spoke in a calm and even tone as he explained the trauma he had been living for years.

Will got up and refilled his coffee cup and refreshed J.C's too.

CHAPTER 31

"When Evelyn died, the nightmares just stopped. I don't know why; maybe when she got to heaven, she talked to God about them." Will chuckled lightly. "I feel so ashamed of how I treated Evelyn and you all those years. J.C., neither one of you had anything to do with my brothers, parents, army buddies, or even Johnnie but my fear was that anyone I loved was going to die, so I tried to stop whatever love was between us. Evelyn never stopped trying. She held me when I woke up sweating and screaming. She would bury my head in her chest so that you would not hear me scream. She truly was an angel sent from God. Maybe that is why we could never find her family. Maybe it was God who left her on those steps." Will stopped and let the information sink in.

J.C. looked at the floor and drew in a deep breath. "Dad, I knew about the nightmares," she said sternly. "Sometimes I heard them and finally asked Mom one day. She told me that you suffered from nightmares. Believe me Dad, I can understand why you had them. What I cannot understand is how one day you loved me, held me on your lap, read books to me, played games, simply just talked to me and that all stopped because Johnnie died of a disease that none of us could control. Was I not worth going to the Veterans Hospital for an evaluation?" J.C.'s emotions were escalating, and she could tell the volume of her voice was raising but she could not hold it in any longer. "Why didn't your God tell you sooner that I needed to hear that you loved me, and that you were sorry? Forty years is forever for a little girl to wonder what happened, what she did wrong, why her dad stopped loving her." Tears were gushing from J.C.'s eyes and she was starting to sputter as she gasped for breaths. "How could you sit there night after night and barely speak to me? So, you watched from afar a few of my softball games but missed the most important highlights of my life. Did it ever cross your mind that I needed you just as much as you needed your mom, your dad, your army buddies, and Johnnie? When we sat in that hospital staring at mom's lifeless body, did you care that my whole world was gone? Dad, I have no one; no husband, no children, no grandparents. When you are gone, I will have no one. I will be completely and utterly alone!" J.C. gasped for breath and dropped her head into her hands.

Will stood and took a step towards J.C. She held up her hand to indicate that he needed to stop. The silence was deafening. Will slowly sat back down on his chair.

Finally, Will spoke so quietly that J.C. was not even certain it was him speaking. "I know it was my fault that things did not work out with Roger."

"What is that supposed to mean?" J.C. shot angrily back.

"You were afraid to have a family that could be destroyed like ours was," Will explained.

"No, Dad! I was afraid that Roger would not be faithful to me because he started seeing other women after I was transferred to Chicago. If you had talked to me about it back then, you might know it had nothing to do with you!" J.C. drew in a deep breath. "Dad, I find it hard to accept your God loves people and then rips their lives apart like He did our family. You are going to have to give me some time to absorb all this." J.C. stood up and walked towards her bedroom. "I need a shower and then we can head out and do some shopping."

As the hot water ran over her body, J.C. realized that she was feeling relief from finally saying some things that she had held onto for so many years. She had wanted answers to her question, "Why?" Could it be PTSD? If that was the case, this seventy-five-year-old man was not about to go weekly and talk to a psychiatrist about his thoughts, feelings, and emotions. If the nightmares had stopped, if his heart recuperated and he returned to farming, his life would be normal. Whatever normal was for Will Mason. She just needed to get him back on his feet, have that 'conversation' that Ken Barr kept referencing and then move on with her life. Maybe once she moved on, she would put some effort into being more connected in a new community. She might even consider dating again. Why not? It had been fun spending time with Vince and maybe there was someone out there for her. Everyone here was way too connected to God. If that God existed, He had made her life one miserable wreck. J.C. turned off the water, dried off, pulled her hair into a wet ponytail, and then slipped into some jeans and a sweatshirt.

"Dad, let's go do some shopping," J.C. said as she opened the door into the living room and suppressed all the earlier conversation back into the deep dark hole, from where it had emerged earlier.

Chapter 32

*T*he next week flew by with physical therapy sessions each day for Will, J.C. finalizing her proposal for IBM, and walking Will through the spreadsheets she had created from his farm records.

It was April 3rd when Dr. Wilson released Will to move back to the farm. "Will, it is amazing that a man of your age has recovered faster than some of my forty-five to fifty-year-old patients. The physical therapist said you were doing extra workouts at J.C.'s condo in-between your therapy sessions. I am impressed. Now, remember that you still need to take it easy–no lifting, pushing, pulling, or farming until I say so. I will see you in Greenfield in two weeks and no driving until then." Dr. Wilson was looking directly at Will when he said that.

"We understand. I will keep him under control. Is it OK for him to walk around the property on the days he does not have therapy?" J.C. asked.

"Certainly; if he has been working out on the treadmill at your condo, he should be good to walk a mile or two each day around the farm," Dr. Wilson said.

"Great," Will said. "I will see you in two weeks and get my release signed for driving," he said with confidence.

Dr. Wilson just shook his head and laughed as he left the examination room.

Will and J.C. had packed up the car prior to the doctor's appointment so they headed straight to the farm when they were done. The ride home went quickly. J.C. used the time to lay down some ground rules.

"Dad, I bought a printer and laptop computer for your office. Since you learned how to use mine this past week, you can use this time to update your historical data and then we can really compute your purchase-to-market expenses for all your livestock. I will get that set up today so that you have something to keep you busy," she explained.

"Thanks, J.C.; that will be nice, and I really appreciate you getting me started on this," Will said.

"I also plan on taking over the daily chores and letting Josh cut his hours back. I will need help when it is time to sell hogs or sort cattle, but I really think I can handle the rest," J.C. said with confidence.

"J.C., you do not need to do that. I can pay Josh to keep doing the chores until I am back on my feet," Will said compassionately.

"Dad, I was helping with the chores before and like I said, I can handle it. I might let you do some laundry and housework to offset my chores." She smiled at Will.

"OK, it is a deal," Will said.

Just then J.C.'s phone rang on the car microphone. "Hello, this is J.C. Mason; may I help you?" she asked.

"J.C., Ken Barr here. I heard that Will is coming home today. Is that true?" Ken asked.

"Yes, I am," Will said loudly into the open air of the car.

"Oh, good, Will. I did not know you could hear me," Ken replied.

"Well, these new gadgets in cars today! We are just passing Dexter right now. Is there something you need Ken?" Will asked.

"Kind of ... I need a signature on the Nelson property so that the kids can sell the machinery, grain bins, and hay," Ken explained.

"I see," Will replied. "They are really in a rush. You know that corn in the bins belongs to me. You need to check the original contract to see if the grain bins were part of the purchase contract. Evelyn handled all of that and I cannot remember off the top of my head if those were included. Is that something you have in your office?" Will asked.

"Yes, I am pulling it out right now," Ken responded.

"OK, then we will stop there before heading to the farm," Will said. The phone call ended.

J.C.'s head spun as she looked over at her father who was conducting business like a seasoned negotiator. "Dad, you know I stopped in to see Ken when I first came home regarding what type of legal documents we should put in place. He told me I needed to talk to you before he was willing to work with me." She wanted to make sure that everything was out in the open before they got to Ken's office.

"I know I should have told you sooner, but Ken and I prepared a will, power of attorney and living will soon after Evelyn's death. We had a number of documents that needed to be updated when she passed away and at Ken's suggestion, I went ahead with these documents also. I will have him go over them with you today, so you are aware of everything," Will said with confidence.

They drove in silence to Stuart and parked in front of Ken's office. J.C. followed Will inside. "Here to see Ken," Will said to the receptionist.

The young girl got up and walked back to Ken's office and immediately returned. "You can go on back," she said.

They walked out of the reception area, past Jim Powell's office who noticed J.C. and Will, and went directly into Ken's office. J.C. made sure the door closed behind her.

"I am so glad that you are better, Will," Ken said. "I was very concerned when I first heard the news, but you look great today."

"Ken, let's get this business taken care of for those Nelson kids," Will urged.

"You were right – all the buildings, including the grain bins belong to you. Only one tractor and mower in the machine shed were Everett's. He must have kept that to do a little mowing around the property," Ken stated.

"The house, barn, shop, machine shed, and grain bins were all listed in the original purchase price." Will was reading from a document that Ken had handed him when they walked in. "They can sell the tractor, mower, household items and their parents' personal things but the rest of it belongs to J.C. and me."

The hair on the back of J.C.'s neck stood up. Why would Will include her in this transaction?

"Sorry, Will I should have read this before calling you. Evelyn was so concerned about the privacy of this matter when we first did it, I did not even want to unseal the envelope before talking to you." Ken seemed nervous.

"OK, you are clear on that now?" Will asked confirming and Ken nodded in agreement.

"Since we are here, can you pull out the new paperwork and go over it with J.C.?" Will requested.

Ken turned around and pulled a large brown legal envelope from behind him onto his desk. The first document that he handed across the desk was 'William John Mason's Last Will and Testament'.

J.C. quickly read through the boilerplate language customary in most wills that identify Will as the living legal heir to the property, personal assets, and investments that he was passing onto her. Next, she reviewed the power of attorney that gave her all legal rights to make financial and health decisions for Will. He had signed a living will that indicated he did not wish to be put on life support. A preliminary contract with the Stuart Retirement Home outlined his current medications, request for a private room and the payment process through Ken's office. The final document that Ken handed to J.C. was shocking. The Distribution of Property Statement.

Upon Ken Barr being notified that Will Mason was no longer able to handle his own affairs the following steps were to be followed:

1. Contact Stuart Sale Barn instructing them to retrieve all livestock from the farm for immediate sale with check made payable to Jacquelyn Caine Mason.

2. Contact Purdy's Auctioneers to sell off all farm equipment and any household items that were not requested to be held by Jacquelyn Caine Mason with sale proceeds paid to Jacquelyn Caine Mason.

3. Contact Vince Martin to liquidate ownership in Veterinarian Coop with check made payable to Jacquelyn Caine Mason.

4. Contact city clerk to sell school and library bonds with check made payable to Jacquelyn Caine Mason.

5. If Will was deceased, contact Link's Funeral Home to retrieve the body and follow pre-paid arrangements for burial and inscribe the tombstone already in place at his wife's grave.

6. Contact his only living heir, Jacquelyn Cain Mason, at the cell phone number listed.

7. Deliver safety deposit box keys and contents: IBM certificates, Bank CDs, Bank Stock Certificates with death certificate to Jacquelyn Caine Mason.

8. Follow instructions from Jacquelyn Caine Mason on the liquidation of 1,550 acres of land with check made payable to Jacquelyn Caine Mason.

9. Finally, deliver the family Bible that William John Mason received from his mother on his twelfth birthday to Jacquelyn Caine Mason.

All legal fees have been prepaid in accordance with the preliminary work provided to William John Mason.

These documents were all signed and notarized approximately forty-five days after Evelyn's death.

J.C. could not move. Her sweaty hands were locked on the sides of the documents in her lap. She could not raise her head after reading the last word. J.C. stared into the background of the documents as her mind raced to comprehend that Will had taken care of everything. If he passed away, no one other than his attorney and the assigned individual corporations on this list would need to be bothered. It was all complete! No wonder Ken Barr was so bold when she had come to his office to make arrangements. They were done, down to the last payment even to himself. Will had taken care of everything. His affairs were in order!

Slowly J.C. shuffled the papers into an organized stack and handed them back to Ken.

"Do you have any questions?" Ken asked.

J.C. shook her head no and stood up. Will stood up and they both turned and walked to the door.

"Will, so glad you are doing OK. I will call Martin Nelson and take care of that matter." Ken Barr was still talking as J.C. walked past Jim Powell's office with Will right behind her.

Jim called out to J.C., but she did not hesitate and walked quickly out the door into the sunlight and got in her car. Will joined her, and she started the ignition and backed out of the parking stall. J.C. drove to the farm in silence.

Chapter 33

*S*ettling in at the farm took all afternoon. J.C. set up the laptop computer and printer in Will's office in the machine shed. She returned the notebooks she had taken to his bookshelves. Finally, she transferred all the files from her laptop to Will's new laptop. He had everything he needed to continue his logs that would eventually build the reports he was looking for.

Josh showed up about 5:30 p.m. and started his afternoon routine. J.C. quickly changed into her chore clothes and caught up with him while he was putting some corn and mineral in the cattle feeder. "Hello, I am J.C., Will's daughter. I have been here the past few weeks helping my dad out." J.C. smiled as she introduced herself.

"Great, I am Josh Davidson. I work with Vince at the vet clinic. He has given me the background on your situation." He returned her smile. "I can continue to handle this until your dad is back on his feet. I really do not mind. Most nights I am looking for something to do anyway. I get through the morning chores in about forty-five minutes so that is not a big deal either."

J.C. was still hung up on 'the background situation'. What was that? Her mind wanted to take off, but she knew today was not the time to let it loose. "Well, I really think I can manage most of the day-to-day and will only need help with the sorting and selling," J.C. spoke directly.

"Yeah, that is what Vince said, but really, I am looking for something to keep me busy in the evenings. What are your plans for the spring planting? How many acres do you have to plant?" This livestock stuff is one thing but if you plan on doing that too it could get to be a lot." Josh seemed compassionate and caring as he spoke.

"It is more than I thought." J.C. hesitated since it had been less than four hours that she learned her father owned over 1,500 acres. How had that information escaped her in the past forty years she wondered?

"Josh, it has been kind of a long day. Moving my dad home and getting things re-established here took more time than I expected. Can we sit down in the morning and discuss some options? Maybe when you come by for chores, we can have coffee and decide what our needs will be and where you can help out." J.C. felt relief as she gave herself some more time to digest all that had happened that day.

"Great, I have been starting around 6:00 a.m. on weekdays so I can be back and shower before going to the clinic. Is it OK on Saturdays and Sundays to start at 7:00 a.m.?" Josh asked meekly.

"7:00 a.m. is great. I will help scrape the hog floors after you do the feeding and then we can talk." J.C. smiled and headed back to the house to check on Will.

Will was still sleeping when she got inside. She looked in the refrigerator and saw a casserole that Nadine had left and popped it in the oven to warm up. She headed upstairs and unpacked her bag, placing the small printer she had purchased on the desk. She heard Will moving around downstairs and headed back down to check on him.

"I see Josh Davidson is out there doing chores," Will commented as he stood at the dining room window looking out across the barnyard.

"Yes, I talked to him. He is going to come in tomorrow morning, and we can talk about what we need him to do over the next few weeks." J.C. informed Will of her conversation with Josh.

"Great. I would like to get to know him a little better," Will said.

"Nadine left us a casserole yesterday. I will set the table and we can eat," J.C. said as she was setting the table.

When Will lifted his head from praying, J.C. asked, "So, Dad, did you think I wasn't going to be around to take care of you?" referring to the paperwork that Ken Barr had shared with her.

"No, I thought you would be busy working and I wanted to make the process of getting rid of all this as easy as possible for you," Will stated.

"Mom never thought you would be able to handle this kind of stuff," J.C. commented.

"Well, I liked to let Evelyn take care of the business side of things. She was good at it and it gave her a sense of purpose, especially after you were out of the house. She really did make some great investments for us. On your first day at IBM, she suggested we buy stock in that company. Every year you were there she added to the stock." Will smiled at J.C.

"Dad, how much IBM stock do you own?" J.C. asked.

"Well, how many years did you work for them?" he asked.

"Twenty-eight," she replied.

"Take that times one hundred, plus some dividend shares. Probably over 3,000 shares," Will said casually.

"Really Dad, between the two of us we own over a million dollars in IBM stock," J.C. stated, surprisingly.

"Good, that would make Evelyn very happy to know that you will be taken care of." Will smiled down at his plate.

"Really Dad, is that what you think I want, to be taken care of?" J.C. shot back sharply.

"No, no, J.C. you misunderstood me. Your mother wanted this for you so that when we were gone, you would not have to work. You could travel, find hobbies that you loved, or whatever you wanted to do. She dreamed of you having whatever you wanted." Will smiled at J.C.

"Dad, I wanted for you, mom and me to be a family. That is what I wanted!" J.C. choked.

Silence remained during the rest of their dinner. Will took his dishes to the kitchen and came back and cleared the table. He took the leftovers to the kitchen and put them away. J.C. sat confused at the table while watching Will clean up the kitchen, dining room, and the dishes. When he had finished, he returned and sat down. This time not in his normal spot at the end of the table but in Evelyn's chair next to J.C. Will reached out and placed his hand on J.C.'s arm.

"J.C., I know that my actions have not shown you the love you wanted and deserved, but whatever you think of me, do not allow one thought to take away what your mother worked so hard to do for you. She spent every living breath making sure that you were happy, safe, and cared for. Even after you left this house, her days were consumed with knowing what you were doing, how you were feeling, and planning the next time she would see you. The investments she made were so that the two of you would be able to travel more and do things together. She would be crushed to hear you say that you do not want what she worked so hard to give you." Will lifted his hand and just sat there.

J.C. felt like her head was going to explode. She had waited years to communicate with her father and now she struggled to control her emotions. What to say first? Her outburst in Des Moines gave her some momentary satisfaction but overall did not answer her question – *Why*?

After a few minutes of silence, she decided to break things down into segments that hopefully would put the

'*Why* puzzle' together if she found all the pieces. "Dad, when did you buy all that land?" J.C. asked very calmly.

"Again, it was mostly Evelyn's doing. She would hear things at church or the library about someone's children getting ready to sell the family farm. She came home and would ask me if the property was a good piece of land. We would go take a look at it. She would pull up soil documents at the library. Once she had all the information compiled, we would make our decision on price. She was a great negotiator. Most people did not push back too much due to her gentle nature. By the time Johnnie was born, we owned over one-thousand acres. It was always our plan to have enough ground to support our children and their children." Will sighed, and J.C. could see him reliving the memories of the early years with Evelyn.

"So, you were farming over one-thousand acres while I was still home?" J.C. inquired.

"Yes," Will replied confidently. "Why?"

"I never realized how much you were doing. I guess, I always thought you just had the one-hundred-forty acres that you owned when your parents died." J.C. admitted her ignorance. "Did you help anyone else out besides Everett?"

Will looked down at the table and then towards the door before answering. "Just Donald Martin," Will said softly.

"Vince's dad?" J.C.'s eyes widened with her question.

"He mortgaged his farm to start the Vet Cooperative when Vince came home from college. The first few years, things were pretty lean. Some of the other investors wanted to foreclose on the Vet Cooperative, so, Evelyn and I bought about half of their land to keep the Martins out of foreclosure and the Coop open. It worked out. Vince could not farm seven-hundred acres and do his veterinarian work, but he seems to get along well with the 150 crop acres and some pasture for his cattle now," Will spoke solemnly.

CHAPTER 33

"So that is why Vince comes by to check on you and help out? He feels like he owes you?" J.C. felt like a light bulb had just gone off.

"I hope not. I never wanted to make Vince feel bad about that transaction. His dad wanted to help Vince start a business and the lean years were just too much for the Martins to swing. Once the Vet Cooperative took off and they were farming a smaller portion of land they seemed to get by just fine." Will seemed to be reflecting on some other thoughts as he talked.

"I know that mom liked Vince from the start. She would always talk about him whenever we were together. He just told me last week how she would put food in his truck anytime he stopped here to take care of livestock. He also said she was very gracious to Teri, his wife," J.C. commented.

"Evelyn loved the Martins. She was fond of most people, but I agree she had a soft spot in her heart for Vince and his family." Will smiled again with more memories than what he shared.

"OK, so now I know about the land. What about the bonds?" J.C. continued her inquisition.

"The school bonds were obvious investments. The town was growing and the school needed expansion. Evelyn loved anything to do with education. So, we bought school bonds every time there was a new issue coming out. The library was pretty much the same thing. The bank bonds were a little different. Evelyn was not convinced at first that we should be investing in them, until one day at Nadine's she heard that the Earlham Savings Bank was going to take them over if they did not sell enough bonds. I thought she was going to buy all of the remaining offerings. We settled on an amount to invest and that ended up being one of our best investments... next to IBM of course." Will chuckled at J.C.

Heaving a big sigh J.C. said, "Dad, I had no idea that mom had such a strong business sense. Maybe I got that from her." J.C. smiled.

"I am sure of that!" Will confirmed.

"Dad, you could have knocked me over with a feather today in Ken Barr's office. I had no idea that you and mom had accumulated so much wealth but more shocking was that you had taken care of all your final arrangements. Mom would be so proud of you. She made me promise over and over that I would take care of these things for you," J.C. said quietly.

"I know. Since I let her handle all the business stuff, she probably thought I wouldn't know what to do. But like I said earlier, it gave her so much joy to know she contributed to our lives that I just let her think I couldn't do it without her help." Will's face was covered with a big smile.

J.C. was exhausted, "Dad, we need to get to bed. Let's plan on talking over breakfast what we want Josh to do going forward so that we are on the same page when he comes in after chores."

"Sounds like a good plan," Will agreed. He walked into the living room and sat in his chair and opened his Bible.

J.C. stopped in the bathroom to complete her nightly routine before heading upstairs.

Chapter 34

J.C. checked her phone and saw that she had two missed calls from Vince and one from Nadine. Nadine's had come in the middle of the afternoon while she was setting up Will's new laptop and printer. Vince's were both after dinner. She decided to wait and call Nadine back in the morning. Flopping on her couch she dialed Vince.

"Hope I am not calling too late?" J.C. said with a question in her voice.

"No, just catching up on some bookwork. How is Will doing?" Vince asked.

"He is fine. He took a longer nap today than what he has been doing in Des Moines. I bought a laptop and printer for him and set those up in his office so that he can continue inputting his livestock statistics. I hope that will keep him occupied these next few weeks. I am also thinking about ordering a treadmill. He really seems to like getting in extra workouts between therapy sessions and I would love to maintain my workouts while I am out here." J.C. stopped herself because she sounded like she was rambling.

"Not a bad idea." Vince confirmed.

"Josh seems extremely conscientious. We are going to sit down in the morning to discuss a schedule going forward. He said he wants to continue doing the chores and even asked about the spring field work." J.C. relayed her conversation with Josh.

"I know he likes being re-engaged in day-to-day farming. It is your call, but my advice is let him do as much of it as he can. You are going to keep busy with Will's appointments and housework, garden and yard work will start in another couple of weeks..." Vince was making a good point J.C. thought.

"You are right," she interrupted him mid-sentence, "I had not even thought about the lawn and whether to plant anything in the garden. Will said he would help with the housework and started that tonight after dinner. Completely surprised me when he cleaned up the table, dishes and kitchen." J.C. spoke with actual surprise in her voice.

"Well, he has been taking care of all that himself for this past year," Vince confirmed and then changed topics. "I wanted to give you a heads up that Kelsey might call. She wants to talk to you about prom next weekend. I told her not to put any pressure on you because your plate was full right now. So only say yes if you really want to, *promise!*" Vince insisted.

"I had mentioned that we could get her nails done at a salon in Des Moines if she wanted to. Prom is a week from Saturday, right?" J.C. asked. "I will be careful not to over commit, but I do want to help make her day special if there's anything I can do. I owe you both so much." J.C. smiled thinking about Kelsey wanting her help.

"Stop it. You owe us nothing and you do not need to take her to Des Moines for that; there are some options closer that will be just fine." Vince was stern in his response.

"OK, I get your point... but this is one of those girl things that I am not sure even how to explain it. She wants that *wow* factor where no one knows or sees what the end result is going to be until that special moment." J.C. caught herself.

CHAPTER 34

She was engaged in a very personal conversation with Vince, and it seemed normal. She pulled herself up on the couch and took in a deep breath. "Vince, I better get going, I have some things to do before bed and tomorrow I am back on farm time with early morning chores." She knew that was an exaggeration but felt like she needed to bring things back to a more neighborly kind of conversation.

"Sure, get some rest. We can talk later. Good night, J.C." Vince spoke softly as he said, 'good night, J.C.'

It sent a shiver down her spine. A good shiver!

J.C.'s alarm went off at 5:00 a.m. She hurried, dressed in her chore clothes, and headed downstairs. Will was sitting in his chair with his Bible open on his lap. "I will get breakfast started," J.C. said as she passed through the living room.

J.C. made scrambled eggs, sausage, and toast. It took less than fifteen minutes. She fixed two plates and put them on the table with two glasses of orange juice just as Will came in and sat down. She returned to the kitchen to get the coffee.

"Dad, I was thinking I can help Josh with the hog floors and silage dump like I was doing with you each morning. That should cut fifteen to twenty minutes out of his morning schedule. Mid-afternoon I can take the corn and protein out to the feeder cattle and put out hay when they need it. That should cut his afternoon chores to about an hour. We will need to sell hogs next week; maybe Vince could come one night and help me sort those off and I could take them into town the following morning." J.C.'s mind was walking through the list she had come up with the night before preparing for the meeting with Josh.

"Slow down, J.C.; we need to see what Josh thinks after doing these chores for the past ten days. He might have some recommendations for us that I had not considered in all the years of doing things the same old way," Will cautioned.

J.C. sat back in her chair and realized her dad was a sharp and savvy man. "Dad, that is a great idea. I would have recommended that to any client; a third-party review should

255

bring some new ideas and efficiencies to the product." She smiled across the table at Will. Her father's strong business sense surprised her.

When J.C. had finished breakfast, she set her dishes in the kitchen sink and walked into the mudroom. She had just gotten her coveralls and boots on when Josh pulled in. She walked out the door to greet him.

"Good morning, Josh. I will let you lead since you have been doing this for over a week. I am pretty good at opening gates, moving things, and scraping the hog floors. Just point or tell me if you want me to help with anything." J.C. smiled at Josh. He nodded.

Josh headed to the machine shed and came out with the tractor and silage wagon. J.C. helped him through the lots opening all the gates. When he reached the silage pit, J.C. was on the tractor attached to the end loader and began dumping the silage in. When the silage wagon was full, J.C. parked her tractor and cut across the lots to open the gate at the end of the cattle trough. Josh drove in, turned around, and began dumping the silage as he drove back. When he finished, J.C. closed the gate behind him and he drove back to the machine shed.

Josh drove in and re-emerged with the honey wagon attached to the tractor. J.C. headed to the hog barn to start the hog chores. When Josh walked in, she was scraping the first pen. Josh grabbed the feed buckets and started filling the feeders in the individual pen. Once that was done, he headed back outside and started the motor that sucked a load of manure into the honey wagon. When that was done, he left to spread that manure while J.C. scraped the second pen. They continued in tandem until the pens were all cleaned.

Josh returned the tractor and honey wagon back to the machine shed and J.C. cleaned her boots at the water hydrant and headed into the house. She took off her boots and coveralls in the mudroom. She stopped in the bathroom to wash her hands and readjust her ponytail. Will had cleaned up the breakfast dishes and set three empty cups on the table.

"Thanks, Dad. Josh should be in any minute." Just then they heard a knock on the door. J.C. answered the door and introduced Josh to Will. "Josh this is my father, Will Mason," she said with a smile.

Josh extended his hand and shook Will's hand. "Nice to see you again, Mr. Mason," he said.

"Pleasure is mine, son. I cannot thank you enough for helping us out while I recover. Can I get you some coffee?" Will asked.

"No thanks, I'm not a coffee drinker, a glass of water would be great," Josh said.

J.C. came back from the kitchen with a glass of water and the coffee pot. She filled both her and Will's cups with coffee and returned the pot to the kitchen. "Have a seat, Josh," J.C. said as she pointed to the chair next to the dining room table. Will sat on the end, J.C. took her normal spot, and Josh sat across from her.

"Well, the two of you did those morning chores in record time," Will said with a smile. "I know that our lot situation is pretty cumbersome, Josh, so if you have any advice for us on how to make these chores more efficient, we are all ears."

"They aren't bad, but there are a couple of things that would reduce some steps. Have you ever considered automatic feeders? I bet you could buy some good used ones online and that would cut down on the labor of moving the grain from your grain storage to the feeders each day," Josh recommended.

"I agree. Last fall I went to a neighbor's farm sale and tried to buy a couple but got outbid at the auction. J.C., can you find what we need on your computer and have them delivered?" Will's decisiveness reminded J.C. of her own.

"Sure, Dad. I will check those out today," J.C. said.

"Anything else you think we need to change?" Will asked.

"I would put screens on your waterers in the hog barn. They get straw twigs in them from the birds and that can destroy them after a while. You have the rotary motor that cleans out the drains but these small items falling in get caught in the intakes. You really do not need anything fancy just some fine screens cut to fit the top of each water tank," Josh commented.

"We will pick some up in Greenfield on Monday," Will said. "I think that is a project I can even do." Will smiled at J.C.

"Josh, you have definitely impressed me with your knowledge and care of my livestock. Let's talk about what you would like to do and what we need done this spring." Will had completely taken charge of his business and J.C. watched in awe although there was a pit in her stomach. Was it a feeling that she was not needed?

"Well, Mr. Mason, I enjoy my work at the clinic, but as you know the low man on the totem pole stays in the office most days, so I get very little hands-on with larger livestock. I see mostly cats and dogs." He wrinkled his nose to indicate that was not the work he enjoyed. "I am a farm boy from northeast Iowa. My parents have a large hog operation outside of Dubuque. They have 1,000 acres of crop ground that we raise corn and soybeans on. I can run every kind of farm machinery and do not mind working long hours. My days get pretty boring living here without family and very few friends close by." Josh nodded towards Will.

"Josh, you are just what we need. I have approximately 1,200 acres of crop ground, going to corn and soybeans; seventy-five acres of hay ground and the rest is in government programs. The fall field work is done, and I usually hire the elevator in town to spread the spring fertilizer. We need to rotate the manure distribution to another farm which is about three miles away for the next few weeks. That could add some extra time to the chores. You have been in the machine shed so you know what equipment we have to work with." Will waited to see what Josh thought.

"Mr. Mason, I would be thrilled to help out and your equipment is in great condition, so I am certain it will be just fine for this season. Could we scrape the hog floors in the evening instead of the morning? I should have plenty of sunlight to get that done with the evening chores. If you are fine with me working evenings for planting, I do not mind working after dark. On weeknights, I will probably stop around 9:00 p.m. so I can be alert for work at the clinic in the mornings. If the weather cooperates, I can cover a lot of ground on Saturday and Sunday. Except for the one weekend a month that I am on call." Josh was talking faster, and J.C. could read the excitement in his tone and body language.

"Hey, guys, I am still here and able to help out also," J.C. said with a nervous laugh. The knot in her stomach was getting tighter as she thought Will was deciding that Josh was more capable than she was.

Both Will and Josh stopped and look directly at J.C. "Sure, J.C., you can do whatever you want, and I will just pitch in where you need me," Josh said humbly.

Will did not comment.

"Josh, I owe you for the work you have already done, and we need to agree on a rate going forward. Is an hourly rate good? I was thinking we would match whatever your wages are at the vet clinic," Will said.

"Oh, Mr. Mason, I think that is very generous, but what about $55 per hour?" Josh said.

"No, I am on the Board at the vet clinic and know that we pay you more than that. I insist that your wages here match those at the clinic." Will was very direct.

"That is very generous, and I appreciate that." Josh was extremely humbled in accepting Will's offer.

"OK, then each week you drop off your hours in my office in the machine shed, and the following Monday there will be a check waiting for you." Will stood up and shook Josh's hand.

J.C.'s head was spinning. She had laid awake the night before outlining in her mind how this conversation would go.

It was done and she had said next to nothing. Will Mason was a master of taking care of his business. How in the world had he kept that from Evelyn all those years? She felt like she was the outsider in the conversation instead of Josh Davidson. J.C.'s mind wanted to take off, but she forced herself to stay engaged with Will and Josh.

Josh stood up and walked to the door. As he leaned down to pull his boots back on, he turned and asked. "Do you know of a place that I could rent? My lease in town is up in May and I really would prefer to live out in the country."

Will looked at J.C. and smiled. "Let's go for a little ride. Come on J.C.; you have not seen this farm yet either." All three of them headed out the front door and climbed into Josh's pickup. Will instructed Josh to turn south at the end of the driveway. They drove to Everett's place three miles south. "I own this farm and the house with building site will be available on May 1. You can move in here when your lease in town is up," Will said with a big smile.

Josh shook his head and looked at J.C. who nodded affirming what Will had just said. "This is also the corn stalks that you can start spreading the manure on from the hog pens. I would have rotated here about a week ago but if we plant this field last and the rains hit right, we should still be fine." Will was talking to himself more than to J.C. and Josh.

"Mr. Mason, you have already been so generous, I almost hate to ask for one more thing," Josh said sheepishly.

"What is it, Josh?" Will asked.

"Can I bring my horse down from my parents' farm keep her here in this barn?" Josh looked down humbly.

"Bring your horse, your chickens, sheep, cows and pigs... use this farmstead as if it were your own, Josh." Will smiled broadly at the young man.

Chapter 35

When J.C. got back in the house, she called Nadine. They talked for over an hour getting Nadine caught up on the trip home, meeting at Ken Barr's office, Josh, the new hired man, and Everett's farm. J.C. cautioned Nadine not to spread the news about Everett's farm but knew in the back of her mind that it was a matter of days, if not hours, that the gossip would hit the streets of Stuart.

"J.C., you sure have kept things exciting since you moved back. My life was pretty boring two months ago but since you got here, I feel like a new soap opera has just hit the air waves!" Nadine was laughing as she delivered her last zinger.

"Nadine, that is not funny at all. Why do you think I caused this excitement? Will's plans were done eight months ago and the fact that mom did not tell you or me about some of this stuff is still very unsettling. So, do not blame me for the new excitement in your life. Oh, my phone is buzzing, it's Kelsey, I have to go, Nadine," J.C. said hurriedly.

"Another soap opera that is just waiting to blossom!" Nadine chuckled as she hung up.

J.C. shook her head, "Hello, Kelsey, how are things going?"

"Great, we just had our final planning meeting for prom. Everyone is going to be at the gym at 7:30 a.m. next Saturday to decorate. The plan is that we should be done by 9:00 a.m. so everyone, particularly, the girls, will have plenty of time to get ready the rest of the day." Kelsey was talking fast, and J.C. could hear the excitement in her voice.

"I can tell you are excited... what can I do to help you?" J.C. offered.

"Well, I do want to get my fingernails and toenails done in a color to match my dress; but I do not want to go to a salon. Would you be willing to paint them for me if I can find the perfect color?" Kelsey asked in an almost pleading voice.

J.C. drew in a big breath. She had not painted her own nails in almost twenty-five years... what if she messed up? "Oh, Kelsey, I am not sure you want me to do that," J.C. responded hesitantly.

"J.C.! I am not a drama queen and they do not have to be perfect. I just think it is crazy to spend $50 to get them painted at a salon and then ruin them on the way home. So many girls do that every year and talk about it for days!" Kelsey sighed loudly. "I stopped at the Ben Franklin in Stuart after school and they do not have the right color, so, I might ask my dad if I can go to Greenfield or Winterset to see if I can find a color that is closer to what I need. Please!" Kelsey pleaded.

"Well, if you are sure you will not be upset if they do not turn out perfect, I guess I can try." J.C. really did not want to do it, but she opened with 'what can I do to help', so was caught in her own trap.

"Great. And .... will you also come with dad to watch me walk the red carpet?" Kelsey's enthusiasm was over the top.

"Walk the red carpet, what is that?" J.C. could not imagine what Kelsey was talking about now.

"Each couple is announced when they arrive at prom once they are done with dinner. We are going to have a runner of red carpet coming down the hallway from the elementary section of the school over the staircase and into the gym. The parents line the hallway and walls to take pictures as each couple gets announced. Then, of course, the parents leave before the dance starts. It is really fun! I went last year with a friend who had a sister that was a senior; it was awesome!" Kelsey took a breath.

"Kelsey, I will think about that." J.C. was not ready to make that commitment yet. "When do you think you will start getting ready next Saturday? Are you still planning on having someone do your hair?" J.C. asked.

"Yes, I am getting my hair done at 10:15 a.m. at the Stuart Salon. I told them something really simple. Pull one side up or something but *no up-do*! So, we should have plenty of time to do my nails after lunch," Kelsey replied.

"OK, just let me know when you find the polish and the exact time you need me to stop over next Saturday," J.C. committed.

"Thanks J.C. You are the best. I would not be able to do all this prom stuff without you," Kelsey said as she hung up the phone.

J.C. looked at her phone and shook her head. How in the world did I get myself completely emersed into the teenage drama of prom, she wondered?

J.C. logged into her computer and went to Craig's List to look for livestock feeders. She was surprised to see various options available. One that caught her attention right away was in Winterset, Iowa. Winterset was about a thirty-minute drive from the farm. She took her laptop and went downstairs. Will was just getting up from a nap. "Dad, look at these feeders. They have four automatic hog feeders and are located in Winterset." J.C. set her computer on the corner of the dining room table.

"Wow, that is amazing that you can find this stuff so quickly on-line," Will commented as he studied the items on the screen in front of him.

"Should we call and see what we can find out?" J.C. asked.

"Sure," Will replied.

J.C. dialed the number listed on the screen and handed her cell phone to Will. He looked shocked at first but when he heard someone speak on the other end he said, "I am calling about those automated hog feeders you have for sale. How old are they and what is the asking price?" Will waited to hear the reply. "Sounds pretty reasonable. How many head have used them, would you estimate?" Another pause. "OK, would I be able to stop by and see them tomorrow?" Pause. "Where are you located?" Pause. "OK, we will call before we come over. Thank you." Will handed the phone back to J.C.

"Can you drive the pickup and trailer over there with me tomorrow and if they are as good as they look, we can bring them home?" Will asked. "Did you see any on there for cattle?"

J.C. nodded affirmatively that she would take Will to Winterset the next day. "No, I have not found anything for cattle, but we can continue to look." She pulled the website up again and started to make inquiries regarding grain feeders for cattle. The only ones that came up were in Texas. J.C. closed down the Craig's List site and did an open search for cattle feeders and immediately found that the implement store in Greenfield sold new ones.

Will looked at a couple of different styles they had advertised. "I like this one that measures the feed out based on the programmed amount set on the feed cycle," he said.

"Dad, how do you know if more than a couple of cows are eating all the grain with this method?" J.C. inquired.

"Good question. It is not a perfect science, but the more they eat the faster they get out of the lot and the next group moves up. So, it kind of takes care of itself." Will smiled at J.C. "The more aggressive cows eat more of the feed until they are sold, and that cycle continues downward until each group is moved out."

"I get it, top of the food chain eats until they become the food chain." J.C. and Will laughed at her joke.

"Something like that," Will agreed.

"I am going to go see what our options are for dinner. I think we have some chicken in the freezer. I can boil that and make some noodles to go with it." J.C. looked at Will for confirmation.

"Sounds good. I think I will go for a walk outside. Remember the doctor said I could do that." Will stood and started toward the mudroom.

"Dad, a couple of things. I was thinking about ordering a treadmill to set up in your office, so you can walk on the days you do not have physical therapy. Secondly, walk on the pasture side of the fence, not in the lots!" J.C. said sternly.

"OK, I will stay out of the lots. That treadmill idea is a good one, we could both use it," Will said.

J.C. smiled to herself as Will walked by. He knew she wanted to have a treadmill at the farm also.

After J.C. put the chicken in her mother's old pressure cooker, she began mixing up the noodles. It had been years since she helped Evelyn make noodles, so she had to use the cookbook to make sure of the correct measurements of flour, eggs, and milk. Once she had them rolled out and cut, J.C. sat down to enjoy a cup of coffee. She was still amazed at how masterfully her father had handled the meeting with Josh this morning. It was almost eerie how he reminded her of herself conducting business transactions back at IBM. J.C. still could not get past the fact that Will and Josh had made all those decisions without her. Maybe she really wasn't needed at the farm. Will's paperwork was in order. He had a hired man to help out with the farm. Her time at the farm might come to an end much sooner than she thought.

J.C. picked up her phone and decided to text Kelsey to let her know that she could check Winterset Drug when they went to look at the hog feeders the next day. 'Kelsey, need to drive my dad to Winterset in the morning. Will check Winterset Drug Store for Fuchsia polish.'

Immediately a text returned. 'You are the best. Thanks.'

Just as J.C. was finishing her coffee, Josh drove in to start the evening chores. J.C. got up and put on her overalls, boots and gloves and headed out to help.

"J.C., you do not need to help. I got these," Josh shouted as he stepped down from his pickup.

J.C. walked over to Josh. "We found some hog feeders in Winterset that we will look at tomorrow. If Will likes them we will bring them back with us. So, I wanted to discuss the best locations for them in the pens," J.C. said.

"Great, that was fast. Your dad makes quick decisions. *Wow*, my head was spinning this morning when things happened so quickly," Josh said with a big smile on his face.

"Yes, Will is a surprise." J.C. did not elaborate. Josh headed into the machine shed and J.C. walked down to the hog barn. Once inside she began cleaning the floors. The floors were pretty light since they had just been cleared in the morning, but this was part of the plan to move them to the evening shift.

Josh hooked up the honey wagon and came inside to fill the feeding troughs. While he filled the feed troughs he motioned to J.C. where the feeders would fit along the inside gate line. She nodded back in agreement over the squeal of the hogs. When he was done, he headed back out and sucked up the first load of manure and headed down the road to Everett's old place. J.C. continued to scrape the floors and was almost done with the last pen when Josh got back. He was able to get it all into the second load, so J.C. finished before he pulled out the suction hose. Josh drove off and J.C. cleaned her boots and the scraper before heading back to the house.

When Josh got back, he left the honey wagon in the machine shed and put the hay fork on the tractor to hay the cows. Once he had filled the hay feeder, he took four buckets of corn to the feeder cattle and closed down the machine shed. Just as he was finishing up, Will returned from his walk. J.C. looked out the window and saw the two men leaned on the side of Josh's pickup talking. The knot returned in her stomach.

Will came in and stepped into the bathroom to wash his hands. "It felt good to get out in the fresh air," he said. "Josh sure is excited about Everett's place. He said he called his parents, and they are going to bring his horse down and help him move in."

"That is great, Dad. It is very generous of you to let him stay there," J.C. commented as she brought the chicken and noodles to the table.

"Smart is what it is," Will said. "It will keep vandals away. They won't bother the buildings if they know someone is living there."

J.C. nodded and smiled, and Will bowed his head in prayer.

Chapter 36

*F*riday went according to plan. Josh and J.C. finished morning chores in under thirty minutes. J.C. and Will headed to Winterset, picked up hog feeders, and of course nail polish. Will called the implement store in Greenfield and put a hold on two new cattle feeders and a roll of fine screen wire to be picked up Monday when they went in for physical therapy. J.C. went online and ordered a treadmill to be delivered by UPS to the farm. After lunch, Will wanted to go out to his office and work on his new computer. J.C. insisted he rest for a least an hour first. When Will got up from a nap, J.C. sat with him until he was comfortable inputting data on his new computer. When J.C. headed back to the house to finish some laundry, she stopped in the middle of the driveway and looked around. Will Mason had spent his entire life right here with the exception of three years when he was in the army. He was in control here and until he took his final breath – no one was going to take away that control; not even J.C.

Doris called to check on things once J.C. was back inside. "Dad is doing great. He is eating well, sleeping well, taking walks. We go to Greenfield on Monday for therapy. I am sure he is right on schedule for his recovery plan," J.C. stated.

"Well, that is great. I sure am glad that you are there to help him. He seemed a lot more outgoing than the first time I met him years ago when your parents came for Christmas Eve dinner," Doris commented.

"Yes, he is opening up more," J.C. confirmed.

"You got a letter from IBM that looks important. Do you want me to send it to you?" Doris asked.

"No, it is probably a check for the consulting work I completed for them. I will be in soon and pick it up," J.C. confirmed.

"Well, you take care of yourself, dear," Doris said before hanging up.

Wow, that is the shortest conversation I have ever had with Doris, J.C. thought. She had put a ham in the oven after lunch and it was starting to smell delicious. Some baked beans would go well with it she thought. She chopped up some onion, added brown sugar, mustard and molasses to the dish of beans and set them in the oven with the ham. J.C. checked her watch and noted it had been two hours since she left Will in the machine shed. She headed out to check on him. When she opened the door, Will was still on the computer entering numbers. "OK, Dad, I think that is enough for today. You need to get up and walk around a little before dinner," J.C. cautioned.

"Yes, you are probably right. I am feeling a little stiff," Will said. "J.C., on Monday I need to call the elevator and tell them to deliver my seed corn so that Josh can start planting when the ground temperatures warm up."

"OK, I will remind you on Monday," J.C. said.

J.C. went inside and put on her coveralls and boots just as Josh was driving in. They headed down to the hog barn together to assess how to move the hog feeders that J.C. had left parked on the trailer earlier that day.

"I think if we put the bale fork on the tractor, we can move these feeders right up to the gate and one of us can swing the gate into the pen holding the hogs back while the other one lowers the feeder onto the floor. Once it is in place, we can slide the gate behind it," Josh stated.

"I am game to try that," J.C. committed.

Josh headed to the machine shed and returned with the tractor and bale fork. J.C. opened the sliding door and Josh pulled in and loaded the first hog feeder off the trailer. They started with the east pen. J.C. unhooked the corner gate and slowly walked it forward backing the hogs up and watching to make sure none of them went around the open end. Josh quickly came in behind her and lowered the feeder onto the floor. Once it was in place, he got down and unhooked the opposite end of the gate J.C. was holding and they slowly walked it around the feeder and reattached both ends. Josh high-fived J.C. when they completed the first one. She smiled thinking how old she was compared to this thirtyish guy helping her. They repeated the process in the next two pens. Once that was done Josh pulled out with the tractor and returned with the honey wagon. J.C. was already engaged in her scraping routine. The floors were a little heavier tonight. Josh filled the feeding troughs, sucked up the first load of manure, and drove the tractor to Everett's. J.C. continued scraping and was almost done again when Josh got back. They were both surprised that even though it seemed heavy, it all fit into the second load. J.C. cleaned up and then headed towards the pickup. She returned the trailer to the machine shed. Josh brought the honey wagon and tractor back and carried some corn to the feeder cattle. When he was finished J.C. told him, "we will pick up the cattle feeders on Monday in Greenfield."

"OK, this is my weekend to be on call, but it looks like we will need to grind feed either tomorrow or Sunday. I can come over at 6:00 a.m. tomorrow so we can get started but I may have to leave if a call comes in. With these new feeders, we can grind more at one time and should only need to do that a couple of times per month going forward. If we take the grinder down to the hog barn, we can dump it directly into the new feeders," Josh informed J.C. "We should pull the old feeding troughs out of the pens tomorrow too. If they are not used for feeding, they will become a nuisance in there."

"OK, I will be up and ready at 6:00 a.m.," J.C. confirmed as Josh headed to his pickup to leave.

"Did you get those new feeders in place?" Will asked as J.C. came though the kitchen door.

"Yes Dad, we set them on the north edge of each pen up against the gates. Tomorrow when we grind feed, we will fill them and then pull out the old feeding troughs. What do you want me to do with those old ones?" J.C. asked.

"If Josh wants them for his horse or any other livestock he decides to add to his new place, he is welcome to them," Will said.

The table was set, and Will had pulled the ham and baked beans out of the oven. J.C. finished in the bathroom and then sat down to dinner. Will bowed his head and prayed. J.C. just sat in silence.

"Dad, do you have a protein or vitamin mix that needs to be added to the corn tomorrow when we grind feed?" J.C. inquired.

"Yes, there should be some bags in the machine shed next to my office wall. The ratio is on the outside of the bag. I think there is enough for a couple of grinders full and that should fill those new feeders. I will call and have the elevator send out more next week," Will said. "I do not add anything to the cattle feed. They get pure ground corn."

"OK, thanks." J.C. paused. "You do remember that I can run the field disc? Mom showed me when I was in high school so if I need to start getting fields ready for Josh to plant, I can do that, Dad," J.C. stated.

"J.C., I don't think that's necessary. Josh is planning on starting field preparation next week and should be ready to

THE FARMER'S DAUGHTER

plant corn in about three days if we do not get any rain. That is right on schedule to where I would be if I was doing it myself," Will responded.

J.C. ate in silence. She did not initiate any other conversations. When she had finished, she stood up, went into the bathroom, and prepared for bed. She walked out of the bathroom and went upstairs without saying anything else to Will.

Will cleaned up the dishes and kitchen while J.C. was in the bathroom and was still doing that when she went upstairs.

As J.C. plopped on the couch, she wondered if Will noticed she was giving him the silent treatment. What is going on she asked herself? It was great that this young farm kid comes along just at the opportune time to help Will out. He seemed capable and willing to do everything they needed done. If Will's health continued to progress, J.C. would be free to head back to her 'normal' life soon. Isn't that what she wanted when she arrived eight weeks ago? Why did it bother her that she was not needed? Why, why, why? She was really annoyed. Especially since she *never* seemed to be able to answer it. Just then her phone rang. It was Vince. J.C. hesitated before answering it.

"Hello, ...Vince," she said slowly.

"Hi, J.C. How is Will doing?" Vince asked.

"Fine," J.C. responded.

"Thanks for running that errand for Kelsey to get nail polish. This is a never-ending favor that you have gotten yourself wrapped up in." Vince laughed.

J.C. didn't laugh, "It was no big deal, I had to take dad to Winterset to pick up some feeders that Josh suggested we get for the hog barn. So, we went right by the drug store." J.C. just stated facts.

"Josh, oh my that guy is on cloud nine! He stopped over here after you guys showed him the farmhouse. He is so excited about living out in the country and getting to have his horse down here. The farm he described sounds like Everett's place?" Vince said with a question in his voice.

"Yes," J.C. responded. "We are grateful that Josh is available to help out so much this spring too."

"So, is Martin hiring Will to manage that farm until he gets it sold?" Vince asked.

"No, not exactly," J.C. hesitated. "Will has owned that farm for the last forty-five years." Silence hung in the air.

"Oh, I guess that makes sense." Vince did not say any more about that topic. "Did Kelsey mention to you about the red-carpet thing?"

"Yes," J.C. said with hesitation in her voice.

"Well, she really would like you to come, and I would appreciate having some help taking pictures; so, if you are willing, I thought we could maybe grab a burger beforehand." Vince's voice seemed to have some excitement in it.

J.C. was already lost in an internal mind war. She was grateful that Will had opened up and she understood more about his past and she was relieved that his affairs were in such good order. She was flattered that Vince trusted her with his daughter and it seemed like he might even have some feelings developing for her, but there was this knot – really big knot in her stomach! She might be experiencing shock! All the information that she had gained over the past eight weeks had not sunk in yet. What was it that was still bothering her? And why, why, why?

"J.C., are you still there?" Vince asked softly.

"Oh, sorry." J. C. drew in a long breath. "Vince, I can help Kelsey with her prom prep and help you out with pictures, but I'll have to pass on the hamburger," J.C. said and with some sternness in her voice.

"OK... thanks," was Vince's response. "I switched weekends with Josh, so he can grind feed with you tomorrow and I will have next weekend off for prom; it worked out well for both of us. He said that some of the hogs are starting to get close to market weight so let me know if you guys need help sorting next week."

"Thanks, Vince. I'll let you know. Good night." J.C. ended the conversation.

"Oh, good night," Vince said with surprise in his voice.

J.C. threw the phone on the couch in front of her in anger. Why, what, how—so many questions in her mind surrounding these past few weeks. She really could not understand how after forty years of silence in this house, Will had snapped out of it completely. He seemed so *normal* now! But what is normal when it comes to her father? And now Josh? Was Will replacing Johnnie with Josh? Her stomach grew tighter, and her eyes focused on Johnnie's picture on her desk. Evelyn and Will had purchased Everett's farm for Johnnie, not Josh, and now Josh was going to live there. How could Will so casually make that decision? The knot in J.C.'s stomach grew tighter. Maybe it was more than a knot. She felt sick. Her heart started to race, and she was perspiring as her mind continued to stir. Just then she saw the light flicker in the floor register and knew that Will was in his chair with his Bible in his lap. That Bible! The Bible verse from the hospital flashed through her mind, 'If you do not believe, you will not be welcome in heaven.' Her anger grew more intense. She needed to get out of this place. She had not found any answers here. Everyone seemed to believe in something and someone that she did not. She did not fit in here. Her promise to her mother was invalid. It was time to go. She got up and walked into her dressing room. She pulled out the big suitcase and started to throw things in it. Her body started to tremble and shake... I really am ill, J.C. thought. Halfway through her mental rant, she ran into her bedroom and threw herself onto her bed in tears, sobbing until she fell asleep.

Chapter 37

What was that awful sound and what time was it? J.C. rolled over in her wrinkled clothes and looked at the clock radio beside her bed. It was 6:15 a.m. and that sound... was the auger loading corn into the grinder. J.C. shot out of bed and back to her dressing room and kicking her open suitcase to the side, she sorted through a pile of clothes looking for her chore clothes. Out of the corner of her eye she caught a glimpse of herself in the full-length mirror. She was wearing her chore clothes, her eyes were swollen and blood shot, her hair was a tangled mess. She ran out of the dressing room and down the stairs. Will was making breakfast in the kitchen. She went directly into the bathroom, brushed her teeth, combed her hair, put it in a bun, and washed her face with cold water. Standing up, she looked into the mirror again to confirm that she was ready to go face Josh in the barnyard. It was not a pretty sight, but slightly better than what she had seen upstairs. She opened the bathroom door.

"I made some eggs, bacon and toast," Will stated.

J.C. shot Will a look to kill then turned and walked out into the mudroom. She slipped into her coveralls and jacket and headed down to the hog barn. She got there ahead of Josh and opened the door so that he could pull in with the tractor and grinder. They unloaded the grinder into the first two feeders and Josh headed back to the corn bin to start the second batch of hog feed. J.C.'s heart was pounding as she stood in silence in the middle of the hog barn. She started talking out loud to herself, "J.C. you just need to get through the next ten days. This prom stuff, physical therapy on Monday, and picking up the cattle feeders in Greenfield. The following week Will should be released to drive, and you will be free to go. Go – where am I going? Maybe I'll take a trip, a *big* trip ... Italy, Spain, or Hawaii. Alone? Yes, you fool alone ... you are alone! Your mother is not here to travel with you anymore and you have not made any lasting relationships in your life, so you are fifty years old and alone!" J.C. was pacing up and down the center aisle of the hog barn, the squeal of the pigs and her own thoughts had drowned out the sound of the tractor reentering the barn so when Josh let the clutch out to back into the last feeder, J.C. almost jumped out of her skin. Josh looked down and shrugged his shoulders mouthing 'Sorry' at J.C. Her face turned red, not because Josh could have possibly heard anything she had just said to herself. She was just embarrassed overall.

The last feeder was full, and Josh left the barn with the tractor and grinder. J.C. started to unwire the gates behind the old feeding troughs. When Josh returned, he had the bale fork back on the tractor and they reversed the process from the previous day of inserting the feeders to remove the old troughs. Using the bale fork, Josh lifted the gates over the old troughs and J.C. held the gate until Josh pulled out the old troughs and set them in the center aisle. J.C. rewired the gate to the barn post when they finished. They repeated that process two more times. When they finished Josh asked, "Where do you want to store these feed troughs?"

"Dad thought you might need a couple of them at Everett's place to feed your horse," J.C. stated.

"Well, that would be great. I guess I could bring my pickup down here and we could load them." Josh nodded as he spoke like he was confirming in his mind already how he would use them.

"Great, go get your truck and I will wait here," J.C. said.

Within minutes Josh was back and they had the feed troughs loaded in his pickup. He drove his pickup back up to the driveway and J.C. followed with the tractor and bale fork. She headed into the machine shed and put the fork away before backing around to the silage wagon. Josh hooked up the wagon for her, so she didn't have to get down and opened the three gates on the way to the silage pit. When J.C. backed in, Josh was on the other tractor with the end loader and filled the silage in J.C.'s rig. She drove to the cattle lot and released the silage and returned the rig back to the machine shed. "See you at 5:00 p.m.," J.C. said as she waved to Josh.

It was just after 10:00 a.m. when Josh left, and J.C. headed back in the house. Will was not there. J.C. went upstairs and grabbed her stuff to take a shower. While taking a shower, J.C. tried to organize her thoughts from last night. Will's paperwork was in order. He was recovering from his heart surgery well. She had cleaned out her mother's and Johnnie's items from the house; and she could remove the rest of her things in the next ten days. Will was becoming more technology savvy, and he had a potential hired man now that could help him as he continued to age. When she was finished with her shower and back upstairs, she started a list of the final things that needed to be done before she moved on.

- Buy Will a cell phone.

- Set up an email account for Will.

- Prepare an employment contract for Josh.

Just then she heard someone pull into the driveway. Looking out her window, she saw the UPS truck. J.C. grabbed a coat out of her dressing room and headed downstairs. She was just stepping into her ankle boots when the UPS guy knocked on the door. "Hello, I bet you have a large box for me?" J.C. said as she opened the dining room door.

"Sure do, where would you like it, Miss?" the UPS driver responded.

"It is going down to that machine shed." J.C. pointed as she stepped towards him onto the porch. She walked in front of him and started towards the machine shed. The UPS driver returned to his truck and followed her. J.C. opened the sliding door and motioned for him to drive in. Once the truck was parked inside, J.C. opened the office door. Will was sitting at his desk looking at his computer. "The treadmill is here," J.C. announced.

Will stood up and turned around. "Oh, great," he said. The UPS driver was at the office door with the large box on his dolly. J.C. motioned for him to leave it at the end of Will's desk. She moved a chair back into a corner while he unloaded it. When he was finished, he asked J.C. to sign his form, returned to his truck and left.

Will reached into his desk drawer and pulled out a box knife and began opening the large container. Once the side panel was open, they were able to pull the treadmill out onto the floor. "Wow, that is a nice one, J.C.," Will said with a smile on his face. "I think I'll head into the house, grab my tennis shoes, and give her a test run. I have been sitting for about three hours and need to get up and move."

"That sounds good, Dad. Where should I put this box?" J.C. asked.

"I will cut it up and take it out to the trash barrel behind the garage," Will responded. "You can just leave it in here for now and I will take care of it after I am done with my workout." J.C. wished she had not just taken a shower. It would feel good to go for a hard run on the treadmill. She would give it a try in the morning she said to herself.

CHAPTER 37

The next week went by just as expected. Will's new physical therapist was impressed with how well he was doing. The cattle feeders were exactly what Will wanted so they bought them and brought them home. Josh filled them Monday evening when he got done with the regular chores which were now taking thirty minutes in the morning and forty-five minutes in the evening. On Tuesday, Josh got off work early and helped J.C. sort the fat hogs. On Wednesday morning, J.C. and Josh loaded the hogs before morning chores and then Will rode along with her to deliver them to the sale barn. While J.C. was unloading, Will went inside to take care of the sale. When they got back to the farm, J.C. changed into her workout clothes and headed down to the machine shed to work out. Josh started some field work on Thursday evening disking the forty acres just south of the hog building. Things were falling into place for J.C.'s new plan.

Chapter 38

*I*t was 1:30 p.m. on prom Saturday when Kelsey texted that she was headed home from her hair appointment and was ready for J.C. to do her nails. J.C. had just finished cleaning up the dishes from lunch. Will was napping after working in his office that morning. She left a note on the dining room table that she would be back for chores at 5:00 p.m. and headed over to help Kelsey get ready for her big night.

J.C. pulled into Vince's driveway at 2:00 p.m. She had a knot in her stomach and was anxious about seeing Vince since their last phone conversation had ended so abruptly. She took a deep breath and gave herself a pep talk as she headed towards the house. *You can handle this; it is only painting nails and telling her she looks pretty.* She knocked on the door and waited …. knocked again. It took Kelsey five minutes to answer the door.

"Sorry, I thought my dad was home. He must be out in the barn," Kelsey said with a big smile on her face.

The knot in J.C.'s stomach loosened a little bit. "I like your hair; it looks very natural and not all made up," J.C. said sincerely.

"I let them pull both sides up and drop these curls down the back," Kelsey said as she turned to show J.C. the back of her head. It reminded J.C. of her hair style for her senior year prom.

"Well, it looks very nice." J.C. stepped inside and out of her ankle boots. She hung her jacket on the hook at the end of the counter where Vince normally put it. Kelsey was in the kitchen filling water glasses and turned to J.C. "I am sorry, would you rather have coffee?" she asked.

"No, water is just fine," J.C. replied.

They headed through the archway, down the hall and into Kelsey's room. Her prom dress hung on the back of the closet door, the shoes from Doris directly below it and Kelsey's makeup was spread over the top of the vanity in her bedroom.

"Kelsey, sorry I left the polish in my coat pocket, let me grab that," J.C. explained.

"Wait," Kelsey said excitedly. "I am not sure this is the best light, plus should I put the shoes on first, or do my makeup before my nails?"

The anxiety in Kelsey's voice stopped J.C. as she could tell that Kelsey was a little frazzled. "OK, let's sit down." J.C. patted the end of Kelsey's bed. "What time is Jason coming to pick you up?"

"5:30 p.m. Our dinner reservations at the country club are for 6:00 p.m. His dad made them!" Kelsey drew in a deep breath.

"OK, then we have plenty of time to make sure you are ready and relaxed when he gets here." J.C. was not sure where this advice was coming from. Maybe Evelyn had used those words during her teenage years, and they were just coming from deep inside her. It just sounded like the right thing to say. "I also picked up a fast-dry topcoat for your nails so that should help." J.C. spoke slow and calmly. "How long does it normally take you to put on your makeup?"

"Fifteen minutes. You know I do not wear much." Kelsey smiled sheepishly.

"What time would you like to be completely ready?" J.C. asked.

"5:15 p.m.," Kelsey stated.

"Great, we have plenty of time. Do you have a basin that is big enough for your feet?" J.C. asked.

"Yes, I think my mom had one in her bathroom. Sometimes she would sit in front of the fireplace and soak her feet. She said it was relaxing." Kelsey started to stand.

"I think that is a great idea," J.C. said as she followed Kelsey out of her room. Kelsey went straight down the hall and into her parents' bedroom. J.C. headed back to the front room and collected the nail polish items from her coat pocket. "Kelsey, bring some bath salts or bubble bath if you can find them along with a few towels," J.C. called out.

Just then Vince walked through the door. "J.C., has the transformation process began yet?" he asked.

J.C. took in a deep breath, "No, but your timing is perfect. We need your help. Will you build a fire in the fireplace for Kelsey?"

Vince smiled and nodded his head affirming he would do just that. He turned and went outside to retrieve the wood.

Kelsey came through the archway with a square plastic tub that contained two kinds of bath salts, bubble bath and towels. She spread one down on the floor in front of the couch just as Vince was returning with the wood. "Oh, great Dad, are you going to build a fire?" Kelsey smiled to show her approval.

"Yes, you do know it is sixty degrees outside today?" he said looking inquisitively at the two of them.

They both smiled, and Kelsey responded, "Oh, Dad!"

J.C. took the tub to the kitchen and filled it half full of hot water. She then added some bath salts and a couple of drops of bubble bath. She carefully walked back to the living room and set it on the towel in front of Kelsey. Kelsey had already removed her socks and slid her feet into the warm suds. "Oh, J.C. this feels great," she exclaimed.

Vince stacked the wood in the fireplace and within minutes had a small blaze going in front of Kelsey. J.C. had gone back to the kitchen where she took two small towels from a drawer, sprayed them with water, and placed them in the microwave for a minute. Opening the refrigerator, she surveyed the beverage selections. She saw some orange juice, cranberry juice and Seven-Up. Taking a glass from the cupboard, she filled it with ice added orange juice, cranberry juice and Seven-Up, grabbed the warm towels, and returned to the living room.

"Miss Kelsey, here is a refreshment and may I place some warm towels around your neck to relax you?" she asked with a big smile. She gently pulled up Kelsey's hair placing the warm towels against her neck and over her shoulders and placed a dry towel around the hair to protect her recently styled curls.

Vince stood up from tending the fire and smiled down at Kelsey sitting on the couch. Kelsey's smile matched Vince's, "J.C. this is better than the spa!" she gushed.

J.C. just smiled. "She is right!" Vince echoed.

J.C. turned her attention to Vince. "Thanks for the fire but I think it is time for you to make yourself scarce, so we can begin the transformation!"

Winking at Kelsey, Vince headed through the archway and downstairs to the basement. "You ladies call if you need more wood or anything else," he said over his shoulder. Within a few minutes, soft jazz started to flow through the house stereo system.

Kelsey was sipping her drink and relaxing her shoulders as J.C. sat down in the chair next to the fire.

"Did your mom do this for you on prom day?" Kelsey asked.

"No, I do not remember if I even painted my fingernails for prom; that tradition came along later than my prom years. I would soak my mom's feet and put towels around her shoulders when we would get back from her chemo treatments though," J.C. said gazing into the fire. They sat in silence and their own thoughts for a while.

When Kelsey was done with her drink, she dried off her feet and J.C. took the tub to the kitchen and emptied the water. J.C. painted Kelsey's toes first and put an extra coat of the fast dry on them to help avoid chipping. Then they moved to the dining room table and J.C. painted Kelsey's fingernails. She worked slowly and surprised herself at how steady her hand was. She applied two coats of color and one coat of finish on Kelsey's fingernails. They were both pleased with the results.

"See, I told you that you could do it." Kelsey gave J.C. a big smile of approval.

"Well, let's see what they look like in thirty minutes after they are dry. Can I get you anything?" J.C. asked.

"I could use a little snack. I did not eat any lunch and I probably will not eat a lot at dinner. Can you get some crackers out of the pantry?" Kelsey asked.

J.C. walked to the pantry and pulled out a box of crackers, "Are these Ok?" she asked. Kelsey nodded her approval.

J.C. went back to the refrigerator to grab some cheese and grapes she had seen earlier. She washed the grapes, sliced some cheese, put them on a plate, and took them to the dining room table. She then returned to the kitchen and poured Kelsey a glass of milk. "This should give you some energy but not fill you up," J.C. explained. As Kelsey finished her snack, J.C. noted the time on her watch. It was 4:15 p.m. I think your nails should be good and dry, so you can start putting your makeup on if you like. Kelsey stood and walked carefully back to her room. J.C. cleaned up the snack remains and put the dishes in the dishwasher.

When J.C. got back to Kelsey's room, she was comparing her nails to the dress. "The color is a perfect match," she said holding her hand up to the prom dress hanging on her closet door.

"Yes, it looks like it. Do you need any more help?" J.C. asked.

"No, thank you. My hair is ready, nails are perfect, and I have plenty of time to put on my makeup and slip into my dress. Thanks, J.C., you are the best! You are coming for the red-carpet entrance to take pictures, right?" Kelsey's voice had a pleading sound to it.

"Wouldn't miss it," J.C. replied. "OK, I'd better get home to take care of some chores, make dinner and clean up so I can see how amazing you look on the red carpet." J.C. drew in a deep breath and walked out as she heard Kelsey yelling behind her. "*Thanks, J.C.!*"

J.C. slipped her boots back on and grabbed her jacket. She did not put it on as Vince had been right, that this early spring day was nearly perfect. When she got to her car, she found a note on her windshield. *Pick you up at 7:00 p.m. – V.* The knot tightened in her stomach.

Evening chores went like clockwork and J.C. was back in the house by 5:45 p.m. She quickly opened some canned beef and added some vegetables in a pot on the stove to cook while she took a shower. Will came in while she was upstairs dressing. He was just getting out of the shower at 6:30 p.m. when she put two bowls of soup and some rolls on the table for dinner.

"I am going to the high school tonight to watch Kelsey walk in for prom. It is something new they do, I guess." J.C. was in the nightly update mode.

"That should be fun," Will responded when J.C. took a bite of her meal.

J.C. looked up and Will was looking at her and she lost her train of thought.

"I think Vince is looking forward to it as well," Will stated.

J.C. shot her father a quizzical look. "He mentioned that he was coming by to take you to this red-carpet affair to take pictures tonight," Will said.

"When did you talk to Vince?" J.C. asked.

"He was over earlier today. Hey, you better let me clean up tonight, I think Vince just pulled in the driveway." Will smiled at his daughter.

J.C. shot up out of her chair and quickly headed upstairs to grab a jacket and her purse. She heard Vince knock on the door and Will answer it. "Vince come in. J.C. just ran upstairs for a minute. She should be right down. Now, you will have her home at a reasonable hour?" Will said with a chuckle as J.C. reentered the room. Her face immediately flushed. She shot her dad a disapproving look.

"Ready for the big night?" Vince asked with a big smile on his face.

"Not my..." J.C. caught herself as she was about to say something sarcastic. "Yes, I can't wait to see Kelsey in her dress," she said passing Will who was still holding the front door.

J.C. needed to get things under control, so she gave herself a pep talk as they walked to Vince's pickup. She was doing this for Kelsey as the final piece of her good neighbor deed. Well, she owed Vince too for bringing her car back to her while her dad was in Des Moines. She was just paying off debts. That is all this was, she thought, as Vince opened the passenger side of his pickup and helped her get in.

"The weather sure turned out nice for the kids tonight." Vince opened the conversation while backing his pickup out of the driveway.

"Yes, I think both of my proms were cold or rainy," J.C. recalled.

"You know I do not remember what kind of weather we had for prom. I just remember being so nervous the first year I thought I was going to throw up when I walked up to Debbie Nelson's door. You remember her dad was a policeman. He opened the door and looked me square in the eye and said 'son, no funny business tonight'. I remembered that line for the longest time and kept wondering what he meant by 'funny business'." They both laughed and J.C. felt a sense of ease pass over her.

The parking lot at the high school was full when they pulled in. Vince drove through the lot and confirmed there were no spots left. He headed to the west side of the building along the street. It was full also. He pulled into a little house and J.C. recognized Josh's pickup. "I am going to see if Josh will let us park here," Vince stated.

Vince shut off the engine and walked around to open J.C.'s door. After helping her step down, he headed up to the house and knocked on the door. Josh nodded to Vince and then waved at J.C. They walked in silence towards the high school. Halfway across the street, Vince stopped. "Oh, no, I left Kelsey's camera in the truck. I will be right back." He quickly walked back to his truck. J.C. continued to cross the street and waited for him on the sidewalk.

Vince led her into the old elementary portion of the building. J.C. was shocked to see the hallways were lined with people on both sides. Vince was not intimidated at all by the crowd. He led J.C. through them with ease, down the steps and into the gymnasium. It was decorated beautifully. The rain wall was on the north end and raindrops made from blue cellophane hung from the ceiling. The lights were all on, but J.C. imagined it would be even more impressive once the lights dimmed. When Vince stopped and selected a spot about six feet from the base of the stairs, he pulled J.C. back gently with their backs to the south wall. "Is this OK?" he asked.

"Fine," she replied.

Vince checked his watch and then his phone. "No text from Kelsey yet," he said, updating J.C. "She said she would text when they parked. I cannot imagine where these kids are going to park since the parents have taken all the parking." Vince took the camera out of his pocket and handed it to J.C. "It is pretty simple, zoom here, contrast here, big button on top takes the picture." J.C. sensed a little tension in his voice as he was explaining the camera. "The reason you have the camera is because I miss the best pictures. At least that is what Kelsey and Teri always said."

"Well, I am no photographer but at least I only have one subject to capture so maybe I can get a few good shots. You just relax and enjoy watching your daughter." J.C. smiled at Vince. When she raised her eyes to survey the crowd, she made eye contact with Janice, one of her old high school girlfriends. Janice raised her eyebrows and mouthed 'what are you doing here?'

J.C. swallowed and mouthed back 'taking pictures'; knowing that was not at all what Janice meant. Janice had been one of those friends that earlier mentioned what an eligible bachelor and great catch Vince would make for someone. J.C. diverted her eyes away from Janice. Taking in a deep breath she tried to move behind Vince a little bit.

Shortly after Vince and J.C. had gotten settled in their spot, students started arriving. J.C. used the first few couples as a test for the lighting and setting the camera up so she would be ready when Kelsey and Jason came down the stairs.

"They're here," Vince leaned into her and whispered. She could hear the anxiousness in his voice.

J.C. brought the camera up and focused it on the stairway. Ten or so couples came through before she recognized Kelsey and Jason coming down the stairs. J.C. clicked, clicked, clicked, each step they made. She had shot twenty-plus pictures by the time they were right in front of them. Kelsey stopped and turned Jason towards them once she spotted her dad. J.C. continued to snap pictures. When Kelsey thought J.C. must have gotten the perfect shot, she said, "Dad, come stand here with me." Vince immediately obeyed.

J.C. snapped five or six more shots and then lowered the camera to see what she had been taking pictures of. Kelsey looked amazing in the fuchsia dress with a classy white baby rose corsage on her wrist. Jason had done well in his selection.

J.C. smiled at the beautiful couple. "You guys look great. The best-looking couple in the place," she said.

"Did you get us coming down the stairs?" Kelsey asked.

"Yes," J.C. reassured her "I took twenty or more shots for you to pick from."

"Thanks, J.C. Oh, Jason, I am sorry, this is J.C. Mason, the friend that I told you about. She helped me with all my prom stuff. She is amazing." Kelsey introduced Jason who held out his hand to shake J.C.'s.

"We met at the spring musical a few weeks ago," J.C. reminded him.

"Yes," Jason said with a big smile.

"OK, you kids go have fun," Vince said and with that command they both turned and walked into the maze of kids standing in the middle of the gym floor under the raindrops.

Vince grabbed J.C.'s elbow and led her down the wall to the southwest exit doors of the gym. He pushed the lever and the door swung open and they were outside in the fresh air. J.C. took a deep breath that felt like her first in the last half hour. Vince turned and smiled at her with a big smile. "Now, let's go have some fun!" he said with excitement in his voice.

Chapter 39

*B*efore those words could settle into J.C.'s brain, they were back in Vince's truck and headed west on Highway 6. Vince was talking non-stop about how nervous he had been for Kelsey, but she looked beautiful and confident. Jason had shown up early and talked to Vince which made him feel more comfortable about Jim Powell's son. Vince drove through Menlo and turned south on Highway 25 towards Greenfield. J.C.'s palms were starting to sweat a little. She wanted to know what Vince meant by fun.

Just over the interstate, he turned left at the Country Club sign. What? Her heart started beating faster. She was not dressed to go to the country club. The eyebrows raised in the gym would be nothing compared to those that would raise if she walked into the club with Vince Martin, the widowed veterinarian. Vince pulled around to the back side of the club and looked at J.C. "Wait here," he said with a smile. He hopped down from the pickup and entered the backdoor of the kitchen. J.C.'s heart was beating faster and before her mind could analyze what was happening, Vince returned with a bottle of wine and two glasses. He opened her door and handed them to J.C. He walked around to the opposite side of the pickup, got in and drove back along the access road of the golf course. He pulled over, stopped, and then reached behind his seat for a couple of blankets. Vince got out of the pickup, walked around to open J.C.'s door and helped her down. He guided her through a hedge and onto the golf course. "The thirteenth hole!" Vince announced as he spread one blanket down on the green and took the bottle of wine from J.C. "I thought this would be a little more private and raise fewer eyebrows," Vince said with a chuckle.

"So ... you saw those curious looks too, back at the high school?" J.C. asked with a smile.

"Of course, and I am sorry that I put you in that position. I should have known showing up in public for the first time with a beautiful woman would cause this town to go into a tither!" Vince laughed and motioned for J.C. to sit down.

He draped the second blanket around J.C.'s shoulders and then he pulled a corkscrew out of his shirt pocket and opened the bottle of wine. J.C. still had the two glasses and held them up while Vince poured. He sat down on the blanket next to her and proposed a toast. "May the stars always shine brighter for you and may my nights always be this perfect. This is really amazing weather for early April!" He smiled as he looked into J.C.'s eyes.

J.C. felt a warm sensation rush through her body as she swallowed her first sip of wine. Vince Martin was sitting next to her under the stars. She did not know what to think. Her escape plan was less than ten days away. This was not the time to start falling for this guy, who she was still convinced was just nice with no ulterior motives.

"So, J.C. can you name any of the constellations?" Vince chided.

"Big Dipper?" J.C. scanned the sky above her trying to locate it.

"That is too easy, but can you show me Orion or Pleiades?" Vince laughed and changed the subject. "If you were still working for Big Blue, what would you be doing on a beautiful night like this? I guess what I'm asking is how did you spend your free time?" Vince seemed sincere in his questioning.

J.C. took a long drink of wine and hesitated before answering. "Well, Vince, I would have probably been working out, reading a book, or working. I really lead a very boring life especially now, after my mother passed away."

"That reminds me, did you say once that your mother was an orphan? Left on the church steps as a baby?" Vince's smooth transition of topics resembled the smoothness of the wine J.C. was consuming.

"Yes, she grew up in an orphanage in Omaha, Nebraska. After finishing high school, she went to a teacher's college and became certified to teach elementary education. The school posted a list of schools in the Midwest looking for teachers in the spring before her graduation, so she bought a train ticket and came to Stuart, Iowa. The rest you could say is … history." J.C. shared this information without anxiety.

"Wow, that had to take a lot of courage for a young woman to do that in her day!" Vince was looking into his wine glass with a very serious look on his face. "I wonder where she learned to be so caring. I told you how she went out of her way to be nice to me and Teri. Your mother was a really special lady."

"Yes, she was," J.C. said with sadness in her voice. "She had to be to take care of Will all those years."

Vince refilled their glasses and said, "And, Will, what a transformation he has made since you have been back. It has really been good for him; he has really opened up. When I stopped over today, he was showing me all his production charts and plans for this next year to minimize his costs for both pigs and cattle. You could introduce IBM to some new farming software products based on what he is creating. Maybe that was your plan all along to come here and revolutionize on-site farm data tracking." J.C. knew he was kidding but it felt like a compliment, too.

"Yes, Will has changed in the past two weeks," J.C. confirmed. Neither one of them said anything for a few minutes. Both of them tipped their heads back and gazed up at the stars.

Vince broke the silence. "J.C., I really do not know how to thank you for tonight. The first time I stopped at the house after you moved back, I knew it was a long shot that you would say yes to helping me with Kelsey and her prom preparation. I will admit now, with two glasses of wine under my belt, I was pretty nervous that day. Why would a successful IBM manager, a classy and composed businesswoman, care to help out a local farmer with his teenage daughter? I was not even sure you would remember me. You left for college and never looked back, so I was not sure what to expect when I asked about where to shop for prom dresses. These past few weeks have been so perfect and today treating Kelsey like a princess as she got ready for her big night was more than I could have ever expected. J.C., thank you." Vince paused and drew in a deep breath. "Teri would be so happy to know that you turned her little girl into a beautiful princess tonight." Vince's voice cracked and he turned away from J.C.

J.C. did not respond right away. She needed some time to compose herself too. "Vince, this is all the thanks I need. A great glass of wine under the stars. No one has ever gone out of their way to treat me with such class. As for Kelsey, she would have been a princess without any help from me. You and Teri raised a beautiful daughter who is very mature for her young age. You could have gotten any dress and she would have made it look amazing. It is what's on the inside that makes it beautiful." J.C. stared into her empty wine glass. What a beautiful moment in time she thought. A father caring so much for his child and missing his wife who should have been on the blanket to share this moment with him. J.C.'s heart felt a deep sadness in her chest, and it sent a shiver through her.

"Oh, we better get going. You are getting cold. Let me help you up." Vince extended his hand and pulled J.C. to her feet. She followed him back through the hedge to his pickup. Vince opened her door and held the glasses as she stepped inside. He handed her the empty bottle and glasses before taking the blankets and getting into the pickup himself. Vince put the pickup in reverse and drove back up to the kitchen door of the club. J.C. handed him the glasses and empty bottle and he disappeared inside.

When Vince was back in the pickup, J.C. asked, "So how is it that you can come here and take stemware and wine outside? Do all the members have these privileges?"

"Well, I am club president! And the club manager is a great friend. Sometimes I do him a favor so occasionally he lets me have a few extra privileges," Vince said confidently with a big smile and then winked at J.C. They drove down Highway 25 to a gravel road west of Fairview Church, turned east on the gravel and headed towards the church. When he turned right heading to Will's farm, Vince broke the silence. "Thanks for going with me tonight, J.C. I know the town will be talking about this tomorrow, so I want to apologize in advance for making you the center of Stuart's gossip cycle this week."

"You know, you are the ultimate nice guy. Who else would care about what people are saying about me? I am a big girl and can take care of myself, Vince, but thank you anyway." She smiled at him and opened her door as the pickup came to a stop in the driveway. She did not wait for Vince to come around and open her door. She knew he missed his wife and loved his daughter; there was no reason to pretend that Mr. Nice Guy was anything more to her than that.

Chapter 40

*S*pring field work was rolling right along. Josh was working almost every night after evening chores and had half of the acres planted to corn by April 15th.

On the morning of April 16th, J.C. took Will into Greenfield to see Dr. Wilson at the Adair County Hospital. "Will Mason, how are things going?" Dr. Wilson asked as he entered the examination room.

"Great, never felt better, I'm ready for that release to drive." Will got right to the point.

"Well, let's see." Dr. Wilson paused as he reviewed Will's chart. "Your physical therapy has gone well. They are ready to release you. All of your bloodwork has been normal for the past month. Let's listen to that heart." Dr. Wilson stepped over and placed the stethoscope over Will's chest. "Sounds pretty good." Dr. Wilson spun around and looked at J.C. "How is he doing? Is he following orders and not lifting, or exerting himself?"

"Yes, Dr. Wilson, he really has followed the rules. He walks a couple of times a day on a treadmill in his machine shed and now with the nicer weather, he takes a walk around the pasture every once in a while, but no lifting, driving, or exerting," J.C. reported.

"Well, Will, I have to say you have surprised me. I know Evelyn would be happy to know that we finally got that old heart of yours fixed, so yes, you can drive and slowly start building up your strength to lift feed buckets again. Promise me you will take your time and not rush back into that kind of work all in one week. I will see you back here in three months. You can make an appointment at the desk when you leave. Really great to see you doing so well, Will." Dr. Wilson looked down at his clipboard and started writing.

"Thanks, Doc; no need to worry about feed buckets. J.C. automated that work while I was laid up. We hired a young man to help with the planting this spring and may even keep him around for harvest, we'll see when the times comes. I will take it slow and surprise you in ninety days!" Will had a twinkle in his eyes. They stopped at the front desk to schedule Will's next appointment. J.C. thought Will was going to skip out the door; he was so happy to get the driving release.

"Dad, no lifting seed bags, yet!" J.C. said sternly as she backed the car out of the parking lot and headed back towards the farm.

"Not planning to do that, J.C. I think Josh has got the spring planting schedule under control and I plan to let him finish that. Maybe tonight we can talk about what chores I can get back to doing. I kind of miss doing them," Will said.

"Well, you can scrape those hog floors any night you like. I will give you that chore in a heartbeat," J.C. said with a smile.

Will changed his clothes as soon as they got back to the farm. "Before lunch, I am going to drive around and check the fields Josh has planted," he announced to J.C.

"OK Dad, I will start lunch and work on getting your cell phone set up," J.C. replied.

"Not sure why I need one of those things," Will protested.

"Because when I leave, I want to make sure you carry it in your shirt pocket in case you go down again; that way you can call for help. You might even find it is useful when you're in the hog barn, so you don't have to come back to the house to call for price quotes." J.C. nodded as Will headed out the mudroom door.

J.C. was in the final stages of her exit plan. She had set up email for Will and they had practiced emailing back and forth from his laptop in the machine shed to hers. She planned to use that also as a means of communication with her father once she moved back to Des Moines. Now, with the addition of the cell phone, she could really check on him anytime to make sure he was getting along OK. If necessary, she could face time him and see for herself how he was doing.

J.C. started boiling some chicken to make vegetable chicken soup for lunch. Her phone rang and she looked to see who was calling. "Nadine, how are you doing? Just got back from Greenfield and Dr. Wilson released Will to drive again. So, of course, he has gone out in his pickup already to check the fields that Josh has planted." J.C. quickly ran through the information she knew that Nadine was calling about.

"Great, I assumed Will would get released today. He has recovered very quickly. What's new with you? Spending your spare time at the Martin place, I am sure," Nadine said with some sarcasm in her voice.

"I am fine and *no*, I have not spent *any* time at the Martins. I got a beautiful handwritten note from Kelsey with a picture of her and Vince on prom night. My work there is done. He asked me to help get his daughter ready for prom and I did that." J.C. spoke sternly to let Nadine know that this topic was closed for discussion.

"Well, with Will mended and now that Kelsey's prom is over, what is your next project?" Nadine asked.

"Moving back to Des Moines," J.C. stated.

"What, why so fast?" Nadine asked.

"I did what I came to do. Will does not need me anymore and I plan to move back before the weekend," J.C. outlined.

"The old J.C.," Nadine said with confidence in her voice, "is back! She is in control and headed on down the road. I hope you find what you are looking for J.C. I really thought you were getting close to finding it here but maybe you got too close and that scared you."

"Nadine, what in the world are you talking about? Sometimes I don't understand you at all!" J.C. spoke with frustration. "I did what I came here to do. Dad's finances and end-of-life paperwork is in order. He has help on the farm and even confirmed today that he plans on keeping Josh as a hired man. Mom's and Johnnie's things are taken care of. The remainder of my things will be gone this week. That leaves dad's personal belongings and the furniture, which he has outlined to be sold at a farm auction upon his death. My work here is done! I need to start looking for another job and may have to move." J.C. ended with a big sigh.

"Well, I hope you do not move too far, too fast. I think once you put a little space in between you and Will you might discover you like having a father again," Nadine spoke with confidence. "You are more like Will than you think, J.C."

J.C. shook her head but did not respond to Nadine's comments. "I do want to see you before I move back. Can I take you to lunch sometime this week?" J.C. changed the subject almost as keenly as Nadine could do.

"Oh, well that would be nice," Nadine said, "there is that new hamburger place in Dexter I have been wanting to try. Does Thursday work for you?" she asked.

"Great, I will come in and pick you up around 11:30 a.m. and we can try it out," J.C. said. "I better get lunch fixed so it is ready when Will comes in. I will see you on Thursday."

Will and J.C. sat down to lunch and before J.C. could say anything Will said, "Josh has really done a nice job with the planting. I checked the depth of the kernels on the four fields he planted so far, and they are all at exactly two inches. He really is a good farmer. I have been noticing the weight gains on the hogs are improving also. We reduced three days off that last load of hogs that went to town, even with the slight increase of feed consumption, using the automated feeders will save us about twenty to thirty dollars per head on our feed expense." Will was talking like this was a normal conversation and J.C. did not know what to say.

"J.C., I would like to talk to him about an employment contract. You mentioned that last week and I kind of pushed it off. I think that makes good sense. Do you have a document that you have used in the past or should I call Ken?" Will asked.

"I think I can put something together that should work, Dad," J.C. replied. She sat in her chair amazed at how sharp her seventy-five-year-old father was. He knew that this young man could do things faster and smarter than he could, and with his recent heart attack he could spend the remainder of his days doing the things on the farm he enjoyed. This was even more evidence that she was not needed and would be in the way. "I think I will move back to my condo on Friday this week." J.C. looked across the table at Will.

"Really?" Will looked directly into her eyes. "I will miss having you here, J.C.," he said softly. Will dropped his head and finished eating.

J.C. felt a knot in her chest. Was she doing the right thing? Really, with Will doing chores, Josh's support and – what *and*—her internal voice shouted inside her head. No, and … Vince was just a guy who still misses his wife and is raising his teenage daughter. She needed to get back to her life and find her new reality! When she pulled her attention out of the rant going on in her head, Will was setting his dishes in the sink and headed through the mudroom door. J.C. cleaned up the kitchen, put a beef roast in the oven with potatoes and carrots, and headed upstairs to sort and pack. When J.C. got upstairs, she sent a quick note to her former boss asking if he would send her a generic employment agreement.

Chapter 41

J.C. went into spring cleaning mode when she got back to the condo. Dust lay everywhere and there was a stale smell to her place. The weather was warmer, so she was able to have the windows open during the day. The fresh spring air filled her condo as she deep cleaned everything. It felt good to go through each room moving, sorting, and taking things to Goodwill that no longer had purpose in her life. Whatever she had started on the farm was carried over to her place in Des Moines. She found she was transitioning to a simpler lifestyle. Less clutter was her motto each day as she worked her way through the condo. If she needed to move, it might make sense to sell the condo, and the simple classy look was more appealing to buyers she told herself. When J.C. finished her condo overhaul, she scheduled a spa day to reward herself.

It had been exactly two weeks since she left the farm; no calls, no texts, no contact at all from Vince or Kelsey. She lay in the lounge sipping her wine at the spa and confirmed to herself that she had read the signals correctly. Vince was the ultimate nice guy raising a normal teenage daughter who just needed some female assistance for her prom. They had

CHAPTER 41

moved on and she needed to do the same. When J.C. pulled her phone out of her purse, she was surprised she had missed a call from Vince. Her chest tightened. She pushed the voicemail button and heard his voice say, "Sorry, been busy with spring work. Hope you are doing well. I was wondering if you are free Friday night and could join us for Kelsey's birthday? No big plans–just Kelsey, a couple of her friends, and me grilling burgers on the deck. Call me. And oh, Kelsey wanted me to ask if you would mind bringing the *cake!*" J.C.'s heart quickened and her mind started racing. Was he just being nice, or did he really want her to come? Had Kelsey asked; did she want to go? So many questions were racing through her head.

J.C. checked out at the front desk of the spa and walked out into the late afternoon sun. Her car was warm as she settled in and turned on the AC. As she drove to her condo, she reassessed what she had seen that last night with Vince on the golf course, the fact that in two weeks neither Vince nor Kelsey had made contact and the biggest issue was that her life was so different from theirs. It was obvious that this was a friendly call and she needed to keep moving forward to execute her plan.

She had completed the employment agreement for Will and Josh but thought it best if she met with them to go over it in case they had questions. She called Will as she drove. "Dad, it's J.C. How are you doing?" she asked.

"Good, getting used to this new gadget in my pocket. I kind of like it. You were right; it does make it easier to do business from outside. What's new with you?" Will sounded chipper.

"I have that employment agreement ready for you and Josh to sign. I was thinking maybe I would come out on Friday and we could go over it with him then." J.C. laid out the plan.

"Sounds good, I will mention that to Josh tonight and see if that works for him. I am glad you are coming home this weekend; I have another idea I would like to run by you," Will stated.

"What idea is that?" J.C. shot back a quick question.

"It's about Everett's place; I think it might be time to sell," Will responded.

"Well, Dad ..." J.C. drew in a sigh. "I am not coming home for the weekend; I'm just stopping by to go over the agreement and now I guess to discuss the potential sale of Everett's farm. I will plan on being there mid-afternoon so we can finish our discussion before Josh gets there. If you guys want to review the agreement first, then I will head back while the two of you do the chores." J.C. hurried through her comments hoping that Will would just agree.

"J.C., have you talked to Vince?" Will asked.

"No. He left me a message today, but I have not returned his call yet." Strange that Will would ask that question she thought as she shot back her sharp response.

"OK. I guess I will see you Friday," Will said as he hung up. J.C. shook her head as she pulled into the garage underneath the condo.

When J.C. got into her condo, she flopped on her couch and listened to Vince's message again. He sounded like always laid-back, no pressure, nice, and inviting. She decided to text her response, 'Vince, thanks for the invitation. I am sorry that I will not be able to come Friday night, but I will make sure that Kelsey's cake is there. J.C.' She read and re-read her message before hitting send.

On Friday morning, J.C. went through her normal routine. Up at 6:30 a.m., hit the gym downstairs for a forty-five-minute workout, and then back for coffee and a shower before she started to make Kelsey's cake. J.C. lost herself in her memories about Kelsey as she prepared the sour cream chocolate cake and fudge frosting. Using a butter knife after frosting the cake she marked '18—-18—-18—-18—-18' all around the cake. She smiled as she finished it but lost the smile when she realized she would not see Kelsey's face when it was time to cut the cake. It is best this way, J.C.'s internal voice confirmed. She placed the cake in the carrier and put it in a cooler with two bags of ice to keep the frosting firm for the drive from Des Moines to Stuart.

J.C. went into her office to pick up the employment contract and put it in her bag that contained a small box from Joseph's Jewelry. Picking up the cooler, she headed out the door and to her car. It was 11:30 a.m. and she was right on schedule. On her drive to Stuart, J.C. called Nadine. "Nadine, can I stop by for coffee later this afternoon? I have to take some legal papers to the farm for dad and Josh to sign and thought I could see you before heading back into Des Moines tonight," J.C. asked.

"Oh, J.C., I am sorry, but I am going with a group from church to Adair tonight to try out a new restaurant. We are leaving at 4:30 p.m. so we can beat the 6:00 p.m. rush. You can go with us. It is Marjorie, Delores and ..."

"No, thanks!" J.C. interrupted her, "I will see you next time I come out this way. Are you doing OK?" J.C. asked.

"Fit as a fiddle. Did you get all your cleaning done?" Nadine replied.

"Sure did. I took three carloads of items to Goodwill. It feels great to have all that clutter gone." J.C.'s voice almost sounded lighter as she spoke. "Well, I will let you go; have fun with the ladies tonight." J.C. smiled as she envisioned the carload of women headed out for the evening.

It was just before 1:00 p.m. when J.C. pulled into Vince's driveway. She was certain he would be at work and Kelsey would be at school. She parked and looked around cautiously before turning off her car. J.C. pulled the cooler from behind the driver's seat and walked to the deck. She drew in a deep breath and knocked on the door. No answer. She heaved a sigh of relief, slowly turned the handle, and released the front door. She stepped inside Vince's home with butterflies in her stomach. Quickly looking around she walked to the counter and set the cake carrier on it. J.C. returned to the car to leave the cooler and reached into her bag and pulled out the small gold box and card addressed to Kelsey. She quickly walked back to the house and left them on the counter next to the cake. Turning around, she stood for a moment taking in the Martin home one last time. She felt sad that this was the last time she would be here.

When J.C. walked into her father's house, he was sitting at the dining room table with a cup of coffee reading a magazine. "Dad, what are you doing? I have never seen you read anything other than ..." J.C. stopped herself before she said Bible.

"Josh gave me this because it has an article on winter wheat. He has used that up in northern Iowa and thinks it is good for the soil. Pretty interesting stuff and I might consider trying some on a couple of fields this fall." Will smiled at J.C. as he explained. She nodded and headed into the kitchen to pour herself a cup of coffee. Returning to the dining room, J.C. sat in her usual spot and pulled out the agreement and pushed it towards Will to review.

Will slid the stack of papers to the side of the table. "J.C., I don't think I need this anymore. These past two weeks working alongside this young man, I no longer think of him as a hired hand. He is just a neighbor helping out a neighbor. Now, don't get me wrong, I still plan on paying him for the field work but tonight is the last night Josh will need to help with chores. I can handle them on my own now." Will stopped, but J.C. could tell he still had more to say and after a few deep breaths Will said, "I do not want to rent the building site to Josh. I want to sell him that property. He is the kind of young man that we need in this community .... farming and taking care of things ... like neighbors in need." With a deep sigh Will stopped and looked at J.C.

"You said that mom's plan was that Johnnie would someday live there and farm with you. How can you give it to someone that you barely know?" J.C. spoke sharply with anger in her voice. "I do not want any of this land and couldn't care less who farms it when you're gone, but how can you make this decision so quickly and without any respect for mom's feelings?" Tears were streaming down J.C.'s face as she stared at Will.

Will's tears began to fall, and he slowly replied, "J.C., this has not been a quick decision. Josh is an answer to my prayers. He is the right person for that land. He is the kind of young man that Evelyn would want to farm in Johnnie's place. He came here and made things better. She would love his resourcefulness. As for Johnnie, you need to understand that Johnnie is happy where he's at. He would not come back for one minute to this old earth even if he could. He is in *Heaven!*" Will's voice was strong, and he had a twinkle in his eye. "I know you and I have a past of pain and suffering that I wish I could wipe away, but you have to be willing to let it go too, Jacquelyn. I was broken and no words that I know will ever erase the pain I caused you. Please try and forgive me so that we can start ..." Will spoke gently and reached out his hand toward J.C.

"*Stop!* I do not care if you want to sell the farm to Josh, sell it to him. I know Johnnie is not coming back. I am *not* a child; and do *not* call me Jacquelyn. Jacquelyn died with Johnnie and she is not coming back either, Dad!" J.C. stormed into the bathroom sobbing.

When J.C. came out of the bathroom, Will was gone. She stood in the dining room for a few minutes then opened the front door, left the house, and slowly walked to her car. J.C. turned on the ignition, put the car in reverse and backed out. One hour later she was back in her clean, quiet condo, completely alone.

Chapter 42

*A*t mid-day on Sunday, J.C. stepped out of the shower and wrapped her hair in a towel. She pulled on her yoga pants and T-shirt. Comfort was what she needed today, her last day of self-pity because tomorrow she was making calls to find a placement company that could land her the perfect job in a new location to start her new life. As J.C. stepped into her kitchen to grab another cup of coffee, there was a knock at her door. Doris must need to borrow something she thought. J.C. opened the door without checking the peephole.

"Vince!" J.C.'s voice showed her shock.

Vince Martin stood in the hallway with a spring bouquet of flowers cradled inside his right elbow and her cake carrier in his left hand. He was dressed in grey slacks and a dark grey V-neck sweater over a black and white checked shirt. "What happened?" J.C. said pointing at Vince's right shoulder where the right sleeve of his sweater fell flat to his side.

"Broken arm. Cow kicked me square on the forearm and snapped it right between the wrist and elbow," Vince said with a big smile on his face.

"Oh, Vince, I am so sorry. When did that happen?" J.C. asked, as she took the flowers from him and moved backward inviting him into the condo.

"About three weeks ago. I was in a hurry and did not check the kick bar on the shoot. It came loose and hit me in the head." He turned, showing J.C. the stitch lines over the right corner of his forehead where his hair was shaved. J.C.'s right hand started to raise towards his stitches, but she awkwardly pulled it back down.

"As I turned away hoping to miss the bar, my arm came right into the direct line of impact. They had to leave it open for about ten days so that the skin could heal before putting the cast on. The doctor said it could have been a lot worse. I was lucky I saw the bar coming. I could have lost my eye if it had hit me any lower." Vince stopped as he could see J.C. was struggling to take it all in.

J.C. laid the bouquet of flowers on the counter. She turned and examined Vince's head injury. "Vince, I am so sorry; you should have called." J.C. was still in a state of shock as she examined Vince.

Vince motioned towards the bar stool indicating that he would like to sit down. "Of course, I am still shocked to see you and hearing this, I am completely disoriented. Would you like some coffee?" J.C. hurried around the kitchen reaching for a second cup and pouring it for Vince before he had a chance to reply.

"J.C., I'm fine. I just wanted to thank you for surprising Kelsey with the cake and the beautiful gift. I will let her thank you properly when she sees you," Vince said.

J.C.'s mind was starting to catch up, processing what she was seeing, hearing, and aligning it with reality. "How did you get here?" she asked Vince.

"To Des Moines or upstairs to your condo?" he said with a sly smile.

"Both!" J.C. responded, sitting next to him with her cup of coffee.

"Well, Kelsey drove us to Des Moines. I remembered your garage combination and so we parked in a visitor space downstairs. I hope that is all right?" Vince waited for J.C. to give her approval.

"Of course!" she replied.

"I took them to a restaurant, ordered lunch for them and then came back here to deliver these to you. Plus, we wanted to ask you to go to the show with us this afternoon," Vince said.

"Show, what show? And who is with Kelsey?" J.C. was starting to stammer again.

"Jason is with her. Remember you told me Kelsey would like 'Phantom of the Opera'. Well, I gave her four tickets to today's matinee for her birthday. You just happen to be the fourth person she wants to take. If you say no, we may have to find a bum on the street to go with us," Vince said jokingly.

At that instant, J.C. realized her hair was still in a towel and she looked hideous! "Oh, my! Vince, I must have scared you when I opened the door looking like this. I forgot I had this silly towel on my head." Horror covered her face as she stood to dart to her bedroom.

Vince reached out with his left hand and pulled her back down to the barstool. "J.C. you look fine. The show starts at 2:00 p.m. so you have plenty of time to get ready before Kelsey and Jason come to pick us up. "Finish your coffee and if I could impose a little ... would you make me a sandwich? Eating in front of people is still a little awkward but I can manage a sandwich pretty well." Vince smiled sheepishly.

"Of course." J.C. shot out of her chair and around the island to the refrigerator. She grabbed some turkey, swiss cheese and bacon that she had planned to use for her lunch and quickly made two sandwiches. "Now tell me exactly how all this happened and why no one called me!"

"They kept me in the hospital overnight to make sure I did not have a concussion and then I was down flat for three more days at home. My arm was in an immobilizer so the outside skin could heal before casting. Once I got the cast on, I have made steady progress of taking care of myself. I am not the best with my left-hand, but I can brush my teeth, feed myself and get most of my clothes on and off without too much trouble. Kelsey has been such a great help. Since it was near the end of the school year, her activities were over, and she's been able to help out more. She comes home after fifth period every day and gets most of the housework done before Josh and Will get there to help with chores. She thought she could do it all, but they have insisted on doing the majority of the outside work. They even finished planting all my acres before Will let Josh finish his. I do not know what I would have done without those two guys." Vince took a sip of coffee as J.C. set his sandwich in front of him.

"Will and Josh did your planting?" J.C. asked meekly.

"Yes, Will on my rig and Josh on yours. They had it done in the three days while I was on bed rest," Vince stated.

"Vince, why didn't anyone call me?" J.C. asked courageously for the third time not sure she wanted to know the answer.

"It was my pride." Vince looked down at his chest. "Kelsey had your number dialed at the hospital that first night. We thought you were still at the farm. Then Will showed up alone and said you had moved back to Des Moines that day, so I told Kelsey not to call. I could tell you needed some space on prom night and thought I should give you some time."

Silence filled J.C.'s condo. The hum of the refrigerator was all that either J.C. or Vince could focus on. It was a deafening sound. "Vince, I didn't need space." J.C. was the first to speak. "I saw how much you missed Teri and ..."

"I know," Vince interrupted her, "Nadine came by last week to drop off a casserole, change the bedding, wash some towels, and make sure Kelsey was doing OK. She told me what fools you and I both were. She said she knows you better than anyone. Nadine was certain that I had strong feelings for you; so, her advice was that I had better do something quick or you would be gone. She told me that you would never want to take Teri's place for either Kelsey or me." Vince heaved a sigh like he had just gotten something major off his chest.

"Nadine! I never said, she always thought, how in the world!" J.C.'s mind was reeling to think that Nadine had talked to Vince about her feelings. Wait, her mind was scrambling again ... she had never told Nadine how she felt about Vince. A schoolgirl crush that started on a school bus one day and blossomed under the stars one night on a golf course. How could she have told Nadine? J.C. had never admitted to herself that she had fallen in love with Vince. It has only been three months ... no one falls in love that fast. Her mind made a quick turn; did Vince use the words 'strong feelings' for her? She gasped, "Sorry, I never said any of those things to Nadine and do not know why she thinks your personal life is any of her business anyway," J.C. said abruptly.

"J.C., it is OK! I would have gotten here eventually. Nadine just has a way of getting to the point quicker. Like I said, it was my pride, and I should have handled our evening on the golf course better. Teri would want me to be happy again. I know you make me happy, and you make Kelsey happy. It doesn't seem possible, but I am in love with you, J.C." Vince had turned his bar stool and was looking deep into J.C.'s eyes as the words crossed his lips.

Emotions started stirring in the depths of J.C.'s stomach. She could feel them rising and wondered how to stop them. Run! Was the first thought that came into her head. Instead, she heard a gentle voice telling her to 'let go'. Evelyn's face flashed through her mind 'someday the right guy will come along, and you will not know what hit you'. Her mother had told her this would happen. J.C. sat frozen on the bar stool next to Vince.

"I can tell that you are caught off guard. I wish I had said something before you got out of the pickup the other night. I was struggling to believe that in three short months I had fallen for you. Nadine and Kelsey knew it right away, but it took me longer to admit it to myself." Vince was trying to explain.

J.C. took a deep breath and tried to put into words her hesitations. "Vince, I know that I have feelings for you too and I adore Kelsey, but I am not like the two of you. You both believe in a God that I cannot understand. You both have a peace that seems to permeate your lives even though tragedy has taken someone that you both loved dearly. I try to understand how your God could take so much away from people that seem to be doing all the right things. Nadine lost her husband before she was thirty. My mother never even knew her family. My dad has lost so many people he loved at such critical times in his life. Johnnie was only six years old and loved life to the fullest when your God took him. You and Kelsey lost Teri who was in the prime of her life. What kind of God does all that and then in the middle of my mess brings you into my life?" Her face was filled with questions.

Vince smiled with the most genuine smile and said, "That is what makes God–God. J.C., we were never meant to understand all these things while we are on earth. God created each one of us for a specific purpose. Johnnie was too special for this world; just like Will's two brothers. Their time was so short because their purpose was more heavenly than earthly. Teri's role was to bring Kelsey into this world and give her a strong foundation so she would be ready to move forward on her own. Evelyn touched many lives in her lifetime and created this beautiful woman that is sitting next to me. God did not promise us lives without troubles. He does, however, promise rewards for those trials if we are willing to accept His way. You don't realize it, but you are one of those rewards that God has brought into my life and Kelsey's. I think you are also a special blessing to Will, Nadine, and Doris. Your business mind tries to make all these things balance out like a strategic plan. Well, God's plan is a little different. The good news is that all we have to do is believe."

Hebrews 4:3, 'you must believe if you want to enter heaven'. The words that J.C. had read in the Bible that day at the hospital came back to her. J.C.'s mouth opened, and she heard words coming out but could not explain where they came from. "Vince, I want what you and Kelsey have. I want to believe in your God." If Vince was willing to take this chance; if Will could come back from the depths of sorrow that he had lived; if Nadine could care more about others' happiness than her own; if Josh could help total strangers that he had never met, then their God must be a miracle worker. J.C. wanted to be a part of that.

Vince wrapped his arm around her shoulders. Vince invited J.C. to join him as he prayed. "Father in Heaven, I believe and let go of all my sins and give myself to you. Please forgive me and accept me as a child of God today. Amen." Just then someone knocked at the door. Vince walked to the door and Kelsey and Jason rushed in. J.C. was wiping her eyes as she stood up. Kelsey ran towards her and threw her arms around her. "Thank you for this beautiful locket. I put a picture of my mom in it. She is right over my heart. Are you going to 'Phantom' with us?" Kelsey's questions were gushing out so fast that J.C. could not possibly answer all of them. Kelsey released her hug on J.C. and stepped back.

J.C. looked at her clock and then towards Vince who was nodding that there was enough time. She quickly headed into her bedroom and put on a midnight blue cocktail dress while her curling iron was warming up. She put on some eye make-up, bronzer on her cheeks, curled her hair, and stepped into a pair of heels. Before returning to the living room, J.C. picked up her phone and called Will. "Dad, I am sorry about our last conversation. I have some amazing news for you and will share that when I get back to the farm tonight." She paused before saying softly, "Dad, I love you." J.C. hung up the phone.

Chapter 43

The Fairview Church candlelight Christmas Eve service was more crowded than usual that year. Kelsey sang a solo, '*Silent Night*', to open the service. Both of Vince's sisters had come home at Vince's begging and brought their families. Josh was there with his parents. Jason Powell and his mother also attended. The pastor read the gospel of Mark's version of Christ's birth - the traditional nativity story of Mary, Joseph, and Jesus in the manager. He talked about shepherds that came when they saw the star, the wise men who traveled from afar and the lowly animals that stood around; somehow relating that to each and every person that attended the service. It was the most powerful message of the Christmas story that J.C. had ever heard. Kelsey and Jason sang a duet of '*O Holy Night*' to close the service. J.C. felt shivers run down her spine again, hearing them sing. When the service ended, Vince, Kelsey, J.C., Will and Nadine all headed back into Stuart to the newly renovated historical Stuart Hotel. Vince had booked rooms there for his two sisters' families and also catered a special dinner so the families could celebrate Christmas Eve together.

The hotel was exquisitely decorated for the holiday season. It seemed odd that on Christmas Eve, a small jazz quartet was playing but it created a wonderful holiday atmosphere. The tables were preset with white linens, china, crystal, and red rose centerpieces. As soon as they arrived, Vince headed into the kitchen to check on the caterers. Will and Nadine spent time catching up with Vince's sisters and their families. No one seemed to notice that J.C. and Kelsey immediately disappeared. Two waiters were serving hors d'oeuvres and drinks as people gathered and mingled. A few other people began to come in just before 7:00 p.m. Will nodded towards Josh and his parents. Nadine thought it odd that Jason and his mother walked through the door around 7:00 p.m. also.

At exactly 7:00 p.m. Vince returned to the dining room in a charcoal grey tuxedo followed by Reverend Johnson and asked everyone to gather around the base of the staircase. He nodded towards the quartet who began playing 'Mandel's Wedding March'. The room fell silent as Will stepped to the bottom of the staircase and all eyes looked up. First, Kelsey came down in a scarlet velvet dress trimmed in white fur around her shoulders and cuffs. She carried a white fur muff. A single gold locket hung around her neck. She gracefully descended the staircase smiling at Vince the entire way. When she had reached the bottom step, the music crescendoed and J.C. appeared in a soft white stretch velvet gown that draped gently off her shoulders into a v-neckline. The bodice was covered in snowflake sequins accented by tiny rhinestones that sparkled like snow. The beading cascaded gently down the flowing skirt almost like scattered snowflakes until it gracefully touched her toes. Her veil was a small cluster of snowflake beads that matched her dress and covered a hair comb attached to tulle. J.C.'s hair was pulled up on both sides to the top of her head where her veil was clipped. She carried three red roses wrapped in white satin as her bouquet. One simple gold locket was the only jewelry she wore. She too smiled at Vince the entire time as she descended the stairs.

CHAPTER 43

Will was smiling from ear to ear as he took J.C.'s arm and led her to where Vince and Kelsey were waiting in front of Reverend Johnson. After Will responded to "Who gives this woman to be married?" with a response of, "I do." He stepped up next to Vince as the best man.

The ceremony was simple. Reverend Johnson described what marriage means based on scripture. Instead of vows, J.C. and Vince had both selected songs to be sung. J.C. asked Jason to sing *'You Needed Me'* by Anne Murray. Vince asked Kelsey to sing *'You Light up My Life'* by Debbie Boone. After Reverend Johnson prayed for Vince's and J.C.'s union, Kelsey and Jason closed out the ceremony with *'Happy Together'* by The Turtles; everyone was clapping and laughing. Nadine rushed to J.C. with tears rolling down her cheeks. "I knew it, I knew it, remember I told you from the very beginning, I am nobody's fool. But how could you not tell me? J.C. you know, Evelyn is dancing in heaven tonight. She is at Jesus' birthday party right now looking down knowing that she created this beautiful night. She brought all of us together so that this could happen. You know that don't you, J.C.!" Nadine was smiling and crying as her words blurted out.

"I know, Nadine, I know. Thanks, mom!" J.C. smiled towards the ceiling.

"Did everyone know besides me?" Nadine inquired, still short of breath.

"No, only dad and Kelsey. The rest of the guests were invited just for dinner by Vince, or Kelsey, or dad ... they are all in the same state of shock that you are!" J.C. said with a big smile on her face.

"Even Jason?" Nadine asked.

"Even Jason thought he was the entertainment for Vince's Christmas Eve dinner party," J.C. assured Nadine.

Just then the photographer that had been sent by Talesse' Designs to capture this custom made, original wedding gown stepped up and touched J.C.'s elbow. "Can we get a few pictures of the wedding party on the staircase?" he asked.

Nadine turned and looked surprised as she had not noticed him in the back of the room during the ceremony. Kelsey, Will, Vince and J.C. posed on the stairs as their guests watched. One quick picture with the reverend and the wedding party signing the license and then Vince announced that everyone was to be a part of the final picture.

The photographer arranged the thirty-plus people around the large Christmas tree in the front window of the hotel. It was exquisitely decorated and made it the perfect focal point for his shot. He positioned the younger cousins standing on chairs in the back. A row of adults stood in front of them. On the right were Vince's two sisters and Kelsey; and on the left, Will and Nadine were seated in chairs. He carefully placed two small boxes between Kelsey's and Will's chairs and positioned Vince and J.C. on them. Snap! Snap! Snap! "That's good," the photographer said as they all stood up shouting and clapping.

Dinner began immediately. J.C. hired one of her favorite caterers from Des Moines. The tables were positioned in a square formation with the center of the square left open. Vince and J.C. sat down at one end and invited everyone to sit where they were comfortable. Every person there could see the bride and groom and enjoy their happiness. Soft music played in the background, guests dined on steak, chicken or salmon accompanied by garlic mashed potatoes, steamed vegetables, and Nadine's homemade dinner rolls that J.C. had prearranged to be made for Vince's Christmas Eve dinner. When everyone had finished the main course, a beautiful three tier chocolate cake frosted in chocolate-fudge frosting was brought in for the bride and groom to cut. J.C. and Kelsey had baked the cake together earlier in the day and of course used Evelyn's sour cream chocolate cake recipe. Will nodded his head towards Josh who left momentarily and came back with a homemade ice cream freezer from his truck, that Will had asked him to pick up from the farm before heading back into town. Everyone smiled as their desserts were set in front of them.

As the guests enjoyed their dessert, Will stood, cleared his throat, and said, "No one expects me to speak but I think it is customary for the best man to say a few words. These two families have experienced so much sorrow and pain but tonight our pain is replaced with joy. Vince and Kelsey, thank you for bringing my daughter and me back together. Thank you for making our family complete again." He cleared his throat and said, "J.C. and Vince, no wedding is complete without gifts, I wanted to make sure you had at least one gift tonight." He reached into his inside pocket and pulled out a folded set of papers. He handed them to J.C. She opened them, and as she read them a tear ran down her cheek. She passed them to Vince who read the description of a property that once belonged to his father and saw that the deed now said it belonged to Vince and Jacquelyn Martin. His eyes filled with tears as he rose and shook hands with Will. "Thank you," was all he could whisper.

Once Vince collected his emotions he spoke, "All things work together for good to those who love God and are called according to His purpose. We are all here because God loves us, takes care of us, and blesses us with joys beyond measure. Thank you for your love and support over these past few years as J.C., Will, Kelsey and I lost loved ones, but God has brought so much good out of all that sorrow. J.C., thank you for saying 'yes'..." Vince took a long pause, "... to helping with the dress!" was Vince's toast as the room erupted into laughter.

All J.C.'s 'whys' had been answered. Jacquelyn Caine Martin was loved by Vince, Kelsey, Will, Nadine and God.

Epilogue

*E*velyn was walking in the garden one afternoon when she saw The Teacher up ahead. She quickened her step to catch up. "Teacher, Teacher," she spoke excitedly, "Thank you for bringing me back to teach the children. I get to spend every day with Johnnie. I am so blessed!"

"I am pleased to hear that you enjoy training the children. They are so important to My Kingdom." He smiled and continued the conversation. "Evelyn, your veterinarian friend is getting remarried today."

"Oh, that is wonderful. He was so nice, and I was sad when his wife was killed. Is he marrying someone from the community?" she inquired.

"Someone that recently returned to the community," was His response.

"A nice woman, I hope." Evelyn was enjoying this unhurried conversation with The Teacher.

"She has become more like her mother with each passing day," Teacher replied.

"Was her mother someone I knew?" Evelyn asked.

"Evelyn, he is marrying Jacquelyn." The softness of His voice caught Evelyn off guard and her heart leaped inside her.

"My Jacquelyn?" Evelyn asked with hesitation.

"Yes, your Jacquelyn and your Will is the best man." Teacher was smiling as he delivered the news.

"Oh, Teacher, you are so wonderful. Thank you for this blessing today!" Evelyn's entire being was filled with joy.

"Well, your friend, Nadine, is giving you all the credit," Teacher said with a chuckle.

"Sounds like Nadine!" Evelyn's sigh was full of love.

CPSIA information can be obtained
at www.ICGtesting.com
Printed in the USA
BVHW091105260122
627129BV00008B/215

9 781662 820847